CL SE PROTECTION

Blood Brothers #2

MANDA MELLETT

Published 2016 by Trish Haill Associates
Copyright © 2016 by Manda Mellett

Editing by Kate Marope at The Ribbon Marker Editorial Services
(https://theribbonmarker.wordpress.com/editorial-services)

Book and Cover Design by Lia Rees at Free Your Words
(www.freeyourwords.com)

All rights reserved. This book or any portion thereof may not be reproduced or used in any manner whatsoever without the express written permission of the author except for the use of brief quotations in a book review.

www.mandamellett.com

Disclaimer

This is a work of fiction. Names, characters, businesses, places, events and incidents are either the products of the author's imagination or used in a fictitious manner. Any resemblance to actual persons, living or dead, or actual events is purely coincidental.

ISBN: 9780995497627

AUTHOR'S NOTE

Close Protection is a standalone novel, and is book number two in the Blood Brothers Series.

Although you will enjoy reading *Close Protection* in its own right, it does provide some further background to the events in the first book, *Stolen Lives*.

Likewise, characters introduced in the first two books will reappear in *Second Chances*, the third in the series, which will be published shortly.

CONTENTS

CHAPTER 1
Mia

Seven Years Ago

Y*ou are not going anywhere! Not dressed like that!" Saliva flew from her mouth as she spat out the words.*

I couldn't help rolling my eyes, though I knew even that small sign of mutiny would only infuriate my mother further. Compared to the other girls who'd be at the party, what I was wearing would probably be considered modest. Black leggings hugged my legs, and yes, okay, so my red tank top was on the clingy side, but I'd covered it with a loose black jumper which hung off one shoulder and was long enough to conceal my bum. That was teamed with a tasteful chain around my neck, with beads to compliment the colours I was wearing. Hooped earrings adorned my ears—clip on, of course, Mum would be in her grave before she'd allow me to get my ears pierced—and my make-up was light; just a touch of mascara and eyeliner, and a little blusher on my cheeks. I thought it looked quite tasteful seeing as it was the first time I'd attempted it, working only from tips in the magazines I'd sneaked in and hidden under my bed. I was seventeen; I should have been able to go out looking halfway fashionable at least.

"You look like a slut!" She was getting more and more riled, her cheeks flushing red as her anger flared.

"Mum," I started, trying to appease her.

"You're not going out to any party. You get back in here now!"

Not listening to me, and after with a quick glance up the street to make sure no one was looking, she grabbed my sleeve roughly and tried to pull me back in from the doorstep.

"Mum," I began again, shaking her hand from my arm. "It's only some girls from school. It's at Anna's house. You know her."

At last, my calm voice and reasonable tone seemed to get through to her. She put her head on one side as if considering whether to change her mind. Crossing my fingers behind my back, I started to hope there might be a chance she'd relent and let me go.

"Are her parents going to be there?" she asked suspiciously at last, her eyes narrowed.

I sighed deeply. I'd been brought up to tell the truth, and had never been able to lie to my mother; something on my face gave me away every time. Looking down at the ground I shuffled my feet and answered quietly, "No, they're away for the night."

She stood back from the door, giving me space to squeeze past her and into the house where I'd lived since I'd been born. "Then you're definitely not going. Come back inside."

I'd always been the good girl; the girl who never got into any trouble, the girl who always did what she was told without question. At seventeen, I might have been a bit late in going through a teenage rebellion, but suddenly all the things I was missing out on raced through my head. The other girls in school were learning to drive, going out with boyfriends and going to the parties held with frightening regularity and to which no one had ever invited me before—and doing all that while I'd sat at home with a book or TV.

Knowing it was well past time to break out of my cocoon, my eyes flashed with anger as I stepped away from the porch and out of her reach. "I'm going. And you can't stop me!" I turned and ran, not hanging around to hear any more of her objections.

But that didn't stop her parting shot reaching me as I ran

through the garden gate. "You look like a slut, Mia Fable! Don't come crying to me when you get what you're asking for!"

Present day

"For fuck's sake!" I scream out and quickly cover my mouth. I don't often swear in public, but for once I just can't help myself as, when of all things, a flipping taxi drives straight through a large puddle sending a shower of cold water splashing all over me.

Quickly looking around in embarrassment, I see most of my fellow creatures behaving like typical Londoners, ignoring my outburst entirely. Each handling the misery of the torrential rain and cancellations on the Central and Northern Underground Lines, in their own individual way. A middle-aged man with boyish features glances at me as he goes by, and offers up a sympathetic grin. A similarly drenched older woman momentarily meets my eyes, silently acknowledging our shared misery before looking away. And all the while the dirty puddle water drips uncomfortably down my legs that are already soaked by the lashing rain. But there's simply nothing else for it but to get myself moving again.

Resuming my tedious journey, I catch a vague glimpse of a large guy wearing a soaked light blue hoodie, leaning against a doorway on the opposite side of the road. He's looking straight at me. When he spots I've caught sight of him, he steps away from his shelter and marches quickly out of my line of vision. *Strange.* Was he self-conscious I'd caught him ogling me? Glancing down at myself, I don't believe I look very remarkable or different to anyone else. Now I'd noticed him something twinges at the back of my brain. *Have I seen him already today?* Maybe, but I can't be sure. Everyone's looking the same, unprepared for the turn in the weather that the forecast certainly hadn't predicted. But as I watch him stride away I feel sorry for him, he looks like he's been out in the rain even longer than me; his wet fleece hanging heavy on his frame.

Turning my thoughts back to my own predicament, I realise it's no use getting riled. I, blue hoodie man, and hundreds of thousands of other people have no choice but to plod on through the crowded streets trying to get home as best we can. I should have guessed it. If someone is going to be desperate enough to throw themselves in front of a tube train, the chances are likely that it will be on a gruesome wet, windy Tuesday when I've travelled into the city for a working lunch with Val, my literary agent. Only a fool would drive into Central London during working hours on a weekday. And couple that with the fact part of the lunch was, predictably, going to be very much of the liquid variety, my car had stayed safely in the garage today, leaving me at the mercy of delays on the tube lines, over-crowded buses, and black taxi cabs with their orange signs markedly unlit.

With no option other than to resort to my own two feet, I traipse on through the streets of the city just like everyone else. But my best foot very quickly gets tired of being put forward, and I need to make yet another stop under a shop's awning to rub my aching toes. *Why, oh why didn't I bring a pair of flats with me? And an umbrella. That would have been useful!*

Catching snippets of conversations as people hurry by, it's easy to hear everyone's just like me, totally fed up with the situation. If truth be told, I've more compassion for the poor bastard of a train driver who probably started his day with higher expectations than to end it scrapping blood and guts off his windscreen. And don't get me started on the Northern line. Delays due to adverse weather conditions? It's England, for God's sake. Yes, hello-o. It rains here! My mood worsens with every step.

Standing at the kerb for a moment in the vain hope I might see a vacant cab, I'm jostled by dozens of others doing exactly the same thing. Competition is fierce, and the likelihood of me being able to wave one down before anyone else is about as probable as hell freezing over. The only taxi I'm likely to get close to today is the one that just splashed water all over me.

Moving back to the side of the pavement closer to the shop windows, seeking the relative shelter from the rain as well as safety from thoughtless drivers I carry on, stopping every few hundred yards to see what the queues for the buses look like. Ever optimistic, I keep an hopeful eye out just in case a taxi discharges its load in front of me. Having been walking for nearly an hour, now I'm prepared to take on all comers to get to it first.

I stop again, bending down to rub my aching feet, certain I've already got blisters. Raising my head my eyes fall on the guy in the blue hoodie, he's about a fifty metres away on the other side of the street. It's definitely the same man as I saw before. An uneasy shiver goes down my spine. *Could he be following me?* Oh, for goodness sake, I'm just being paranoid. Just like me he's probably just stopped off to shelter for a moment, and then, again like me and everyone else realises the futility of waiting for a break in the weather. With no visible breaks in the dark clouds, anyone can tell it's not going to stop pelting down anytime soon.

I make it only a couple of hundred metres further before I need to take a rest again, wondering whether I should stop and buy some new shoes, but shelve the idea, I don't like spending money unnecessarily, and am ashamed to try on new shoes with sopping wet and quite possibly bleeding feet. A quick pep talk to stop feeling sorry for myself, I continue walking, trying to concentrate on something other than my misery, namely how I'm going to fit Val's suggestions into the plot when the guy in the blue hoodie passes me *again*. This time, on my side of the street. Okay, he's walking past without giving me a second glance, but the number of occasions I'm noticing him is getting bizarre. Casting my eyes quickly over the rest of the passers-by I don't think I'm seen any of them before. None of them stand out as either striking or memorable. *So why do I keep seeing him?*

It's probably just coincidence, but I start to feel more than a touch uneasy. What are the chances of seeing the same man time and time again? He's going in the same direction as me, but why is it he seems to keep crossing from side to side, getting behind, and now in front of me? With an intense sense of disquiet coming to the fore, I try to put extra impetus into my steps as I carry on with my now hobble-type walk, going as far as possible, and then waiting just as long as necessary for me to be able to put my weight on both feet again. The next time, when I stop, I look around me with more care. *Shit!* There, gazing avidly into a shop window a few doors behind me is the man in the blue hoodie again. My first thought is how did I come to pass him? Last time I saw him disappearing ahead of me. Logic suggests he'd probably stopped off somewhere, but my survival sense is now on high alert, and somehow I can't imagine he finds the display of clothing for the larger woman as fascinating as he's making it out to be. My uneasiness evolves into outright concern, my breathing becomes erratic and despite the cold I begin to sweat as I start to panic. Whether it's my fevered imagination or not, I'll be a whole lot happier if I could stop seeing him.

Noticing I'm standing next to a department store, I make a quick decision to go inside. The warm and dry interior helps ward off the trepidation I'd felt outside as I waste some time browsing around the sort of clothes I'd never dream of wearing. Then the footwear section tempts me, and that's where I end up making an impulse buy of some comfy looking shoes encouragingly called 'Footgloves.' Hoping they'll be as comfortable as their name suggests and having made my purchase, I sneak into a quiet corner where I swap them for the four-inch heels I'd worn to look the part of a moderately successful author at my agent's. I swear my feet sigh in relief as they fit perfectly and fulfil their advertised promise of being soft and bouncy, and most importantly, flat. Now far more comfortable, my worries return to the man who seems to be following me in a creepy horror film sense. *Has he been shadowing me since I left Val's office?* Racking my brain I try to remember where I first noticed him.

If he's been following me all this time, does he know who I am? I go cold at the thought; memories of my past, which I'm usually able to keep at bay, assail me and I shake my head to dismiss them. *It was seven years ago. Put it behind you!* But experience has taught me what happened *then* still influences my behaviour *now*. Sure, I'm more cautious than the average person, but who wouldn't be with the baggage I'm carrying? Forcing myself to breathe, I try to think it through. *Who exactly is this man shadowing?* Myself, quiet living Mia Fable, or my alter ego, the outgoing erotic fiction writer, Dexie Sanders. My heartbeat speeds up, as I try to decide what I should do.

Checking around the shop I quickly discover there's no convenient back entrance, and I'll have to go out the same way as I entered. Should I call the police? *What would a normal person do; one who didn't live with the nightmare of their past?* Pulling out my phone, I hesitate, my finger hovering over the first nine. *A normal person would probably check there was actually something to worry about before getting the authorities involved.* Deciding I'm being stupid and quite possibly not a little paranoid, I realise I need to find out if the guy is actually still there waiting for me before I make what could be an unnecessary cry for help. Otherwise, I could end up looking like a hysterical female. Safe in the warmth of the shop, I convince myself I'm over-sensitive; it was probably just pure coincidence. Never being comfortable in crowds, my nerves are simply getting to me and no one's following me at all.

I've been in here for a good half-an-hour now, long enough for anyone to have given up and moved on unless they had a good reason to linger. So taking a deep breath, and letting it out slowly, I force myself to be calm. *Come on, Mia, pull yourself together; blue hoodie's got to be long gone.* Heart rate back to near normal, I wait for the whoosh of the automatic doors then step out once more into the rain that's still coming down cats and dogs.

He's standing across the street, staring at the entrance to the store, looking like he's been waiting for me to emerge. I freeze. There can be no doubt about it. He is following me! He's looking straight at me. The way his back straightens, and that he immediately turns away shows he knows I've clocked him. There can be no doubt about it. *He is following me! What the heck do I do?* If I go back into the shop, he might follow me in. *What if he's got a knife or a gun?* He could attack me before I have the chance to call for help. Shit! Sometimes it's not a blessing to have a vivid author's imagination.

My heart beating wildly, I quickly realise my number one goal is getting out of sight. Scanning my surroundings I note the alleyway beside the shop, turn and run down it, hoping to find some place to hide. While he's caught up dodging double-decker buses and trying to cross the busy London street, I duck down behind a large wheelie bin. It stinks a bit, but hopefully I won't be here long and will just have to endure the assault on my nostrils while I wait. Sure enough, he comes down the alley at a pace. I hold my breath, but luckily he doesn't slow and hasn't given the bin a second glance. The other end's not far away, and he does just what I'd hoped he would; he runs straight past me.

As soon as he's out of sight, I double back on myself, returning to the main road, cross it, and go down another side street opposite. I'm running as fast as I can, thanking God for my new shoes, but eventually come to a breathless halt, bending over with my hands on my knees as I try to get much-needed air into my lungs. *Fuck! He came so close!* Why the hell was he chasing me? What did he want?

While my breathing returns to normal, I take a good look around and find no trace of blue hoodie in sight. I'm shaking like a leaf, but the danger seems to be over now, but I don't want to return to the main road and risk seeing him again. To give myself a chance to calm down, and to lose blue hoody completely, I need to find refuge of some sort. It's then I see a tea shop up the street. *Perfect!* Heading up the road, I stop at the entrance under the fading sign. A quick glance inside shows it's relatively empty; a typical old café with tables covered with Formica table tops that have clearly seen better days, much like the waitress hovering by the till. Wanting to be inconspicuous, I enter quietly and take a seat at a table in the back, ensuring I'm facing towards the door. Just in case.

When the waitress comes to take my order, I ask for what will be a very welcome coffee, something both to calm my nerves and warm me up. Discretely, I watch her as she returns to the counter and pours hot steaming black liquid into the cup, checking out of habit how she's preparing it. There's nothing amiss, so as she returns and places my drink in front of me with an optional pot of artificial creamer and a sachet of sugar, I start to relax and even begin feeling chuffed with myself. I've successfully managed to lose blue hoodie. *Go me!*

The beverage is too hot, so I lean back in the chair waiting for it to cool, my weary, aching feet grateful for the rest. *Dammit.*

Who the hell would be stalking me? And what do I do now? Call the police? But what could I tell them? I didn't recognise him, and couldn't think of any reason why anyone would be stalking me. Hmm. *Perhaps it was a case of mistaken identity?* Even as I think of that comforting explanation, a small shudder goes down my spine. Was that likely?

When my coffee's cooled to the right temperature, still hot enough to give a warming glow but not too hot to scald, I pick up the mug and start to drink. One-handed I check the London transport app on my phone, finding to my great relief that the tubes have begun running again, so once I've finished here I'll be able to head to the nearest Central Line station and continue home that way. I must have successfully lost blue hoodie man now; it will be safe to resume my journey.

Perhaps I had imagined it all? Maybe it was all in my head. I frown, going back over the events, not knowing what to think. He'd seemed to run after me, but what the hell could he want from me? My autograph? I smile to myself; even I'm not vain enough to think I'm that famous.

My café retreat is warm and dry, tempting me to stay a while longer to give the tubes time to become less crowded. Noticing the waitress looking pointedly at my empty cup, I realise she's expecting me to vacate my table, even though the place isn't exactly crowded. Not wanting to move just yet, I look around for an excuse to stay, and see the counter opposite holds an enticing display of some yummy looking cakes. Something sweet and sickly would decidedly hit the spot, especially after the calories I'd burned running. As I get to my feet, unable to choose between Coffee and Walnut or Sticky Chocolate, the café door opens, and a man walks in. He's wearing a blue hoodie, and he's heading straight for me.

What the fuck? There's no exit behind me so I'm trapped at the back of the café. Already half standing, I push myself up back against the wall. *Christ, what's going on?* He's a big man, intimidating looking, tall as well as broad. Most of his face is in shadow as his hood is pulled down low, so I'm unable to make out any of his facial features except for a cruel-looking mouth with and a dark five o'clock shadow on his chin, and he has a menacing air as he stalks towards me. Grasping this cannot be good, I part my lips to call for help, but he moves swiftly forward, very quickly for such a big man, and puts one hand over my mouth and the other around my throat, holding it so tight I struggle to breathe.

"Today is just a warning, slut," he tells me in a low rasping voice, "He's coming for you." Taking his hand from my mouth he pulls an envelope out of his pocket and waves it in front of my face, my brain somehow registering that the hand he's holding it with is missing the little finger. Having got my attention, he throws the message onto the table top, then pushes me back hard, viciously knocking my head against the exposed brick wall behind me. He pauses for just a moment, unhands me, spins on his heels, and leaves the coffee shop as quickly as he'd entered.

I fall forwards, gasping for breath, my hands clutching at the table for support. The waitress, having witnessed the incident sees my distress, and is by my side in seconds. "Are you alright, dear? Did he hurt you?" The older woman, who'd seemed a bit standoffish earlier, now sounds genuinely perturbed as she puts her arm around me in a motherly fashion, trying to offer some comfort.

I'm stunned, shocked and shaking like a leaf. I try to say something, but can't get out any words. I cough. When at last, I'm able to speak, my voice sounds hoarse and trembles, "Can you call the police, please? I need help; he's been following me."

She nods, her eyes widening and her shoulders drawing back

as she goes off to perform the important task I've given her. It's then I look around, to start with making sure blue hoodie has really gone, then noticing while there are only a few other patrons, they are all staring at me as if wondering what I've done to deserve such attention. Not one of them had come to my assistance, but I'm not surprised; the whole thing had been over in seconds, and it takes longer than that to shake off the typical reaction of not wanting to get involved in someone else's business. I also can't blame them for not wanting to take on someone of blue hoodie's wrestler-type build. As I remain the subject of mass appraisal, I drop my eyes to the table, disliking being the centre of attention; embarrassed that I was the cause of the kerfuffle. And as I look down, my gaze falls on the partly forgotten envelope he'd left.

The outside of the envelope is damp from the rain but not so sodden that I can't open it. While knowing I really ought to wait for the police to arrive before sliding out the contents, impatience and curiosity get the better of me. I grab a knife and gingerly slice it open, mindful not to leave my fingerprints on what is presumably evidence, and extract the piece of paper inside.

I don't need anyone to tell me I've gone white as a sheet; the blood drains from my head as I start to feel dizzy and faint. I put a hand to my mouth and get up to run. The waitress isn't stupid and directs me straight to the toilets, where my coffee comes up quicker than it went down. Wiping my mouth with a tissue, I stay hunched over the porcelain as I see words on the paper that have become imprinted in my mind.

YOU OWE ME, BITCH. NOW IT'S TIME TO PAY! I'M COMING FOR YOU!

CHAPTER 2
Mia

Seven years ago

For the first time in my seventeen years, I'd gone up against my mum. I was shaking with a mixture of triumph and fear as I walked down the length of our street, but already starting to have regrets by the time I reached the corner, nervous about the ear bashing I could expect to receive when I returned home. Mum wasn't violent; she'd never physically abused me, but she could flay me with just her words. Silence was her other tool. It wasn't unknown for a week or more to pass with her not saying a single word to me, punishing me for even the most minor of infractions, such as being five minutes late coming home from school. What on earth was she going to do this time? All I was wanted was to be a normal teenager for once!

Pausing automatically to check for traffic at the zebra crossing, I crossed over the road and made my way to Anna's house; luckily only a couple of streets over from my own. I tried to stop thinking about Mum, not wanting her to ruin my night, but it wasn't easy. My excitement at going out, ruined by her disappointment in me. Could I come up with something to placate her? Actions do speak louder than words, if I only stay out for a couple of hours and get home at a decent time, maybe that will calm her down a bit and show her I could be responsible if she just loosened the leash a little? Oh, to heck with it. She'd just have to get over it.

I'm going to a party! That was something in itself! It's not that

I was a victim of bullies at school, but being brought up the way I had in a strictly religious home made me the quiet one, the one the other girls typically tended to ignore as part of the background. Not someone they issued invitations to or involved in their lives. So having received the invite out of the blue I certainly wasn't going to turn it down. I'd longed for so long to be part of the crowd. Did this mean the other girls were starting to accept me? A grin came over my face as I raised my fist in the air and pumped it down. Yes!

I was just a few months shy of being an adult. Surely it was well past time to break out of the control of my stern and fanatically religious mother.

But there was still a little voice inside of me that hoped tonight would be worth all the hassle. Like any girl, I still needed my mum, whatever her shortcomings. She's the only one I had and with no other close relatives, the only person I could turn to.

I'd bring her round. I'd have to.

Present day

I'm still sat at the same table in the café when, forty minutes later, the police eventually arrive. Despite my state of distress, I almost smile when the waitress quickly greets them, and takes charge, describing the afternoon's events in great detail before leading them across to me. Even now in author mode making mental notes, I note her behaviour; the attack on me seems to have made her day; she acts as if she hasn't had so much excitement in years. All the time she's talking and describing blue hoodie's threatening behaviour, her hands gesticulating wildly. From the way she's recounting it, I start to think they must be surprised I'm still alive and breathing. I let her have her moment. In truth, she's saving me a lot of explaining.

There are two police officers, a man, and a woman. He looks

in his early thirties; she seems a bit younger, but they're both wearing that worn 'seen it all before' expression. The woman sits down opposite me, and when she deigns to glance at me properly, she winces and throws me a quick look of sympathy. I see her eyes taking in the redness around my throat. I know just what she's looking at, I'd already spotted just how visible the marks were in the mirror in the Ladies and had accepted I'll probably bruise later. After taking in my appearance for a good few seconds, her eyes flick to the envelope and paper still lying on the table. I notice the exact point when she reads the words written on the note, as she flinches, then lifts her chin at her companion. His eyes narrow as he, too, takes in the threat in front of them. She regards me carefully, introducing herself and her partner, and then starts her questions. "I'm PC Starkey, and this is PC Smith. What's your name, love?"

Well, it's not 'love' for a start, but I shrug off the condescension. She's probably trying to put me at my ease. Keeping my voice quiet, aware of listening ears, I tell them, "My real name's Mia Fable, but my pen name's Dexie Sanders." I offer both my identities, not sure whether blue hoodie was following me or my alter ego. Or, whether as some small part of my brain keeps hoping, he might have thought I was someone else entirely.

She starts, frowns, and glances up quickly, a disapproving look appearing on her face. Her companion does the opposite, grinning widely. "My wife loves your books," he informs me, "I'm not into them myself, but…" As his voice trails off, he shrugs; wry amusement on his face. I resist the urge to shake my head in despair. It's not uncommon for people to tell me my writing has put a spark into their love lives. The female police officer's reaction is also fairly universal. The mistaken assumption I have the same active sex life I tend to write about is the reason I protect my privacy so fiercely. If my plots were about murder, they wouldn't be bringing out the handcuffs, but due to the openly sexual and often deviant lifestyle of my characters I'm immediately found guilty and convicted of participating in the same kink. And that couldn't be further from the truth.

My glare causes the police officer to recoil. Realising she's let her prejudice show a bit too openly, she backtracks and almost overcompensates by becoming ultra-friendly. Plastering a fake smile on her face, and lightening her tone she asks, "So when did you first notice someone following you?"

Shrugging, glad we're back on track I tell her, "I can't be certain. I may have noticed him outside my agent's office in Westminster, but I wasn't paying too much attention at the time. With so many people having to walk home today, I was more bothered with avoiding being crushed in the crowds and didn't notice particular individuals. Looking back, I think he was there, but that might just be my mind playing tricks, you know? It wasn't that much later, though, when I really noticed him, and at that point twigged I'd seen him more than once."

After a pause for breath, I continue, "Of course, at first, I just thought he was going in the same direction as me. He wasn't the only person taking the same route, so I didn't think anything of it at the time. But when I kept seeing him…" I break off, remembering how scared I'd become and shudder. "When I kept noticing him, I started to think it couldn't be a coincidence. When I loitered in a shop for a while, and he was still there when I came out, I ran, hid behind a bin, and figured I'd lost him. And then, well, you know the rest." I nod towards the waitress who's already brought them up to date. "He found me."

"Any idea why he would have been following you?"

That's the question that's been bugging me, but I can't come up with any rational explanation to offer. And the note made no sense at all. "I have no idea. I'm hoping he's got me confused with someone else."

She listens intently, scribbling frantically in her notebook. As I stop talking, she looks up. "Hmm, we'll have to consider that possibility of course, but for now, let's work with what we've got, the assumption he meant to follow you. Can you give me any description?"

I heave a sigh, not really is the answer, but I make an effort. "He was wearing a light blue hoodie. No logo that I could see. The hood was pulled up and down over his face. He seemed to have a heavy build, muscular I'd say. Oh, and his little finger on his left hand was missing." I shut my eyes, grimacing as I try to recall as much as I can remember, "I can't tell you much more. He had a dark five o'clock shadow on his chin, so possibly he has dark hair? But then, he could have been bald as I really couldn't see him. And he had thin lips." In all truth, I know I haven't given them much to go on.

The waitress, who's been hovering within earshot, backs me up, confirming he hid his features well. Then I have to sit, and watch as PCs Starkey and Smith go to take statements from the other people who were present at the time, but it takes a fair bit of time for them to sort out who they should be speaking to. In the time it took for them to arrive the customers had changed; some sneaking out as soon as they heard the police were being called, others coming in to satisfy their curiosity about what's going on. Then there are the regulars who just want to give their opinion even if they didn't see much at all. As they sort out the actual witnesses, I start to get tired and lose patience. My throat's hurting, shivers of fear still plague me and I just want to get everything over and done with. I want to go home, preferably without being followed. I hate all the fuss, normally I'm a very private person and very shy. Drawing all this attention is quite unnerving.

In the end, because of the plausible threat on the table in front of me, and because I'm a "celebrity" they decide to take me to the police station to talk to a detective. I'm pleased they're taking it all so seriously but instead of dissipating, my stress levels seem to be rising. *Breathe, Mia, breathe. Soon you'll be home and opening that bottle of Chardonnay you put in the fridge to cool.*

I stand up, dragging my sodden coat back on, musing that at least I'll be in a heated police car, and won't have to walk the streets in the wet. Outside the rain is still coming down in such a way it's making me wonder whether somewhere out there a man called Noah is building an ark.

I'm tired and cold, and not a little scared and uncertain. I've written about police cars and criminals, and watched them on TV like most other people, but have never actually been in one myself. So it doesn't surprise me to feel a hand placed on my head as I'm helped into the back of the police car even though I'm going willingly. I suppose it's become a habit for the PCs, but it makes me feel like I've done something criminal. And then there are the passers-by who are stopping to gape, giving me curious looks, wondering what I've done wrong. Trying to ignore them, I take out my phone and glance at the screen. It's already seven o'clock. I left Val's office at three. *No wonder I'm so weary.* Suppressing a yawn, once the car is underway I look out the windows as we drive through the traffic that's now begun to clear as the main rush hour is over. Ironically, there are hundreds of taxis passing, their orange Taxi signs now glowing as they're on the hunt for customers. *Too late, mateys,* I think to myself. And I have to wonder whether I'd be here now had I been able to get a ride earlier on today. Would I have shaken off the stalker? Or would he just have followed me another day?

The police car isn't as warm as I'd hoped; for some reason they've got the air conditioning on instead of the heater, so I'm shivering as the PCs lead me into the police station. I'm taken to a room and offered a cup of tea while I wait for a detective to be assigned to my case. Once alone, my shivers turn to uncontrollable shaking as the shock of the day catches up with me, made worse by the fact I'm sitting waiting for someone to interview me in a police station. It makes it seem all too real. *Why me? What have I ever done to upset anyone?*

I know some people are offended by my books, but no one's forced to read them. Why would someone stalk and threaten me? The sound of the door opening interrupts my thoughts. Looking up, I find a middle-aged man with a tired looking face coming in carrying two hot steaming mugs. He puts one tea in front of me and places the second on the other side of the desk where he seats himself. I sip at the drink cautiously.

He watches as I put my hands around the hot mug, trying to soak up the warmth, his eyes examining me intently. "I'm Detective Waring, and your case has been allocated to me. But before we go further, do you need a doctor?" he asks, apparently noticing the bruises on my neck which must be darkening by the second, and the violent trembling I seem powerless to stop.

Shaking my head, I dismiss his suggestion, "No. I'm alright. Thank you."

He still looks concerned. "You've had a shock and have been assaulted. Are you sure you don't need to see someone?"

The thought of seeing a doctor, as usual, makes me more than a little apprehensive. Adding to that, I've not been in a police interview room before and find it bleak and unnerving even though I'm innocent of any crime. Right now, all I can think of is getting this over with and going home to my comfortable little cottage where I always feel safe and nurse my hurts myself, medicating myself with that nice chilled wine.

"I'm all right." I tell him, trying to put strength in my voice. In truth, my throat is more swollen now, making it painful to speak, and my head throbs from where blue hoodie had banged it against the wall, but I don't need, can't face, medical attention. Clearly, I want my attacker caught, so I have to stay and go through this, however uncomfortable I'm feeling. I take a small sip of the tea even though it's still close to boiling; the simple action providing some comfort and helping to settle me.

"Okay." Giving me an intense stare, he doesn't seem happy with my response, probably preferring I get checked out, but he accepts my decision. My injuries are superficial; they look worse than they are.

Opening a folder he looks carefully at the contents, and I try to see what he's reading. He appears to have copies of the statements taken in the café, and two plastic evidence bags; one containing the envelope, and the other the note blue hoodie gave to me. He turns the envelope over, and back again, and then reads the writing on the piece of paper. Finally, he looks up, "I'm sorry, I know you've had a bad experience, but I need to ask you some questions so we can try to get to the bottom of exactly what's going on here, and I'd like to do it while it's still fresh in your mind. The first question is the obvious one. Did you recognise anything about this man at all? It was definitely a man; I take it?" he starts the interrogation.

"No doubt he was male. I can't even think of anyone I know with that build. He was tall," I put my hand over my head, trying to show how much taller than me he was, "Bulky. It looked like he had muscular legs and arms, and his body was broad. I didn't see his face, properly, only the lower half. I'm sure I've never come across him before. I can't remember anything I haven't already put in my statement."

"Nothing else you can remember from the assault?" He consults the notes police officers Starkey and Smith must have passed on to him.

I think back. Ah, there was something else, "His hands were

calloused. Possibly a workman? And as I told your colleagues, he had a finger missing on his left hand. His little finger."

He jots down the additional information. "Did you get the impression the note was from him or was he delivering it for someone else?"

"Someone else," I say without hesitation, "He told me 'he' is coming for me."

Lifting his head, he stares at me, tapping his pen against his teeth as he seems to be deliberating something. "You mentioned to the PCs that you thought it might be a case of mistaken identity. Obviously, we can't discount that, there was no name on the envelope, but if he *was* following you from your agent's I think it unlikely, I'm afraid. We have to work on the premise that he knew who he was after. So who do you think he was stalking, would you say? Mia Fable or Dexie Sanders? Or is it common knowledge you're one and the same?"

I shrug, that's what's got me worried. "Though it might be wishful thinking, I'd say Dexie Sanders. I protect my identity, only my publisher and agent know my real name."

"Hmm," he considers for a moment, "And the Inland Revenue, your accountant, your bank probably. I expect there are more people than you think."

Reluctantly I nod in agreement. He's probably right, but I don't like thinking about that. I pick up the tea and drink some more.

"Friends? Family? They'd know your pen name, wouldn't they?"

"I haven't had contact with my family for years. But yes, my mother does know my pseudonym. And a few of my close friends, other writers."

He snorts as if he's been clever catching me out. "So quite a few people."

I don't like being made to feel stupid. Even if that's not his intention, that's the result his words are having on me. "I can't think of anyone who'd want to threaten me. And before you ask, I don't owe anyone anything." The idea that someone close to me might do something like this is making me distressed.

"Who knew you'd be at your agent's today?" He changes tack.

I know that I'm to blame for that. "No one knew Mia was going there, but all my fans knew Dexie was. It's on her Facebook page." Remorsefully, I think back to the status I'd posted last night. 'Hey folks, off to see my great agent Val tomorrow. Lots of laughs and booze will be involved.' I regret writing that now.

He looks confused. "You talk about yourself as two different people." Picking up his drink, with a hand covered in liver spots showing his early aging, he gulps it down noisily, finishing the whole mug in one go. Then he tilts his head to one side, waiting for me to explain.

Laughing softly, I try to put it into plain words so he can understand, "I am. As Mia I'm myself, quiet, shy, but Dexie is outgoing and confident. Dexie's the one who can talk at conferences and book signings. I hide behind her. It's like an actor on stage playing a role." By the way he's shaking his head I don't think he gets it. I know it must seem as though I'm schizophrenic, but sometimes I find it easier to play the part expected of me as Dexie. Dexie's the extrovert.

"Your books," he begins, and I think I know what's coming. "There are obviously people who are offended by them. And think that you're immoral to write the way you do. I understand your descriptions are quite explicit?"

His words give away that he's seen my Facebook page, or my Twitter account, already. The vast majority of comments are from fans, usually positive and full of praise. But occasionally I get the odd one on there from someone with a rather bizarre take on the content of my novels, telling me I've got no morals, that I'm encouraging abuse or something of that ilk, making the assumptions that I'm into the same things as my characters. *The same assumption he is making.* I start to get angry. "So if I wrote a story involving drugs you'd pull me in on a suspected dealing charge?" I challenge him.

"So you're saying you don't have the same proclivities as your characters?"

"I'm saying that's none of your business!" I snap at him, starting to get outraged. Suddenly Dexie wakes up. "I'm not a suspect here. I'm a victim! Now, can you just tell me what the next steps are to find out who's threatening me; how I can stay safe, and then let me go home?"

He has the grace to look sheepish and his eyes turn away from me, looking back down at the documents in front of him.

When he stays quiet, I prompt him, "What happens now?" If I know some action is being taken, something positive is being done to find who's behind this, it might help me to keep it together. At the moment, I'm a hairsbreadth away from falling apart. *Who could possibly be threatening me? And why?*

"We'll see if we can lift fingerprints off the envelope and paper, I'll get our forensic team to look into it." Now he looks at me. "Would anyone know Dexie Sanders' address?"

I'm pretty sure they don't. "No. As I said, the link between my pen name and my own is quite hidden, and I'm careful with my real identity as well. I don't give it out unless I have to. I don't use business cards with my physical address on, only details of my website." But I still know I'm more hopeful than positive with my answer. *For goodness sake, I hope to God he doesn't know where I live.*

"Just to be on the safe side, I'll get a squad car to take you home, Ms Fable, and as a precaution, one of the officers will check your house before you go in. But for now, I have to tell you there's very little to go on." He breaks off and frowns as something occurs to him. His eyes narrowing, he adds, "Assure me that this isn't a publicity hoax, Ms Fable? It wouldn't be the first time police time's been wasted as a way to increase sales."

Pointedly rubbing the marks round my neck, I stand up, furious, and lean over the table, Dexie very much in control of my actions. "Detective Waring," I shout, well, as much as possible with a sore throat, "I've been scared out of my wits today. Someone's followed and threatened me. At lunchtime, I was enjoying myself, accepting congratulations on the sales of my recent book, and discussing the new project I'm working on without a care in the world. I'm now frightened and scared, and that's just not fair!"

He mimics me by also rising to his feet, but in contrast to my outburst speaks quietly. "I understand your frustration, Ms Fable, but I've been on the force for a very long time, and unfortunately day after day I see people like yourself, who, through no fault of their own, become victims in some way or another. You do have my sympathy, but I have no magic wand to wave and miraculously get answers. We'll try to get to the bottom of this, and try to give you back some peace of mind. Now, for tonight, let's just get you home."

As he stretches his hand across the table for me to shake, I begrudgingly reach out mine to take it. He's right; I know. I write about victims; often my characters have something in their backgrounds that they need to recover from, abuse, and neglect. My temper evaporates as quickly as it came, but I need to make no apology. My reaction can't be anything he hasn't seen before. "You'll let me know what you find out from the note?"

"We'll be in touch. In the meantime, I suggest you have a think about who might have a grudge against you. As I said; we haven't got a lot to go on at the moment."

"You think blue hoodie will contact me again? Or the person who's putting him up to this?"

He seems to be considering his next words carefully and then tells me gently, "I'm afraid the wording of the note and the verbal message suggests there's more to come. Be very careful, Ms Fable, and don't publicise your or your alter ego's whereabouts or plans anymore."

I nod. At least that's one area where we're in total agreement. I've certainly learned that lesson today.

* * * *

The one benefit is I get to travel home in comfort, sitting in the front of a police car instead of battling with the crowds on the tubes. A different police officer is driving, a young constable. He's not exactly talkative, which suits me. I'm happy to stay silent as I'm driven away from the city, through the suburbs and out into the countryside near Epping, to the house that I call home; a small cottage, dating back over two hundred years. It sits on the edge of the forest that nowadays is a mere shadow of its former self, yet still a beautiful area. I was able to move here from the flat I was sharing with my student friends, with the proceeds from my first four novels and, of course, a hefty mortgage to my name. But notwithstanding the substantial amount I owe to the bank, it's *mine*.

When we pull up outside, I obey the instruction I'm given to wait in the car. The police officer takes my keys, and my eyes follow him as he unlocks my front door and disappears into the house. It's a traditional two up two down with an extension on the back, giving me a large kitchen and conservatory that would be perfect for entertaining if I had many friends living nearby. The sad fact of the matter is that my closest friends are mostly virtual, and we connect more via instant messaging more than we do in person. Writing isn't a job with a lot of socialisation involved, except for the occasional conferences I attend.

I see lights appearing in each of the rooms, as he methodically goes through the building top to bottom and watch as he puts on the security light in the garden, using a torch to peer into the darkened areas, appreciating his thoroughness. He's back in a few minutes and opens the car door for me.

"You've not got a security system, ma'am?" he asks me as I step out of the car. I notice he doesn't make the unnecessary statement that he'd found nothing of concern in his search.

"No," I confirm, starting to frown, "I never thought I needed one."

"Might be a good idea to get one installed," he advises.

I nod. The idea had already gone through my mind on the drive back. I'll have to look into it. The lack of security never bothered me before, but after today, well, I have to give it some serious thought. But where the heck would I get one from? What type will I need? And then I'll have to find someone to install it for me. I think of asking the constable for help, but he seems anxious to get on his way, and I'm just too tired to take in many details tonight. I'm also angry; I was so pleased to find this cottage affordable in my price range, and it's always felt a comfortable haven to me. Now I'm unnerved at the prospect I might not be safe in my own home. I'm banking on the hope the person was following me because he doesn't know my address. *God, I hope that's true!*

"You've got decent locks front and back, ma'am," he continues, looking back at the house. "Make sure the doors are locked and bolted, and if you've got window locks, use them too."

To be honest, his recommendations are making me even more nervous; it's almost as if he expects someone's going to break in. As he prepares to go, I turn and thank him for the lift home, take back my keys, and then, at long last, make my weary way to my front door. It's been one heck of a long day.

At least the heating has been on, and the house is warm and cosy despite the rain that is still coming down heavily, blowing against the windows and making them rattle. Walking through the house drawing the curtains shut, checking the window locks, and bolting the doors following the instructions the police officer had given me, I start to jump at each little noise from outside. I'm a bloody bundle of nerves! Trying to get myself together I take a bottle of wine from the fridge, a glass from the cupboard, and make my way to the lounge where I collapse onto the sofa. I pour the first glass of that Chardonnay I've so been looking forward to, and down half of it in one go, feeling I deserve it. Only then do I take my phone out of my bag, but before making my call, top up my glass expecting I'll be on the phone for quite a while.

I press the pre-set number, the phone rings a couple of times, and then the familiar voice answers. "Hi?"

"Hey, Val. It's Mia."

"Hi, kiddo! How's it going?" My agent seems puzzled to hear from me when I only saw her earlier today.

Then she sounds even more perplexed when my only answer is to burst into tears, sobbing my heart out on the phone. It surprises the hell out of me as well. I've managed to hold it together all afternoon, and all it takes is one friendly voice, and I'm a complete mess. But this is Val. As well as being my agent she's become someone I'd call a friend, close enough to stay on the line for the few minutes it takes for me to compose myself, staying silent until I'm ready to tell her what's got me in such a state.

By the time I've finished explaining she's lost for words herself. "Val?" I prompt her.

"Just give me a minute." Again there's silence. I suspect she's pouring her preferred brand of fortification. I top up my wine again. Half the bottle's already gone, but I'll need some help to sleep tonight. Tomorrow can go hang itself.

Back on the line, she makes me go through the afternoon's events again and again until we've thrashed the very little we know to death, going round and round in circles, asking the same questions and coming up with no answers. In the end, I know we're just repeating ourselves when she asks for the umpteenth time, "Mia, are you okay? Is this going to set you back?"

Val knows something happened to me in my past, but she doesn't know any details. No one does. When I first met her, I was a mess, jumping at everything, scared of people brushing past me, suspicious of their intentions. Gradually I've become stronger and what I do know is I'm not going to let anything or anyone chase me back to that dark place. I refuse to let them, so I reassure her, "I'm fine, Val."

There's a moment's pause, and I suspect she's considering my sincerity before she leaves that avenue there and gets back to the main topic. "And you've absolutely no idea who could want to hurt you, Mia?"

"None at all." And that's the honest truth. I don't know anyone I've upset, or at least not to the extent they'd want to hassle or stalk me. Okay, maybe I was a bit abrupt when I was shortchanged at the newsagent's last week, but I can't see the shop assistant taking that to heart.

Eventually, she tells me, "I've got a friend who might be able to give us some help. Can you leave it with me tonight, while I try and contact him, Mia?"

I'm a bit puzzled, "What friend? What could he do?"

"He has a security firm. He'll be able to give you advice if nothing else. Are you okay if I contact him?"

Knowing any help might be better than none, I tell her,

despondently, "There's not a lot else for me to do, is there? At the moment I'm just stuck with the police seeing if they can find anything from the little they've got."

By the time we've said our goodbyes and Val's off the phone, it's getting on for midnight, and the bottle of wine is almost empty. I finish it up, double check all the locks, switch off the lights and make my way to bed. Having eaten nothing since lunch, the effects of the alcohol on a nearly empty stomach make me a little woozy as I climb the steep cottage stairs and stumble into the modern bathroom. Doing just the absolute necessary, I get ready for bed and then settle in for a restless night, expecting the old familiar nightmares from my past to resurface tonight, as well as new ones conjured up from my horrendous day.

I'd wanted to get home, to the place where I have always felt safe. But the thought someone might be after me makes me toss and turn, unable to relax. Then, when I force myself to lie still, I'm alert to every creak in the old building, having to try to convince myself it's nothing more than the usual sounds of the aged timbers settling. I hear owls hooting in the distance, the sound of the rain still lashing down against the window panes, and gradually, despite my nervousness, my eyes start to close as I give into the stress-induced exhaustion and eventually drift off to sleep.

* * * *

Tuesday morning, I awake after a surprisingly good uninterrupted rest. Even the bottle of wine only left me a bit fuzzy, and the expected and well-deserved headache is happily absent. Refreshed, the events of yesterday seem like just a bad dream. Safe and cosy in my bed, with the sun streaming in through the gap in the curtains, memories of being stalked through the rainy streets of London seem far, far away. But my bruised throat, and the lump on the back of my head, remind me what happened yesterday was all too real and I shiver. *Is someone really out to get me?*

Dressed and ready for the day I wait anxiously to hear from the police, but there's no update, and gradually I stop looking at the phone to make sure I haven't accidentally put it on silent. Slowly I convince myself, if they haven't bothered to rush to get back in contact they can't think it's as serious as it seemed at the time. My mind starts to blur over the facts, as I refuse to let myself feel intimidated. The bright sunshine and blue skies, replacing the ominous dark of the day before, help to lift my mood.

The morning passes quickly. Despite everything I manage to get in my word count and more, as a sudden unexpected blast of inspiration hits me. In one day I'd experienced more than I normally would in a year. The range of emotions I'd gone through, the people I'd met—the ebullient waitress, the police officers, and the detective—being in a police car and police station for the first time as well as the encounter and attack itself; all fuel for my plots. My characters come alive, and start rambling off in directions I'd neither planned nor expected, and I know I'm doing some of the best writing I've ever done. *Hmm, I make a joke in bad taste to myself. Perhaps I should get out and get stalked more often.* Although, that does seem quite a high price to pay for some inspiration!

While I'm churning out words by the dozen, as usual, I lose all sense of time. Lost in another world, I work all day and by the evening, when I eventually emerge from my study, I realise I've forgotten to organise an alarm system for the house. But I've also forgotten any real urgency to do so. I'm happy with the work I've completed, pleased with the progress I've made and having heard nothing further from the police and still unable to conceive anyone could want to hurt me; I no longer feel under threat. At least here, in the safety of my cosy home. I'll be a lot more cautious if I have to go into London anytime soon. No one knows where Dexie Sanders lives. Yes, I'm sure of that.

"Hi, sweetie. How are you doing?" Val rings around seven, just as I'm putting a ready meal for one in the oven.

Pleased with myself, I tell my agent that I've doubled my word count today, and start to enthuse about how the new novel is shaping up until she stops me, laughing. "Not much keeps you down, does it? I'm ringing to see how you *are*, not what you've *done*."

I smile, my phone balanced between my shoulder and ear as I get out a plate and cutlery. "Sorry, Val. Everything seems different today. I'll just be ultra-vigilant when I'm out in future."

"Did you sort out your alarm system?"

"No, I'll get round to it sometime. I haven't had time today. It will be fine, I'm sure."

"Mia, it sounded serious to me!" She sounds exasperated and reminds me again of the precautions that I should be taking in her view. Then she adds, "Look, I've pulled in a favour from someone I know at Grade A Security. They're a protection and security company with great rep. They'll be sending someone to see you tomorrow about what exactly it is you need."

"There's no point, Val. I'll get round to sorting it out." Eventually, but I add that under my breath.

She sighs loudly, "You're a celebrity, now, Mia. I think you need some expert advice on this."

"Actually, I'm bloody angry I need to pay out money just because someone doesn't like the content of my books," I suddenly snap. I've started making a decent income now, but it's not a fortune and just as hard earned as anybody else's, often as a result of fourteen-hour days and no weekends off or holidays. "Why don't they just bloody well not read them, if they hate them that much?"

"I'm trying to help, here, Mia," Val retorts sharply, stopping my tirade.

At once, realising it's wrong to direct my anger at her, I apologise. After she reminds me someone's coming from Grade A tomorrow, I thank her for taking the time to arrange it, and we say our goodbyes. Putting down the phone, I eat my dinner for one. *Christ Val, I was just feeling comfortable now you've unnerved me all over again!* Glancing around my kitchen, I check the window is locked, and in the silence realise how alone I am. I've always lived by myself, and so far have never felt lonely. With all the characters talking in my head I don't need anyone else's company. But all of a sudden I realise how vulnerable that makes me, a twenty-four-year-old woman, living on her own, out in the country, at least a quarter of a mile from the nearest neighbour.

A shiver runs up my spine as though a ghost has just walked over my grave.

* * * *

As darkness gives way to light, my fears once again begin to evaporate in correlation with the sun rising, and the next day starts much like the last. The police still haven't made contact, I've heard no more about the stalker, and once again, my writing's on a roll. I pause only to make a few notes on my iPad to remind me to see if Detective Waring, who'd given me his contact details and card, might be amenable to talking me through some police procedures I've been getting confused on. I do like to get authenticity into my work.

As I'm pondering whether the detective would mind answering some questions, the rattle of the letterbox signalling the post has arrived interrupts the flow of my thoughts and jolts me back into reality. I don't live a great distance from the town of Epping, but far enough away to be considered resident in a rural area. Hence, I'm almost the last on the postman's round, and he often doesn't get to my road until late morning, sometimes not until after lunch so I never know when to expect him. I don't bother moving at first, not until I hear the knock on the door which probably means there's a delivery I need to sign for. Sighing, I back away from the keyboard and check my watch. *Eleven o'clock. The postie's made good time today.* Calling out for him to wait for a moment, I run down the stairs from the sparc bedroom which serves as my study, and open the door to him. He's my regular, so he greets me with a smile.

"Only a few bills for you, love," he says, passing the brown envelopes over, then he waves his hand downwards, "But I didn't know if you realised you had these? I didn't think you'd want them left here to spoil." Having pointed out the delivery left for me, he nods and leaves, quickly exiting down my short front path, and jumping into his van to continue his round.

But I don't watch him go. Instead my eyes are focused on what he so kindly pointed out to me. Someone had left a bouquet of white lilies against my front door. My mouth goes dry. *I don't know anyone who'd send me flowers.* And while relatively innocuous, if you like that type of bloom, to me it looks like something you'd put on a coffin. With a feeling of dread, I suspect that is exactly the effect they are meant to have. *Shit!* Sinking to my knees, I gingerly extract the card that's attached to the cellophane wrapping. Carefully I open the envelope, which has my address clearly printed on it, then, with shaking hands, I hold it up, letting the contents slide it out, still hoping there's a possibility it's from a friend. But reading the words printed on the card in big bold type, I rock back on my heels and put my hand to my face. *Dear God! He does know where I live!*

Fuck! My hands tremble so much I drop the card. Tears of

frustration and fear come to my eyes and I angrily wipe them away, annoyed at myself for my weakness. Glancing down, I read what's written on the envelope again. It's addressed to Mia Fable. I'm right to be afraid. Another threat, and this time there's no doubt he knows my true identity, as well as my address.

I leave the flowers where they are; I don't want to touch them, and I don't want to bring them inside and have that sickly sweet scent wafting through my home. I shut the door, so they are out of my sight and waste no time grabbing my phone and ringing the detective I spoke to on Tuesday evening at the police station in London. He answers, and I tell him what's happened. There's some confusion as he's with the Met, the Metropolitan Police Force covering London, but the local Essex Police are the ones who deal with the area where I live, so he's going to have to contact them and pass my case over. I just teem with exasperation. *I don't care whose jurisdiction it is.* I just want them to bloody well get it sorted!

It takes two hours for them to decide who's doing what, and to get someone out to me, but I suppose an unexpected delivery of flowers is not generally classed as an emergency. When they do arrive, they come mob-handed suggesting the notes of my interview last night have finally been transferred and they're now taking it as a serious threat. Different police officers come tasked with various jobs, one starts to fingerprint the front gate, which would have to have been opened to deliver the flowers then, finished with that task, uses tweezers to pick up the card and place it in a plastic bag, berating me for handling it. I snap my patience now almost non-existent. What did they expect me to do? He bags the flowers and takes them out to the police car and I breathe a sigh of relief once they are out of my sight. But it's impossible to forget the words that I'd read:

RIP BITCH! ONCE YOU'VE PAID YOUR DUES.

Apart from the forensic expert who, on returning to the

house, continues to mutter about me contaminating his crime scene, there are three other police officers; a detective, a crime scene officer, and a constable; the latter standing as if on guard by the front door. The detective, who quickly introduced himself as Detective Sergeant David Coulton, takes me into my sitting room and starts to question me, taking me through every possible scenario where I might have made an enemy.

But nothing's changed from Tuesday night; I still can't think of anyone who would want to threaten and scare me. He seems focused on the demand that I pay my dues for what I owe. But I owe nothing to anybody. Shaking my head and narrowing my eyes I'm perplexed and puzzled as to what the hell this could be about. I honestly have no idea! *Who'd want to do this to me?* I think he's on the wrong track. Although it doesn't make any sense, the only thing that occurs to me is that some nutter has got extremely upset by the content of my books. But in that case, why weren't the flowers sent to Dexie Sanders? Why were they addressed to me?

"Is there someone you can stay with for a few days?" Coulton asks me when we've exhausted just about every avenue to explore as to who might have a serious grudge against me. "If you can go somewhere else, you would feel safer. At the moment, we can't say whether this is a credible threat or just a hoax. It could just be someone playing a cruel joke, getting their kicks from upsetting you. But as the person knows where you live, well, I must admit that makes me more than a tad concerned. He might remain content with just leaving these messages, but we can't rule out that his actions might escalate into actual violence."

I don't have to think about it for long. There's no one I'm that close to that I could impose on to give me house-room. So I shake my head as I tell him, "Not unless I stay at a hotel. And how long would I have to go away for?"

He shrugs. "The problem is we have no idea who is threatening you or why. Until he crawls out of the woodwork, it's impossible to say."

What the hell do I do? I'm scared and feeling very alone. My stalker is already winning, and that infuriates me. "Then it's impossible for me to leave," I tell him, firmly. "I haven't got unlimited resources. Can't you provide protection for me?"

"I'm sorry, but unless we know who or what we're protecting you from, or have evidence there's a real risk of physical danger towards you, we just haven't got the manpower after all the recent cuts. We're spread too thin already." He looks at me sympathetically, "I can have a squad car include your house in its regular rounds, and obviously, we're only a 999 call away, but, horrible as this might sound, the situation needs to escalate before we can do much about it. I know that doesn't give you much comfort, Ms Fable, but I'm afraid that's how it is."

Nodding slowly, I accept that in the scheme of things my stalker problem probably appears insignificant. To them, maybe, but not to me. He looks around. "You need to have a security system installed. One with a panic button connecting you directly to us."

I'm an author; I'm not a practical person, and it probably sounds pathetic when I start to ask him for his advice. "Who can install a security system? What type do I need?"

Suddenly an unfamiliar but authoritative voice interrupts us. "You can leave that to me."

I spin round. My eyes open wide, and my jaw drops. All the air has been sucked from my lungs, as I struggle to take in a breath. I've written about scenes such as these. The immediate attraction to someone on first sight, but I've never experienced anything like it in real life. Having to put my hand on the back of a chair to steady myself, I can't tear my eyes away from the man standing in the doorway, his massive frame making my sitting room seem far too small.

He's wearing a leather biker jacket, tight fitting black jeans which cover his long legs and, to complete his ensemble, biker boots. In his hand, he's holding a helmet. He's so tall; I have to lift my chin to look up at his face. His eyes are dark, almost black as they focus on me, his nose straight and aquiline. His lips are slightly parted, revealing straight white teeth. He's got designer stubble – more than just having missed a shave but less than can be called a beard – on his chin, and dark brown hair just long enough to reach below his collar looking neat and styled even though having been flattened by his helmet. All his features add up to one thing, and the reason for my immediate irrational reaction; if I'd dreamed about a man I couldn't have conjured up someone who appealed to me more. It's as though one of my favourite fictional lead characters has come to life. My stomach clenches and my body's unwanted response to this devastating man scares me almost as much as the threatening notes I'd received. This man, whose very presence makes my house feel like it's shrunk; not just because of his size, but there's something about him that oozes power and dominance and which makes me want to give myself over into his care. I've *never* had this kind of reaction to a man before and never believed I ever would. *I do not get attracted to men.*

"Who … Who the fuck are you?" I manage to stammer out, my voice sounding so unlike my own, shaking and full of trepidation.

CHAPTER 3
Jon

Six years ago

I read the email again. Then I lifted my head and gazed up at the burning hot sun floating in an unbroken sky of blue, as I considered the job offer I'd just been made. Was I really at the point where I wanted to change what many would see as my dangerous career?

If it had been from anybody else, I might not have given it a moment's thought. But Ben Carter had been my Captain; Special Air Services Capt Carter to give him his full title, and I'd been one of his Squadron Sergeant Majors. We'd worked together in that elite unit of the British armed forces, commonly known as the SAS. We'd been seconded at the same time to the Counter Revolutionary Warfare team, conducting training in close protection techniques to prepare bodyguards to protect VIPs. Billeted in the same accommodation, we'd spent both days and nights together. We'd parted company when I was transferred to the mobility troop and shipped out to Afghanistan.

This was where I was now, stood on the hot desert sand, my phone in hand. Once more I re-read the message Ben had sent. Having left the service a year ago, he was setting up a security company, and was inviting me to buy in as a partner. He'd approached me firstly as a good friend and comrade and secondly because of my expertise in close protection. It was an intriguing offer, but was it for me right now?

I looked around at my team of four men waiting for me as we prepared to go out on patrol, and knew I had to put Ben's proposal out of my mind, needing to focus on my current career. Switching back to soldiering mode, I checked my weapons and ammunition, getting myself in the right mindset for the mission ahead. We were tasked with clearing a village of insurgents and hopefully freeing the residents from their oppressors. But despite the seriousness of the work in hand, the tempting idea lingered. Did I want to leave the service and take a job with a private security firm? I hadn't got the funds to buy in, but I knew I wouldn't mind working for Ben. I'd be doing close protection work, something for which I was more than qualified. I'd always enjoyed Ben's company, both as my senior officer and as a friend. We were very similar in our approach to life and, it has to be said, have the same taste in the female sex. We're both Dominants, and we'd both headed for the nearest BDSM clubs when on leave. We'd even shared the same woman on occasion. Yes, he was a good friend, and would probably be a good employer.

I glanced at my watch and watched the second hand approach 0900 hours. Time to leave. The nod I threw towards my troop signalled I was ready to go, and they followed me as I led the way to the armoured vehicles ready to move out.

This life is all I'd ever known. I'd been in the military since the age of eighteen, and having put in the requisite time, managed to pass the arduous tests required to join the crème de la crème of the British Army. Could I change and do something different?

As we emerged into the scorching heat of this god-forsaken desert, I laugh at myself. I must be mad, but I couldn't really see me doing anything else but being a soldier. Although this place could well be the death of me, for now this is my life.

Present day

It shocks me when I arrive at my destination to find it looks like all hell's broken loose. Curious to discover what's going on, I pull up my motorcycle in the driveway between two police cars. As I tug off my leather gloves, tucking them into my helmet, I can't fail to notice the admiring look my mode of transport is receiving an from a young constable who's hovering by the front door. To be quite honest, I'm still giving the bike appreciative glances myself, finding it hard to believe that the lovely and very rare Agusta is mine. Acknowledging his obvious envy, I nod at him, then step forwards getting down to business. My credentials are already in my hand.

As I approach the doorway, the constable holds out his arm effectively blocking the entrance and, bike forgotten now, he gives me a suspicious look. "Can you tell me your business here, sir?"

In answer I hold up my card which identifies me as a privately employed CPO or, in layman's terms, a Close Protection Officer or bodyguard as we used to be called, working on behalf of Grade A Security Ltd, Security Consultants. In fact, I'm one of the three partners, but there's little need for him to know that. Or that the reason I'm here is on behalf of Ben Carter, the senior partner who apparently owes a literary agent friend of his a favour. As he's up to his neck in an important case at the moment, I stepped in to help.

Of course, realistically I could have sent one of the many experienced ex-police or ex-military officers that we have working for us as CPOs, but I decided to come in person after spending last night reading one of Dexie Sanders' novels as background research. Just remembering the scene of the submissive servicing her Dom and the very detailed and competent way in which it was handled has me shifting my legs to avoid exposing the developing bulge in my jeans. I don't want to be arrested for public indecency. *But boy, that girl can write!* Perhaps the plot didn't interest me with its happily ever after ending, but even *I* learned something from the intimate scenes she wrote about, and I'd thought I'd seen it all! *Whoa. Down boy!* I half turn away as I will my unruly cock to behave.

I hear the commotion still going on inside and realise it's time to get my mind back to the business in hand, and ascertain what the fuck's going on. I didn't expect to turn up to find police swarming around, and the sight is disconcerting. But I take heart there's no ambulance here, which hopefully means I've still got a body to protect. "What's happened?" I ask the police officer at the door. Ben's already briefed me on Tuesday's stalker issue.

Having accepted my credentials, and luckily oblivious to my now, fortunately, receding state of arousal, the constable tells me. "A bunch of white lilies was delivered earlier today. And another threat."

"Delivered here?" I check. As he nods I still, realising the implications that quickly have the effect of entirely dousing my ardour. The stalker knows where she lives. That puts a difference connotation on the case. "Can I go inside?" I wave my hand to the front door, requesting permission with the gesture. He's not going to keep me out, but I go through the appropriate motions which will keep him happy, and avoid certain argument were I just to barge in. He's clearly a stickler for following the rule; a 'job's worth' type.

After a short hesitation during which he gives me a careful scrutiny, his thought processes apparently running through the procedures he's been taught to follow, he stands back to let me through. I walk across to another police officer who appears to have custody of a card in a plastic evidence bag and introduce myself all over again. I find taking the initiative and dotting every 'i' and crossing every 't' right from the start usually helps me gain co-operation more smoothly. So once more I show my identification and give him the extra information that Grade A will be providing any required protection and security arrangements for Ms Fable. Then I request sight of the latest threat. He clearly knows of Grade A and our stellar reputation, so doesn't appear to have a problem with either my presence or request, and shows me the note, watching my face to see my reaction. I whistle quietly through my teeth, knowing that while the threat is worrying, the delivery address and the name it's addressed to, is of most concern.

Nodding my thanks and handing the evidence bag back, I make my way on through the small, homely lounge and down a short hallway with the stairs off to one side. I arrive at the entrance to the kitchen where a detective is evidently going through the motions with Mia Fable, the identity behind Dexie Sanders. Holding back before entering, I listen in to the discussion. It's soon becoming clear the police aren't going to be of much help, but no one could criticise them for that – there isn't a lot to go on, I'm stumped at the moment too. The detective tells her that a florist could have delivered the flowers – an apparent effort to calm her fears that the stalker personally came to her house – and that they'll be checking with the shop whose name decorated the card. As I listen to their conversation, I take the opportunity to glance around her small home.

It's not large but wouldn't have been cheap considering the area that it's in and it's proximity to London. She's a successful writer, but that's not a particularly high earning profession. There are monetary implications for Grade A of taking this case on; I've already drawn down Mia's financials, and the bottom line is if she needs a full-time CPO, and with the latest threat it's likely she does, she won't be able to afford our standard rates. But we've taken on cases before pro bono, or at a considerably reduced fee if we think the case is worthwhile. And of course,

Ben's already committed us to helping her out. I have to admit I'm curious as to exactly what favour he's repaying, but that's none of my concern for the moment. Though perhaps one day I'll get him drunk enough to find out.

Putting my thoughts about that particular mystery aside, I hear an opening when there's a pause in the conversation happening in the kitchen, and step into the room. Realising as I do so, how unlikely it is that a twenty-four-year-old woman who seemingly spends her life locked up with her books would know where to start looking for a security system or a company to fit it. Especially, when it needs to be installed in a hurry. "You can leave that to me," I say, firmly.

As the words leave my mouth, Mia Fable turns, and as I get my first glance of the author behind the sexy novel I'd read. And it's at that point I immediately regret coming here in person today, and not assigning the case over to somebody else. I'm not arrogant, and my looks aren't your typical definition of handsome, but I've been around long enough to know that something about the way I'm put together makes me attractive to a significant proportion of the opposite sex. I could have a different woman in my bed every night of the week if I so wish and, I have to admit, often do. But to give my full attention to a person I'm supposed to be protecting, it's preferable that they're immune to my charms and I to theirs. I'm a man, after all, and wouldn't be a very effective bodyguard if I'm balls deep fucking the daylights out of the woman I'm supposed to keep safe. And the way Mia's devouring me with her eyes shows she's very far from immune to my charms. But what surprises me most is my own immediate, visceral reaction to her.

There was no photo on the jacket of the novel I'd read and Grade A hadn't had time to compile much of a dossier on her, so I'd been prepared to be disappointed. My mind had conjured up this writer of such erotic fiction would turn out to be a not particularly attractive, possibly overweight young woman, living vicariously through the lives of her characters. But my rather low expectations turn out to be one hundred percent wrong. Now, my cock will stand at attention for females of all shapes and sizes, but it's rare I do anything other than admire from afar unless it's a playmate who'll have no qualms about a temporary arrangement. But this woman, with such delicate, ethereal beauty about her, and a figure I want to get my hands on, looks so lost I just want to fold my arms around her and hold her tight. And I'm not sure if I'd ever want to let her go. *Mine!* Unbidden the thought comes into my head.

What. The. Fuck?

Utterly disturbed by this strange reaction, I watch as she gets to her feet, her hand clutching the back of the wheel-back chair as though she needs the support. "Who the fuck are you?" she asks. Her voice is unsteady, but the tone is soft and melodious, the swear word sounding harsh coming from her lips.

Fuck, I've got to get out of here. Her voice stirs regions which have no business being stirred while I'm working, and my desire to protect her has nothing at all to do with me being here in my professional capacity. I look at her face, instantly captivated by her large brown eyes, currently open wide and fraught with worry. *Freaking hell, they're pretty.* As her scrutiny meets mine, she can't hold my eye and her gaze drops to the floor, and I have to suppress a grin. Continuing my examination I see chestnut brown shoulder-length hair hanging down in waves, framing her oval face. If I wanted to be critical, her nose is a little large and not perfectly straight, but it works to give her a unique attractiveness. My gaze drops lower, and any feeling of arousal fades and turns to anger when I see the darkening bruises around her neck where the bastard grabbed her two days ago. Immediately I want to cause serious injury to the man who caused the damage.

The challenge to stay calm and collected is not one I've ever had to fight with on a job before. Usually, I've no trouble staying dispassionate and focused. The intensity of these feelings, quite foreign to me quickly make me realise how wrong it would be for me to offer her my personal protection. In my head, I run through the other CPOs who work for Grade A and who are currently available. Sean or Ryan, perhaps? But something inside of me flares at even the thought of either of those experienced Doms being anywhere near this obvious submissive. Harry, maybe? He's in Amahad at the moment, but I could call him back. At least he's happily married and in his forties. There has to be someone. Quickly I rack my brains.

She's staring at me, and I realise I haven't answered her question. "My name's Jon Tharpe." I introduce myself, walking forward and holding out my hand for the requisite handshake. She hesitates, before tentatively taking my hand in her own and shaking it and I swear sparks fly as we make contact, skin to skin. Carefully schooling my features to hide my reaction, I extract yet another business card from my wallet, and hand it over to her. As she reads the information on it, my mouth opens, and the words came out before I have a chance to filter them. "Your agent has contacted us to provide close protection for you. I'll be staying with you as your CPO until we find out just what's going on here." In case she doesn't understand, I clarify, "I'll be your bodyguard."

What?

Fuck, what the hell's got into me? Why did I tell her that? I should have told her that I was just here to assess the situation; that someone else would be doing the actual work, but my thought and speech centres seem disconnected as I find myself committing to giving her my full, personal attention. She needs someone here to protect and reassure her, and somehow my subconscious has decided that person is going to be me, and no one fucking else.

She takes a step back, putting some distance between us. The flush making her cheeks pink suggests whatever the attraction is between us is mutual. *I fucking hope so!* I'm angry with myself. This is a crazy situation and not one I've ever had to deal with before. But I just can't bring myself to be the one to walk away. *If she's sensible, she'll demand someone else.* I hold my breath, knowing I'm hoping she won't take the prudent option.

"Thank you, Mr Tharpe, but I'm certain I won't be able to afford…" she looks at my card, "Grade A Security." There's a slight tremor in her voice, but whether it's her reaction to my presence or to the events of the morning I have no way of knowing.

With a wave, I brush off her concerns, "We'll talk about the finances later. But for now, let me go and organise that security system for you." My voice is quiet, but purposely full of authority, leaving her no room for argument without revealing an irrational response to me. For her to make a refusal of help at this point would be difficult to justify.

Even so, she seems about to protest when the detective coughs, drawing her attention back to him. "Someone staying with you here is probably the best option for now." He nods at me, "Thanks for coming. I'll leave you to take this from here." Glancing back to Mia he tells her, "We'll be in touch if we have any new information for you." With that parting shot he ups and leaves, gathering up his team of police officers with him.

I smirk, realising he's metaphorically kicked the ball at me and run off the field as quickly as he can.

Seeing Mia is about to speak and to forestay any further objection to my presence, I hold up my hand to stop her, "Let me make this call first, and then we can discuss how this is going to work."

Calling up one of my pre-set numbers, I get straight through to our security department and request the system she needs, emphasising that it has to be installed today and dismissing Howie's protests at being giving yet another rush job. When I explain the situation, the security consultant agrees to make it a priority. As I end the call, she raises her eyes to look at me, having to crane her neck as she only just reaches to my shoulder. My cock twitches. A small woman feeds my protective instinct; I'd be able to tuck neatly under my arm. A woman I can lift and fuck in the shower, against a wall… *Fuck Tharpe; get your filthy mind back on the work in hand.* I force my thoughts out of the gutter and lower my head to meet her eyes. As she raises her eyebrows, I see she's surprised by my side of the phone conversation I just had, and what I was asking for.

"Cameras? That will cost a fortune." She's biting her lip, concerned and reluctant.

I know it will seem expensive to her, but the question has to be asked. "How much is your life worth, Ms Fable?"

She stills, and then a mirthless laugh comes out of her mouth. "Probably more than I can afford," she says, disparagingly.

I need to touch her, comfort her; it's the last thing an experienced CPO should do, but I reach out my hand and gently rest my fingers on her arm. "I know your financial situation, Mia, down to the last penny. It's the first thing we do when we take on work for a new client. Our fees will not be outside of your budget. The most important task for us is keeping you safe; the cost doesn't come into it." I know she's going to protest the intrusion into her personal life, but that's how Grade A functions. We fleece the likes of wealthy oil sheikhs and millionaires when we work for them, so we can lower our charges for people who need us. It's a system that works.

"How dare you access my personal information!" she hisses at me.

I just shrug, and let her think about it for a moment. Then, as she's about to challenge me I forestay her, "The upshot is, you can afford us. And, sweetheart, you need protection." The endearment slips from my lips without me being consciously aware of it. *Fuck where did that come from?* Luckily she doesn't seem to notice.

She walks away from me; her frown showing wheels are turning in her head. She'd be stupid to turn us away, and she's soon going to realise she's no other option. I give her a few minutes to process what I told her, and feel something in the air alter around us as she reaches the obvious conclusion. Her shoulders slump when she realises this is the only path she can take. "So, the security system," she begins, but then, as she remembers, adds with her eyes narrowed, "But you said you'd stay…?"

I nod.

She's shaking her head, her eyes narrowed and a slight flush to her cheeks, "I'm not sure I'm comfortable with that. I don't want anyone here." Then she adds with emphasis, "I don't want *you* here."

Asking her why would be stupid. There's no denying there's something inexplicable between us, and if it's scaring her, it's terrifying me. I've never felt such a strong connection so quickly with anyone else. Sure, I've seen women I've immediately wanted to strip and fuck, but this goes far deeper than that with the woman standing in front of me. My head tells me to run away as fast and far as possible while my dick tells me to stay close and explore what's happening. My heart tells me… Christ, what the hell has my heart got to do with it? That organ is covered in cobwebs and dust and has never been involved in any relationship before.

I'm an experienced Dom; I should know how to keep myself under control. But today, acting logically seems impossible.

Despite common sense dictating I leave before things get complicated, I find words coming out of my mouth to convince her to let me stay. "It's not safe for you to be alone. The threats might just be a cruel joke to upset you, or they could be very real. Do you really want to stay here by yourself knowing that there's a fucking lunatic out there and that he knows where you live? Keeping you safe isn't a nine-to-five job. Your stalker isn't going to conveniently time his threats, or attacks, to take place during normal working hours. You need twenty-four-hour protection."

I watch as she takes a deep indrawn breath. Even though I get the feeling that I'm playing with dynamite, I continue to persuade her, "I'm here; I've made the necessary contact with the police, and I'm up to speed with what's happened." I run my hand through my hair as if thinking and then lie, another thing I don't normally do. "We don't have anyone else available, Ms Fable." I resist the impulse to touch my nose to see if it has lengthened.

I don't miss the point when she accepts the inevitable, and her face drops as she gives in. "You'll be staying overnight?"

"Until we catch the bastard, yes. Either myself or one of my colleagues, if I'm tied up elsewhere." Or tying someone up. As soon as I get my head on straight, I'll appoint someone to provide me with back up and time off – twenty-four-seven with Mia Fable might just be the end of me. The quicker I'm out of here and get back to my usual self the better. A boy's gotta play sometime, and a night in the BDSM club I frequent might be just what I need. But she'll need someone else to provide cover if I'm not here. *Damn it! I don't want anyone else near her!* And then I wonder what playing with her would be like. Fuck, is my cock doing all my thinking today?

"I use the spare room as an office…." She's still struggling to come up with excuses.

"The couch will be perfect." It looks lumpy and not big enough for my tall frame, but maybe I won't be sleeping there for long. I freeze, as I realise a very particular part of me is hoping to get into her bed. *No Tharpe. That's NOT what you're going to do!* Fuck, what the hell is the matter with me? I've been a CPO for long enough to know you *don't* get involved with a client. It's the number one rule in the book!

"Oh." She fidgets; her hands clasp and unclasp as if she's not quite sure what to do with them. She seems lost, which is not far from the way I'm feeling. Looking up at me with those large brown eyes, she asks, "What happens next?"

That one's easy. "Next, I take you to lunch, and we try to make some sense of what's going on. Is there a pub nearby?"

CHAPTER 4
Mia

Seven years ago

Checking the number to make sure it's the right house, I paused by the front gate while I summoned up the nerve to go to the door and knock. This was the first – and, as it turned out, the last – teenage party I went to, and I had no idea what to expect. Fortifying myself with a couple of deep breaths, I started up the path.

While I was in the middle of deciding whether to use the knocker or ring the bell the door opened and to my surprise, Anna immediately stepped out and drew me into a tight friendly hug. "I'm so glad you came, Mia." She beamed at me.

I gave a weak smile, feeling a bit suspicious as I shrugged and replied, "I don't know why you invited me."

Putting her head on one side, she gave me a serious look and then nodded as if making a decision. "My mum meets yours at the Ladies' Fellowship Group at church. Says she's a mad old bat?" Her voice rose on the last word as if asking me a question.

Part of me felt I should be defending my mum, but the description was wicked, and Anna's grin was taking the sting out of her words. So I laughed. "That's one way of putting it."

"Apparently, she tried to veto a Bingo session as it was an invention of the devil!"

I looked down, feeling embarrassed. Yes, I'd heard all about that. I could only hope she hadn't been quite as virulent in front *of the other church ladies as she'd been at home telling me about it.*

"Anyway," Anna continued without waiting for a response. "I felt a bit sorry for you – I thought my mum was bad enough. Hence the invitation!" She finished with a flourish and threw open the door. "Come on inside!"

Present day

He's taking me out for a drink? I suppose it's a sensible suggestion to get out of the house for a bit. A change of surroundings, after the intense morning I've had, might help me put things into perspective, but there's something about the way he has walked in and taken over that I don't like. I hate the way he's so dominant, so sure of himself. Telling me, not asking. Not giving me the opportunity to decline his services. Deep down, I understand I need what he's offering; what the hell do I know about the kind of security of protection I ought to have? And I have to remember it's Val who's organised this, I trust her, and that she knows what she's doing. She wouldn't put me in touch with a firm that wasn't reliable and didn't have a good reputation.

I've got a stalker who's come right to my door, and categorically I don't want to have to deal with him on my own if he turns up to make a personal visit. Having someone here should be a very comforting thought, but I just wish it wasn't going to be *this* man who's providing that protection for me. My irrational attraction to him unnerves me. *I shouldn't feel like this, I've never had this kind of reaction before.* When he touched my arm, a bolt of electricity went through me, making me want to turn and run, to get out of this house, to another place, another country, another continent. Anywhere, I don't care where. As long as it's as far away from him as possible! How can he affect me like this? Deep down on a physical level, he's made parts of me awaken that I thought were completely dead. I'd figured I was immune from the baser instincts, and the realisation I might not be – *dammit, it scares me stiff.*

And apart from my strange response to his presence, I'm irritated that Grade A seemed to have checked my financials and violated they've obviously hacked into my personal accounts. And even if he knows down to the last penny the amount I've got saved, I still have concerns whether his view of what is affordable is the same as mine. I don't want to spend the money I've put aside in case my career goes down the drain; my reserves are there, so I never need to go back to living hand to mouth, skipping meals to have enough money to pay the rent. I did that for long enough after I left home and struggled to manage on a student grant. As I glare at him, I'm lost in my memories, reminiscing on those days I survived with hardly any money, or food for that matter. He coughs, pulling me back to the present.

Unable to think of any other option that wouldn't leave me exposed and unprotected, I glower and stand up straight, needing to take back some control. Before I agree to go anywhere, I want to check where I stand. "You'll give me a breakdown of your charges?" I ask.

He grins, realising the question means I'm giving in, and lifts his chin. "The office is sorting it out now. But you don't need to worry about the cost, Miss Fable. You *need* us. I'm not walking away leaving you at the mercy of this bastard."

I realise until now his face has been stern and unyielding; the new expression makes him look younger and more approachable. Butterflies flutter in my stomach and I have to look away. *God! He's even more attractive when he smiles.* His words, though, give me some comfort; I'm not mentally or physically equipped to face this alone. Turning back, I study my new protector. Goodness knows how frigging tall he is; he must be well over six foot. At five-foot-seven I'm not short myself, but this man dwarves me. He's broad, and it's obviously not fat, but muscle. As a bodyguard, he's probably going to be a good one. As someone who's going to be offering close protection, he's a threat to my well-being. Trying to clear my head of my unexpected reaction to him, focusing on the practicalities instead, I take a breath, and then a leap into the unknown and at last answer his original question. "There's a decent pub down the road," I tell him.

* * * *

Within easy walking distance, the fairly typical country pub strangely named The Blazing Donkey advertises its fifteenth-century origins on a squeaky swinging sign out front. Inside, the low beams mean my companion has to duck his head, but the setting is quaint, the epitome of an English ale house. At this time of the afternoon, it's nice and quiet; just right for the type of conversation we're going to have. Knowing he's probably going to be asking me all kinds of personal details to try and identify the stalker and, preferring no one to be within earshot, I lead the way to a small table beside a large inglenook fireplace. A fire's been lit, and it casts a cheery glow over the room; flames flicker, their light dancing and reflecting on the horse brasses which adorn either side and up and over the chimney breast. I let out a deep sigh as I sit down and start to relax for the first time since finding the flowers left on my doorstep. It's good to be in a different environment and, I have to admit, to not feel like I'm dealing with all this on my own.

A log basket is full by the grate. The landlord comes over and throws another on the fire. "Bit chilly today," he greets us, rubbing his hands together, as the thick wood begins to smoulder.

We both nod and agree out of politeness in the way people do, and would, even if the truth was entirely different. As the barman goes back to take his place behind the bar, Jon asks me what I'd like to drink. Leaving my coat behind to reserve the seat, I get up, indicating I'm going with him and wait beside him as he orders himself a half of bitter as well as my white wine. Carefully, I watch the barman as he gets a bottle of wine out of the fridge and pours the correct measure into my glass. I carry my glass back to the table; while Jon brings his drink and a couple of menus with him. It's only now I realise that I completely missed lunch and that I'm hungry. Food would be good! It's basic pub fare, and luckily their kitchen is open all day. Quickly I decide on lasagne – I just need to eat, and I don't care what. Jon says he'll have the same. As he gets up to place our orders, I offer him the money for my meal, but he won't take it, informing me he's already started a tab. Sipping my wine my sceptical self-expects, despite his protestations, the cost of the food will appear on my bill for Grade A services at some point in the future. But I'd noted the prices; luckily the food is relatively inexpensive.

My gaze follows this man who'll apparently be my bodyguard. He's standing at the bar, his back towards me. As my eyes take him in from head to toe, I appreciate the fit of his jeans over his taut backside, his muscles clenching as he rests one foot on the brass rail surrounding the bottom of the bar. Suddenly I have the desire to trace his firm buttocks with my hands. Shocked at myself I look away, not understanding what's happening to me. *I don't fucking ogle men!* I lift my glass of wine and take another long sip, forcing myself to look away from him.

God, what's got into me today? Is it the shock of everything that's happened? Is my disturbed state of mind having an effect on my libido? Bloody hell, I've got to control myself. Heaven help me, if he realises he's only got to look at me to start me trembling in anticipation of his touch. What would his reaction be if he knew? He'd probably laugh himself silly. He's just... Wow. He probably only has to crook his little finger to get any girl he wants, he would never be interested in someone like me in a million years! Putting down my glass, I lean forwards and place my head in my hands, my eyes staring into the dancing flames of the fire. I've got to play this as shy retiring Mia. *Keep a bloody back seat, Dexie; I don't need you to come out with any clever comments that could get me into trouble.* What a joke. The first time I find myself interested in a man, it's someone who probably wouldn't look twice at me. Ruefully, my lips curve into a smile. Someone that handsome, that virile, must have to beat interested women off with a stick.

Want me? That must be the biggest joke of the century. My smile turns to a frown, as I realise doubtless I'd just be one of a very long line. No, I must hide any sign of my interest in my new protector. Given that I'm just a job to him, it would only make him feel awkward and embarrassed. Let's face it, apart from my theoretical knowledge I've no experience to deal with a man who simply oozes sexuality.

CHAPTER 5

Jon

Five years ago

I had no inkling before it happened, no prior warning or premonition, but this was to be my last tour of duty. My final assignment; an extraction. We recovered the target; he got out alive, but half my team was taken out by a dirty bomb as we'd made our retreat. I was one of the lucky ones, alive, but in hospital needing shrapnel removed from my chest and a particularly nasty chunk from my lower back which for a short time had caused talk of permanent paralysis. I was better off than most; in time, I'd make a near complete recovery, but not full enough for the SAS to allow me to resume active duties. But mentally? There the healing would take much longer. The explosion played in my head on a loop. What could I have done differently to have prevented the deaths of my men? What sign had I missed? I didn't know how I'd ever get over the guilt that something had been overlooked; a change in the ground, movement of the enemy I hadn't seen. Something, anything that could have changed the outcome.

So there I was, unemployed. An ex-army man with no experience with anything else, I was left with little option other than to accept the job offer Ben Carter first enticed me with the year before. Unable to afford to buy in as a partner, I signed on as a Close Protection Officer. With discharge papers in hand, I entered the employment of Grade A Security but barely managed *to get my arse in my seat before Ben sent me out on a long term posting as CPO for one Sheikh Nijad Kassis, Prince of Amahad and third in line to the throne of his country. Knowing it was quite a coup for Grade A to secure such a lucrative contract, it demonstrated the trust Ben had in me, and I was determined to make the most of what could be either a monotonous and dull, or exciting and extremely dangerous – and probably a mixture of both – role. To top it off, from my research Nijad was a typical playboy sheikh, and had nothing visibly hiding in his closet. I was looking forward to meeting the man for whom I'd be a constant companion, for quite probably, the next few years.*

Present day

The pub is homely and welcoming, and the landlord jovial; the perfect atmosphere in which to question Mia. Returning to my seat, I see she's already started to relax. Out of her house and away from the police, the lines start receding from her forehead and, as she sips her wine, I see the first real smile from her, and it transforms her face, making me hold my breath as I realise she's even more beautiful than I'd first thought. Watching her, I find myself wanting to know everything about her, far more depth than I need to run the case. I want to know all her likes, dislikes, and how she prefers it in bed. *Shit, there I go again.* Rubbing my hand across my eyes, I wonder what the fuck is wrong with me. *This is the wrong time, the wrong place, and definitely the wrong woman.* However much I want to get to know her, to understand the pull she seems to have on me, I need to focus on the task I'm here for and be one hundred percent hands-off. We've no time for idle chit-chat. Particularly, as right now I'm going to have to steel myself to be a brute; we've got things to talk about, and she's not going to get away with lying to me. Stalkers don't stalk for no reason, there has to be something that's triggered it, and that's what I need to find out. I can't let her hide anything from me.

Preparing myself for an awkward conversation, I down a good part of my beer – only a half-pint as I need to keep my wits about me – and then school my features carefully. "You know him, Mia. I'm sure you do." I use her name for the first time; she doesn't correct me.

"What makes you say that?" Puzzled, she turns her head away from the fire that's been mesmerising her and looks straight at me.

That's right; I want to see your eyes for this. "The way the notes are worded. You *owe* him. This person thinks you've taken something from him."

To give her her due, she takes a moment to think about it. "I've been thinking about it ever since Tuesday. But I can't begin to imagine there's anyone I owe anything to. Not in the money sense or otherwise. No one's done me any favours that I haven't repaid; I'm certain of that." Sounding frustrated, she picks up her glass for another sip. "I wish I could say 'oh yes, there was that person who' as it would make everything so much simpler. But there's no one I can point the finger at."

The barman comes over with two sets of cutlery wrapped in a napkin and then places two mats on the table. He reaches over to the next table and puts salt and pepper pots in front of us, together with an assortment of sauces in little plastic sachets. "Won't be long now."

We both acknowledge him with a nod and a 'thank you'. She's back to watching the fire. I need to know all I can about anyone who's close to her. There's something personal about how those notes are worded. Knowing the police have already questioned her about likely suspects, I'm approaching from a different angle. Reaching out my hand, I gently grip her chin, moving her head around to face me. "Will your boyfriend mind me staying over?"

She quickly moves away from my touch as if it burns her, but laughs softly. Her humour seems to be directed at herself. "I haven't got a boyfriend."

I'm surprised but admit I'm pleased, more than I should be. I scold myself that it shouldn't matter, but it's good to know I haven't got any competition. Then give myself a mental slap on the wrist, I really mustn't get involved. The fact she's available, however, does open a line of questioning. "Your last boyfriend? Did you part on friendly terms?"

A red flush crosses her face. *Ah*, I think to myself. *There's something here. Something she's concealing.* But at that moment, our food arrives, and she makes a fuss of putting dressing on her salad and salt on her chips, the normal accompaniments to typical English pub fare. I stare at her while she's preparing her meal, shaking my head at her evasion, but then do the same to mine. We start to eat. I give her a few minutes; it looks like she's hungry.

She glances up at me watching her eat and smiles, "I didn't eat breakfast and missed lunch. Thanks for this, I was starving!"

"You're welcome," I smile back at her, suppressing the comment that it's her Dom's job to look after all her needs. *Her Dom? What the fuck?* The frown that comes to my face is as much for me, as for her evasion. "You didn't answer my question. Your last boyfriend?" I prompt.

She takes a few more mouthfuls, puts down her knife and fork then blots her lips with her napkin. "No need to go there, there are no ex-boyfriends with or without an axe to grind waiting in the wings." She looks away, and then back, and after a sigh, adds, "I suppose you need to know that there have been no boyfriends at all, axes or no axes."

I can't hide my look of surprise, not immediately able to compute what she's telling me. To gain some time to process her admission, I indicate she should continue eating; she needs to look after herself. I don't want her to stress out, so I give her some peace while she finishes her food. But as soon as she's done I start again. "Have you ever been married?"

Shaking her head, she laughs without any real mirth. "You didn't understand me. There's never been a man in my life at all."

Am I stupid? Did I misinterpret the look she gave me back at her house? I'm sure it's not true and if it is my gaydar needs a tune up. "Girlfriends?"

This time, she snorts a laugh, "Not in a sexual sense."

I lean back in the chair and stretch my legs out in front of me, crossing them at the ankle and fold my arms, relieved I'm not off base. But as I try to fathom out her answers there's something's amiss, and I'm having difficultly working it through. She writes erotic fiction, but has never had a boyfriend? That makes no sense at all. I try again, "So you have short-term liaisons? One night stands?" Perhaps she's into playing like me? Writing the kind of books she does, she needs a certain amount of experience.

She turns her head away, looking anywhere but at me, and replies far too quietly; I'm only just able to hear her. "No. I've never had a one night stand. I don't have any relationships with men."

My brow furrows as I frown, trying to comprehend what she's telling me. I'm aware I'm perhaps straying outside of the professional arena; I started this conversation so we could trace ex-boyfriends to find out if anyone might want to harm or frighten her. Now I'm interested in the answer on a very personal level. Sitting up straighter again, I reach out and touch her arm, waiting patiently until she turns back to me. Again I feel a slight flinch as my hand makes contact, so as soon as I have her attention, I remove it. There's a question on my mind that I need to keep inside for now, and her apparent aversion to personal contact is another clue I'm filing away in my mind. It's not the time or place to ask for such intimate details, but before my brain can kick in and stop it; once again the words somehow escape from my fucking mouth before I can censor them to my immediate regret. "Are you a virgin?" I knew it was a mistake the second I asked.

My question brings tears to her eyes. Her mouth falls open, and she's looking at me in shock as though she can't believe I've asked such a personal question, and being honest, neither can I. My directness has upset her. She shakes her head, whether to give me my answer or as a refusal to respond it's hard to tell. But she can't meet my eyes for long. Her head hangs down, and her shoulders slump making me feel the nastiest motherfucker alive. It's clear from her posture that she's closed herself off. I'd felt we were getting a rapport going; it had been all too easy to sit and talk with her. But I've gone and destroyed that now. What a bloody arsehole I am, rushing in with that type of question, just like a bull in the proverbial china shop. *How much damage I've done? How can I regain her trust?* And at the back of my mind, an unwelcome thought niggles at me, something I don't even want to consider in relation to this sweet woman sitting across from me. *Fuck no! Don't let it be that!* I'll have to press her at some point, but I know she wouldn't be answering that particular enquiry right now.

Suppressing the unpleasant direction of my thoughts, it's clear all we're doing now is sitting in an awkward unproductive silence and, unusually for me, I'm at a loss for something to say to make things right between us. My thoughts are making me tense, and I'm loathe for her to pick up on, and possibly misinterpret it. After letting a few minutes tick by, I stand, go settle up the tab, then return to her, holding up her coat and passing it to her. She takes it without protest; knowing as well as I do there's no point staying here any longer, any progress towards a rapport has disappeared. She comes with me willingly enough, but walks stiffly, the earlier friendliness completely gone. As I hold the pub door open, it's easy to read the pained expression on her face, and I hate that I've put it there. But worse, I get a feeling of dread in my stomach as I become sure I'm interpreting the clues correctly. I'm not often wrong when I read people, but now I'm still trying hard to think of any plausible alternative, not wanting the quiet, mild woman beside me to have gone through the ordeal my brain's coming up with.

As we walk along the path leading back to her house my phone rings, slicing through the silence between us, and providing a welcome release from my darker thoughts. Glancing at the screen, I see it's our security guy. "Howie, are you at the house?" I'm glad of the interruption.

"Yeah, we just arrived. Only to find she needs new locks as well now." To say Howie sounds pissed off is an understatement.

I narrow my eyes, not understanding. "I thought they were okay?"

"Until they were busted in they were!"

"*What?*" I step away from her to make sure she doesn't hear too much of the conversation until I've had time to understand what's happened.

"Yeah, we got here about ten minutes ago. Someone's broken the lock on the front door, and has obviously been inside."

"Fuck! We've only been gone an hour or so. Christ, he must have been watching the house. Have you been inside?" I hold my breath, a hundred different scenarios flicking through my head.

"Yes." Howie takes a breath. "Someone's been in her office; it's a mess in there."

"Shit! Have they taken anything?" I ask him.

"Not that I can tell, her laptop's here, other computer equipment. It seems like someone's swept everything else off the desk. But there's an envelope that's been left on the keyboard. I don't want to touch it."

Howie knows better than to handle anything that might have fingerprints on it. I ask him if he's called the police, he hasn't, thinking I might want to speak to my contact direct. Agreeing, I end the call. Mia is looking at me with distress on her face; she knows there's something wrong. I turn to face her. Putting my hand on her arm, I feel how tense she's become, and her stress only increases as I give her the gist of Howie's call.

I can't help but frown as her face crumbles. "He's been in my house?" She's shaken, and I appreciate how frightening the news must be for her. As I nod in answer to her question she continues, almost mumbling to herself as the implications sink in. "He was watching the house, wasn't he? Waiting to see the police leave. What would have happened if I'd been there alone?" She looks up at me, her worry palpable. Her previous anger at me seems to have been forgotten in the light of this most recent invasion. "I'm scared, Jon!"

"I know, sweetheart," the endearment slipping out again before I can stop it. I put my arm around her, pulling her into my side, trying to give her comfort, telling myself I'm not stepping over the line, and this time, she doesn't pull away. "He left another note, for now, it seems like he's toying with you, wanting to frighten you." I think about it for a second, "It might be that's all he wants." I give her a gentle squeeze. "And rest assured I won't be leaving you alone until we've caught this bastard, so don't worry about that. I've got to ring the police now, so bear with me for a moment." Fumbling my wallet out of my pocket one-handed, I take out the card Coulton gave me and place a call direct to the detective. He's not there, but I leave a message. The whole time she's looking at me with those big brown eyes making it hard for me to keep my distance. Once again, everything that I am wants to protect her and comfort her, and not in a Grade A approved way. I force myself to take a step back, my arm dropping to my side, "Come on; we've got to get back. I'll be with you, don't worry. That's why I'm here, remember? To keep you safe."

She hesitates, looking straight into my eyes. I can see her pupils are dilated, not with the passion I'd like to see, but with fear and dread. Then taking in a deep breath, showing me she's drawing on strength from somewhere deep inside her, she allows me to lead her down the road, back to the pretty cottage that up until now must have been her safe haven.

As we go through the front gate, I call out a greeting to Howie's crew who have continued installing the tiny cameras that are almost impossible to see, but which provide high-quality pictures of anything happening around the house, equipped with night vision. Expensive, but Grade A had often found they come in very useful, and will mean at least from now on the stalker won't be able to approach the house undetected. The team will be fitting a state of the art security system inside as well, together with panic buttons which will send an alert straight to the local police station, as well as to Grade A and, as the CPO for the case, direct to my phone.

Howie joins us, but Mia's shows her reluctance to step through the front door, and it's not hard to understand why; having an uninvited visitor to your home is never pleasant, and particularly so under the present circumstances. I take her arm and encourage her in, knowing she'll be feeling violated. The intruder couldn't have been there long, but however many minutes he spent in her house was that many minutes too long.

As Howie has already told me, nothing's been touched downstairs; he only targeted her study; the room in the house that's probably most important to her. Walking beside her up the stairs, my hand hovers behind her back, but I don't touch her; wanting to provide reassurance, but desperately trying to maintain a discreet professional distance. A desire that gets increasingly hard to resist as, being taller and able to see over her head, I get the same first glimpse through the open door as she does.

The room's a total mess. Paper and index cards she apparently uses for planning have been swept off her desk and onto the floor, and other furniture has been overturned. Nothing that can't be put back into place, but the mess is distressing all the same. And right in our line of vision, the whole purpose of him coming into her house, the envelope propped up against her laptop. The message is clear; it's to make her feel exactly what she's feeling; insecure and nervous in her home. And, as her study is the only room touched, strongly suggesting the reason for her stalker's attention has something to do with her writing. By coming into her office and the positioning of his latest missive, his attack is aimed at the very heart of her work.

The envelope is lying in the middle of the keyboard, Mia's name typed in large font on the front. Stepping closer to the desk, I take a penknife from my pocket and using a piece of paper to protect it from my fingerprints, I slice the envelope open, flicking out the card that's inside. Bending over to examine it, I shield her from the writing until I've had a chance to study it first.

GETTING CLOSER! NOWHERE'S SAFE, BITCH! YOU'RE GOING TO HAVE A TASTE OF WHAT YOU LOVED SO MUCH BEFORE.

CHAPTER 6

Mia

Seven years ago

I was so naïve! *The party was due to start at eight o'clock, so that's the time I arrived, not realising that most people typically wouldn't turn up until later. At first, I found myself in the company of Anna, and a couple of girls I'd seen around school. I hadn't shared the same lessons with them so didn't know them that well, but they seemed pleasant and friendly enough, and I was lulled into a false sense of security, thinking the party tame enough to satisfy even my mother.*

By ten o'clock, the numbers had increased and the crowd grew rowdier. By eleven o'clock all thoughts of leaving early had gone from my head. I'm enjoying myself! Dancing to what my mum would call the devil's music and having a whale of a time listening to the typical conversations of teenage girls which seemed to revolve around sex, sex, and more sex; a topic on which I could only listen but not contribute. Their discussions shocked me, and I spent most of the time with my hand over my mouth smothering my embarrassment and giggling while thinking this is what it's like to be a teenager! As I hadn't brought any myself, I refused the offers of alcohol – how was I supposed to know what's expected for this type of party? I did, however, try a cigarette offered to me which made me feel dizzy and resulted in a bout of coughing making everyone laugh good-naturedly. I was enjoying myself; my new friends seemed to like me.

Around half-past eleven, the large sitting room was already full, and bodies were overflowing all over the house. Some boys had arrived, and to my new friend Anna's horror pairs started to form and disappeared upstairs to the bedrooms. She looked worried when she told me there were also a few gate crashers, people she hadn't invited and didn't even know. I saw she was becoming concerned about the state the house was going to be left in. Many of the newcomers looked far older than our average age of seventeen. But after another couple of drinks, even she stopped being so anxious.

As the sexes paired up, my circle of girlfriends around me diminished. The music was loud; the odour of sweat and cigarette smoke mixed with perfume began to fog my brain. I started to feel uneasy, and it was at that point I began to think it might be a very good time to leave.

Present day

Leaning over Jon's shoulder, I read the words and shudder. Christ almighty! Just when I think I can't take anymore, there's another of those bloody messages. Reeling back I run out of my office, unable to stay there a minute longer. It's only a mess of paperwork; he hadn't damaged any of the equipment, but the mindless destruction and intrusion into my home hurt me. It's too personal; he's got too close. With shaking hands and a feeling of nausea, I go back down the stairs, all the while looking around my cosy cottage and remembering how proud I was when I earned enough to buy my own place. It was everything I wanted, quaint with character, something I could put my mark on. I've lived here for three years, and thought it represented security. But no longer. My emotions are a mixture of fear and outrage. *How dare he?*

After a few minutes, Jon comes down and joins me. There's

pity written all over his face, but behind that – *is that suspicion I can see?* Does he think I've done something to attract attention such as this? Does he think I've brought it on myself? Is he thinking I write filth, so I deserve it? Although I'm trying so hard to be strong, I can't hold his eyes for long, and lower my gaze to the ground. He reaches out and squeezes my shoulder, the touch one of comfort and not censure. *Don't you dare go back there, don't think this is your fault. Not again.*

As he leaves his hand where it is, his warmth pervades through the layers of clothes I'm wearing, even though I've not yet taken off my coat. I don't stop to analyse why I'm neither shrugging off his touch nor the fact I welcome it, even finding it calming. I'm just so grateful someone's here with me, hating to think what state I'd have been in if I'd discovered that note on my own or, even worse, had been in the house when the stalker turned up. Just the thought makes me shudder, and tears prick at the corners of my eyes.

I'm finding it hard to hold it together. But before I completely descend into hysterics, there's a knock at the front door, and it almost immediately opens. Well, the knock was a formality really, the lock's broken so the door's useless, just hanging on its hinges. Jon tenses behind me and then relaxes; it's just David Coulton, the detective back again. Not wanting ever to read it again, I leave Jon to show him the new message, and watch as another police officer is waved in. The card goes into an evidence bag, and thankfully they remove it from my sight. But that doesn't stop the message from going round and round my mind.

"Can you make us some tea, sweetheart?"

I throw Jon a look. I'm not his sweetheart and never will be, and I'm certainly not a lackey. But as he inclines his head towards the detective, it's clear he wants to have a private word, and it's a ruse to get me out of the way. I shrug. Half of me is thinking I ought to stay as whatever they have to say surely concerns this situation, but the rest of me is so bloody well fed up with trying to answer unanswerable questions that I'd relieved to be sent on an errand. *Who the hell is doing this to me? And why?*

I might as well keep busy, so going into the kitchen I put the kettle on and then notice Howie working out in the back garden. Going out to ask, I find out he and his two colleagues would appreciate a drink as well, so I get out enough cups for all of us. The everyday actions of boiling water, getting tea bags and coffee from the cupboard; seeing who wants what and whether they take sugar, and/or milk are helping quiet my overactive mind, as well as giving my hands something to do. Once the drinks are made and distributed, I lean against the sink and stare out of the window. *Will I ever feel comfortable here again?* I doubt it, or at least, not until my stalker is caught. And even then it might be difficult. *Perhaps I should think about moving?* Damn this man whoever he is. *How dare he disrupt my cosy life?*

I hear footsteps behind me, but don't need to look around to know it's Jon. I've already become tuned into his presence, the heavy sound of his footsteps on the wooden floors, the waft of his aftershave and that special something only he brings into the room.

"Will you come and sit with us? There's something we want to ask you." I sigh, get my cup and wave to indicate he should pick up the two sitting on the worktop, and go into the lounge. Jon follows with the other cups and sets them on a table. Coulton indicates my settee, so I sit down, putting my tea on the side table. He sits in a chair opposite; Jon remains standing.

The detective glances up at Jon, frowns, and then turns to me. "Do you mind Mr Tharpe staying?"

It hadn't occurred to me that he shouldn't be present, so I move my head from side to side. If he's providing me with protection he needs to know everything. I've no secrets I need to keep from him. Well, nothing that has any bearing on what's going on, I'm certain of that. The only skeleton in the closet I have is from long ago in the past and I'd rather that stayed locked away.

Again Coulton looks at Jon, and I see them exchange glances. Whatever it is I just wish they'd get on with it. As the detective seems to have difficulty putting his question into words, Jon comes round and sits at the other end of the sofa. Coulton clears his throat. "Miss Fable, you write erotic fiction. Mr Tharpe has apprised me of your recent conversation and that you have, let's just say, a very limited number of liaisons with the opposite sex. But despite this, I interpret from the intrusion into your study and this last note, that there might be someone who believes your books, or something in your stories, relates to an experience which involves them?" He considers me for a moment. I grow anxious as he skirts a little too closely to the truth. Not in the way he thinks, of course, but I glare anyway. My expression makes him back off a little, and he goes in a different direction. "If not a personal experience, someone you've spoken to perhaps? Someone, who may have unwittingly provided you with material for a plot?"

I try hard to suppress my shiver. The skeleton I'm not prepared to expose is rattling his bones, but I'm not going to be prising the nails out of his coffin. Not just yet. Not unless I absolutely have to, and I can't see it could ever come to that point. Surely something that happened seven years ago should have no bearing on the present? So I concentrate on thinking about the people who've I've spoken to about my work. While I'd like to have conducted research with someone actually in the lifestyle I write about, I've never met anyone who'd admit to it. So it doesn't take long before I give a firm shake of my head, and say adamantly, "There's nothing I can think of. No one I discuss my work with. Beta readers, editors and of course, my agent might give me suggestions, but I develop the plots and write the scenes purely from my imagination. I started writing five years ago, and my support group, if you like, have been with me all that time. If it was anything to do with them, why wait until now?"

His stare is hard, and I know he doesn't believe me as he probes further, "I want you to think very carefully, Miss Fable. We could be dealing with someone who thinks you've written their story. Are any of your support group, as you call them, male?"

"No, all female. If I think of anything, I'll let you know without delay, but I don't think there's any merit in going down that route," I assure him. "Surely, it's more likely it's someone I don't know, and they've just got a fixation on me?"

He shrugs. "It could be, and I'd be inclined to think that way if he's addressed the notes to Dexie Sanders. But it's your name he uses, Miss Fable, not your pen name. That suggests the stalker's got something against you personally."

He seems to be glaring at me as if he thinks I'm hiding something. Which I am, but I'm not going to share. It's not something I talk about; I've never told anyone. Saying it out loud would bring it all back. Would negate the years I've spent almost successfully convincing myself I've moved on. And anyway, it all happened so long ago; there's no way there could be a connection. Lifting my eyes, I notice Jon watching me carefully; as if he's able to read my private thoughts.

"Have you had any hate mail previously? Anything that you thought was suspicious?" Coulton continues.

Grateful that he's now on a different tack, I turn my full attention back to the detective, and I think carefully, "No. Snail mail doesn't come here; anything would go straight to the publishers or my agent. And then they forward anything I need to deal with on to me. But there hasn't been anything at all of any concern. They certainly haven't told me about anything out of the ordinary." I narrow my eyes, remembering, "I did receive a couple of emails direct, from people who wrote and commented they didn't like a particular scene or thought I'd got something wrong."

Coulton sits up straighter. "Have you kept those communications?"

I nod, "I'm dreadful at deleting anything so yes, any emails will be on my laptop."

"Can you dig anything out that might now seem suspicious in the light of recent events?"

I can do that. "No problem." I agree.

His disdainful expression makes it clear he thinks I know more than I'm letting on, or as if I've brought it all on myself. But what am I expected to do? Change the way I write my books which millions of fans enjoy just because of a fucking nutcase who doesn't happen to like them? What's happened to freedom of speech in this country?

I don't need to feel guilty! Instead, I find myself growing angry; my facial muscles tighten, and my cheeks start to flame. Jon coughs as if to clear his throat. It has the effect of breaking the tension.

"And our suggestion?" He glances at Coulton as if to prompt him.

"Ah, yes. As the stalker has got up close and personal by breaking in here, we've been discussing moving you to a safe place until we've got a better handle on what's going on here."

I sit up straight; I'm not at all happy with that proposal. Which is perverse; earlier I wanted to run and never come back. But my anger has got the better of me, and I don't want to be chased out of my home. So I protest, "I've already told you I've nowhere to go, and I can't afford to stay indefinitely at a hotel. I might be safe if I leave here, but what happens when I come back?" If they hadn't picked up on it before, my tone would leave them in no doubt I'm getting annoyed. "You've just installed a state of the art security system, Jon," I address him directly; "You've offered to stay with me. Surely it's better to wait this out now and try and catch this fucking nut?"

Jon narrows his eyes at me, as if I've said something he objects to, but then he raises his eyebrows and looks at Coulton. They appear to have an unspoken conversation and then Jon speaks "She's right. It's the best way to draw him out." He comes over and squeezes my shoulder. "If Mia's up taking the risk of staying here, I'll ensure she's got twenty-four-hour protection."

Coulton's jaw tightens as though he's clenching his teeth, perhaps trying to stop inappropriate words emerging. I gather he's not particularly happy leaving it to Grade A Security, but has nothing he can offer instead; the police can't provide one to one support in the same way. We thrash out the pros and cons for a while longer, but I remain adamant my stalker's not going to drive me out of my home, and in the end, the detective grudgingly agrees it might be the quickest way to bring the case to a swift conclusion. With the cameras all set up, if the stalker does come here again there's a good chance they'll be able to catch him, or at least, have some footage to help identify who he is.

When Coulton and his colleagues finally leave, it's not long before Jon follows, needing to go back to his place to collect the necessities sufficient for a couple of nights away from home. This morning, he hadn't expected events to take the turn they had and hadn't come prepared to stay. But before leaving, he reassures me the security guys are still installing the alarms, and will be around at least until he returns. As he zooms off on his motorbike, some of my tension leaves me, my relief showing the extent of the strange effect he has on me. Causing me to wonder just who exactly is the greatest threat to my life; Jon Tharpe or the stalker.

CHAPTER 7

Jon

Five years ago

I took the flight to Dubai, and then the connecting flight to Amahad, not sure exactly what my new job would entail. While providing close protection, my job would be to shadow the sheikh wherever he was to go. I quickly found the palace in Al Qur'ah, the capital city, was opulent, shamelessly displaying its wealth and heritage. But Sheikh Nijad, himself, seemed down to earth and more European in his outlook than I expected, speaking English like a native and, even in this Muslim country, having a fully stocked bar in his room; the contents of which he didn't hesitate to share. Nevertheless, the otherwise archaic customs of this small Arabic state didn't hold much appeal, and I was pleased to find we'd be spending most of our time in Europe, and that he only paid the occasional obligatory visits to his home and family.

We clicked immediately; him being an ex-military man himself, and fast found common ground. Living in Europe for most of his time, it was only a matter of days before we were quickly on our way to Paris, his favourite city and where he shared an apartment with his brother, Jasim. It was in that cosmopolitan city that I soon discovered Sheikh Nijad's lifestyle choices were very close to my own, and being his bodyguard was no chore at all. Especially when it meant I gained membership to some of the more exclusive BDSM clubs in the French capital.

Nijad and I quickly dropped any formalities between us – once you've seen a man getting his cock sucked in a kink club it's hard to stand on ceremony – and we fast became close friends.

Our relationship made my job so much easier; in fact, it hardly seemed like work at all. Gone was the uniform – I dressed to merge into the background – no longer did I have to rise at godawful hours, and also absent was the responsibility for my men, my only duty keeping myself and my client alive. My main weapon was a Glock I carried in my shoulder holster and which I hoped never to have to use in civilian life.

My service training served me well, and however strong my friendship became with Nijad, I remained vigilant, never forgetting I was being paid to keep him safe. On duty, I was always alert, on the lookout for the smallest detail, never wanting to miss anything ever again.

Present day

On my return to Mia's cottage near Epping, I find the woman herself outside, discussing the security arrangements with Howie. As the guys finish up installing the equipment, passing the new keys to the door and window locks over to Mia, they call out their goodbyes and leave. Collecting my bag from my car, I follow Mia into the house, finding it hard to keep my eyes away from her denim covered arse, the tight material emphasising the enticing sway of her hips as she moves. Reminding myself to keep my mind firmly on the job, I lift my eyes to focus further north and force myself to concentrate on the fact that this woman is in danger, and it's my responsibility to keep her safe. The thought that there's someone out there who wants to hurt her slams into me with such force it makes me pause my forward motion. A sudden rage burns inside me, and I know I'll do everything in my power to protect her. Even if that has to mean, protecting her from myself as well as the stalker. I must be the CPO, not the man.

Moving on into the house, I carry my holdall into the lounge and put it down by the side of the couch. It's not heavy; I don't carry a lot with me, the bag only contains a change of clothing and necessary toiletries, no weaponry. The major downside to working in England is that it's not legal to carry a gun. For the last few years, I've worked abroad in countries where the laws are less stringent so here I feel naked without a holster. The strict gun laws in the UK mean there is far less crime involving shooting, but notwithstanding that, while I can't be armed, there's nothing to say the person Mia and I could be facing will be so law abiding. I'll need to be even more on my guard and on my toes. Lucky I'm well able to defend myself, and my clients, with my fists.

Mia offers me food, but time's getting on, and it's well into the evening now. Having eaten late afternoon, she's not hungry herself, so I'm quite happy to settle for the can of lager she offers. My preference is beer, but if that's all she's got I'll take it. I'm not surprised when she pours herself a glass of white wine; it seems to be her preferred tipple. Sighing, seeming tired, she sits down on the sofa, and leans her head back, rolling her shoulders as if to relieve tension there. I take the chair opposite. For a moment there's an awkward silence, and raising her head back up she throws me a nervous look. Having a man staying in her house is probably new for her, particularly someone she doesn't know. The way her hands are twisting in her lap suggests she's not quite sure how this is supposed to go. I know one way I'd like this evening to end, but that's not going to happen. Winning the struggle to bring myself back to business I give her an update, hoping my matter of fact approach to the conversation will put her at her ease.

"I've got Vanessa, head of our investigation team back at the office, going through the comments on the Dexie Sanders' Facebook page. But, we were wondering, were there any you had to delete?"

My business-like approach seems to settle her. She's quiet for a moment, her brow creasing as she thinks. "No, if there was an adverse comment I just tried to answer it reasonably. There haven't been many. Most are about when's the next book coming out, or discussing the latest one. Or discussions about where I've taken the plot. Of course, I deleted some which weren't relevant to my page, adverts in the main. But there were only a few of those."

"I'm not sure what we'll get from your emails, but it's worth a look tomorrow. And Vanessa will be contacting your publisher and your agent to see whether they've had any communications with them that they haven't told you about."

Nodding, thoughtfully she dismisses the idea, "Val wouldn't hide anything from me." She pauses, and then asks, "How do you know Val? She's the one who contacted your company for me."

I smile, "I don't know her, but my partner, Ben does. I don't know the details, but apparently, he owes her a favour." *And one of these days I'm going to get to the bottom of exactly what it is. It must be a big one; this case is going to cost us thousands.* The security system wasn't cheap, but on checking with Ben he's happy to run with it. He had, however, raised a quizzical eyebrow when I told him I was personally taking the case on.

"Oh." She picks up her wine and sips it. A drop glistens on her lip, and I ache to lick it off.

I close my eyes for a second, as if blocking her from my sight will help me get my shit together and remember just why I'm here. If I'm right, what I'm going to ask next is going to hurt her, but there's no way to avoid it, not if I want to get the information which might save her life. Somehow I have to approach the question that's been going around my head since the talk we had in the pub, however much I wish the seed had never been planted. Was it really only a few hours ago? Already it seems a lifetime away. I take a moment to prepare myself mentally and to find the right tone of voice. If the answer is as I expect, I'll need to school my features carefully not to reflect my rage.

I lean forward, looking straight into her lovely eyes. My gut churns as I dread hearing the answer. If there's ever been a time in my life that I wanted to be wrong, that time is now.

"Mia," I start my voice as gentle as I can make it. "I need to ask you something." When she looks up and puts down her glass, showing I have her full attention, I continue, "Have you ever been raped?"

I've caught her completely unawares. Her hand goes over her mouth but isn't successful in smothering that giveaway gasp. As she starts to shake violently, her reaction confirms what I suspected even while I was hoping to God it wasn't true. I can't help myself, in one swift move I'm sitting beside her, putting my arm around her, trying to pull her close. She tenses, fighting me, but I'm insistent, not allowing her to break loose, and gradually she stops struggling, and instead leans against me, giving into my touch, accepting my support. I'm boiling inside, but she needs comfort from me, not an outburst of anger. Although it's definitely not in my job description or any close protection manual, I place a kiss on the top of her head, and for a second, all I can think about is her scent as it fills my nostrils, her hair tickling my nose.

"I'm so sorry, Mia." I'm apologising in advance for the line of questioning her response has opened up. "What Coulton was getting at, is whether someone thinks you're basing your writing on an actual sexual experience, and that's the reason they believe you owe them." I take a deep breath before I continue. I'm surmising here, but I reckon I'm going to be right on target,

"Mia was your only sexual experience your rape?" I hug her to me, and again my lips nuzzle her hair. "I know it's the last thing you want to do, but you do need to tell me everything, it may have a bearing on the threats now, and I have to be armed with any and all pertinent information if I'm going to be able to protect you."

She shivers, even though the house is warm. I touch her hand and find it cold to touch. Reaching up, I grasp her chin gently and turn her head to face me only to see silent tears running down her face. My gut churns, I want to kill whoever did this to her, slowly and very, very painfully. "Tell me," I ask again, gently, but firmly, keeping my inner reactions on a tight rein, not letting them show.

Shaking her head, she starts to speak, her voice so quiet it's hard to hear her. "I can't believe there's any connection. It happened seven years ago; it's something I don't talk about, or even want to remember. I've never told anyone before. Ever."

"I'm sorry," I repeat, keeping my voice soft and low, but also commanding. "But there might be a link." I hate doing this do her, but it's important she shares everything with me; otherwise I'll be working in the dark.

"I don't know how it would help. I didn't know them, never knew their names. But I heard their voices. I'm certain I've never come across them again; I'd know. I'm sure."

Fuck! There was more than one? My jaw tightens, and my teeth grind together. Steeling myself, so I don't give away the growing anger inside me, I force my fists to loosen and take her hand, rubbing my fingers across the back in a gesture of support.

"Definitely not the man who was stalking you?"

Another shudder, "I don't think so, but then, he, blue hoodie, only said a few words in the café."

If one of her rapists had been her age when it happened, in the intervening seven years a young man's voice may have deepened. I'll leave that for now, but I can't rule out the possibility that her stalker and one of her abusers are one and the same. My arm still around her, I encourage her to go on, "Tell me what happened to you, Mia."

I watch as she swallows a few times, realising how difficult it is for her to speak about her ordeal, especially if it's true she's never talked about it before. I give her a little time to get her thoughts together, and when she starts telling me the details, I can do nothing but admire the strength she manages to summon up and put into her voice. Now she's decided to disclose the circumstances, it all comes tumbling out.

"It was seven years ago when I was just seventeen. I went to a party; my mother didn't want me to go." She pauses, and just before I need to prompt her, she carries on, "I must have been given something, Rohypnol I suppose? Next thing I knew I woke up tied, blindfolded and gagged in some sort of building. There were two of them. They both raped me. I didn't know them." Her voice trails off.

I want to swear, to rant and rave. I want to know who they are as they're both fucking dead men; they just don't know it yet. No, killing's too good for them. I'll castrate them, cut off their cocks and force them down their fucking throats. I swallow down my anger, trying to keep my voice calmer than the thoughts raging through my head as I sense there's worse to come. She's trembling in my arms, the memories so painful; I wish I could do something to take them away. But there's more she's not telling me. So I encourage her, "And then?" Though it's a battle to keep my voice composed my apparent easy acceptance without criticism seems to ground her.

She continues in a flat voice. "I was there two nights. Then they dropped me back near where the party was. Literally, threw me out of a van. Luckily it was also close to home."

Inside I'm seething. Two men. Two nights and a day in

between. At least thirty-six hours. I try not to imagine what depravities they put her through. I roll my shoulders and breath in a deep breath in an attempt to reduce the tension that been building up while Mia's been recounting her ordeal, knowing the last thing she needs is for me to let my fury show. It's nigh on impossible, but I force myself to stay composed. I'd floated the idea with Coulton, but when he checked, he found the police had no records of any rape case linked to Mia Fable. But still, I ask to check. "Did you report it?"

"No."

I've seen rape victims before and understand the misguided guilt they carry. So I think I already know part of the answer, but continue to ask the question. "Why not?"

She takes a deep breath; it's difficult for her to get out the words. "I got home. I was in a pretty bad way. My mother opened the door and called me a slut for going to the party. She said if I'd got hurt I'd brought it on myself. When I tried to tell her what happened, she said I deserved everything I got. All because I wanted to be a normal teenager for once." She breaks off; I give her a reassuring look and tighten my arm around her, waiting for her to carry on. At my gesture of support, she picks up her heart-wrenching story.

"Mum was a religious fanatic and kept repeating it was my entire fault, that if I'd been a good girl it would never have happened. She wouldn't let me go to school until the bruises faded. She'd made some excuse for my absence. No one ever knew, or even suspected. After two weeks of her ranting, I came to believe what she was telling me; that I brought it on myself." She stops and looks straight at me, "At first, I wanted to go to the police, Jon; I didn't want them to get away with it and do it to anyone else. I asked, begged her to let me contact them. But she locked me in my room and refused to let me out. She said no one would believe me, and she didn't want everyone to know what kind of daughter she had. In the end, when I was eventually able to leave, I was too embarrassed and ashamed to talk to anyone."

I breathe in sharply, and look away briefly, not wanting her to see the disgust on my face. Not directed at her, of course, but her fucking mother. How can someone treat their daughter like that? Rape is brutal and devastating at any age, and the person closest to her should have been there to give her support. And it's worse as Mia was still a child yes; she was above the age of consent, but not yet an adult. And she certainly had not consented in any way to what had been done to her. The men had committed the crime, not Mia. *That woman deserves to be shot!* "I'm so sorry," I tell her quietly, when I've got myself under control. Then I switch to my most dominant voice, "You were not to blame." Again I turn her to face me, "It wasn't your fault, you did nothing wrong."

She shrugs, and I'm angry and worried she still seems to be taking the guilt on herself. So I tell her again, "You had no choice; you didn't ask for them to abduct and rape you. You were a victim." Her reaction surprises me.

Pulling up a little straighter in my arms, her gaze becomes intense. "I know that now," she tells me emphatically, "But it took me two years to understand that I hadn't 'asked for it'. It was only after I hit rock bottom and came close to committing suicide that I began to realise whatever I was wearing, whatever I'd looked like, it wasn't my fault. The only reason I didn't take that bottle of tablets was I couldn't have my flatmates coming in and finding me dead; I couldn't do that to anyone. But I came close. I sat there, staring at that bottle, for a very long time. Once I'd washed the tablets down the drain, I cut down any contact with my mother to just a couple of phone calls a year to let her know I was still breathing. I never saw her again, it was the only thing I could do to remain strong. Every time I'd make contact, she'd remind me what a slut I was. She never forgave me."

I don't know which part of her story is worse, her abduction and rape, or her fucking mother's reaction. Or the fact it's only her inner strength, and that she didn't want other people to have to live with the nightmare of finding a body that she's still alive today. All thoughts of any seduction I might have had have fled. I pull her back to me and give her a brotherly hug. She notices the difference and pulls away.

"I'm still a woman, Jon. They haven't taken that away from me."

I have to admire the force in her voice, but the fact she's not had a boyfriend since her ordeal belies her words. I think carefully about where to go next, and know I should avoid any discussion about her sexuality. Tonight is not the right time. "Do you have any idea who abducted you? Any clues at all, however slight, as to who they might be?" I probe gently.

She looks at me as if she was expecting me to say something different, but then realises I'm still fishing for information. "That's the other reason I didn't tell anyone, there wasn't much point. I didn't know who they were, absolutely no idea. They kept me blindfolded the whole time I was kept captive. There were so many people at the party; I didn't even get a good look at the man who gave me the drink. I only know he was a bit older – well, that was my impression – and quite tall." Her eyes are staring unfocused into the distance as her mind apparently drifts back. "It was two years later that I realised I was the victim, not the instigator. Sitting, debating whether to end your life somehow brings clarity that wasn't there before. I thought about my friends, how they dressed when they went out – far more provocative than anything I wore to that party. I never thought of them as being sluts or going out looking as though they were advertising their availability for sex. A woman should be able to dress how she wants, without it being taken as a blatant invitation. I know that now.

"But I still felt – *feel* – dirty, that will never leave me. I wanted them punished, but if I'd reported it two years after the fact, what could I say? It was too long after for any proper investigation. And I could have given them nothing to go on. All the DNA evidence was long gone." She comes back to the present, "Don't think it doesn't bother me that they might have done it again. That gives me nightmares. And that's what I feel most guilty about. If I'd come forward at the time, had a proper examination, then they might have been caught. And stopped. *That's* what I agonise about the most."

"But your mother prevented you from going to the police. You were seventeen, Mia, not yet considered an adult." I run my hands through my hair and bring them down to rub my chin. "It's a fucked up situation. You could be right they went on to do it again. It's impossible to know. But you shouldn't beat yourself up about it. It was out of your control, sweetheart. Everything was out of your control."

Reaching forwards, I pick up her wine glass and hand it to her. If there was ever a time, she needed a drink that time is now. I wonder whether she's got something stronger in the house, but decide not to ask, just wait until she's taken a few sips. Then, as Jon, the man, not the CPO, I question her, "What did they do to you, Mia?" I reconsider, realising the pain it might put her through. All that I require is any description of them or where she was taken. I know they raped her; I don't need to know more, so shaking my head I state firmly, "No, you don't have to tell me the details, not if it's too much."

But it seems now she's started she wants to get it all off her chest. There's a brief pause before she looks at me and shivers, then proceeds to give me the answer in a quiet monotone. "Everything." She turns her head, and then swings back quickly and frowns in disgust, whether at herself, me or the rapists I'm not too sure. "Fuck, Jon, it's so hard to put into words." Again she looks away. I open my mouth to tell her it doesn't matter when the details come spilling out. "They raped me, repeatedly. They took my virginity and then they kept taking turns. I don't know how long it lasted, or how many times. Then they used me together as they forced me to give oral. They choked me and laughed as I gagged." She pauses for a moment. "They must have improvised a spanking bench and a St Andrews Cross; at least that's what it felt like. They handcuffed and tied me to different things. They spanked me, caned me and whipped me, Jon. I've got scars."

For a second I wonder how she knows what the equipment is called, then I remember the book I'd read, she'd obviously done her research, and has become familiar with the apparatus in retrospect.

Suddenly she bursts into tears and throws herself into my arms. I hold her tight, giving her comfort through my touch, unable to find the words, I rub my hand up and down her back, trying with my actions to convince her I don't think she's dirty or deserving of the treatment she received. Remembering this is the first time she's talked about her ordeal, I let her cry it out, hoping she'll find some relief. Her hand grasps my shirt. I hold her close as she cries. Her sobs are killing me, my T-shirt getting soaked. I rock her gently as though she's a child. Eventually, her tears start to dry, and when she's only giving an occasional sniffle, I push her slightly away and look deep into her eyes. "Mia," I start to tell her, purposefully lowering my voice and putting as much conviction as I can into it. "You're one of the bravest people I know. I've so much admiration for your strength." She looks at me strangely, as if she can't understand what I'm trying to say, so I continue, "You came through, Mia. You've coped and rebuilt yourself. You've moved on where a lot of people would have fallen apart. A lot of people would have taken those tablets, Mia. *You* came back."

She wipes her eyes on her sleeve and then looks around her. "I need a tissue," she says, then gets up and goes into the kitchen. I hear her blowing her nose loudly before returning. When I hold out my arms in invitation, she settles beside me once more. Gratified she trusts me enough for that, I give her a moment to compose herself then, just as I go to say something, she asks me a question. "Do you believe one of those men think I'm writing about what happened to me?" She pauses, as if in thought. "I never write about rape. Everything I write is consensual."

"It's not what I think that's important. The bastards that did that to you were warped and twisted. Who the fuck knows how *they* think?"

She seems to consider my words for a moment. "But it's a moot point. I don't have any clues as to who they are. One was the leader, the chief instigator of everything, the other one deferred to him and did what he was told to do. But I have no clues as to their names. And no description other than one was probably tall."

I wonder how strong she truly is. "We could try to find out," I suggest, not sure what her response will be. Identifying those motherfuckers would be hard for her, and might undo the healing she's managed to do to become the woman she has.

But she surprises me by sitting up a little straighter, asking only, "How? How could we start to do that?" The eagerness in her voice shows me she needs this. The whole ordeal is still an open book in her past, and I suspect she needs it closed before she can properly move on.

I mull it over for a moment, "We can start with the person who held the party, and then track down other people who were there. They might have seen something. Can you do that, Mia? Are you up for it? I'll be with you every step of the way."

Pulling away from me, she stands and collects her empty

glass. I'm taken aback to see a faint smile on her face as she indicates my empty bottle and I nod, realising she's going to get us more to drink. But she speaks before she leaves the room. "Jon, if there's anything positive I can do, let's get on with it. I don't want to be a victim any longer; I want to tackle this head on."

I grin as she goes out. What a girl! Fuck, too right, what a girl. But not the fucking girl for me. She's been through too much, and somehow she's come out the other side. She needs a man in her life, one she can trust to help complete her healing, and that's certainly not me. The things I'd want to do to her. Hell, I fuck, I don't make love. I dream about having her over a spanking bench, beneath my whip. I'm a Dominant, and anything I'd want to do would only scare her and remind her of the most traumatic experience of her life, bring back memories of the worst thing that can happen to a woman. And I'd never be happy in a vanilla relationship, even with someone like her; I know myself too well. Even before I knew there was a name for it I couldn't concede control in the bedroom, and I have an insatiable appetite for sex. No, I'm completely the wrong man for Mia Fable. I stare into space, not focusing on anything in particular. I'll do my job here and protect her, *but then I'll have to let her go.* She deserves, *needs,* so much more.

After she's refreshed our drinks, she disappears for a short while, returning with her arms full of blankets and pillows. As she places the spare bedding by the two-seater couch I suppress a shudder. I'm going to be in for an uncomfortable night.

CHAPTER 8
Mia

Seven years ago

The party seemed to get even crazier, and I wanted to go home. But the sheer number of bodies I'd have to push through to get to the front door stopped me leaving. I was too hot, my skin damp and clammy and feeling claustrophobic and overwhelmed. Alcohol was flowing freely, and by then there was more staggering to the music than actual dancing. Voices were getting louder, and I was more than ready to go home. But I'd already been groped twice as I tried to make my way through the drunken throng, so, for the moment, I stayed put, out of the way, my back up against the wall waiting for the crowd to thin. Or pass out, which currently seemed the more likely.

"Here. Have this." A gruff voice beside me told me, as something was pushed into my hand. Automatically, I took it, before looking to see what I'd been given.

It was a bottle, an alcopop. "Thanks, but I don't drink." I tried to pass it back. The man who'd given it to me had to lean down to hear me, and even then I had to shout into his ear. I kept my eyes lowered, not wanting to draw attention to myself.

"Go on. One won't hurt." he encouraged.

Looking at the bottle, I assessed the crowded room and realised I'd be trapped in my corner for a while. Suddenly I was aware just how dry and thirsty I was and was ready to drink anything to ease my parched throat, even if that meant I was about to try my first *alcoholic drink. He'd already been kind enough to open it for me, so putting the bottle to my lips I took a small sip, surprised to find it just tasted like normal lemonade with only a slight aftertaste. I was thirsty, so I carried on drinking until the bottle was empty.*

My new friend remained beside me, but he didn't talk to me again, so I assumed that he was like me, keeping out of the fray which continued getting wilder by the minute. I glanced at my watch; it was gone midnight. Oh God, I really shouldn't have left it this late before leaving. Suddenly I felt drained and knew I had to make a determined effort to get out, so pushed away from the wall with renewed resolve. No longer having a solid support behind me, I stumbled as I tried to stand up straight.

"Whoa, there," his rough voice rumbled in my ear. "Steady." His hand came out to hold me, and I was grateful for his help and leant on him to get my balance. "Where you off to?"

"Home," I told him, "I've got to get home." My head was spinning, and I was starting to feel sick.

"I'll help you out."

Grateful to him, I accepted both his offer and supporting hand to help me steer my way to the door.

Present day

Waking Friday morning, I'm surprised to find I'd slept the whole night through without interruption. Despite having to relive my ordeal as I recounted it to Jon, the resulting nightmares I'd been expecting hadn't materialised. Maybe talking about what happened, getting it out into the open had been cathartic. There'd been no indication that Jon had judged me, as I told my sordid tale for the first time in my life. Perhaps I should have spoken to someone years ago, but I veered away from counselling, too worried I'd be found guilty and convicted, in the way my mother had. Then, two years later, when I realised it hadn't been my fault, I'd become my own therapist.

But now, as the new day dawns, I'm feeling refreshed, as though some of the heavy weight has been lifted off of me. I've still got a stalker, but I've also got Jon on my side and staying close. I don't feel so afraid, he makes me feel safe, and today I'm going to start taking action, not just sitting back and letting things happen.

Having gone through the morning routine of showering, dressing, and breakfasting, I'm ready to go. Picking up my bag I follow Jon to the front door, but before leaving the house, make sure to set the new alarm behind me. He's watching carefully, and gives a nod of approval, looking pleased I've remembered the instructions Howie gave me the day before.

Trailing after him across the drive, he opens the door to an amazing sports car that he tells me is a McClaren Spider in a beautiful royal blue. I smirk at him; the car screams sex and speed, I can't remember even having seen that make before on the road. It seems a bit excessive for a bodyguard, and I'm shaking my head in disbelief as I find myself repeating his words, "A McClaren?"

He grins back. "A present from a wealthy sheikh," he tells me.

I can't resist; I walk around the gleaming car that seems entirely out of place on my driveway behind my old, but reliable, Ford Fiesta. The author in me is taking notes. "What's the top speed?"

"It will do over two hundred miles per hour, and reach sixty in three seconds." He smirks. My mouth falls open, and my concern must show on my face as he pre-empts my question, resting his hand on my arm for reassurance, "I'm a safe driver, Mia. Yes, I've pushed the car on a race track for fun, but I stick to the speed limits on the roads. Well, close to, anyway."

The car doesn't pretend to be anything other than a rich man's toy; its sleek lines, huge exhausts, the styling, all built for speed and power. Just the two seats, definitely not a family car and I don't miss the opportunity to learn something else about the man.

"No family to carry around, then?" I keep my voice light, but my insides tighten as I wait for his answer.

He throws me a searching look, "No, I'm single."

Annoyed at the extent of my pleased reaction to his statement, I try to deflect his attention. "Nice, you must have impressed your sheikh!"

He waits a moment then shrugs self-depreciatingly, "I stopped a bullet for him. He was grateful."

That knocks me back. Suddenly my view of my bodyguard changes, and I shift uncomfortably. This man standing before me is prepared to step in front and take a bullet instead of allowing the individual he's protecting to be shot? *What kind of person does that?* For some reason, his bravery gives me a warm and fuzzy feeling inside.

It's not easy getting into the car, and I'm glad I'm not wearing jeans and not a tight skirt as I settle my bum in and then swing round my legs, suspecting there's a technique I've yet to learn for getting into such a low-slung car; I'm so close to the ground I could be sitting on it! The butter-soft leather of the sports seat feels amazing, but the inside of the car bemuses me. And while I don't have a clue about the control panel, part of me is wondering if he'd ever let me drive it. But I'm too nervous to ask. As I marvel at the luxury, a voice inside continues to ask, *was this worth risking his life for?*

Then Jon gets in the driver's side and starts the engine. Bloody hell! It roars! The sound as loud as a Harley but far more refined. I'm glad I have no close neighbours to disturb. Initially, I find the noise disconcerting.

"Open or not?"

Jon's voice pulls me back to him, but I don't understand the question. He points to the roof. "It's got a retractable hard top; I can open it up if you like?"

The sun's shining, so why not go for the whole experience? "Open." I throw him a grin.

It takes only a couple of seconds for the roof to slide open, letting the sun stream in. *This is the life!* Looking across at my personal bodyguard, I realise how much the car suits him. His large, powerful hands, resting on the steering wheel which looks like it should be in a racing car, remind me how it felt to be held me in his arms last night, how he made me feel so secure and protected and something else, something I don't want to analyse. Usually, I'd flinch any from any man's touch, other that an introductory handshake, but I'd let him hold me and accepted his comfort. *Why him? Why do I feel so safe with him? And how did he get me to spew out all my dirty secrets?*

It hurt to relive my past, but somehow, getting it out in the open has helped me beginning the journey to put it behind me. I've let my abuse haunt me for too long. *What if it's possible to put all that in a box; lock it, throw away the key, and get on with my future? What if that future could include a man like Jon? Could I be ready for that? Maybe I don't have to be alone anymore.* Not actually this breath-taking specimen sitting beside me, of course, I need someone less threatening. Less... everything. I have to suppress a shiver. And just as I'd like to take the McClaren for a test drive, I know I never would. It would be just like its owner. Too much for me to handle.

As Jon expertly turns the powerful car and starts up the road, it dawns on me that, for the first time in my life, I'm considering the possibility of letting a man into my life, and starting to believe that allowing myself to feel feminine isn't asking for trouble. And then, reluctantly, however much I don't want to admit, it's not the thought of just any man, it's Jon himself who's awakening my dormant sexuality. The sexuality that my characters feel and act on with ease, but I'd only ever thought that was make-believe, things I could write about and imagine, but could never feel or do myself.

Everything about this man is as erotic as hell. He shouldn't be allowed to look so damn good, or do everything with such a masculine grace. To my mortification the combination of sexy sports car and the dangerously attractive driver is lethal, and the result is my knickers are becoming decidedly damp. *Is this actually happening to me?* Shifting uncomfortably in my seat, I drag my eyes away from him and concentrate on looking out of the window. The fact he's playing the part of my knight in shining armour must be fooling around with my libido. I mustn't allow myself to think of him as anything other than what he is, a bodyguard employed to protect me. Once his work is done, he'll disappear out of my life.

Berating myself for starting to get hung up on a man who couldn't possibly reciprocate my interest, I force myself to think instead about this morning's destination. We're on our way to try to track down Anna Smith, the girl who hosted that fateful party. All symptoms of arousal leave me when I begin to picture her in my mind, and more particularly, the house where the party had been held. I've never been back. Even when I still lived in the area, I avoided walking past it, and just the thought of the place summons nightmare images in my head. *Can I actually go through with this?*

As if he knows what I'm thinking, Jon reaches out his hand and rests it on mine. I glance at him.

"Okay?"

His simple question reveals he's tuned into my thoughts and understands how difficult today's trip down memory lane will be for me. Well aware there's no way on earth I could do this without him; I squeeze his hand in return. "Yes."

"If it gets too much, tell me! I'll take you straight home." He's slipped into a way of talking, a deep tone of voice that's different from his usual. "Promise me, Mia."

Feeling grateful, knowing I have an out if I need it, although I'm determined not to use it, but answer, "I will. Thank you, Jon."

We drive on in a silence broken only by the dispassionate instructions from the sat-nav easily audible over the purr of the powerful engine, each of us lost in our thoughts. I'm about to return to the area I left seven years ago without once looking back. Nowadays, it's rare I even think about my mother, and I have to say I don't miss her. It took me two years to shake off her influence and control once I'd left home, and that was the best move I'd ever made. She should never have had a child. My Dad had died when I just was a baby; I was too young to have any memories of him. My mother hadn't known what to do with me and had no idea how to bring up a child on her own. But we'd jogged along adequately enough, until that time I genuinely needed her, the time when I found out that appearances mattered more to her than the emotional well-being of her only child. I've no doubt she feels well rid of me; has by now probably forgotten she ever had a daughter. I didn't go back to see her after I left, restricting our contact to telephone calls on birthdays and at Christmas, but even that stopped four years ago when I foolishly told her about the publication of my first novel. She didn't want to risk anyone connecting her with the author Dexie Sanders and disowned me. It didn't come as much of a surprise.

Jon reaches for the radio and cocks his head at me. I nod, interested to discover his choice in music. He switches it on, and a national rock channel blares out. I grin; it's what I would have chosen. A song by Journey comes on; I can't help myself; it's one I love, and I automatically start to sing along softly. Although I'm quiet, he's heard me hum and smirks, then belts out 'Don't Stop Believing' in an impressively melodious baritone.

I laugh, and rather impudently ask him, "Is there anything you aren't good at?" Then I turn away to conceal my blush, hoping I haven't given anything away.

He's laughing out loud now. "Oh, baby, some things I'm extremely good at."

His deep sexy tone makes me glance back to see a playful leer on his face and that he's waggling his eyebrows. I have to suppress a gasp. Baby? Is he *flirting* with me? The shiver running down my spine isn't one of fear.

He continues, still chuckling. "The rest of the stuff I'm just pretty good at." The moment's gone.

"Okay, then," I rise to the bait. "What don't you do well?"

He pretends he needs time to think about it. "Ah, Sheikh Nijad beat me in a fencing duel. Once. Or it might have been twice. But then, he was a champion."

I smile widely, enjoying this playful side of him. "So modesty is not your strong point?" He laughs again.

We drive on, radio playing, the short conversation lightening my mood. The sat-nav tells us there's a ten-minute delay ahead of us but helpfully adds that we're still on the fastest route. Jon looks rueful but doesn't protest or seem impatient, impressing me with both the way he handles the car and his attitude. Let's face it; I'm captivated by everything about this man.

Forcing my attention away from my companion with some difficulty, I try and concentrate on why we're here. We've discussed what the next step will be if my old friend, Anna, is not in; it's going to be the middle of the day by the time we get there, so it's probable she'll be at work even if she still lives at home. Her family remains at that address, though – Jon's already confirmed that for us with his office – but he thinks going back to the scene of the crime, so to speak, might help jog some of my memories. Memories I've tried to suppress for seven years but am now making a conscious effort willing them to return. Creasing my brow, I try to recall the faces and names of people who were there, making a mental list that I'll write out later.

Suddenly I'm chilled, even though the heater's blowing out hot air. I've remembered the last conversation I had with my mother. My intake of breath is audible, and he looks at me.

"What is it?"

I frown, as the conversation comes back to me. "The last time I spoke with my mother was when I'd sent her a copy of my first book," I hesitate, gathering my thoughts, "She only got as far as reading the blurb on the cover, but that was enough for her to tell me I'd do better to forget my experience, not try to make money out of it. She thought, Jon, that that was why I wrote my book. To glorify what had happened. If she could believe that, maybe you're right. Maybe someone else does too."

He swears under his breath. "Your mother's a right piece of work. Letting you cope with all that alone, and then criticising you for it? Christ, babe, you were just a child!"

"I was seventeen," I remind him. "But you're right. She didn't like me going out; I wasn't allowed to have boyfriends. I was so naïve back then, shit, I hadn't even had a drink before that night. My first real drink, just an alcopop, and that had to be spiked. I don't drink much out of the house now, not unless I'm with people I trust, and even then I keep a careful eye on my glass all night."

"I don't blame you. But after everything you told me, I understand the way you write what you do."

Sitting up straighter I look towards him, he's caught my interest, and I want to hear his analysis of my motives for choosing my particular genre, "Go on."

"You turn something devastating into something good. Your

characters aren't forced, they're not hurt, they enjoy themselves, have fun pushing their boundaries. You're writing it out of your system. And you're excellent at it."

As I look out of the window, I realise that he gets me. "It's my therapy, Jon, the way I cope with what happened. But I never glorify rape." I confirm it again, as much force in my voice as I can get.

Again he reaches over and presses his fingers to my arm, before he has to remove them, needing his hand to flick the indicator. We've turned off the M25 now and start to drive down towards Croydon. Soon we'll reach the area where I was born and bred. My hands are becoming clammy, and I'm starting to question whether this was such a good idea. My hometown brings back no happy memories for me, not having had the ideal childhood, even before the events of that night. I was so relieved once I'd got my place at Uni, there was no need to come back, and working any job I could to finance me through the holidays. The first year I spent in Halls on campus, and after that, I was lucky enough to flat share with three great girls until we finished our course. I'm still friends with them, though we're scattered far and wide now.

I can see the area hasn't changed very much in the last six years, but there's a roundabout built to serve new housing which wasn't there before, and it throws me for a moment, making me lose my bearings, so I'm glad we've got the sat-nav to rely on for directions. But all too soon Jon makes a turn into a road I do recognise, just two streets away from my childhood home. The house where Anna Smith lived and the location of that fateful party.

Residential parking restrictions haven't as yet extended this far out of the town which means he's able to pull the McClaren up almost outside Anna's house. After a second's pause while the roof folds up back into place above our heads, he cuts the ignition. I wait as the ticking engine cools, staring straight ahead, reliving the moment I was thrown out of the van, broken and violated. Remembering the excruciating walk home, which was part stagger, part crawl in the early hours of that fateful Sunday morning. I see the blood on the pavement where I caught my head when I landed. I see the white van driving away.

Shit! I see the *white* van driving away.

I draw in a sharp breath. "White van!" I whisper. He turns to me, quickly, giving me a probing look. "I was dropped off out of a white van." Then I lift and drop my shoulders in dismissal, "Not much, but it's something I didn't remember before."

He takes my hand and rubs it in his. "It's a start, Mia. Someone might know who at the party had one." He continues to look searchingly at me, and his fingers go to my wrist.

I realise he's feeling for my pulse. I raise my eyebrows questioningly.

"Breathe slowly, Mia. Take deep breaths. Hold it, and then let it out."

I hadn't realised how tense I'd become, but he knows. He reads me so well. "How do you do that?" I ask him.

He chuckles, "It's my job."

CHAPTER 9

Jon

I t was one of those events that happen for no good reason; a mad man in the wrong place at the wrong time, Nijad wasn't even the target: the gunman was just firing randomly.

As we left the theatre that night I had a prickling feeling at the back of my neck; a sixth sense that something was wrong, my perception honed in the armed forces. You don't go out on SAS missions without developing a constant awareness of your surroundings, the ability to soak up the atmosphere and sniff out anything that seems even the slightest bit out of place. That's how I, and my team, survived as long as we had.

There was fear and anticipation in the air; I could almost taste it. Fanciful perhaps, but it was there, nonetheless. And I knew better than to ignore such premonition. As Nijad reached the exit, stepping forwards, joking and laughing with the stunning model who hung off his arm, I swung around, pushing them both back into the shadows, coincidentally also blocking the way for other theatregoers to come out.

Apparently, I saved a number of lives with that action, that balmy summer evening in Paris. The gunman started shooting indiscriminately at the crowd, and almost as soon as I turned to propel Nijad back, I was caught full in the upper chest, a bullet sent straight into my lung.

The police never discovered the precise reason for the gunman's *actions; he was just an unpredictable little man with a rage against the world. Before being killed himself, he'd shot me, wounded another and killed two passers-by. The death toll could have included a sheikh and many others if my body hadn't blocked the door.*

Present day

It's my job. I tell her, knowing she'll interpret it wrongly. *It's a Dom's job to monitor his sub's reactions carefully.* Certain skills come in useful. It's not just her personal safety that matters to me anymore, but her mental stability. I'm pushing her, I know. I could have done the investigation on my own, but that would have meant leaving someone else to babysit her. And the positive side is her presence will mean people will probably open up more than they would with a stranger. But just being back, where her nightmare started, is stressing her out.

As I gaze at her lovely face, seeing the nervousness in her eyes, thinking of ways I could relieve her tension, I remember the resolution I made last night. She's not for me; especially now I know the nightmare of her past. She deserves someone gentle, someone caring, and someone who'll stay around for the long haul. Not a Dominant like me who wants to take her in any and every way, to tie her up and fuck her until she screams, to push her boundaries far beyond even anything she's written in her books. She wouldn't be able to meet my appetites, not after everything she's been through. Hell, she's not even had a vanilla relationship in her life, so she's certainly not ready for a kinky one.

I watch her take a few more deep breaths; my fingers remain on her pulse, and I feel it slowing. I think she's as ready as she'll ever be. "Shall we go?"

I see her head dip in a nod, watch her swallow, and then grab the door handle with a new determination. Brave girl.

After checking back to make sure the McClaren has automatically locked the doors, we walk up to number nineteen and I notice we're approaching a tidy looking terraced house with a neatly maintained small front garden. At the door I turn around, and automatically scan the road as she rings the bell. My hand goes to my non-existent holster; old habits die hard.

The door's opened by a pleasant looking woman in her early fifties. Casually dressed, she has a cautious expression on her face as she stands motionless for a second, giving us the once over. Before she can dismiss us as hawkers or Jehovah's witnesses, I nod and say, "Good morning."

Mia takes my cue and addresses her by name, "Mrs Smith?"

The woman looks wary and answers with a slight inclination of her head.

"I used to be friends with your daughter, Anna," Mia continues, once the identity's confirmed. "Does she still live here?"

The woman relaxes a little, but her expression remains guarded. "She's here." she tells us.

Mia turns to me, her face looking pleased. She turns back, smiling warmly at the woman, "Can we speak to her, please? I'm Mia Fable. I was at school with her."

A tentative responding smile appears on Mrs Smith's face. "Yes, I think I remember you now. Wait here, a moment, and I'll see if she's awake. She works nights, but I did hear her stirring a little earlier."

She doesn't close the door completely but leaves us waiting on the doorstep. It's only a couple of minutes before the door opens for the second time, and another woman appears, a younger version of the first, wearing baggy sweatpants and an old T-shirt. I take a good look at Mia's old school friend. She's on the plump side, with a welcoming and friendly expression on her face. She looks first at Mia and gives her a broad smile, and then meets my eye, briefly reciprocating my appraisal, apparently curious. "Come in," she invites, waving her hand to usher us along. "Mia, it's lovely to see you. It's been ages! You haven't changed much, have you? What have you been up to?"

She continues throwing questions at us as we follow her into a comfortable looking sitting room. "Please forgive the way I look. I work nights now and have only just woken up. I'm a nurse." She pauses only to take a breath. "What are you up to nowadays?"

Mia's smiling at her old friend, I'm glad there's no awkwardness. Especially since the party probably took place in this very room. "I write books, novels."

Anna's eyes open wide, "Wow! That's great! Would I have seen them?"

I step in, not wanting Mia to broadcast her pseudonym. I don't know this girl from Adam, or how far she can be trusted. I clear my throat to get their attention. "Anna, I've not introduced myself. I'm Jon Tharpe; I'm providing protection for Mia."

If possible, her eyes widen even further. "*Protection?*" Shock makes her voice go up an octave. "Mia? Why do you need someone to protect you?"

Mia puts out her hand and touches her arm. "I seem to have picked up a stalker, Anna. I've no idea who he is, so we're trying to explore all avenues. I've come to see whether you can help me. It might be linked to something in my past."

Mia's revelation seems to have struck her old friend momentarily dumb. Anna glances first at me, then at Mia, as she digests the information. When she speaks again, she gets directly to the point, her chatty personality growing serious. "A stalker? No way! What do you need from me?" I find I'm beginning to like this woman as she wastes no time offering her help.

Now comes the tricky part, and I let Mia find her way through it. "Anna, I came to a party here seven years ago, when we were seventeen. We want to know who was at the party, and in particular if you know the man or men I left with?"

Narrowing her eyes, Anna scrutinises Mia carefully. "We didn't see much of you after that, did we?"

Mia shakes her head.

"Did something happen?"

Mia doesn't answer.

For a moment, Anna stares at her old friend intently and then flicks her eyes to me. Slowly she nods her head, and again she goes up in my estimation as she doesn't press for more information. Instead, she gets up, and crosses to the room, going to stand and look out of the window. Her head is bowed as though she's trying to remember. After a few seconds, she raises her head, still staring outside, and starts to speak. "I remember you arriving, Mia, as you were once of the first. I think you came alone?" She turns and looks at me, "The party got a bit crazy. I'd only invited school friends, but some gatecrashers showed up. I was worried they'd destroy the place, so most of my time was spent trying to keep everything under control. It was the first and last party I ever had here!" She grins conspiratorially, "My parents darn near killed me after. There were people in the bedrooms, on the floors, some still there the next morning when they returned home. It got a bit wild. I didn't notice you go, Mia, I'm sorry."

I've been to enough parties like that, so I'm not surprised. Mia, on the other hand, looks deflated. Personally, I wasn't expecting answers so quickly. "Can you give us a list of the people who you remember were here? The ones you knew? We'd like to question them to see if anyone else can recall anything."

"Yes, there's no problem with that. I'll have to rack my brains, but I'll do what I can and get it to you later today." She seems pleased to be able to help in some small way. I pass over my business card, indicating my email address.

"Do you remember anyone who had a white van at the time?" I probe. White is a popular colour, so I'm not hopeful of anything coming from that line of enquiry, but it's worth the question.

She thinks about it. "We were all the same age, my friends, that is. Some only sixteen, most seventeen. Most of us hadn't passed our test yet, let alone owned any vehicle." Another quiet moment of thought. "I'll ask the people I'm still in contact with if they remember anyone having one? It might have been the gatecrashers; they seemed to be older. But someone might have recognised them."

"That would be great!" Mia brightens up a bit, realising this isn't necessarily a dead end.

Something niggles at the back of my mind. "You say most of you were sixteen or seventeen, yet there was alcohol at the party. Who got it for you?" My train of thought is that it might have been one of the older blokes.

Anna snorts a laugh, "Come on, sixteen and seventeen-year-old girls? Some of us had fake ID, and we certainly knew how to look older than our age. And the Off-License down the road never asked too many questions. Where there's a will and all that."

Although that line of questioning didn't bear fruit, I still grin at her. I'd been seventeen once, and corner shops selling alcohol often turned a blind eye.

With no more questions to ask, we decline the offer of refreshment, but Mia doesn't seem ready to leave just yet. As she chats with Anna, trying to condense seven years into as many minutes, I send a quick text to the office asking Vanessa, one of the office staff, to expect a list of names to investigate later. By the time I've finished, the girls are done with their catch up, and we say our goodbyes. As we're at the door, Anna suddenly gives Mia a hug, while looking at me, and addressing her comments my way, "Take care of her, Jon." Then, glancing back to Mia murmurs, "I don't know what happened to you, Mia, but I can put two and two together. Look after yourself, and don't be a stranger."

Thinking the way compassion comes easily to her probably makes her a very good nurse, I shake her hand, and we leave the house.

As the front door closes behind us and Mia's walking to the car, I grasp her arm to hold her back. "Hold up a minute, Mia," I turn her to face me, "I'm sorry, but I want to see if you can remember anything else. Whereabouts on the road were you dropped off?"

She stills. Dragging up long-buried memories is painful, but it has to be done. With a sigh, she seems to pull that cloak of determination over herself again and starts looking up and down the road. Suddenly she shoots out her hand and points to the corner, "There."

I look across, noting the position. "Was the van driving up the road, or had it just turned into it?"

"Up." She sounds firm on that. "Why?"

"So we know the direction they came from. Okay, let's get in the car." I give a quiet chuckle as I watch her awkwardly folding herself to get into the bucket seat, then move to the driver's side and slide into my seat with ease of long practice.

After we've buckled up our seatbelts, I turn to her again, "Can you remember how long you were in the van for?"

"I don't know," she frowns. "I was unconscious when they took me; when they brought me back, I was in agony." Her face creases and I know she's thinking hard. "I remember the van shaking and juddering at first; I was being thrown around until I was going to be sick with the pain. Then it smoothed out. But how long I was travelling for I don't know. It could have been ten minutes, but it felt like ten hours."

"And you could see nothing at all?" My voice is calm, but my fingers grip the steering wheel so hard my knuckles go white. How could anyone treat her or any young girl, in that way?

"No. I still had my blindfold on until they threw me out. When I took it off, all I saw was the van driving away, as I said."

"Hmm." I glance at her, noting her hands are relaxed in lap, and there's no obvious tension in her, making sure she's able to cope with her memories. Then I reach for my laptop. Calling up our position on Google Earth I take a look. It sounds likely the jolting could have been because they'd been driving up a track. Possibly to a farm? The direction the van came from leads out into a rural area, so that makes sense.

"What are you looking for?"

"A barn or outbuilding, away from any occupied areas." From the map, it appears there are quite a few possible structures. Looking back I see her face is now showing some strain and decide the thought of trying to find the place where she was held is a step too far for today. She's had enough. "I'll get the office to look into it. Let's get back to your place."

I start the McClaren. The engine gives that satisfying roar, which still hasn't got old, and check over my shoulder before pulling away from the kerb. As it's going to take a while to get back to Epping, I put the radio on again. Music helps me think, and as I drive my thoughts surround my inappropriate feelings about the woman beside me. Everything inside me is screaming out to protect and help her, to give her what she needs – my cock is particularly resolute on that. How she was strong enough to bring herself back from her ordeal, and without professional help, I'll never know. I'm amazed how far she's managed to come. But the reality is, she's so innocent, so pure; she wouldn't be able to handle my lifestyle. While at times I might have a regular sub, it's only with a time-limited contract, so we both know what to expect. I don't do relationships. And a contract wouldn't work with Mia. She needs someone who can commit for the long term, and that isn't me. *I have to keep my distance.* My throbbing dick in my pants disagrees.

Her phone rings, so I turn down the music so she can answer. I do listen, and I won't apologise for that. I'm protecting her after all. It's necessary to know everything about her. But what I hear turns me cold. The more excited and animated she becomes as she speaks into her phone, the more my fists tighten on the steering wheel as I start to seethe. *She's going to a fucking BDSM club with a seedy reputation? Not on my watch!* Somehow, I manage to restrain myself from grabbing her phone and ending the connection long enough for her to complete the call. Gritting my teeth, becoming increasingly angry I wait for her to finish talking, preparing to have my say. But before I'm able to get a word in, she puts down her phone and gets in before me, her voice so eager and happy.

"I'm going out tomorrow night, Jon!"

She thinks this is good news?

There's a layby ahead, and I turn into it, making an abrupt halt and pulling up the handbrake harshly. I'm too fucking furious to drive at the moment; I'd be risking both our lives and probably a few other people's if I was to carry on. The rage rises in me, and I deserve a medal for not reaching over and shaking her. As it is, my fingers grasp the wheel even more tightly to help resist the urge to take them off and grab her. She throws me a curious glance and recoils a little at my expression. My tension is palpable.

I look straight ahead as she tells me, her brow creased as she tries to understand the way I'm acting. In a more cautious voice, she repeats, "I'm going out, tomorrow."

Slowly I turn to look at her. My behaviour has dampened her excitement. She's twisting her hands in her lap, so I know she's nervous. Anxious, about her outing? Or telling me about it now she's seen my reaction? Suspecting it's a mixture of both, I decide to take charge.

Through a clenched jaw, I tell her firmly, "No you're fucking not." Her eyes widen, both my words and my tone have startled her. I continue, "I heard where you're going, Mia." Thoughts are chasing through my head. I remember the book she's written. "Have you been there before?" Just the idea horrifies me. I can't imagine she has, I don't even want to imagine her in such a place. Her innocence would make her a target for exactly the wrong type.

"No, I haven't. What's the matter?" She turns away, and then comes back at me, determined, "You can't stop me."

Oh, she shouldn't go there and challenge me like that. She better bet I can, I'll tie her up if I have to. I look back and stare out the windscreen. It's starting to rain, the clouds black; the weather a direct correlation to my mood. "Why the hell would you want to go to a place like that?"

Her eyes are on me as she twists in her seat, facing me once again. "I need to go for research. Val's put me in contact with one of her friends who goes there, and I'm going to go with her," she pauses, and takes a breath. Her voice composed, full of conviction. "I've written about clubs like this, but only based on what I've read or researched online. I've never been to one in real life. I want to go and see it for myself, soak up the atmosphere then I'll be able to make it all come to life in my writing. This is my work, Jon. And let's face it, the only good thing that's happened to me this week. I'm not going to miss this opportunity. You don't get to tell me what to do. "

I remain focused on the drops of water running down the glass in front of me, preparing to set her straight on a few facts.

"So you want to go to an underground BDSM club, with no dungeon monitors and few rules just for research purposes? Hell, they'll eat you alive in there." I can't help myself; I try to hold the words back, but they come out anyway. "Fuck it, Mia. You're all but a goddamn virgin!"

She gasps loudly and covers her mouth with her hand. I've shocked her.

"How dare you throw that at me?" I hear the sob that escapes. As I turn my head, I see a tear roll down her face, but the blotchiness of her cheeks and the tension in her neck shows she's also angry. Then she tells me something which makes me realise how innocent she is. "I'm not going to *do* anything there, Jon. I just want to experience the atmosphere."

I close my eyes for a moment, and breathe deeply, willing myself to calm down, there's no point making this an argument, I've got to find the right words to convince her. "It's not safe. I understand why you want to, but believe me, that's not the place for you to go." The rain has eased off so I get out of the car to get some fresh air, to remove myself from the tension, to allow me time to decide if the answer that's come to me is indeed a good idea. The sound of her door opening reaches me; then I hear her swear and let out a gasp of pain behind me. Immediately I go to her.

"Damn it, Jon. Did you have to park next to stinging nettles?" She's rubbing her leg furiously and frowning.

Without thinking, I lift her up and over the offending weeds and put her down on the gravel next to me while continuing to hold her. I like the feel of her in my arms; she's soft and huggable, her head only reaching to my shoulder, her frame so much smaller than mine. I reach out my hand and turn her chin, so she's looking up at me. Her brown eyes return my stare. If I hold her too tightly, the effect she has on me would be all too apparent. But my hard and throbbing cock makes it easier for me to come to a decision.

"You're not going to that club," I tell her, firmly, but this time without the ire. As she begins to protest, I put my finger to her lips, and then continue as I discover I don't have to think about it, I've already made the decision, "You're not going there because you're coming to Club Tiacapan. With me." She pulls back, eyes wide open, her eyebrows raised, showing her confusion. Raindrops start falling again, so before she can question me, I sweep her in my arms again. "Come let's get back in the car." She doesn't protest as I carry her around to the passenger door and gently ease her into her seat. "There, I've protected you from the deadly nettles." As I grin, a giggle escapes her lips. The moment lightens the mood.

I return to the driver's side and strap myself in, checking her seatbelt is fastened too. It's the protector in me; I'm unable to turn it off. Starting the car, I pull away and get back on the road.

CHAPTER 10
Mia

Seven years ago

The party continued to rage around us, as my new friend gave me his arm to help me across the room. Without his support, I doubt I'd have made it as far as the front door. The odd notion that I ought to say something to Anna, to thank her for having me, rattled round my head, but I couldn't summon up the right words nor had the inclination to search the house to find her. I was hoping fresh air would revive me, but as I stepped out into the coolness of the night, it seemed to do the complete opposite. I tripped over the front step, ending up sprawled over the path. I heard a hearty laugh; someone was mocking me, but I couldn't summon up the energy to protest.

Then strong arms lifted me, and I felt myself being carried, then placed in the back of some vehicle. It wasn't very comfortable, I wasn't on a seat in a car, but my mind was too fogged to worry about what it was. At least some kind person was taking me home. I couldn't have walked.

Senses fading fast when I tried to speak to offer up my address my voice didn't work. The last thing I was conscious of was the engine starting.

Present day

Club Tiacapan? That's only the most exclusive BDSM club in London! The hardest to get into; you need to be a multi-millionaire to afford the membership fees. I know. I've come across whispers about it in my research. How the hell does Jon think he can get me in there? If he really could, it would be an incredible opportunity and give me amazing insight and material for my books. Probably the best experience I could get. Well, in the UK.

He's not said anything more. He's waiting for my reaction, waiting for me to ask the obvious questions. But right now I'm just trying to soak it all in, totally gobsmacked. Not only has he said he could get me into the best club in England, he's said *he'll* take me. Sneaking peep at the man sitting beside me, I realise even the thought has given me goosebumps. He drives along the road, seeming at one with the fast, powerful car, handling it as he does everything, with utter competence. When he carried me over the nettles, I'd wanted him to hold me closer; my normal concerns about a man touching me never ended my head. His arms felt so strong and muscular, so safe, and not for the slightest moment had I any fear he'd drop me. I'd rested my head on his shoulder and drawn in his masculine scent. I wanted more.

But what had he said before? My cheeks redden, recalling his harsh comment and the description he'd used about my lack of sexual experience; though there's no doubt he's right, I just didn't like it being spat out at me. Especially in that way.

I've already recognised his self-assurance, his confidence. Have already deduced he had to have had so much experience with women as to put him out of the reach of such a novice like me. But now I'm learning he's in an entirely different league. He goes to Club Tiacapan; he has to be sexual Dominant, as he's certainly not submissive! *Why hadn't I cottoned on to that earlier?* It should have screamed out at me, the way he acts, the way he behaves. That low, authoritative voice. I've written about enough Doms, trying to describe their psyche. So how could I have missed that this man sitting beside me is all Dom? As the realisation dawns, I turn my head to look out of the window, too nervous to even look at him now I've fathomed what he is and conscious this new fact about him both thrills and terrifies me all at the same time. I never expected him to know about, let alone be involved in the BDSM lifestyle. And he's suggested taking me to Club Tiacapan? What would he expect of me there? Any expectation would be more than I could give. I look down at my hands, clasped tight together in my lap. Though he could have phrased it more kindly, he's right; it's only a technicality that I'm not an actual virgin. I shiver, feeling uneasy.

He takes one of my hands in his; I feel the pressure of his fingers against mine. "Ask," he invites, economically.

I swallow, suddenly timid, wanting to check my intuition is right. "How can you possibly get me into Club Tiacapan?"

"Simple," he chuckles, "I'm a member."

I turn to stare at him. "But the fees… are you that rich?"

He seems to grow a little tense, as if there's something he's not telling me, then relaxes and smirks, "I know a sheikh."

"The same one you got shot for? The one who gave you this car?"

I watch him give an uneasy nod. He doesn't glance at me again, and from his posture, I take it he would prefer I didn't question it further. But I suppose it's sufficient to resolve that mystery; I'd be very grateful too if someone had saved my life. So I get back to the main topic, "And you can really take me as a guest? Tomorrow?"

He considers it for a moment, and then confirms it. "Grade A Security has thoroughly investigated your background, Mia. There won't be a problem with your temporary membership in that respect. But there will be some documents you'll need to sign. Discretion and confidentiality are critical due to the type of members we have."

"Do I have to sign in blood?" I try to lighten the mood.

He remains serious. "No, but understand you'd be risking being ruined financially if you broke the agreement."

I'm not worried; I have no intention of doing so. "How do I get the documents?" I already know that there's no website on the internet. Or not that I've been able to access.

"I'll get them sent to me by email. Your printer works okay, doesn't it?"

I tell him it does, well, when it hasn't had a falling out with my laptop that is. Wifi, the ban of my life.

We drive on in silence, heading back round the M25, which is surprisingly clear at the moment, though probably won't be for long. Although the variable speed limits and fourth lane seem to have helped, particularly around Heathrow accidents happen with frightening regularity and traffic can build up in a flash. I find some amusement in the keen attention the McClaren is drawing, and almost preen in my seat with reflected glory, but my mind's taken off the cars around us when he starts speaking again.

"Really you need to have health tests done before going to the club and have the paperwork to show you've tested clear. But in your case, there's not much doubt about that and I can vouch for you. You won't be allowed to play in the private rooms without medical clearance, though."

So seven years abstinence qualifies me for the club. Hmm. Not being allowed into the private rooms? No worries. I don't intend to play at all, so that doesn't bother me one bit. I see him cast a sideways glance at me.

"Mia, we're going to need to talk about this. You'll be going to the club with me, but you'll be going as a sub. A submissive."

I know what that is, but I've never thought of myself in that way. *Could he be right?* Hiding my thoughts, I smirk. "I could be a Domme."

His barked laugh is one of disbelief. "Mia, I really can't see you leading a man by a collar and leash or attaching a cage to his balls." He continues laughing as I huff, but to be honest, he's right. I wouldn't have a clue what to do if someone wanted to be dominated by me. Which causes me to wonder, perhaps I am a sub? I'd really never thought of myself that way.

"You're a Dom?" I summon up the courage to ask for the confirmation I don't really need. His manner and his caring, protective nature have given him away. Again I shiver, wondering what it would be like to place myself utterly and literally in his hands and under his control. Despite my fears, I shift a little in my seat, trying to get more comfortable as the thought makes my stomach muscles contract. *I wonder just what he likes.* If I'm going to the club with him, will I be *his* submissive? No, of course, I won't, he's probably got someone there he'll be playing with.

Don't be stupid, Mia, you don't want to be anyone's submissive. The thought, almost shouted in my head, brings me back to my senses. Having been forced and raped, I'll never willingly give up control. My visit to the club is purely for research. A tremble shudders down my body as memories return; of being tied up and unable to defend myself in any way. No, Jon's just getting me into the club. He can go play while I watch, listen, absorb, and learn. I'll fade into the background; I'm used to that.

After a while, I realise he hasn't answered my question; he hasn't confirmed or denied my assumption. But then he doesn't have to. I already know the answer. There can be no doubt about it. He's a Dom.

Turning off the motorway Jon takes the Epping road. As we get closer to home, I have something else to worry about as I start dreading what might be waiting for me at home. Tension starts to creep over me again as I wonder whether my stalker paid another visit. Could he, even now, be lying in wait for me? As if anticipating my concern, Jon drives straight past my house and pulls into the car park of the Blazing Donkey. I give a sigh of relief as he cuts the engine, and find it hard to believe it was only yesterday we were last here So much has happened it seems much longer ago that that. I look at him questioningly as he parks the car.

"Food," he says, aptly giving the reason with just one word, then gives me an apologetic smile. "Do you mind going in and ordering for us? I have a couple of calls to make first."

Gently teasing him, asking if this is his way of getting a drink out of me, and then waving his protests away, I tell him, of course, I don't mind. After checking what he wants, I go inside to be greeted by the landlord like an old friend, although I've not been here very often. To be honest I resent paying the cost of one glass of wine when I could get a whole bottle to drink at home for the same price from a supermarket.

It's mid-afternoon, and once again the pub isn't crowded. The landlord confirms they're still serving food so, having bought a wine and Jon's choice of real ale; I collect a couple of menus from the rack on the bar, and take them to the same secluded table we were at before. Coming to the Blazing Donkey is becoming a habit, I smile to myself as I sit down and wonder what calls Jon's making that he needs privacy for, then realise that I'm probably not his only case.

The case, a job. That's all I am to him, and I've got to remember that. *No use yearning over something that's out of reach to me.* Yearning? I pull up sharply. My body may be having a perfectly normal, albeit very unusual for me, reaction when I'm forced to be in close proximity with an extremely attractive member of the opposite sex, but that doesn't mean I'm going, or even want, to act on any physical urge. And though I can't help but like the man well, who wouldn't? He's so sexy, kind, a natural protector, but I certainly can't afford to form any emotional attachment. It must be the situation we're in and his role as my bodyguard that naturally makes me dependant on him causing me to see things which aren't there. God, what would he think if he knew some of the thoughts going through my head? *In your dreams, Mia! And don't forget he's a Dom, not a man someone like you should get involved with.*

And then the man in question enters the pub, pausing in the doorway to scan over the occupants, before coming striding across to me as if he owns the place. Confidence oozes off of him. He sits, pushing back strands of dark hair which have flopped over his forehead and flashing that charismatic smile. Even though I'm wary of that look, as if he's laughing at a joke which I'm not privy too, his attractiveness zooms up into the stratosphere. I admit it; this man is sex on legs, and a woman would have to be dead not to respond. My mouth purses as my welcome dies on my lips, and I turn and look in the other direction, afraid I'm going to give myself away. My pep talk had no effect on my libido at all.

Oblivious to the thoughts going through my head, he peruses the menu. I order a burger; he goes for the steak. Once he comes back from placing the order, he gets out his laptop which, having been caught up with assessing his physical characteristics, I've only just noticed he'd brought in with him. He opens it and calls up a program. Leaning forwards, I can see pictures of my house, all taken from different angles. Raising my eyebrows, I glance at him.

He nods, thoughtfully, and offers an explanation. "I thought it best to check what's being going on while we've been out before we go back to your house. We don't want any surprises."

I cock my head to one side. "We can do that?"

"Yes, the cameras have motion sensors, so we can see anything that's triggered them since Howie installed them yesterday. I'll set up the program on your laptop too, later."

"Hopefully they won't have picked up anything," I say, sipping the wine that I'd watched the barman pour, and hadn't taken my eyes away from while I was standing at the bar.

"Here's something." He presses a button, and a video starts to play. Something had caused the cameras to start filming during the night, the pictures are black and white from the night vision cameras, but they're surprisingly sharp and clear. I hold my breath, worried about what I'm going to watch, but it's certainly not my stalker, it's a pair of deer, jumping over my fence and munching on my plants!

"Huh!" I laugh with relief and surprise. "I wondered what was eating them."

We watch for a while until the deer jump away again, and the camera shuts down. Apart from the postman arriving this morning, nothing else triggered them again. "See," Jon says, looking at me reassuringly. "It's safe to go home."

He thinks of everything to make sure I've both physically and emotionally safe. Just like a Dom taking care of his sub. I shake my head to get that thought right out of my mind. He's good at his job is all!

The food, while not exactly gourmet is satisfying, but we don't linger after we've eaten it. When we arrive home, I'm nervous when I open the front door and see the pile of letters on the floor beneath the letterbox. Having a quick scan through them, I'm relieved when there's doesn't immediately appear to be anything amiss; it looks like I've got a couple of credit card statements and some flyers for things I don't want or need. There have been no messages on the home phone either. My stalker appears to have given me the day off. Or perhaps he's seen Jon with me and given up? That thought is a bit concerning, what if he's holding off while I've got protection, lulling me into a false sense of security? If nothing else happens,

Jon will probably close the case and leave me alone. *You're thinking too far ahead, woman, just deal with it day by day.* I don't tell Jon my worries; I keep them to myself. For now, I'm safe, and that's enough.

The rest of the day passes quickly. Jon settles himself to read more of my books, which makes me uneasy. It's awkward watching him reading the words I've written; I don't want to see his facial expressions, or hear any comments he might make. Generally, I don't care what anybody thinks – like it or not, buy the book or don't – but with him, it's as if I'm baring my soul. And now I know he's got the experience to know what he's talking about. What if he can see things I've got wrong? I try my best to be accurate, but lack the practical experience to be confident I've got everything right.

Seeing my uneasiness, he did take the time to explain he's not reading them for fun or titillation, instead using them to get a feel for anything that might have triggered my stalker. But even so, I'm still too embarrassed to stay in the same room while he reads, so I secrete myself in my upstairs office, quickly getting lost in the goings on of my characters and putting in half a day's word count; far more than I expected to do. I'm on a roll, this could be my best book yet, and the emotional turmoil I'm going through continues to inspire what's appearing on the page.

In the middle of the evening, I'm brought out of a particularly intense scene when he comes up to ask to use my printer. Giving him the printer name I stretch, rolling my neck and shoulders. Goodness, it's already dark outside! *I'd totally lost myself there.*

The printer jerks into life beside me. When it stops churning out paper, Jon picks up the sheets, collates them, and, after helping himself to my stapler, brings the documents over to my desk. Pulling up the spare chair, he sits next to me, giving me a probing look as he hands them over. There are two documents, one fairly thin, one thicker, and both have the heading *Club Tiacapan* on them written in gold script. Engrossed in another world with my characters I'd almost forgotten about our previous conversation, and that I would need to sign them. If I wanted entrance to that exclusive club, that is.

"You sure you want to do this?"

I cock my head to one side, querying his question.

"To come to the club tomorrow?" He clarifies.

As a response to his searching gaze, I give a definite nod. After a second, he looks away and points to the top one. "This is the confidentiality agreement."

Picking it up, I start to read it through. As I interpret the paragraphs of legalese I realise what he'd told me had been right; they'll basically bankrupt me if I break the agreement. But I have no hesitation signing it; it provides protection and the promise of anonymity for me as much as anyone else.

Then he picks up the second document and lays it down. "You know what this is?"

I glance down, and for a second I forget to breathe. Looking over at him, I gasp softly, "A limits list?" Of course, I should have expected a club with the reputation of Tiacapan would go through all the formalities. At the other type of club I'd been planning to go to I'd probably either be given a brief checklist on arrival or even, nothing at all. Having thought about it, Jon is right. Going to that kind of place would have been a risk. Belatedly I realise how grateful I am he'd stopped me.

He nods, confirming that is indeed what he's just laid down. "You write about limits, so I know you're familiar with them. Have you ever filled a list in before?"

I snort. "Of course not!"

He smirks. "I thought you might have filled one in for fun or as part of your research. Anyway, you need to have this completed before tomorrow."

With a dismissive shrug, I pass it back to him without writing anything. "I don't intend to play, so it's pointless."

For a second, he just stares at me as his face tightens into a frown. He doesn't look particularly happy with my response. "You're the one who wanted the experience. Deciding what you are and aren't comfortable with is all part of that. How can you write convincingly about something you haven't done?" His knuckles knock twice on the papers on the desk, and then he stands and strides to the door. Pausing, and turning back before leaving the room he tells me, "You won't get entrance unless you complete that form and sign it, and it's put on record at the club. So, if you want to go with me tomorrow, I suggest you give it some thought. I'll give you some space to decide what to do. If you want to come to the club, complete it. If you're having second thoughts, then don't. There's no problem either way, no harm if you've changed your mind. I'm not pushing you to do anything you're not ready for. It's your decision, Mia."

Before I can stop them, or consider how wise they are, words fly from my mouth, "If I don't come with you tomorrow, Jon, will you still be going to the club?"

He looks astonished I've asked, and so am I. Why should I care what he does on his down time? And surely he must get time off at some point, although up to now he hasn't left my side. Holding up his hands, his palms facing me as if to ward off any further personal enquiries he finally replies, "Perhaps not tomorrow, but sometime, yes. I regularly go, Mia. I'm a member, as I told you."

Not wanting to analyse why that answer hits me like a rejection, I turn back to the papers he's left on my desk as I hear his heavy feet clomp down the narrow wooden stairs. It appears futile to protest. If I want to go to the club – and boy, do I want to go – I need to complete the blasted form. *Dexie, I may need some help here!* With one finger I slide the paperwork towards me.

The instructions are clear. I have to put 'No' to things I absolutely wouldn't try under any circumstances and 'Yes' or 'Maybe' for other activities. My first inclination is to put a resounding negative response on every item on the page; every single entry on the list terrifies me, but I'm certain he won't be letting me get away with that. And worse, if he's right, it will deny me entry to the club. I suppose that makes sense, why would anyone want to go to a BDSM club when they weren't prepared to take part in any activity at all? Unless, of course, they're an author like me and simply going to get some ideas to spice up their books. I grin to myself, I've no intention of playing in the club, but to gain admittance, I have to pretend and go through the motions. So, now I'll just have to pull up my big girls pants and get down to the task I've been set.

The list is in alphabetical order, I notice as I start to read through, and therein lies my first problem. Almost at the top of the initial page is the heading 'Anal' and my first reaction is to put NO in huge capital letters. The bastards tried to do that, but I was too tight, and they weren't successful in taking me that way. But they hadn't given up before I was torn and bleeding. There's no way I'd ever attempt that again. *But they'd gone about it all wrong.* I've researched, I've *written* sensual scenes where the Dom carefully prepared his sub for what I've then described as an incredible experience. My abusers had gone about it all wrong; I know that. Am I always going to let my past dictate my future? Perhaps it would be different with someone I trusted? I tap my pen against my teeth, glad now that I'm on my own, and Jon isn't staring over my shoulder as I complete this. *But he'll see what you've written.* Then I tell myself I'm being stupid. Why would he be interested? Completing this form is just a formality for entrance to Tiacapan; it doesn't mean it would have any significance for my bodyguard. Just because I seem to be developing something akin to a teenage crush on him doesn't mean he feels the same way. He's a Dom for God's sake; I'm not able to even begin to imagine the level of experience he must have, nor the proficiency he expects in his partners. Forcing my mind back to the task at hand and, before I lose my nerve, I put 'Maybe' against Anal.

Then I continue through the list. Many activities are definite 'Noes' that I don't consider other than for a split second or just reject out of hand, and a very few I'm happy to put 'yes' to without too much deliberation. But there are several which give me food for thought. The idea of bondage, any kind of physical beating, blindfolds, rape simulation, the use of gags, fellatio, even cunnilingus, knife play, any type of pain or sensory deprivation or asphyxiation takes me straight back to the worst two days of my life. I've written about and imagined people enjoying some of these activities, but I've never considered experiencing them myself.

I begin to sweat as I go through the list, the pen shaking in my hand. Is the next step for me to try and trust someone enough to help me attempt to conquer my fears? What if I put 'Maybe'? I'll always have the option to say 'No' at the time. Before I can reconsider I put 'Maybe' against some the activities I've been hesitating over. Then immediately want to go back and change them all to a negative response. My pen hovers over the page. "Fuck it!" I exclaim loudly to the empty room and change my responses back to 'Maybe's again. Then, before I can have a second, or even third thought, collect all the paperwork from my desk take it downstairs and literally throw it at the man who's made himself comfortable and very much at home on my sofa. Now mortified, as I realise I've no reason to take it out on him, I walk over and apologise.

I stay standing in front of him as Jon puts down his book – which I notice is my latest novel – and throws me a strange look before bending over and picking up the papers from the floor. After he's collected the documents together, he folds them in half and places the pile on the coffee table without, to my utmost relief, checking what I've written. Then, leaning forwards, he takes both my hands in his and examines my face, carefully. It occurs to me how often he does this. It's far from the first time I've felt he's been trying to read me, assessing my state of mind. Now I know he's a Dom it all falls into place. I stay silent, waiting for him to speak.

What I've just done has shaken me. Of course, I've written about limits in the past, but never thought of applying them to myself. The thought of taking part in any of the activities listed scares the shit out of me, but also, I have to admit grudgingly, *turns me on!* I've become wet between my thighs, and there's a throbbing between my legs that could do with some relief. And here I am, with an incredibly attractive Dom sitting right in front of me. Shifting my weight from leg to leg, trying discreetly to ease the tingling, knowing it's the thought of trying some of the 'Yeses' and 'Maybes' with *Jon* that's making my body respond, thinking that it's a shame he's not interested. And terrified in case he is.

"You're certain you still want to go to the club?" He's still holding my hands, his fingers gently caressing my skin.

My heart's beating fast, and I know he can tell, but I'm hoping he doesn't how much, and in what particular ways, completing the list has affected me. My nipples have hardened, and I fight the impulse to look down to check if they're visible through my jumper, not wanting to draw attention to them in any way. *God, please say he can't see them!* I hope he doesn't choose this moment to check my pulse, because if he does, he'll find it racing. And that burning flush on my face? Hopefully, he'll put that down to embarrassment.

What did he ask again? *Am I certain?* I make sure my eyes

meet his, and try to put absolute certainty into my voice. "Yes," I tell him fervently.

"Okay."

It's impossible to read his expression; I'm unable to say whether he's pleased or annoyed. He isn't giving anything away about what he's thinking. I only wish I knew.

CHAPTER 11
Jon

Four years ago

I t's too much, Nijad," I told him, frowning at the cheque he'd just put into my hand. "I'm providing you with close protection; it's my duty to take a bullet if necessary. It's in my job description, and I'm already being paid well enough for that."

Narrowing his eyes and glaring, he reminded me, "You nearly died, my friend."

I shrugged. "But I didn't." Apparently, my collapsed lung and internal bleeding had caused some concern for those around me at the time, but as I'd been out of it throughout, the only words I heard when eventually regaining consciousness was that I'd make a full recovery. My close dance with death had caused more concern in others than in me.

"Has Ben sent someone over to take my place?" However nice it was to hear Nijad referring to me as a 'friend,' I was working for him. Even while I was out of commission, I still saw it as my job to make sure Nijad had someone on him at all times.

"For fucks sake, Jon. Stop worrying! Yes, Harry's here, and he doesn't leave my side." He ran his hand through his hair and gave a wry grin, letting me know just how frustrating Harry's version of 'close protection' was. Harry took his job very seriously and probably didn't leave Nijad much privacy. Unlike myself. The sheikh and I had come to an arrangement early on that

worked for us both. Nijad continued, "Just relax, get well, and enjoy the lovely nurses," He paused for a moment, and then smirked, "I have."

"Huh!" I turned my head from side to side in disbelief. Well, it wasn't that hard for me to believe. "So all this time I thought you were visiting me...?"

He had the grace to look sheepish, well, as sheepish as an incredibly wealthy sheikh with good looks to boot could look. He attracted women like shit attracted flies. Leaning down, he whispered conspiratorially into my ear, indicating a female nurse standing just outside the door. "Now, that one..." he started, winking, "She's into a bit of S and M." As if she was aware she was the topic of conversation, the nurse chose that precise minute to turn and come into the room. I noticed with interest that her cheeks flushed as she studiously avoided looking at the Sheikh, giving all her attention to me.

"Lucky bastard." I mouthed at him. He just laughed.

As the nurse indicated she needed to check my dressing, Nijad turned to go. But not he saw me pointedly tear up the cheque he'd given to me. As he scowled, his expression let me know this probably wasn't going to be the end of the matter. Bring it on, Nijad; I thought to myself, you bring it on. You're not going to win this. I'm not taking your money!

Present day

She's come down and given me her list of limits for fuck's sake! I'd have bet a pound to a penny that she would have chickened out. *What the hell do I do now?* Just the mere thought of Mia in a dungeon is enough to send the blood coursing through me in a southerly direction so fast I feel drained. Unable to look at the list right at this moment without giving myself away, I fold it, and put it to one side to study later. I'm intrigued, and eager to see how she's filled it in, what she's prepared to try. Although, after everything she was put through I wouldn't have been surprised to see her just put 'No' to every item. Curbing my impatience to find out, I force myself to ignore the paperwork.

Leaning forwards, in an attempt to hide my throbbing erection – my cock feeling like it's about to burst out of my jeans – I take her hands. She's shaking, so I offer her a chance to change her mind, but she seems surprised I'd even think she would back our now, and remains adamant she wants to go. And it's plain to see the idea excites her. I don't need to be a Dom to read the signs; just completing the list has aroused her; I'd not be so crass to tell her, but I can smell it from here.

But how much does she honestly want to try? My suspicions are it's the idea which turns her on, not the actual activities themselves, which would probably send her running for the hills. I'm not stupid; I know she thinks she's going to get away with simply going as an observer, but I won't allow that. The club won't allow that; no one would appreciate someone standing there taking notes while they play. What she doesn't know, and what I'm not going to enlighten her about just yet, is that *I'll* be her Dom. At least for now. And it's at this point I'm going to start taking take charge.

I tell her to go to bed; it's not that late, but she's got a busy day ahead. Not that she knows that, no, there's a few things I've got planned which she'll remain ignorant of for the moment; hence my need for privacy for my phone calls this afternoon. Hiding my smile, I watch her obey; the tone of voice I use has got her to her feet and bidding me 'goodnight' without argument. I grin as she leaves the room, recognising she's already tuned into me. It bodes well. I'm very much looking forward to tomorrow. My cock agrees, lengthening of its own accord.

Now I'm alone I take a few deep breaths, trying to bring myself back under control before reaching to pick up and then unfold the papers she'd initially thrown at me. *Yes, completing that list affected you, didn't it, Mia?* And looking at it is having a similar effect on me! Reading through carefully, I need to sit back in the chair to ease myself; my control shooting away from me, almost off the spectrum. *Fuck, if I'm this hard just thinking about her limit list, what am I going to be like when we're actually in the club?* There are far more items that I would have imagined that she's ticked on her 'Maybe' list. Not so many marked 'Yes', in fact, I haven't seen any yet – hang on, there are a couple – and, at present, I'm perfectly content with the definite 'Noes.' Reaching for the beer I'd been drinking earlier, it hits me again what a brave and amazing woman she is.

* * * *

Next morning, after another uncomfortable night on her far too small couch, I go into her kitchen. Rummaging through her fridge I find some tomatoes, eggs, and a packet of bacon only a day over its sell by date. *That will do.* In the freezer, I find hash browns, and yes, in a cupboard there's a tin of baked beans. A good old-fashioned cooked breakfast will set us up for the day. It's a shame she hasn't got any black pudding, but then not everyone likes eating blood. Finding a cafetière, I put the kettle on for coffee, get out the frying pan, get the grill heating and start cooking.

There's nothing better in the morning than the smell of bacon sizzling under the grill, and as I suspected it would, the aroma wafting upstairs gets her attention. She comes into the kitchen wearing a fluffy robe, her hair a complete mess and her face makeup-free. Her eyebrows rise in question as she sees what I'm doing, and then her face widens into a broad smile. She looks absolutely fucking beautiful. My cock jerks into life, letting me know the only thing that's wrong is that it's not my bed she's just gotten out of. I turn back to the stove while I will the damn thing to go down again, not an easy task but then it never is around this woman.

After the requisite morning greetings, she busies herself making coffee, and buttering toast when it pops up out of the toaster. She lays the table and gathers together the condiments. We work well together. Breakfast ready, I set it on the table.

She tries each item in turn and groans softly, "Mmm, this is good, Jon. Thanks!"

Shifting uncomfortably as that groan goes straight to my groin, I wonder what other sounds I could elicit from her. *Fuck, Tharpe! Get your mind back on business.* I take a bite of bacon after dipping it in the runny yellow yolk of the egg and bring my thoughts back to the day ahead.

As she puts food into her mouth, I mention casually, "After breakfast, we're heading into town, I'm taking you to Grade A so you can meet the team and we'll be able to catch up on whatever progress they've been able to make."

She puts down her fork. "I ought to stay here and work. I've got to get my word count in, Jon." Her mouth purses, "Can't we catch up by phone?"

"Not today, you're taking the day off, Mia." My tone allows no argument, and I offer no compromise. Although I know how she likes to keep to her routine, I have the whole day planned for her.

Her blue eyes regard me, flashing in challenge, but at my unrelenting stare she backs down with a sigh and then tells me grudgingly, "Oh, alright. I'm slightly ahead anyway."

"It is important, Mia. If we don't catch this bastard, you'll be forever looking over your shoulder." My glower emphasises the point. The Dom side of me is annoyed she didn't immediately fall in with my plans, but she doesn't see me in quite that way as yet. But she will, later. Since she gave me her limits list I can't keep the Dom in me from coming out. *She's going to be my submissive.* Which means I'll do whatever I feel is best for her.

We finish up; then I stack the dishwasher as she wipes down the sides; she's impressed that I've made so little mess. The kitchen clean and tidy, I shoo her off to shower and dress and am pleasantly surprised she makes it down again in just forty minutes; she's dried her shoulder-length hair straight and has pulled it back in some kind of braid. It suits her.

We take the McClaren, but I wish I had my motorbike here, not the single seat Agusta, but my Kawasaki. Going through London traffic would have been a breeze on that bike, even better than the Harley I also own. But at least the car has one benefit, allowing me to cast sideways glances to appreciate my companion and to breathe in the aroma that's part perfume, and part the natural scent of the woman sitting beside me. There's no denying it; she's getting to me. I'm very much looking forward to the night ahead.

After an uneventful journey, we reach Grade A's prestigious building in a newly renovated part of the east end. The office block is expensive to maintain, but its aura of affluence helps us attract the wealthy clientele who we depend on to line our pockets. I park in the underground garage and take her up to meet the team who have already assembled in one of the conference rooms.

Ben Carter, the senior partner and technically my boss, although neither of us stresses that relationship, is sitting at the head of the table; the other founding partner, Jason Deville, being out of the country at present. Next to Ben is the head of our investigation department, Vanessa Hawkins. One of her junior members of her team accompanies her, and for a second I have difficulty remembering her name, but then it comes back to me. *Nafisa. That's it. She only started a couple of weeks ago.* She's from Dubai, and while she doesn't wear a veil, she always has a different colourful hijab covering her head. Sean's present as well, and as normal he's ribbing Ryan, who's sitting next to him and refusing to rise to any of the bait that's being offered; also as normal. All the leading members of Grade A, who are working on Mia's case, are here; our other employees are out on their various duties in the field.

I introduce Mia to everyone, and then we take our seats. Keeping my face neutral, I watch Mia's reaction, particularly to Sean, who would likely be the one to provide cover for her in my absence. Sean's a handsome son of a bitch with his pretty boy looks and slim build. As my gaze turns to my good-looking colleague, I inch my chair a little closer to Mia; I'm making a point, and the responding grin Sean throws me shows he hasn't missed it. *Fuck. What the hell is wrong with me?* I've never been possessive about anyone in my life!

The woman in question has become the centre of attention. Forcing myself to sit back, with interest I watch to see how Mia handles it.

"I've read your books!" Vanessa tells her. "I can't wait for the next one – why did you leave the last one on such a cliff hanger?"

Mia sits straighter in her chair and grins. "What happens next needed a whole book to itself," she informs her. And then adds chuckling, "And of course, it helps with sales. The pre-orders are flooding in." The confidence in her voice makes me realise she's slipped into Dexie mode.

"One of them's mine!" Vanessa laughs loudly.

Mia bows her head theatrically. "Thank you."

After giving her an appraising look, Ben pulls us back to business. "Vanessa, can you bring us up to date?"

After a throwing a quick grimace at Mia suggesting she'd

rather keep discussing her novels, Vanessa opens her laptop, makes an instant switch to her business manner and begins to give us the details. "There's nothing on Facebook, Twitter or other social media, or any communication to her publishers or agent that suggests anyone has a fixation with Dexie Sanders. Mia Fable doesn't have any personal social accounts. Nafisa's looked at the comments on Amazon and other online booksellers, and websites such as Goodreads and while some people don't rate the book as highly as others, again, there was nothing there that she could find of any concern."

Nafisa nods in agreement. "Most of your books are rated five stars, Mia." She's probably telling her what she already knows, but continues. "The average for all your books is four to five stars."

"So that appears to be a dead end for now. It looks more likely to go back to the incident in the past?" Ben referred tactfully to Mia's ordeal for which I was grateful.

Taking over again, Vanessa continues, "Yes, I think so. Mia gave us the names of about eight people she can remember at the party, and her friend, Anna, came up with twelve." She looks up for a moment. "How many do you remember being there in total, Mia?"

Mia shrugs. "Impossible to say, the place was choc-a-bloc." She gives it some thought. "Anywhere between thirty and fifty."

"As I thought. Probably a lot of gate crashers, hangers-on, partners." She glances at her screen again. "Putting the two lists together we have eleven unique names to start tracking down. That's what we're going to do next. Once we've got contact details, we'll phone round the partygoers and see if they remember anything or if they can give us more leads."

Now Ben addresses Mia. "You didn't notice anything unusual before the incident on Tuesday? Did you think that anyone was following you? Did anything out of the ordinary happen? You didn't get into an argument, step in front of someone in a queue, road rage or anything like that?"

She puts her head in her hands for a moment, taking the question seriously and trying to remember. After a while, she looks up. "Nothing that I recall. I'm sorry. I spend most of my time at home writing. I'm pretty boring." She laughs at herself and elicits a smile from the rest of us. Boring isn't a word I'd use to describe Mia Fable.

Slowly nodding Ben wraps up, "Well, I think it's best to concentrate on the party and what we can find from there on in. Mia, I asked Jon to bring you here so you can meet the team. If you need anything, and you can't speak to Jon for any reason, you're welcome to come directly to one of us." He gives her his card with his direct line; the others do the same. I know he's made the offer in case I'm out of action for any reason. But also in case she'd rather speak to a female if she remembers details she can't bring herself to share with me. Being her almost Dom, I'd be very upset if that happened. But it's the protocol I'd follow if I were in the Chair, so I don't protest.

Ben stands. "Jon, can I have a word with you for a moment? Mia, Vanessa will get you a coffee. I'll only keep him a few minutes."

Pausing only to make sure Mia is happy with the arrangement, I follow Ben out to his office which is next door to mine. Ben goes to sit behind his desk. He leans back in his big comfortable leather chair and indicates I should close the door, then waves me to the seat in front of him. Leaning back, putting his hands behind his head, he brings his elbows parallel to his ears. He's studying me, the smile and welcome slipping slowly from his face. I wait for it.

He doesn't keep me hanging for long. "What the fuck do you think you're doing, Jon? Inviting her to the club?" He certainly isn't in the best of moods.

Lifting my chin, I narrow my eyes, "She was going to go to Bates' place. Club Tiacapan seemed a better alternative."

"Bates' place? Tops and Tailends? Fuck Jon, she shouldn't be going anywhere! Especially now." Ben raises his voice, "Couldn't you just stop her?"

"Short of tying her up, no. I'm her protection officer, not her gaoler!" My temper flares because part of me agrees with him, conscious I could have tried harder to put a hold on her desire to visit a BDSM club, but can't admit the honest truth; I want to see her at the Tiacapan for my benefit. But I suspect Ben's well aware of that; he's an experienced Dom himself. He won't have missed any of the signs giving me away. He's known me too long and too well.

His arms return to his sides, and he sits up straight. "Why's she so adamant about going?"

"She writes about BDSM in her books and wants to see a real club in action for research," I explain.

I've raised a red rag to a bull. Ben stares at me in disbelief, then, as the implications sink in, jumps to his feet, his fist crashing down on the desk. "So while I'm playing tonight she's going to be standing there taking notes? For fuck's sake!" Straightening, he brushes his hand through his hair. "That can't happen, Jon. You know how strict the club is about confidentiality; no one goes there to be watched. Christ!" His hand stills, "What's she going to do? Observe us like monkeys in a fucking zoo?"

I also stand, my anger getting the better of me as I spurt out before realising just what I'm admitting, "No she won't, she'll be far too busy playing with me!"

"Jesus Christ!" As my words seem to echo around us, Ben glowers at me looking as irate as I've ever seen him. "Tell me this isn't right. You're taking a fucking client to the club and will be sceneing with her? Fucking hell, Jon! Does she know this?"

I wave at him to sit down again; I do so myself hoping he'll copy me. He does. I lean forwards putting my head in my hands, knowing he's right to call me out. He sits rigid, his palms flat against the edge of his desk. We both need to calm down a bit, so I quieten my voice, "That's the problem Ben, I don't know." I admit as I lift my face to look, at him, my frustration showing on my face.

"She's got to you, hasn't she?" As if he realises the hopeless position I'm in, Ben's face relaxes as his rage starts to dissipate, quickly turning to sympathy. "Never thought I'd see the day when a woman had you by the balls, Jon."

Is it that obvious? "She's a natural submissive, and in trouble."

Ben gazes at me. "You don't normally have a problem keeping it in your pants."

He's right. I sigh, sitting back and putting my elbow on the arm of the chair, resting my chin on my palm. He's been my friend a long time and it's impossible to hide the truth from him. "She's special, Ben. I should have given the case to someone else last Wednesday. Now I can't. I'd kill the bugger."

I know the company's rules like the back of my hand. Sometimes we're required to fraternise with clients or targets, so there's nothing contractual to stop me. Just common morals and ethics, and right at this moment I'm in short supply of those.

He looks at me closely as though I'm a specimen in a lab that's acting completely out of character. "Never seen you like this around a woman before, Jon. Brings a whole new meaning to close protection, mate." He laughs, cynically. I don't tell him I'm not *that* close yet; suspecting he assumes I'm already sharing her bed. His eyes sharpen. "This BDSM stuff she writes about worries me. I'm concerned it might have a connection to the case. Have you read anything she's written? Or have you been too busy?" His eyes twinkle with mischief as he adds the last.

"I've read two books so far," I ignore his insinuation. "The only thing that struck me was in her latest book Mia talks about a wannabe Dom, who takes things too far. While she skirts around what he does, essentially he doesn't abide by safe, sane and consensual. He gets his comeuppance, in the end, is slung out of the club and is made to seem a bit of an idiot."

"I think I know someone like that!"

"We've all come across them." I agree.

"But we try to weed them out at Tiacapan." He looks deep in thought. "Not so much some of the other clubs."

"I did think of going fishing; see if anyone fits the bill."

"At Bates' place, that would be two out of every three!" He's right, and his look of disgust is exactly why I wanted Mia far, far away from that place.

The corners of his mouth turned down, Ben doesn't look happy. "But you can't be the one to investigate. Mia's stalker will recognise you by now if he's been keeping an eye on her." He sits, deep in thought, then his eyes light up as he has an idea and continues, "I'll ask Sean to do the rounds of the clubs. And you'll want to stick close to Mia."

It's immediately apparent his suggestion has merit. Sean is exactly the right man for the job. He's a switch, he can both top and bottom depending on who he's with, and then there's his ability to protect himself. A six-foot-three-inch beanpole, but what there is of him is solid muscle. He's an expert at hand to hand combat so there'd be no worries if he met with any trouble, even in the most sordid of clubs. It's a good idea, so I thank Ben as he assigns himself the responsibility of liaising with Sean and getting him to start on his new task as soon as possible. Of course, we might draw a blank, but currently, we haven't got a lot else to go on. Someone out there has it in for Mia. As the stalking has only just started, if we're right, and it's somehow connected to her writing, it makes sense it could have something to do with her most recently published book.

Ben and I throw around a few more ideas, but it seems following up people who were at the party and taking a look at the darker side of the BDSM scene are the only options we have for now. I leave him once those next steps are agreed, and go to find Mia unable to hide my grin as meet her in Vanessa's office. She's in for a surprise today, starting when she gets down to the underground car park.

After calling out a general farewell to the office staff, we leave Grade A's offices behind and I take her down in the lift to the basement level. As she goes to step towards the McClaren; I stop her by putting my hand on her arm. "Different mode of travel, sweetheart," I tell her, watching her carefully; wanting to see her reaction as I lead her towards the other vehicle I keep here.

CHAPTER 12
Mia

Seven years ago

When I started to regain consciousness, the first thing I noticed was that I shivering from cold and next that my head was throbbing. Thinking I must have kicked the duvet off in my sleep, I went to pull it up only to find my hands were behind me, and I couldn't move them. As I pulled, I realised they were tied there. Slowly, as all my senses returned, I became aware I was definitely not in my own bed and that this was no dream. Panic arose quickly when I opened my eyes, only to find I still couldn't see anything, something had been tied around my brow blocking my sight. But it was obvious I was naked, the cold air flowing over me triggering goosebumps all over my bare skin. I started thrashing my head from side to side, but the blindfold wouldn't budge, and I only succeeded in making the thumping in my head worse. My breath started coming in rapid pants as I grew more and more frightened. Then I found I wasn't alone.

"Thank fuck for that! She's awake at last! I heard a voice and felt a hand roughly grope my breast. Tied so tightly I couldn't squirm away. Oh God, what was going to happen to me? "Time to play, bitch. We were waiting for you to wake up so you can enjoy it."

I was so, so scared. I swallowed rapidly, trying to get moisture into my dry mouth. I had never been so terrified in all my life. Tremors ran through me, triggered by both cold and fear of what I hoped wasn't, but deep down already knew in all probability was, to come. My voice came out as a whisper "Please…"

He interrupted me with a harsh laugh. "That's right, bitch. Beg for it." He ran a rough hand down my stomach and further down, into my most private place. I tried to close my legs, but they'd tied my ankles, keeping them apart. "Bet that's a virgin pussy there, isn't it? And my cock's waiting no fucking longer to get into it."

My worst fears were confirmed when I heard a zipper coming down; it rasped as if moving in slow motion. There's no doubt what he planned to do. No, not me. Why me? What have I done to deserve this?

"Please… Don't!" I tried pleading again, as I struggled against my tight bindings. "Please. No!" But I was powerless to move or prevent it. My fear, already sky high, ratcheted up to an impossible level. I screamed in protest, my voice shrill with horror, "No, don't, please." This couldn't be happening! Let this be a nightmare, let me just wake up. I struggled frantically, but the ropes had been tied tight, and there wasn't any play in them. I started to cry; I was pleading and begging, but it made no difference.

He undid the ties around my legs, and I took my chance, kicking out hard, but he was ready for that and retaliated by walloping me in the face. Christ! That hurt! Momentarily stunned, it gave him the opportunity to grab my legs, pulling them wide open. He was too strong for me, and there was nothing I could do to stop him. I screamed and begged over and over again, but my pleas didn't deter him. He was going to rape me!

Tears flooding down my cheeks, I tried to divorce myself from what was happening to my unprepared body, but the pain, embarrassment, and humiliation were unbearable. It seemed to go on forever.

Present day

I enjoyed my chat with Vanessa, especially when she showed me what actions they're taking to try to identify my stalker, impressing me with the sophistication of their investigation tools. Fascinated by the way they work, I couldn't resist making a few notes on my phone, and jotting down some of the processes they go through, imagining using the information in a book one day. Although there can be no doubt they are putting every effort into their work, it does seem a little like looking for the proverbial needle in a haystack. But both Vanessa and Nafisa assured me they won't give up, and are confident that there's something to be found in my past. Their determination to get to the bottom of who my stalker is, leaving no stone unturned; every single clue, however small, is being followed up. Their diligence is giving me hope. Perhaps with having Vanessa's team and the rest of Grade A on my side, my case can be solved and maybe I won't be looking over my shoulder for the rest of my life.

And, of course, spending time with his colleagues meant I could take the opportunity to discover more about the man who's been assign to protect me; all the while taking care to be discreet so as not to disclose anything other than professional interest in him. Casually I ask about the hierarchy of the organisation, but laughter greets my question about whether Ben was his boss. And it's at that point I find out that Jon Tharpe is not an employee, but one of the co-owners of Grade A Security. *What the heck? Why did I warrant such high up attention?* So phrasing it as innocuously as I could, I ask Vanessa that very question. Only to receive an odd look in response, and the added information that it's very rare for Jon to work outside of the office nowadays, usually overseeing the work of others rather than doing it himself. It seems they are puzzled too.

So why *had* he assigned himself to me? *Could he be affected by me as I am by him?* Could this attraction be mutual? A delicious shiver runs down my spine at the thought. I like his company. I'm getting used to him being around, and I'm starting to dread the day when the case is over, and he'll disappear from my life. He's the first man I've ever come across who makes me feel like a real woman, with all the normal female desires. On the other hand, even if he were interested in me in that way, after everything that I'd been through, I would never be able to let him that close. *Would I?* He must have had hundreds of women, all much more experienced than I. Why would he ever want me? *What would I do if he does?*

Could I try? When he touches me, it's as though there's a current shooting through me; when he looks at me my stomach clenches. It's a million miles away from the way I felt when my kidnappers raped and abused me when all I felt was disgust and degradation. What would it be like if it was Jon caressing me intimately, running his hands over my breasts? Jeez, I tremble at the thought, and immediately my nipples harden. *I might like it.*

Is there a chance he took the case because he too felt that spark the morning I first met him?

With the question of whether my developing feelings are reciprocated running through my head, when I accompany Jon down to the carpark, I feel like a teenage girl on a first date. I don't speak, tongue-tied and nervous, anxious not to say the wrong thing, but not knowing what the right words would be either. There's no way I could just come out and ask him. *Should I encourage him?* But how the hell would I go about that? How does a woman show she's interested? *Shit Mia, you write about it all the time, but when it comes to putting theory into practice you haven't a bloody clue!* It's probably safer to keep my feelings to myself and make sure everything stays on a purely business level. *But what if I never meet someone who attracts me in the same way again?* My hands curl at my sides. *Those bloody abusers. Why can't I move past that?*

My mind might be preaching caution; my body isn't getting the message. In the lift, I try to ignore my physical reaction to the charismatic man walking beside me, biting my lip and flushing with embarrassment and, not a little excitement at the notion that he might be interested in me as a woman. But then, I could be interpreting it all wrong, and he could have stayed close simply as a result of that favour Val called in. And if that's the case I need to make sure I don't make a bloody fool of myself!

The lift descends, my emotions bounce one way then the other. Until finally, as we hit basement level, my heart plummets as well. I'm an author, I've got an active imagination, I see things that aren't there. *Stop it, Mia. Why the hell would a man like this want to take things further with a woman like you?*

At last the doors slide open, and we exit into the garage. I take a step towards the McClaren. Then he touches my arm and feeling like I've had an electric shock. I jump.

"Different mode of travel today, sweetheart," He tells me. And leads me across to a very sexy black motorcycle, littered with shining chrome. The logo on it shows me it's a Harley and is one hell of a beast of a machine. *Oh, I'm so not going there!*

I pull back, shaking my head. "No."

"No?" He's grinning at me. "I'm afraid the correct answer is yes. We've not got much time to get across London, and we'll get through the traffic better on this."

"I've never been on one," I explain, still shaking my head. "It's dangerous."

"Today will be a lot of firsts for you then. And why not take a few risks in life?"

I shoot him a look, unnerved. I'm not quite sure what he's talking about. Is he referring to my upcoming visit to Club

Tiacapan tonight? My first time at a BDSM club? Or something else entirely? Disconcerted I make no further protest about the scary motorbike ride which now seems to be in my immediate future.

Enigmatically, he doesn't elaborate on his strange statement. Moving a few steps away from me, he opens a locker and extracts two black helmets and two black leather jackets. He passes me one. It's obviously his spare, and it dwarfs me.

Standing back, he chuckles as I put the slip my arms into the overlong sleeves then attempt to pull the excess leather around me, "Better than nothing." He does the zip up for me, then places the helmet on my head and fastens it. I immediately feel claustrophobic which, of course, my bodyguard doesn't miss, "Relax. We're not going far." Without giving me time for any further objection, he leads me over to the bike. He gets on first and takes it off the stand, balancing the weight of that scary machine, then gestures for me to climb up behind him. Not at all sure of this massive metal beast, I throw my leg over and manage, not too ungainly, to sit on the pillion. Gingerly, I grip the handles either side of the seat, but immediately feel unsafe. *I'm going to fall off!* He lifts his visor so I can hear him, and turns to me. "Hang on to me; you'll feel more secure."

Tentatively I put my arms around him, but he lets me know that's not sufficient, seizing hold of them and pulling them tight around him. His short jacket is unzipped so my hands land on his T-shirt, and I'm able to feel every muscle of his chest; incredible, solid and warm. Trying to ignore the fact I'm so intimately close to him, I attempt to keep as much of a distance as possible, not wanting him to get the wrong, *or right,* idea. Then the engine fires into life with a loud and disturbing roar, and a tremendous vibration starts, which does nothing to cool the heat between my legs. When we move off, my bum shifts down on the seat and settles into him, gravity preventing me shuffling back. My crotch presses against him, and I've no choice but to secretly enjoy the closeness.

Suddenly the bike lurches forward as he twists the throttle, applying power, and then all my thoughts are about hanging on. Tightening my hold on him, almost to the extent I'm afraid I'll cut him in half, certain I'm going to fall off as we weave in and out of traffic. Terrified, I start arranging my funeral in my head.

It's long before I realise that I'm not going to end up on my backside on the tarmac. He handles the bike as he does his car, confidently and surely, and soon I begin to move with him, leaning into the bends as he does. He reaches his left hand around and pats my knee in a gesture which I translate as approval. I don't know where we're going but begin to enjoy the exhilaration of the ride. *I could get used to this.* My legs are snug around his, the intimacy of the position and the vibration of the bike is making me embarrassingly wet between my thighs. Again. *What the hell is happening to me?*

He pulls the bike up and parks it on the pavement outside a shop, and it's then I realise I haven't a clue where he's brought me. So caught up in the new sensations of being on a bike and so close to the man I'm attracted to, I'd taken no notice of the direction. But what I do know is that it's not the way we'd have come if he was taking me to the destination I'd assumed he had planned, my home. He dismounts, and it's clear we're making a stop here when he helps me step off the bike and, thankfully, helps me out of that restricting helmet. I'm still shaking from the effects of the ride which continue even after I'm standing on the pavement. *Jon and his motorbike, the combination is deadly.* I give myself a second to pull myself together then look around. "Where are we, Jon? And why are we here?"

"Mile End." He says succinctly. "And you're here for your appointment."

"Appointment?" What? I've got no meeting arranged. What the hell is he talking about?

He smiles that wicked smile with does nothing to calm the butterflies in my stomach. "You're going to have a day of pampering."

Oh, shit, no. I heave a deep sigh, wishing he'd discussed this with me before. This is so not me. "Jon, it sounds great, but I need to get home and back to work." In all honesty, such an indulgence would probably be lovely, but it's not something I want, nor can afford to spend neither money nor time on.

But I should have known he'd brush off any remonstration. Ignoring my protest, he puts his hand under my chin and turns my head up to face him. "Trust me, okay? It will do you good, and get you prepared and in the mood for tonight." He waits patiently for my response.

I step back, unsure what he's talking about. "Jon…?"

"Please, Mia, trust me." Suddenly I realise his voice has deepened and oozes authority. *It's his Dom's voice!* And it has the effect of making my feet move as though under his control, as he pushes me in the direction of the door to a very upmarket looking salon. *Shit!*

Although I'm earning good money now, I'm always aware my next book could be a flop, so this is the kind of luxury I would generally avoid. When I get my hair cut, it's just at the local hairdressers, not a chic place like this; sometimes I don't even bother to pay to have it dried and styled unless it's for a special occasion. My suspicions that this establishment is going to be well out of my price range are confirmed once I get inside, and cast a glance at the 'menu' on the wall. Quickly I absorb that as well as hair styling, the place offers massages, waxing, saunas, pedicures and manicures and that the price list is frighteningly exorbitant.

"Jon," I turn to speak quietly to him. "There's no way I'm going to be able to afford this."

His answer is simple. "You're not paying."

As I open my mouth, again to voice my objections, a gorgeous woman comes striding over to meet us. My mouth stays open but no words come out then, realising what a fool I look, I close it. The woman is incredible looking, her mixed heritage lending her an olive coloured skin that glows. There's not a blemish on her smooth complexion, and her chiselled face could be one featured on a glossy magazine cover. Not a hair is out of place, and her make-up is perfect. She towers over me, her stunning clothes accentuating her slim, toned body. I'm intimidated just standing in front of her, and when she reaches her arms around my companion to give him a full body hug coupled with a full kiss on the lips, I wish I had a gun to hand. *I hate her.*

"Morning, Gorgeous," Jon greets her warmly once she lets him go. As she takes a step back from him, he holds her at arms-length, his eyes roaming her body, taking her in. "Beautiful as always," He tells her in that way a man speaks to someone he's very close to.

That's it. She's going to die. There must be a weapon around here somewhere.

"And who's this?" Gorgeous seems to notice me at last and, to her credit, she gives me a genuine welcoming smile. *I'm still going to kill her, though.*

"Dexie Sanders." I introduce myself as my alter ego. Mia wouldn't be able to stand up to this woman. I notice Jon cocking his head to one side; his eyes creased as if amused. Does he know what I'm doing? Yes, the bastard has probably sussed it. I try to damp down my jealousy before it becomes too obvious while wondering what I've got to be jealous about in the first place! *He's not mine; he's quite within his rights to shag whoever he likes!*

Jon takes a step closer to me. "She's had a bit of a hard time of it recently, so a complete pampering's in order. Oh, and she's coming to the club tonight, so it's the full works today."

As a knowing look comes over Gorgeous' face, my brow furrows. What difference does going to the club make? And what exactly are the 'full works'? But I don't have time to query what exactly he's getting me into as Jon squeezes my hand gently. Then, directing his request to Gorgeous and not me I notice, asks her to give him a call when I'm finished. Finally turning to me with a smirk, he touches his hand briefly to my cheek and leaves. As I'm suspiciously wondering just exactly what that look and contact were for, I realise we still haven't settled the business of who's paying. I can't let him pay. Not for something as personal as this.

Gorgeous is appraising me and takes no time before she tries to get things straight. "Is your relationship with Jon professional or personal?" She gets directly to the point.

Hmm, of course, she wants to know. I'd love to say personal and see her reaction, but I have to be honest. "Professional"

Her friendly expression doesn't change; she doesn't show relief, so perhaps I'm reading it wrong? *Maybe I'll simply maim her.* Then she gives me a sympathetic smile. "If you need protection from Grade A then you must be having a hard time. Let's start by getting you nice and relaxed with a sauna and then a massage."

That does sound lovely! Then I falter, she must know Jon well if she knows what he does for a living. *Just how does she know him?* As she puts her hand on my back to guide me to the back of the prestigious looking salon, I remember myself and stop. Facing her, I tell her honestly. "Look, I'm sorry, it all sounds fantastic, but I can't afford it. Can you just do my hair?"

She gives a deep laugh; even her mirth sounds alluring. "Jon gets a big discount here, Cherie. Don't worry about it. And the bill *always* goes directly to him." She turns me back around; her manicured fingernails resting on my shoulders. I notice her fingers are long, her nails bright red with sparkling jewels stuck on. Elegance on legs. In my jeans and blouse, she's making me feel shabby and very unattractive. Bemused, and not a little intimidated, I let her push me through the salon, and the question suddenly hits me as I wonder just why Jon gets a discount, and exactly how many women he's brought here to have earned the right to it? The green eyed monster starts rearing its head again. *This is stupid. I'm lusting after a man so far out of my league it's ridiculous. Oh, stop thinking about him. There's more to worry about now. What the full treatment is for a start. And what his parting smirk was all about.*

Somewhere between the entrance door and the rear of the shop I'm being led to I grasp, despite my objections, that I seem to be going to have a spa day whether I want one or not. A door is opened for me, and I enter to find a huge changing room, more than twice the size of that of any shop I've ever been in. Gorgeous directs me to strip down and shower, then either completely naked or with the option of leaving my knickers on, cover myself with the towelling robe that's hanging on a hook. I take the offered option while wondering why I'm here and why I've given in so easily. Gorgeous seemed so insistent, though, and what woman could refuse a day of being spoiled and indulged? *Oh, bugger it!* I make the decision to enjoy myself putting aside, for now, the issue of how on earth I'm going to pay for it all, determined Jon will not be picking up the tab.

After having followed the instructions, I hesitantly exit the cubicle to find a different, and younger woman waiting for me. With a sigh, as I notice she's just as polished and elegant as Gorgeous, I follow her to the sauna, where she explains the process, and then leaves me alone. As I sit in the steam and relax, I find I'm able to let my mind drift, my worries from the previous week seeping away just like the sweat from my pores. It seems all too soon when I collected, instructed to take my time having a cooling plunge bath, after which I'm taken to a different room, told to strip off again and place myself face down on a massage table.

The massage feels wonderful; I've not had one before and soon start thinking it's something I'll be trying again. My muscles relax, and my breathing deepens as the ministrations of the expert hands have a calming effect, even after the sauna I'd still been tenser than I'd realised. Before long, I find I'm half dozing, with thoughts of the evening ahead floating through my mind.

Now I've met Gorgeous; it hits me just how ridiculous and presumptuous it is to think Jon would look twice at someone like me. *She's* the sort of person he would play with, an experienced and incredibly beautiful woman, obviously comfortable in her own skin. *I want to go to a club for research*; I remind myself. Jon's been kind enough to offer to get me entrance into the prestigious club, but I've no right to make any more demands on him other than that. I can't expect to spend the evening hanging onto his coat tails; that would mean I'd just be ruining his night. All he's expecting to do is to get me through the doors. Then he'll be free to go off and play with one of his obviously many play buddies. Perhaps Gorgeous herself is one of them?

Then, as my stomach churns at the thought of seeing him play with anyone else, especially someone as elegant and assured as the salon owner, it seems like every muscle in my body clenches, making the masseuse pause to ask me if anything's wrong. To cover it my annoying reaction, I stammer out that I'm just hungry and try to push thoughts of watching Jon playing with another woman out of my head.

She quickly finishes up, then, to my astonishment, once the

massage is over, there's a plate of delicious food waiting for me, a hot and cold finger buffet selection, as well as a glass of champagne! Ignoring the voice in the back of my mind telling me to think about the cost, I decide to make the best of it and take in every detail as background for a future book. Reassuring myself that research expenses are tax deductible, after all.

Having consumed as much as I can of my fabulous lunch, I'm taken back to another room, once more in my robe. I have my legs and underarms waxed – a painful experience I have no wish ever to repeat. But when the woman starts to draw off my knickers I grab them and ask her what the hell she thinks she's doing.

She grins, and leaves the room, returning moments later with Gorgeous. Gorgeous looks me straight in the eye, and asks without preamble, "You're going to the club tonight?"

"Yes?"

"Well, you need to be neat and tidy. That means a full wax. Jon will expect that."

While I write about a Dom's preference for a sub to be bare, I've never been tempted to shave down there myself. And I haven't a Dom to please in any event, so I shake my head firmly. "No, there's no need for that."

Gorgeous laughs. "Chérie, you don't want to disappoint your Dom you know."

What the hell is she talking about? I know all about the consequences of disappointing a Dom, I've written all about the lifestyle, and I know if he wants you to do something you do it, or risk a punishment. But she's very mistaken if she's got the idea that Jon's my Dom. It's laughable. So I tell her so.

Shrugging her glossy black hair over her shoulders, she gives a throaty chuckle. "That's what you think, chérie. It's obvious to me Jon thinks something else. Now, shall we get on with this?" She turns to the other woman whose name I hadn't caught and tells her she can go. Apparently Gorgeous is going to take over herself. I stare at her, confident that she's got it all wrong. Jon is *not* my Dom. Not even for tonight. He wouldn't be thinking that way, would he? *Surely not!* But embarrassingly a flush comes over my body just thinking about the possibility, and I wrap my robe around me, hoping to hide my body's automatic reaction.

Gorgeous watches me, waiting for my permission for her to start, a faint amused smile on her face as she lets me work it through in my head. *No, I'm not going to let her shave me. No one is going to see in any event.* As I think about it, mulling over what to do and how to politely refuse, I shake my head. But then a little devil inside me wakes up and suddenly I decide, fuck it, why not give it a try? I write about this, shouldn't I at least experience just once something I only have theoretical knowledge about?

I know many men like their women bare. *Is this how Jon prefers his subs?* But whether he does or not is beside the point isn't it? *Oh, shit. In for a penny and all that.* Perhaps I should go for the full treatment. So hoping this isn't going to be something I regret, a little cautiously I nod my agreement.

Her smile turns to one of approval and she starts to prepare what she needs, pulling on a pair of latex gloves. I decide I have to know. She's about to be getting intimate with me, so I don't see a problem getting personal with her. "What's Jon to you?" My eyes narrow as I wait for her answer to the question that's been bugging me all morning.

She laughs out loud again, a throaty, sexy sound. "I won't lie, chérie, we've been together. But not for a very long time. I played with him on a couple of occasions and I have to tell you the things that man can do with his pleasure stick means you're in for a really fun time!"

"Pleasure stick?" I have to giggle, even though I'm not sure how to take her revelation. She's not with him now, but they've obviously been close. "Not heard it called that before."

"Well," she grins, "Just don't call it that at the club." She glances at me and sees that I'm fidgeting, uncomfortable. "Go on, ask."

Not bothering to tell her I'm highly unlikely to get anywhere near his pleasure stick, or whatever else it's likely to be called, I swallow. She's right; I've more questions, although I'm not completely sure I want to know all the answers, so I hesitate before asking, "Why does Jon get a discount here?"

Smiling, she reaches for the wax as she tells me. "Well, first of all, he did all the security for me. I had a gang after me for protection money, but by the time he sorted out all the alarms, cameras, bullet proof glass and so on, I didn't have to worry anymore. Of course, setting everything up cost a fortune but a lot less in the long run than making regular payments to the gang. They leave me alone now. He recommends me to other Doms and subs at the club too, so I get a lot of business from Taicapan." She pauses, before continuing, "And, to be truthful, Dexie, he's sent me a few girls in the past because we cater to his particular tastes."

"Particular tastes?" I repeat, parrot-like, not sure I like the sound of that.

She gesticulates, waving at the paraphernalia in the room. "Waxing, for example. And the lotions we use, he likes the smell. I tend to use things scented vanilla which is a little screwed up if you think about it." I frown as she gives another delicious chuckle.

She tears off a strip of the wax and tears come to my eyes. I can't prevent the yelp. "Sorry, can't help it, I'm afraid. But you won't mind the bit of pain to prepare you for your Dom, will you?"

"He's not my Dom," I reiterate firmly. "And I'm not a sub!"

My eyes water with the stinging pain, but I realise she's gone too far for me to call a halt now. Having one side of my labia bare and the other like a brush is a bit lopsided.

This time, she covers her mouth as she gives a belly laugh. "Of course, you're a sub." As I glare at her, she continues. "Like me."

"You?" I'm dumbfounded. I wave around at the salon. "You're the owner, aren't you?"

She looks at me, puzzled. "Yes?" And then smirks. "Ah, you think a successful business woman can't want to enjoy submitting to a man?" Focusing on her task, she seems to be considering something. "I've read a couple of your books, Dex, and while you describe the power exchange quite well, you do tend to write about slaves, you know, 24/7 submissives. Submissives, who submit out of the bedroom as well as in it. Most subs are like you and me, strong, independent people who don't need someone to depend on all day every day, who want to be treated as equals in their daily lives. But giving up control in the bedroom? Well, there's no beating that as a stress reliever."

My brow creases as I consider her words, "You saying I write about weak women?"

"Not exactly weak, but you haven't yet used a female lead who leads a life totally independent of her Dom. There are many women, like myself, who just want to play and not have a man in their lives."

Using men for sex? In the same way that men use women? Knowing this is a thought completely alien to me; my only experience of sex was something I wouldn't want to repeat, I realise getting to know Diamond better and understanding her way of thinking might provide some good background for a new novel.

So as she continues to *painfully* complete her task, I reflect on what she's said. It's something I can't understand; for me there couldn't be anything worse than the thought of giving up control. However, I'm enjoying this conversation with Gorgeous, and decide that I'm probably not going to cause her bodily harm after all, especially if I want to pick her brains at a later date. Notwithstanding the themes of my novels, I've never actually come across anyone in the lifestyle before, well, other than Jon, but he and I haven't had this kind of chat. It dawns on me I'd like to know her better.

"I take it your name's not really Gorgeous?" I ask with a smile.

"Yes, it is." She grins back. "At the club, anyway." *Ah, so Jon hadn't called her that as a term of endearment.* "My real name is Madelaine, hence Salon de Madelaine. I didn't choose the name; one day someone called me Gorgeous and it kind of stuck."

I smile. It's easy to see why. And then my brow furrows, and I frown, "Has Jon got a club name?"

"Master Jonathan." She squints at me. "I know you write this stuff, but do you want me to go over the protocol of what to call the Doms?"

"Could be useful." Club Taicapan might be different to others I've heard of.

"Any Dom you meet at the club you should address as Sir, if not, you're liable to be punished unless they're lenient as you're new. A Master of the Club should be addressed as Master whatever his name is. You should only address a Dom with the title Master without his name, if you are in a D/s relationship with him."

What she tells me is fairly standard fare, but serves as a useful reminder. "Jon's a Master of the Club?" Somehow I guessed he would be pretty experienced.

"Yes and…" her voice trails off.

"And?" I prompt.

"Never mind. Some things he'll probably want to tell you himself. Anyway, Tiacapan has some protocols which I expect Jon will explain to you. It's different to some clubs which don't seem to have any at all."

"Like Tops and Tailends?"

I see her grimace. "You've not been there, have you?"

"No, a friend was going to get me in, but Jon went up the wall. That's why he's taking me to Tiacapan instead."

Reaching out to touch my arm she suddenly becomes solemn. "Don't go somewhere like that, Dexie. It can be dangerous. You could find yourself in the middle of something you don't want to be doing. Power exchange means exactly that, an *exchange*. At Tops and Tailends you might end up giving your control over to someone else. *All* your control." She shudders. "They're not too hot on safewords, and last time I went, I saw no dungeon monitors at all."

She gets up and goes to the sink to take off her gloves and wash her hands, her manner now dismissive, as if the conversation is over. I sit up and gingerly reach for my underwear. While having a smooth mound and underparts might eventually look better; I'm not relishing the bright red look I'm sporting right now. Gorgeous brings me some cream which takes away the worst of the sting. Whether I'll be able to walk normally, or will have to stride with my legs apart to stop my nether regions chaffing remains to be seen. Before she passes me onto one of her colleagues for the rest of my 'pampering' which I'm now thinking could be better termed 'torture,' she tells me to enjoy myself tonight, and that she might see me there.

The rest of the day carries nothing else out of the ordinary, and I have no further in-depth chats with the salon's owner. I have my toe and finger nails trimmed buffed and polished, and varnish applied. I go for a dark red, still not sure what I'll pick to wear tonight, mentally running through my wardrobe in my head and coming up short on suggestions. Lastly, my hair's trimmed and styled so that it falls over my shoulders in soft waves, a look I've never been able to achieve myself. And then makeup is applied, a bit heavier than I usually wear, but Gorgeous tells me it's perfect for the club, and I have to trust her. Finally, I'm given instructions on how best to refresh it before going out later on.

And then I'm done. I'm dressed and now have to wait for Jon to arrive to collect me. Glancing into the mirror my new look gives me confidence, and I have to smile at the transformation. Then my face falls, my hair style certainly won't look so good once it's squashed under a helmet again. But I should have known better and that there was no need for me to worry. When I watch out of the window and see Jon arrive in the McClaren, I mentally kick myself. Of course, he's used to collecting women from here and knows better than to ruin an effect that's taken hours, and a lot of money, to achieve.

Standing up from the couch where I've been waiting I grab my bag. The door to the salon opens, and Jon walks in like he owns the place, nodding a greeting and calling out a friendly hello to the stylists working out front, then comes to halt in front of me. He lifts his hand to my chin and moves my head from one side to the other. "Beautiful," he murmurs softly.

Gorgeous has come up to stand behind him. "She's a lovely one, Jon."

Lovely one indeed. *One of how fucking many?* I ask myself cynically. He doesn't understand the quick scowl I throw him before I turn back to thank Gorgeous and her team with a warm smile, making sure they know how much I've enjoyed my day with them.

But he's not my Dom, whatever Gorgeous implied; he's just helping me out with my research. So what does it matter how many women he's brought here? He could have brought a hundred for all I care. Stepping out of the door, I pause, trying to pull myself together before getting into the McClaren. I've had an amazing experience today, not one I'd rush to repeat, perhaps, but pleasant nonetheless. I should be grateful, and remember I haven't any reason to be acting like a jealous cow.

CHAPTER 13

Jon

Four years ago

The Kassis Royal Family owned a number of casinos dotted about Europe, as well as one they were currently building in their homeland, part of their journey towards making Amahad a destination attractive to tourists from overseas. Part of Nijad's official role was to keep an eye on this section of the family business, and in that capacity, tonight he was visiting the Kassis casino in the centre of Paris. I was going with him as his guest, not as his protection officer, as I was still waiting for medical clearance to resume duties after having the bullet removed from my lung.

It wasn't long before the argument starts between us.

"Half a million euros?" I looked incredulously at the pile of chips he's put in front of me.

"I just want to get a feel for how the house is working," Nijad informed me emotionlessly, "I'm here to check how things are running. Have fun and lose the lot. You'll be helping me out." Of course, it was probably just pocket change to him, but a huge amount to me.

I glanced at him; we're about the same height so stood eye to eye. I tried to read him, but his face was inscrutable.

"Come on, Jon, just enjoy yourself for once. Harry's got my back," he cajoled me, shamelessly.

There was no point protesting. Without Nijad's help, I

wouldn't have been able to afford to play for long, I certainly didn't have that type of money in my bank account! Reluctantly I agreed. The alternative was to lose the few pounds I could afford to drop and then having to hang around just watching the action. Even the price of drinks was enough to make your eyes water.

He stood back as if to walk away, and then, almost as an afterthought moved forward again, and rested his hand on my shoulder. "Of course, anything you win you get to keep."

I narrowed my eyes suspiciously. My suspicions grew exponentially as I seemed to have the luck of the devil with me that evening, eventually ending the night ten million euros richer.

Present day

Mia looks absolutely fucking beautiful. Her professionally applied makeup making her eyes look even larger than normal, her lips fuller; cheekbones more defined. My cock twitches in my jeans and if don't quickly start thinking of something else; I'll soon be sporting the customary hard on I seem to suffer every time I'm around her. It will be no hardship taking her to the club tonight; I'm more than eager to play. I suppress a grin at the thought of what's waiting for her at my apartment.

Greeting Gorgeous with a nod, I wryly wonder just how many of my secrets she's shared during the course of the day. As we leave the salon, and I step forwards to open the passenger door, Mia turns and gives me a sharp look. Hmm. Perhaps she's shared a little too much. Oh well, step one to face now: our destination. Time's getting on; it's now almost six o'clock. I start the car and head for home. My home.

Mia breaks the silence. "Thanks for today, Jon. You'll have to let me know how much I owe you."

"Nothing," I tell her softly, "It's on me." I know she doesn't like that, but as I know; she couldn't afford to pay the salon's prices.

I see the hard stare she gives me, and she doesn't say anything more, but I doubt I've heard the last of it. I've already found she's got a strong independent streak. Instead, she changes the subject. "Have you told the police about the party, Jon?" Her voice sounds tense, and I know she's worried about how much I would have divulged.

"I rang Coulton this morning after I left you, and brought him up to speed. We're passing on anything we come across to him, but he's happy for us to follow up any leads at present. To be honest, we can put more resources on it than he can, and he knows that." I indicate right and pull out across the road, automatically glancing behind me to make sure there's not a rogue motorbike or mad cyclist zooming up past.

"That's good." She's quiet for a moment. "You told him what happened to me?"

"He has to know, Mia."

She sighs. "Yeah, I know," she says in acceptance but I see her shoulders slump. Something she's kept so private for so long is now out in the open. In my view, that's all to the good. The more we know, the more likely we are to be able to keep her safe.

The traffic isn't too bad for once, so making my way across to Docklands doesn't take too much time. I notice Mia getting a little restless when I don't take the obvious route out of town.

"Jon, where are we going?" she asks, apprehensively, as if worried I've got any other surprises in store for her. I have steamrollered her a bit today. But that's not going to stop just yet.

"My place."

"But I've got to get home and sort out something to wear tonight." She indicates her clothing. "I can't go dressed like this."

I know, and I've taken that into account. "No need to worry,

I've picked up something for you to wear.

She stiffens. "Jon, you've done too much for me." Her words hide a myriad of feelings, one that she doesn't like me spending money on her, and another that I've taken away one of her choices. I get the feeling she doesn't like being out of control. But she's going to have to get used to it. Tonight, *I'm* the one in the driving seat.

"I'm taking you to my club," I explain, gently, "I've seen your wardrobe sweetheart, and you've nothing to wear that will look right. Trust me; I've got you something that will make you blend in, and make me proud to walk in with you on my arm." I'm impatient to see her in what I've chosen, though I doubt she'll put it on without an argument.

Luckily we arrive at the parking for my apartment which stops further conversation. I pull the McClaren in alongside the three motorbikes I'm proud to own; along with the Agusta and Harley I also have an aging Kawasaki Ninja. I notice she gives the bikes a sideways glance and a grin, and can almost hear her thinking *boys' toys*, before taking my offered hand and walking with me to the lift. And she'd be right, I do love my playthings. Suppressing a grin, I pause for a moment to open my mailbox and take out the post waiting for me there.

I live in the renovated docklands area, and look out over the waterways, which gives me an exceptional view from my penthouse. Mia enters my home, and I step back, curious to see what she makes of it. To be quite honest it's not really me, and I prefer her cottage. The apartment is too new, and olde-worlde stuff would look out of place here, so it's furnished with mainly stainless steel and glass rather than the honesty of fabric and wood in her Epping Forest home. She walks over to the floor to ceilings windows and looks out, and I see the view takes her attention. You can see for miles from here.

When she turns, she nods, as if I'm expecting her to make a

comment and doesn't want to disappoint me. "Nice."

I shrug. "It does. It's close to the office, so it's a short walk instead of needing to drive." Moving into the room I glance at the envelopes I'm holding, and for a moment my attention is taken away from the woman I've unusually brought to my domain. Having ascertained there's nothing urgent for me to deal with; I lift my eyes to watch her, interested to see what she makes of this incursion into my life. She's still standing by the windows, as if unsure what to do. I'm not surprised. In her cottage her warm comfy looking sofa just invites a person to sit down; here the cold looking leather doesn't seem as appealing. "Sit," I suggest, indicating one of the two modern couches.

My phone rings as she places her coat into my outstretched hand before taking a seat. I go into the kitchen to answer the call, but it doesn't take long, and after only a few moments I return to her. She's leaning forwards, her arms crossed and her elbows resting on her thighs. She's not relaxed at all and gives me a quizzical look.

Sitting down opposite, I bring her up to date. "That was Coulton. Just keeping us informed, no real developments," I begin. "They've visited the shop where the flowers were purchased, but the florist can't remember much about the man who bought them. There's no CCTV in the shop, so that's a dead end. But there might be something about the locality. It could be he lives in the area."

She shivers. "Were there any other messages today?"

"No, it's gone quiet."

"How long will you keep protecting me, Jon, if he doesn't do anything else?"

I squeeze her hands to reassure her, understanding her fears. "I'm not leaving you alone until this matter's resolved. I'm not taking the chance that he's waiting to get you on your own." Selfishly, I hope a resolution won't be found too quickly; I want more time to get to know this woman.

Her sense of relief is palpable. I take the opportunity to change the subject. "I'm going to order some food now. Want to come and look at some menus?" Getting up, I walk through to the ultra-modern kitchen which I rarely use. It's not that I don't enjoy cooking, I just don't get much time for it, and cooking for one doesn't hold much appeal. Now cooking breakfast for Mia, that was different, and something I could well get used to, watching her eat the food I'd prepared with such relish was a real turn on.

Opening a drawer I take out some well-thumbed highly colourful leaflets promising a variety of highly stylised dishes, thinking how disappointing it is that the dishes don't match the photos when they arrive in little foil containers.

She takes the menus but doesn't immediately look at them. Something seems to be on her mind. "After the club, Jon, am I going home?"

"Here's closest, Mia. I've got a spare room all made up." Selfishly, I'd much prefer we stayed at my apartment rather than me having to spend another night on her couch with is more than adequate for sitting on, but highly undesirable as a bed. But then again, if my plans for the evening work out we might only need the one bedroom. *Down boy!* I shake my head trying to remove such thoughts from my head. It seems I've had a one-track mind since the day I met her.

We order in food, just a basic Chinese, but Mia doesn't seem to have much appetite, which I put down to her nervousness about the night ahead. It must be strange for her, knowing so much in theory, but never having put it into practice before. It's not as though she's got any sexual experience either. Well, nothing good. Briefly, it occurs to me to question whether I'm doing the right thing. But then, if I don't take her to Tiacapan, she's so darn set on going somewhere she may well end up going to a different club on her own where members aren't vetted properly, and safety precautions aren't so well observed. And fuck it, she might go without me. My body tenses at the thought of anyone else touching her.

After we've eaten, while I'm disposing of the uneaten food and clearing the plates away she resumes her place sitting uncomfortably on the couch, her eyes gazing into space. Once I've tidied up, I walk over to her and lift her chin with my hand. Looking into her eyes, she seems haunted. "You okay?" I ask, quietly.

She takes a second to focus on me. "I'd pushed everything that happened to me out of my mind, Jon. I never spoke about, never thought about it. Now it's all flooding back and it's all I can think about." Then a little shiver shames her body, "I *am* worried about going to Tiacapan, and if I'm concerned about *that* I know how stupid it was to think I could go to a club on my own. I *know* what happens there, I'm happy enough to write about it. But seeing it?" She pauses, and her next words come out almost as a plea for help, "But this is something I want to, *need* to do. If I don't, my writing will stagnate."

I kneel in front of her. "We don't have to go tonight if you've changed your mind, if it's too much for you. We can stay in, watch a film, or if you prefer, we can go back to Epping. There'll be another time when you're better prepared. We don't have to rush it. The Club's not going anywhere." *And neither am I.* Aren't I? The thought surprises me.

For a second she hesitates and then pulls herself up straight. "No," she says firmly. "There's no point in delaying; there'll never be a right time. I want to go, tonight. Seeing a real club is something I've wanted to do for so long. Those bastards have already taken so much from me; they're not ruining anything else. I'm going to go tonight."

Watching her cautiously, part of me wonders whether she is

ready for this, but her words and attitude remind me of her inner strength, even if she doesn't appreciate how strong she really is. And another part of me very much wants to take her to the club and bring her home in the right mood to sink my cock into her, right up to the fucking balls. Well aware of my perverse personal interest in the possible outcomes of the night, I know I'm being a bastard as I make no further move to discourage her. I simply nod, showing I'm accepting her decision.

As I stand, I reach for her hands to help her up. "Come, I left the clothes for you to wear in the spare room. I'll show you where it is." It's her desire to go to a real BDSM club, but I'm leaping on that bandwagon with all two fucking feet, and loving every minute of it. Talk about something dropping into your lap.

I take her to the guest room and leave her alone. Shutting the door behind me, I no longer have to suppress my grin, picturing the expression on her face when she sees the outfit laid out on the bed that I bought for her today while she was at the salon. I took a long time choosing it, and my final choice was completely for me. I suspect she won't like it at all.

I'm counting down from ten and have just got to five when the door is flung open! Mia's standing there, a corset in her hand. "I can't wear this!" Her voice is shrill. "And what the hell is *this*?" She holds up a barely there, wrap round mini skirt.

Leaning lazily back against the wall; my feet crossed at my ankles. "It's fetwear, sweetheart. Trust me. Wearing this you'll blend in; wearing anything else you'll stick out like a sore thumb." Frowning, I look at her intently, "What do your characters wear when they visit clubs?"

Her eyes narrow, and then, after a brief pause she replies, "Fetwear." Then her eyes widen in horror. "But I don't know if *I* can do it." Now they start filling with tears. "It's slutty!"

I don't need to be a qualified psychologist to know what she's thinking. Putting my hands on her arms I hold her little distance away from me, but my grasp is firm. "Look at me, Mia." I wait until her eyes meet mine. "Yes, it's slutty. And tonight I might call you my slut because that's what people wear in a BDSM club expect. It's the language we use, as well you know. You've written that in your books. But how you're dressed won't influence a thing. Anything that happens in the club will be safe, sane and *consensual.*" I put a heavy emphasis on that last word.

Waiting to make sure she's taking my words in, I continue, "You can wear the sluttiest clothes in the world, or even be naked, and *nothing* will happen to you that you don't want to happen. The way you dress doesn't give anyone the right to take advantage of you." Again I pause until I'm confident she's listening and my words are sinking in. As her eyes flit to the floor, then back up to meet mine I can almost see her mind working, and have to keep a tight rein on myself as anger rises inside me, directed towards her fucking mother. *How the hell could a woman tell her daughter she deserved everything she got?*

I know that Mia thinks she's come to accept she was a victim and didn't deserve to be abducted and raped, particularly not because of the way she had been dressed. But because of the lack of support when she fucking needed it most, deep down there's still part of her that believes she influenced the outcome. Something about the way she dressed or acted caused the rapists to pick on her, rather than anyone else. She's come such a long way, providing therapy for herself by way of her writing; her characters behave as they like without being hurt, without being accused of 'asking for it'. But Mia's got to take the next big step and apply that rationale to her. And I'm going to be the one to help her.

I give her the time she needs to process what I've told her, and I know I've successfully got through when she gives a small nod and a tentative smile. *There she is! She's back with me.* So now I change tack. "The clothes are part of the lifestyle; they're for fun." *Well, I'll enjoy them at least.* Squeezing her arm, I lighten my voice, "And we're going to have fun tonight, Mia." I wait until her smile broadens, showing her fear is now at least tinged with anticipation, and then turn her around to face the guest room again. "Now you get yourself back inside and get dressed. Five minutes, else I'll come dress you myself." I use my best Dom voice and give her a light slap on her bum to encourage her to get moving.

"Ouch!" She turns, pretending to be affronted, but runs into the bedroom playing the game.

"Five minutes!" I reiterate sternly, before turning away and leaving her, taking myself off to the lounge.

I'm looking at my watch when four minutes and forty-five seconds later she appears. I draw in a deep breath, using every ounce of control I have to stop my cock standing too obviously to attention. *Bloody hell!*

"Mia, you look fucking fantastic," I exclaim, getting off the couch and to my feet. With a come-hither gesture, I motion her to come and stand closer to me. I make a full circuit around her, and then stop when I'm standing looking straight at her face. Slowly my gaze drops lower, "This needs tightening." The corset laces up the front, but it's too loose. She holds steady as I undo the knot and unthread the laces from the hooks. A panicked expression comes into her eyes, but she relaxes when she realises I'm not undoing it all the way although it's taking a tremendous amount of restraint not to expose her breasts to my eyes. *I'll leave that for later.*

But I will see them. I'm fucking determined on that. I thread the laces back around the hooks. "You know," I tell her, smirking, "I'm far more skilled at taking these off." She gasps as the corset tightens, and the top of her breasts are pushed up over the top. It would only need pulling down a fraction to reveal her nipples. "There. That's better."

"Better for you," she huffs out. "How am I supposed to breathe?" She looks into my eyes in protest, but I can't hide my predatory expression and her eyes quickly flick down. Unfortunately, it's also impossible to conceal my growing erection either, touching her, even in that small way has resulted in my cock is straining at my jeans and this time she notices it. A flush comes over her face, but her sharp intake of breath tells me it's not caused by fear.

I'm evil and wicked, and I'm starting to know my girl. "Turn around, Mia," I instruct her, my voice low and gravelly. She obeys instinctively. Good, that bodes well for the night. "Bend over."

She shivers. I think she's going to refuse, but then she does what I said.

"What the fuck are those?" I ask, incredulously.

"My knickers." Her voice shakes; she knows she's done wrong.

"Go and change now. I left you the underwear you're to wear tonight and I want to see you wearing it."

She looks at me in distress. "But everyone will see…."

"I'll give you one minute, Mia. Else we're not going to the club." I would put her over my knee for such an infraction, but I don't want to frighten her off before we even get there. Later, however, she'll learn what happens when she disobeys her Dom.

I think she's going to refuse, but then she turns and runs down the hallway to the guest room. She's back within the minute. I don't make her show the barely-there thong I trust she's now wearing, not yet. "All ready?"

"Yes." Her voice is soft, with a slight tremor.

CHAPTER 14
Mia

Seven years ago

I'd lost all sense of time. It could have been hours or days I'd been forced to endure this abuse on my body, being used roughly and violently time and time again. It seemed never ending, and I knew nothing but pain. There were two of them, two different voices—both cruel rough, and coarse—but I couldn't see them as they continued to keep me blindfolded.

"Your turn." This man sounded the older of the two; he was the one that gave the instructions.

"You fucking bet!" His voice was too eager. He gave me no time to recover after the first man got off when he started. He wasn't as rough as the first, but it hurt worse as I was already sore.

They had taken, no, stolen my virginity, and I would never get it back. Something that had been mine to give had been so cruelly robbed from me. When the second man pulled out, I lay sobbing; hoping that that was the end of it, that they were going to let me go, but the slap round my face and the harsh tugs on my nipples warned me they were not done with me yet. The first man spoke close to my ear.

"I'm going to fuck your mouth now, bitch."

I shook my head violently, clenching my teeth.

He just laughed. "I've got something for that," I heard him pull away, then only moments later he was back, and something was forced into my mouth, opening it wide preventing me biting down. I was compelled to take what he wanted to give me, with no option to refuse. Gagging, I wanted to die.

Present day

All the breath seems to have left my lungs as I manage to gasp out the words, telling Jon I'm ready. I'm lying. I'll never be ready. But oh boy, I've dreamed of visiting a BDSM club for so long; wanting to make sure my writing portrays the atmosphere accurately, and to get ideas for new material. To see, in person, the dynamics of the power exchange at work, to feed off the emotions and arousal.

But now the opportunity is here, I freeze. I'd always expected to go as an observer, never a participant – not after everything I went through. And I'm standing here, dressed in a way that can only be described as being designed to attract attention, and to incite lust. Bile rises into my throat, and I have to turn quickly away, clasping my hand over my mouth as memories of the injuries I suffered and the hell those men put me through come flooding back to me. I don't mind the theory, but to see, hear it in practice? To watch people being spanked or whipped or whatever they do there? Suddenly I realise what a bad idea this is. *I don't want to go.* My hands start trembling.

What I'm wearing makes me feel more like a whore preparing to tout for business. I'm so exposed it scares me, taking me back to that fateful night when I went to the party, dressed in what I thought looked pretty but what my mother told me made me look like a tramp. And here I am now, *deliberately* looking like a prostitute. And I'm proposing to go out in public like this! *What if it happens again? What if someone else thinks I'm fair game?*

"I'll take care of you, Mia." Jon's level voice cuts through my dark thoughts. "You won't be alone; I'll be with you. Anytime you want to leave, you can. Even if you don't want to put a foot through the front door, we'll come home. The choice is yours. At Club Tiacapan, the choice is *always* yours. Now take a deep breath, and try to relax."

His hand comes out and takes mine, and again he puts his fingers to my pulse. His touch, his care soothes and reassures me. As he suggests, I inhale air as deep into my lungs as I can within the restraint of the tightly tied corset, trying to get my rapidly beating heart to steady. *I want to do this.* I've wanted to have the experience to make my books come alive for so long. *So why am I even thinking of chickening out now? Do I want to let those bastards win again?* Letting out one last breath, I turn my face up to his. "I'm ready." I'm proud my voice sounds firm with only a small tremble.

He raises the hand he's holding to his lips and places a feather-light kiss on my palm. "That's my brave girl."

His touch soothes me, even making it possible for me to attempt to joke. "Are we taking a bike or car?" I ask him, not very seriously.

"Hmm." His eyes sparkle as he looks down at my costume, the skirt so short it barely covers my backside. "That's a good question. I can just picture you on the bike." He steps back as if to get a better view, and then comes forward again, leaning close, "But I think the car has the edge tonight."

Giving me no more time to reflect, he takes my coat from the hook and hands it to me. I put it on quickly as though it's a shield; it's three-quarter length, and I fumble as I do up every single button, right to the neck. I'm surprised and more than a little bemused when he places a gentle kiss on my forehead before putting his hand on my elbow and leading me out of the apartment. *What did that intimate gesture mean?* Friendly encouragement? Or something more? *Just what exactly does he expect from me?*

I'd have to be blind not to notice the effect my costume had on him; it's impossible to miss the zip of his jeans straining to hold in his erection, and for once, the evidence of a man's blatant interest doesn't make me want to turn and run. I'm actually proud that I'm the one to cause his discomfort. I trust him when he says nothing will happen that's not consensual. He's not going to push me further than I can go, I believe him when he says he'll bring me home at any time, even before we set foot in the door. As I realise there's no need to be afraid; I start to interpret signs in a different way.

The sight of his bulging jeans, the illicit sensation of the clothes I'm wearing starts to affect me, resulting in my indecently tiny thong becomes damp with my juices. My body is excited and prepared, but my mind's still got some way to catch up. What had Gorgeous said? *She said he'd be my Dom tonight.* Shit! I hope she's mistaken. However much the idea might turn me on, might elicit physical feelings I never thought I'd have, I know in my heart of hearts I'd never have the guts to go through with it.

I won't be playing tonight, with anyone. And definitely not with him. Casting a glance up at the handsome, self-assured man walking next to me, I know I'd only disappoint him. If he has got any ideas about giving me practical experience of the club, I'm going to have to do something to disillusion him.

In the elevator we're both silent, each thinking our own thoughts. I try to look anywhere but at the man beside me, worried the insignificant piece of satin between my legs isn't sufficient to contain the moisture that just looking at his impressive body invokes. *God, wouldn't that be embarrassing if he knew the effect he was having on me?* I turn my head away and feel the chagrin on my face. *Fuck it, Mia, pull yourself together!* Reaching the car he politely opens my door, allowing me get in first and I remember to wrap my coat around me and keep my legs close together, so I don't flash him. His smirk shows me he knows what I'm doing. I turn my head away.

As we drive he starts talking, his voice dark and deep like rich velvet as he runs through some of the things I'll be seeing tonight, and summarising the rules of the club. I try to listen, being reassured to learn that full on sex isn't allowed in the main room – there are private rooms for that – but half of the information he's giving me goes in one ear and straight out the other as it's impossible to quieten the thoughts in my brain. My mind is racing ten to the dozen as, despite having written books on the subject, I've still don't really know what to expect tonight. *This is a real BDSM club I'm going to – not a fictional one!*

"We've been through your limits, Mia, but are there any triggers, anything you might see or hear which could particularly upset you?" His direct question surprises me, and I give it some serious thought. There's probably nothing I'm going to see tonight that I haven't already written about, and I use explicit words and descriptions in my writing.

"To be honest, I can't give any guarantees. But I don't think so, Jon. The only thing that would upset me is if I see someone being forced to do something they don't want to." I sigh, "Take dental gags, for example, I'd never allow one to be used on me, but I've researched them, and as long as the person isn't objecting, I'd have no issue with it. In fact, it might help me to see what I comprehend as instruments of torture being used for pleasure."

He takes his hand off the wheel and gives mine a squeeze. "If anything does upset you, tell me immediately. We'll either leave or just move on to something else. I'm here for you, Mia. But remember, anything you see has been agreed upon by all parties, and if it worries you, it's only how your brain is interpreting it. Look, I appreciate you can't know how you're going to react, so talk to me, tell me if you're getting concerned and we'll talk things through. At any point, if you want, I'll take you home. Communication is key, Mia, do not suffer in silence."

With that, the conversation seems to be over, so I look out the window at the lights of the town rushing past us. We appear to be heading down towards Hampstead Heath. And when he slows, putting on the indicator, I still have qualms about the night ahead, but now it's too late for second thoughts. We've arrived.

"We're here." Jon's voice breaks into my thoughts as he turns the car into a long driveway, and reaching the end, pulls it into a paved car park to one side, ending up perfectly spaced between two already parked cars. One's an expensive Jaguar; the other's a Lotus. This is one place where the McClaren doesn't look out of place. Then my attention is captured by the building we've arrived at, and my mouth drops open. *This wasn't what I expected at all! It's a fucking mansion! It must be worth millions.* A far cry from the basement club in the West End I had planned to visit. Even the size of the place is daunting. My mouth goes dry. I thought it would be more like a night club down a back street somewhere, maybe in Soho.

I've hesitated so long that Jon's opening my door before I have a chance to get out by myself. Mindful of my lack of covering I carefully swing both legs out together, and take his hand as he helps me to stand up. I turn to look at the mansion again. "It's amazing." I croak out.

"Not bad, is it?" He sounds proud for some reason.

"Is it all the club, Jon?"

"It's the whole building. The dungeon takes up most of the ground floor, the private and themed rooms are on the first and second floors. There are a couple of apartments for staff who live onsite on the top level, but the rest of it is all for play." He turns me to face him, studying me briefly, "From here on in I'm

Master Jonathan or Sir." He waits for my nod, as he confirms what he'd told me earlier in the car. "Come on, let's get inside." He's still got his hand in mine, and he tugs it a little. I need the encouragement to get moving.

Come on, Dexie; I need you tonight. Treat it like speaking at a writer's conference. Trying to suppress the shy Mia, I summon up the confident author in me, forcing my alter ego to come to the fore. Straightening my shoulders, and deciding I'd be pulling up my big girl pants if I were wearing anything worthy of that description, I start moving towards the intimidating building. We walk up the path, my heels catching slightly in the gravel, making me grateful for his helping hand keeping me steady. I'm shaking, as we approach a large wooden door. Jon pushes it open, and stands behind me, his comforting touch on my back serving to settle me. *Jon's job is to keep me safe; nothing is going to happen to me here that I don't agree to.* That bolstering thought enables me to step forwards into a foyer, and my eyes widen as I get my first glimpse inside this exclusive club. Despite my knowledge of the sky-high membership fees, I'm still surprised. Even the reception area is more ornate and richly decorated than I expected.

There's a desk to one side, and a burly looking guard standing on the other. Jon moves forward, taking me with him to greet the receptionist, who, I'm pleased to see, is dressed in fetwear, but she's taken it to more extreme levels than I'd dare to. Like me, she's dressed in a short almost non-existent skirt, but her top is simply a couple of black leather straps that leaves a fair amount of her breasts and her nipples blatantly on display. Swallowing rapidly, I'm disconcerted by the amount of flesh on show and that her semi-nakedness doesn't seem to bother her in the slightest. Now I'm grateful Jon has given me something that seemingly, by comparison, is relatively conservative. While I'm trying not to stare at the receptionist's ample bare boobs, he signs a book, and then passes it to me. Tearing my eyes away I see he's already printed my name, Mia Fable, and I put my signature where he indicates. The guard steps forward, and after giving us his best wishes for a good evening, opens another door, allowing us entrance into the inner sanctum.

But we're still not in the club proper. Looking around, I see we're standing in an anteroom, with cloakrooms off to either side.

"The ladies' locker room's over there, just on the right. Go in, put your coat and other stuff in the locker, and wait outside for me. You can give me the locker key when you come out, and I'll keep it safe for you."

I glance in the direction he's pointing. "What about my bag? I'll need my purse."

"Put it in your locker. You won't need it; you don't need to pay for anything here. Drinks are included in the membership. And no phones are allowed." He pauses, and regards me intently, "Are you going to be alright? I'll be waiting for you when I come out; I'm just popping to the men's room to change. I won't be very long."

Convincing myself, it's only a locker room – probably similar to the one at the gym where I'm a member, but very seldom visit – I tell him I'll be okay. Then I stride off, hopefully looking more confident than I feel, to the room clearly designated for the female sex.

It's not like the gym at all. This lady's changing room is decorated with gold gilt and has colourful erotic images painted on the walls. The lockers are made of polished and engraved wood, not the flimsy metal type I was expecting. I find an empty one, take a deep breath and slowly unbutton my coat, hesitating before taking it off. There are a couple of women talking and getting changed right in front of me, and I watch them out of the corner of my eye, interested in what they'll be wearing. But I look away as I find they're stripping down, removing their street clothes until they are completely naked, continuing to chat to each other the whole time with no modesty at all. Now I'm so glad Jon made me change at home; I would have died if I had to uncover myself in front of others. Their casual disregard for their state of undress makes me feel embarrassed for keeping my coat so tightly wrapped around me. Without giving myself a chance to have second thoughts, I throw it off, instantly feeling like I'm baring everything, though the women take no notice.

I want to get back to Jon and the security of his care, but seeing the usual loos are here decide to take advantage of the facilities before going out to meet him. The extra time will ensure he'll have had time to change; I wouldn't want to wait for him with half-naked strangers walking past. Even the thought of someone I don't know approaching me in a place like this when I'm dressed like a slut turns me to stone. I pull myself together with the reminder I've wanted to come to a proper BDSM club for so long, I can't let my nerves ruin the experience for me. Freeing myself from my inertia I do the necessary, then look around and see there's but also a row of well-equipped showers and take the opportunity to have a quick peep inside. All sorts of lavish toiletries have been provided, along with piles of luxurious looking towels. Well, I suppose considering the annual cost of membership, these extravagances should be expected.

Having no further excuse to linger, pulling down my skirt in a vain attempt to cover as much of myself as possible, I leave the locker room to find Jon, leaning against the wall, waiting for me just as he promised.

WOW in capital fucking letters. Just WOW! He evidently keeps his gear here, as I knew he didn't bring anything with him. He's put on tight black leather jeans that cling to every muscle. He's not wearing a shirt, just a black leather waistcoat which hangs open, hiding nothing of his impressive upper torso. His chest, while covered in small scars, has just enough sufficient covering of hair without resembling a bear pelt. His impressive abs ripple under his skin as he moves, not a six pack but an eight pack, and I have to restrain myself from reaching out and touching. As he approaches me, and the waistcoat falls open further, a larger scar that looks like a gunshot wound comes into view. I quickly realise it's evidence of the injury he obtained when protecting the sheikh. My fingers itch with the need to trace the disfigurements which mar his otherwise perfect looking skin, and I have to curl up my hands into fists to prevent myself from reaching out. His stomach is tight, a tantalising V disappearing into the top of his low-slung leathers. No man should be allowed to look this good! I swallow a couple of times. Just the sight of him proves he's too much man for me. *Some girl's going to get very lucky tonight.*

There's a slight look of amusement on his face as if he flipping well knows how he's affecting me. But I also notice he's checking me out in the same way. Then he frowns. "Shoes off!"

I start at his direct order and raise my eyebrows.

"You're a sub. Take them back to the locker room." My initial response is to disobey, knowing, for some reason, having naked feet will make me more feel even more vulnerable. But I know I have to abide by the rules, he *had* told me in the car, but it was one of the things that hadn't sunk in. So I do as he says, returning only a minute later, now shaking and nervous. When he holds out his hand for the locker key, I give it to him with the odd feeling I'm handing myself over into his care. I won't be able to leave without his say so unless I want to limp back home barefoot and wearing a corset and thong! Hmm. I glare slightly, and he catches my look. The bastard laughs. I'm sure he can read my mind.

"You look beautiful," he tells me, his voice coming out on a long breath. "Stunning." Before I summon up a suitable response to his comment, he holds out his hand. "Ready?" He indicates the door in front of us. I step up to it. Again he rests his other hand against the small of my back; I feel the heat through the material of my corset. Letting go briefly, he turns the door handle and pushes. I step inside, needing the gentle pressure from his touch to encourage me forwards.

This is Club Tiacapan!

I try to look everywhere at once, my eyes flicking right, left, straight in front of me as I compare the sight to the descriptions I've used in my books, pleased to see, to some extent at least, there's a good match. Good enough to let me know that my imagination isn't far off track. The room is huge, the inside of the mansion has been gutted, and steel supports are in place of what presumably were the original walls. At one end of the massive open area is a long bar, and in front of that a large seating area with groups of comfortable looking couches and chairs around small tables. The lighting over the centre is subdued, but not dark. Around the edges are large alcoves with well-lit stages. My wide open eyes take in a couple of St Andrew's Crosses, spanking benches, suspension hooks but before I'm able to take a closer look, Jon urges me forwards again. He takes me across to the bar and slips two white bands onto my wrist. I look up at him questioningly.

"Two drinks maximum," he explains. "You give in a band per drink. It's all covered in the membership fee," he reminds me again.

Quickly I'm concerned. I hadn't given a thought to how much he had to pay to get me in here. "How much do I owe you for the entrance fee, Jon?" Rapidly calculating how much I have in my bank account and hoping it won't be too much, especially since I'm also determined to pay for the spa day at some point. But knowing how prestigious this place is, it could run into hundreds, if not thousands. *I'll have to break out the credit card.*

Smiling broadly and giving a little chuckle, he touches my arm. "It's okay; it didn't cost me anything. I know the owners." It seems too good to be true, so I peer at him with narrowed eyes, but there's nothing in his expression to suggest he isn't telling me the truth, and he simply shrugs under my scrutiny. Okay, for now, I'll take it at face value. I breathe an internal sigh of relief. *The admission fee to a BDSM club isn't something I'd want to declare on my tax return.*

"Do you want a drink right away?" he asks, turning away to attract the attention of a bartender.

Something alcoholic might steady my nerves a little, so I nod, and watch as a man comes over to take our order. The barman looks at me keenly; his close examination making me uncomfortable, but almost as if he realises it, he quickly shifts his gaze to Jon and queries, "Who have we got here, Master Jonathan?"

"Mia," Jon answers him succinctly, "She's my guest tonight." Then, addressing me, adds, "Mia, this is Master Ralph. If you get separated from me for any reason, Master Ralph will look after you." Ralph's eyes flick between us, and then he gives a chin lift and smiles, confirming he's happy with the role Jon's assigned to him.

My surprise that a Master is tending the bar must have shown on my face, and Jon answers my unspoken question, "Staff are members too. Now, what do you to want to drink?"

"Oh." When Jon indicates, I take off one of the bands and hand it to the man behind the bar. His friendly expression brings a reciprocating smile to my face as I consider what to have. I prefer wine, but feel the need for something stronger tonight. "Vodka tonic?" *It's a shame I'm limited to two, more might have given me more courage.*

As Master Ralph's getting my drink, I turn and lean with my back to the bar, observing the room. We've arrived early, just after opening time on purpose. At ten o'clock the doors open, but Jon told me beforehand the club doesn't start buzzing until around midnight. He'd felt arriving early would be less intimidating and allow me to get my bearings without being in the middle of a crowd, and now I can see he was right. A couple of the stages are already in use, but many others remain empty, set up for different types of play. Not too many people are around as yct, and most of those are milling around having drinks and talking. I notice a few pairs deep in discussion and suspect they're pairing up for the night. *Negotiating. That's what they're doing.* The music is thumping heavy metal, but not at such a loud volume to make conversation is impossible.

The crack of a whip on flesh makes me jump. I spin to look, but the recipient of the lash seems to be writhing in pleasure, not agony if her screams of satisfaction are anything to go by. My heart, which felt like it stopped for a moment, starts beating again as I remind myself, this isn't a place for torture and abuse, everything here is consensual. And this is what I came for; to experience everything I've read and written about. Well, to watch others; I'm certainly not taking part in anything myself.

There are stools in front of the bar, so I carefully hop on one, trying not to expose any more than I have to; hard with such a short skirt. But while I'm worrying about preserving my modesty, a girl comes up to us, catching my attention. She's wearing a baby doll costume that's completely transparent, revealing she's got nothing else on at all. On reaching us, she elegantly folds and lowers her body until she's kneeling in front of Jon. Her fluid movement and grace betraying she must have been practising the perfect submissive pose for years. Her knees fall open, and even from the angle I'm looking from she's leaving absolutely nothing to the imagination and obviously doesn't give a damn. Her hands settle on her thighs palm upwards. Head bowed, she addresses my companion.

"Permission to speak, Master Jonathan?"

"Speak." Jon looks down at her as, having received his consent, she brings her head up. His face is stern, and my mouth goes dry, realising all at once he how much he sounds and looks like a Dom. A chill runs down my spine.

"Would Master Jonathan like to play with this sub tonight?"

The chill now turns to the burn of jealousy as I hold my breath, on tenterhooks wondering what he's going to say when he reaches out his hand and touches her head.

"Sorry, Diamond. Not tonight."

I try to quash a profound feeling of relief, as I watch Diamond effortlessly unfold her body and stand again. She bows her head in acknowledgement to the Master and then moves away. For me to be envious is completely wrong, and selfish. Of course, Jon will want to play with someone. Swallowing hard to suppress the green devil inside me, I realise she's given me the opening I was after. *But am I brave enough to go through with it?* Glancing around the club I see nothing of concern; my earlier fears have been alleviated by the professional atmosphere *and* the knowledge that all I need to do is to stay close by the bar and with the kindly looking Master Ralph.

A deep breath to fortify myself, and then I touch Jon's arm to get his attention, I start, "Master Jonathan," and then pause, I didn't think I'd be able to call him by that title, it seemed a bit silly when he'd said it in the car. But he's taken on a different persona since entering the club; I'm in awe of him and well out of my depth knowing no matter what my attraction is to him, he'd want far more than I'd ever be able to give. Jon spins round to face me as he feels my hand on his arm, and arches an eyebrow, so I continue. "I don't want to spoil your evening. I'm happy to stay here while you go and enjoy yourself." I hate the thought of him touching a woman such as Diamond. I'll die a little inside if I have to see him with anyone else, but I have no option. The way Diamond had moved, the way she knew how to approach him, it's obvious she is an experienced submissive. Although I've researched and know the theory, I wouldn't have a clue putting it into practice.

He doesn't understand, and frowns, "I brought you here with me, Mia."

"But I'm cramping your style, Jon." I pick up my drink and take a sip; my mouth still dry. "You came here to play." I sound far more nonchalant than I feel.

"So have you," he tells me.

I give a firm shake of dismissal. "I'm fine staying here by the bar where I can watch what's going on. And you said Master Ralph would keep an eye on me. Go ahead, Jon, have fun."

"That's not what I came here for tonight. I brought you, and I'm staying with you."

Guilt makes my voice waspish, "I don't need a babysitter, Jon."

He reels back, then after a short pause retorts, "What if someone propositions you?"

"You told me everything was consensual! I'll just withhold my consent." My eyes flash a look of challenge.

"I don't want to leave you alone." His expression is chilling. He seems disappointed, and I don't understand why I'm giving him the opportunity to go and enjoy himself. That's what he's here for, after all.

"You're not. Master Ralph is here. You go do what you want to do."

"I'm not happy leaving you, Mia. What if you have a flashback or something?"

Now I'm upset; he's referring to my past, making me feel like a victim all over again. I start to regret I ever told him, and I say so. "I shouldn't have told you what happened to me. Why can't you just treat me like an ordinary person? It may have relevance to the case, but tonight, I'm *not* your case! I'm a woman wanting to enjoy her first visit to a BDSM club."

It's obvious he's taken aback, and for a moment doesn't know what to say. He rubs his hand over his chin as he thinks. "This is your first visit, sweetheart. Whatever your background, I think you'd enjoy it more if you stayed close to me."

And do what? What exactly would happen if I stayed close to him? A shiver runs down my spine as I could see myself begging Jon to do more than just stand with me observing the play around us. *What if I wanted to join in?*

Another beautiful sub is approaching the bar, seeming to be making a beeline for him. That decides me. "No, Jon. Please. I'm not here to cramp your style." Repeating it again, I turn away from him, resting one elbow on the bar as I lift my drink in my other hand. I look thoroughly engrossed with the competent way Ralph is pouring drinks.

There's a mirror over the bar, so I watch his face as he surveys the room. People are coming in through the main doors in greater numbers as time's getting on, and I realise, now I've rejected him, he'll be checking out the sub approaching him, or seeking someone else to amuse himself with tonight. The thought causes pain to shoot through me. God, I wished I have the nerve to do more. Shit! *Why do the chains of my past still bind me?*

After a moment he spins me around so I'm forced to look at him. He's staring at me, his face blank. "If that's what you want, Mia." He questions me with his eyes.

"That's what I want," I confirm, as forcefully as I can.

Jon's gaze stays fixed on me for a moment, then his features tauten as though he's annoyed then, with a sigh, he turns to the bartender. "Keep an eye on her for me, Ralph. I'll be out the back." And without another word to me he leaves.

CHAPTER 15

Jon

Four years ago

Nijad threw me a hard look; his dark eyes cold and fierce, "Let me get this right, Jon. You're accusing the Kassis family of manipulating the fucking odds at our casinos?" Pulling himself up to his impressive full height, he continued, "That we run a crooked fucking house?"

Trying to get Nijad to admit that he had stacked the odds in my favour was proving nigh on impossible. I had to bark out a laugh, knowing him well enough to recognise that his supposed anger wasn't genuine. "Of course, I'm not, but you must admit my winning streak was a bit suspect."

"You won. That's an end to it." He gave his signature shrug. "The luck was with you. That's the way it goes, sometimes the house loses."

Heaving an exasperated sigh, I knew when it was time to give up; we'd spent the best part of the last half-hour arguing without getting anywhere. Nijad refused to sway from his original assertion that I'd won the money fair and square. As I reluctantly conceded, he waved my thanks away.

The result being, out of the blue, I was a multi-millionaire with new avenues opening up for me. I moved from being an employee to becoming a partner of Grade A Security along with Ben and Jason. When, in a surprise move Sheikh Jasim, Nijad's older brother announced his plans to establish a club in the UK I *accepted his kind offer to let me buy into it. An establishment, catering to the kinky desires of the elite of society. A top drawer BDSM club. Having had a wealth of experience of playing in such places alongside the two sheikhs all over Europe, I was intrigued by the opportunity. Not only did I stand to make money from it, but welcomed the idea of providing a safe, well run place to play. So without having to think twice about it, I made my second investment. It proved to be a sound one.*

Nijad's generosity set me up for life. But once given the all clear from the medics, and despite my changed circumstances, I continued to act as his primary CPO, knowing I wouldn't hesitate to risk my life to save his again if I needed to. I'd always respected him; now he'd become so much more to me, he'd become my brother.

Present day

As I leave Mia sitting at the bar under Ralph's watchful eye, such a myriad of emotions flit across my mind I have difficulty separating them. The principle ones being anger that she's dismissed me, disappointment that she obviously has no intention of playing with me, and jealousy that she might end up with someone else. I'd been so certain there was a spark between us; that it had been there from day one. I saw her checking me out earlier – have I read her wrong? Or has she noticed someone else she likes better? Shaking my head in confusion, I can't understand why she sent me away. I thought she'd have wanted me close for reassurance at least. But she was so adamant I leave her, she left me no choice. Asserting so confidently she wanted to be left alone, I can only assume it's Dexie in the house tonight. All I can do is hope she can keep that up. At least the bartender's looking out for her. But I'll go back out and check on her soon, unable to shake the apprehension that scared and innocent Mia might rear her head again. *Fuck!* Again I shake my head. *Women!* Trying to fathom out what they're thinking is difficult. Even for a Dom.

Unclipping the velvet rope separating the VIP area from the rest of the club, I storm through, throwing myself onto a sofa. Blinded by my emotions, it takes me a moment to see I'm not alone. Sheikh Jasim, one of the other owners of the club is already there, seated in a relaxed position on a couch. He's looking at me with a smirk on his face and his eyebrows shoot up.

"Don't ask." I rasp out.

He chuckles, but then, of course, he has to probe. "I thought you were bringing a guest with you tonight?"

I scowl. "I did."

"Where is she then?"

"At the bar."

"With?"

"With no one. Well, Ralph's keeping an eye on her."

His eyes widen as he looks at me searchingly. "You left an uncollared neophyte alone?" He's shaking his head. "She'll be fair game."

I shrug. "She thinks she's capable of fending them off."

Jasim's sharp eyes don't miss anything, "What did you do to upset her? It's unlike you to be turned down by a sub."

"She's not my sub." I can't understand it myself; I thought we'd been getting close, "She said she wanted to give me a chance to play with someone else. She made it clear she doesn't even want my company."

He snorts, "So why aren't you playing, then?" Then his eyes narrow, as he regards me thoughtfully. Too quickly he summons up the answer. "Because the only person you want to scene with tonight is her, isn't it? Have you made that too obvious and scared her? You said she had a history of abuse. Perhaps this was not a good idea, brother."

I'd told him the headlines, but hadn't shared the details. That secret is Mia's to disclose if and when she wants to. But Jasim deserves to know who is playing in his club. And I can't deny it's worries me too; her history could mean some of the sights she's exposed to tonight might overwhelm her. So my answer's a measured one as I respond to him, "As long as Mia stays near Ralph she should be okay. He's a good Dom, and would quickly recognise if it gets too much for her. And I'll be going back out shortly, to keep an eye on things. I just needed a moment to cool down." I sigh, and make my confession, "Yes, I wanted to do a simple scene with her, something that wouldn't frighten her." I look up and him and grin, my anger rapidly fading, "She's a beautiful woman, Jas. And a sub, although she hasn't admitted to that yet. And even if we don't play, I'm responsible for her. She's my guest tonight; I haven't forgotten that."

"You want to be the one to introduce her to our lifestyle?"

"I shouldn't." My smile disappears. "She needs someone who could commit to her, and you know me, Jas. I'm the same as you. I'll scene with virtually anyone, perhaps go home with a sub for the night; maybe have a contract that lasts a few weeks, but after that? The women I'm with here all know the score, we negotiate that up front."

He nods, "It's what this lifestyle is all about. Communication and making sure all parties are clear on expectations." Then he laughs, "But someone's got to catch you sometime, Jon. And it might be Mia."

I scowl at him. "She's made it clear she doesn't want me."

"Has she?" His eyes are probing.

Ignoring him, confused as much as he is about her feelings for me as well as my own sentiments towards her, I change the subject. "I thought you said if I had a moment, you wanted to discuss the extension? Well, I'm here. Tell me what you want from me, then I'll get back and see how she'd doing."

He stays quiet for a moment, still regarding me with that intense look of his. He's as much Dom as me, well used to analysing reactions and expressions, and I know I'm having no success hiding my feelings from him. *Fucking woman! She's got me tangled up in knots!* For the first time in my life *I'm* not clear what I want from her, so where the fuck does that fit into and Dom/sub communication?

After a short space of silence, he gives a nod of affirmation, and we start discussing the extension we're considering on the back of the building. The club being so popular, membership is creeping up, and soon we'll be running out of space.

It's only a few minutes later when there's noise of a commotion coming through from the main room. Jasim stands at the same time as I get to my feet, and just as a dungeon monitor rushes in. "Master Jonathan, your guest…."

Not stopping to wait to hear what's happened, preferring to see for myself, I rush out into the club. Mia's standing at the bar, unhurt, but the man in front of her is fuming and rubbing his cheek. He's roaring, "That fucking bitch hit me!" He's attracting attention, and a crowd has gathered around. *Shit! This is not what I wanted for Mia's first time at Tiacapan!*

Pushing through, I claim Mia by putting my arm around her and feel her violently trembling. *She hit him? She's not the violent type!* "What's going on?" I demand my voice crisp and sharp. It has the effect of making everyone else simmer down and quieten.

The man, a newish Dom to our scene, and a junior Member of Parliament in his everyday life turns to me, informing me angrily, "I was trying to negotiate a scene with this, this…" he breaks off and sees the expression on my face. "This sub," he continues, choosing his words with wisely, "Out of the blue, with no provocation she hits me."

I glance at Ralph, who's joined us, and raise a quizzical

eyebrow, it doesn't sound like Mia at all.

"I'm sorry," Ralph is frowning and appears to be annoyed with himself. "I was serving at the other end of the bar, so missed what happened."

Mia's still shaking, she feels cold to the touch. Looking down at her I can see she's gone pale and is probably in shock. I won't be able to press her for answers until she calms a little, so I turn my attention back to the man who she'd apparently struck. There is a fading red handprint on his right cheek. "What did you say to her, Donavan?" remembering his club name at last.

He looks at the ground, and then back up at me, and lifts then lowers his shoulders in dismissal. "Just tried to negotiate a scene. I told her I wanted to tie her up, flog her and lick her sweet little cunt."

When he throws me a challenging look, I guiltily realise that's exactly what I want to do to her, but the difference is, I know something he doesn't. I know she's far from ready for that yet. Becoming angry, I realise a good part of this is his fault, he ought to find out a bit more about the sub he wants to play with before jumping in with both feet, particularly one he hasn't seen before. But the fact that she's hit someone in the club needs to be addressed.

As the participants have calmed down, the crowd around us drifts away, intent on finding better ways of amusing themselves. When Donovan realises he's no longer playing to a full house, his belligerence disappears.

"She's new," I tell him, trying to keep my temper under control. "She's finding her way. With a new sub, you should take the time to get to know their limits first. Everything you've mentioned is a soft limit for Mia."

He knows a Master and co-owner of the club is giving him advice, and that he isn't in a position to argue. To his credit, he thinks about what my words, and nods. "Maybe I did rush in," he begrudgingly admits. "But she slapped me, and she needs to be punished."

Unfortunately, I agree, but I don't want to scare her more. Looking down at the girl by my side, who seems to have regained some composure now the crowd has dissipated, I turn her to face me, and tell her quietly, "Take off your thong, Mia."

She looks at me horrified.

Donavan huffs. "That's punishment?" He asks, scathingly.

"It is for her, and will suffice for now." I glare at him. "*I've taken the time to know her limits*," Again I take the opportunity to stress the point. I'm annoyed, punishing Mia was the last thing I wanted to do tonight unless it was for fun. But in my heart of hearts, I know she can't get away with such behaviour. So I have to reassure him. "*I'll* discipline her later, but first, we've all got to calm down."

To give him his due, he seems to accept this, and his nod shows he trusts me to do what's necessary.

Mia hasn't moved. She's only going to make things worse if she doesn't comply with my demand. "Don't disobey me, Mia; you won't like the consequences. No violence is allowed in this club, for whatever reason. Now remove your thong or your subsequent punishment will be worse."

She looks up at me beseechingly, but my face is firm. She reaches down and removes her thong. She sniffs, and a tear rolls down from her eye. Then, without needing to be prompted, she swivels around to face Donavan, her eyes respectively looking down at the floor, "I'm sorry I hit you, Sir."

He glances at me, clearly understanding she is under my protection. I'm giving him an unyielding stare to signal this matter *will* be dealt with, but by me, not him. With a quick nod and a sigh, he moves away. Crisis over. *But what to do about Mia?*

Master Ralph catches my eye and beckons me closer. "Sounds like something he said must have set her off. I was talking to her just before the incident, and she seemed to be enjoying herself. She was quite relaxed. There was no indication anything was upsetting her."

I study him, he's a good Dom, and I agree with him. It's a shame he didn't witness the incident. "I'll explore that, Ralph. Thanks." I turn to Mia hating that her face is streaked with tears, her makeup running. Scanning the room I see Diamond approaching, and I call her over. Although I turned her down earlier, I know she won't bear a grudge; she's a lovely girl, always offering to clean equipment or serve at the bar when it's busy. I know she'll help. "Can you take Mia to the locker room, Diamond, to clean herself up? Please?"

A broad smile crosses Diamond's face; she's a real service sub, getting pleasure from helping. "Of course, I will." She takes Mia's hand.

My fingers press on Mia's shoulder, preventing her from leaving and getting her attention. She looks up at me, "Go and freshen up; then Diamond will bring you back to me. If you want to go home, just say. We can end this now."

She's softly crying, her free hand coming up to wipe the tears away smearing her mascara even more. "You said you'd punish me? Isn't humiliating me enough?"

Exhaling slowly, I pull her close. "I haven't humiliated you, sweetheart. Just look around you, you're still wearing more than most of the subs here. I'm pushing your boundaries; that's all. I can't ignore what happened. If you stay, I'll have to make good on my promise to Donavan. But I said I'd take you home the moment you feel uncomfortable. And that still stands."

She shakes her head, "I'm sorry, Jon, for causing trouble. I'm more embarrassed than upset. I'd like to stay."

"You stick with Diamond until she brings you back to me. I'm not letting you out of my sight again, Mia. Don't even try to push me away."

When I see her accept that, I tell Diamond I'll be waiting in the VIP area and request she brings Mia to me there. I watch them go, running my hand through my hair, deep in thought. Was it wrong to bring Mia here? Is she not ready, and if not, would she ever be? Does just the thought of playing bring back memories best left forgotten? What exactly was the trigger Donavan hit? Can I help her get over it? Or should I walk away? I remember my impulse when I first met her, and briefly think it would have been better had I acted on it. Maybe running fast in the other direction would have been a more sensible idea for all concerned. Mia would have been better left alone, and well out of my life, *and* my lifestyle. *But then she would have gone to a club alone, and without me there to help her get out of trouble.* The thought is a chilling one and makes me realise we need to have a serious talk. And soon. And for the rest of tonight, she's going to stay right by my side.

Ralph hands me my second whisky of the night; he can see I need it. Returning to the VIP area, I find Jasim is chatting with another of our Masters but breaks off as I approach, throwing me a curious look, so I quickly fill him in on what's happened. He doesn't censure me, seeing I'm berating myself enough for bringing her here in the first place and for leaving her alone. As we discuss the situation, I keep an eye open for Diamond returning, getting to my feet when at last the girls appear.

Dismissing Diamond with my thanks, I stand tall, my features set, and my arms folded in an uncompromising stance. Now Mia is going to find out what I'm like as a Dom. "Mia," I say firmly. "Come." I point to the couch where I've been sitting. She goes as if to sit down, but I put out my hand to stop her. "Kneel," I tell her. With raised eyebrows she questions me. So I repeat my command, my voice strict and unbending. "Remember; just say the word and I'll take you home. But if you want to stay, then do as I ask. Kneel." I'm sure she'll know what I want; she watched Diamond earlier and has written about the submissive pose many times. Her eyes flick towards Jasim and his companion. The sheikh's observing her with interest. He has a smirk on his face as if he's not sure that I'm in control of the situation. I'm wondering that myself.

With unexpected grace, Mia surprises me and complies with my instruction. Now she's kneeling at my feet. Seating myself, I study her pose. It's not bad for a novice, but there's one thing wrong. "Mia, part your knees." She's holding them tightly together, only too conscious she's naked under her very short skirt. She looks up at me pleadingly, but I refuse to bend. I know I'm pushing her, but as her Dom, that's my job, and she's got an out if she really can't cope.

As slowly she pulls her knees apart, I feel so proud, but I don't let it show. "More," I tell her. She takes a deep breath, and this time, she's quicker to respond and comply. She bows her head and puts her hands on her thighs, palm up. "Good girl," I tell her. As I turn to Jasim, he nods in approval. The other Master grins, and then gets up and leaves us.

"I think we should give the architect the go ahead." I continue my conversation with Jasim as though we'd never been interrupted, ignoring the woman at my feet.

"I'm happy with that," he tells me, "Has Jason any comments?"

I'd have a long phone discussion about the plans with our other partner, and he's cool with the ideas and content to leave it in our hands as he's stuck overseas and won't be returning any time soon. As we talk, I idly rest my hand on Mia's head, registering that when I make physical contact with her, she relaxes into my touch. I file that thought away. As I keep my hand there, she moves her head so it's resting on my leg. Slowly, I being to stroke her hair, and she pushes back into my hand.

Once Jasim and I have thrashed out the business we need to, he leaves us.

Now we are alone; the time has come for us to have that conversation. I instruct her, "Come here, Mia." As she stands, I pull her slightly off balance so she's no option but to lie in my lap. "Are you alright? If this is all too much for you, just say."

There's a pause before she answers, but when she does, what she says takes me by surprise as she gets right to the heart of the matter. "While you were talking, Jon, I was thinking — I'd been sitting at the bar, and I felt quite relaxed. I was intrigued, interested by what I was seeing, understanding what you meant when you said everything was discussed and mutually agreed. I saw nothing to make me feel threatened; it was nothing like my experience in the past." She pauses, and swallows, "And then that man came up, so quickly, as if zooming in on a target. I've never, ever hit someone before. I shocked myself! It wasn't just the fact he approached me; it was what he said. Without introducing himself he just simply stated what he wanted to do. And everything he said just sent me straight back into the past. And he used the word 'cunt'."

"But you use that word in your books."

"I know, but it's different to write it than to hear it. They used it differently, derogatively. And a stranger, approaching me like that, using *that* word. His voice, his tone. It was so rough. I immediately thought the way I'm dressed lured him to me, and suddenly, right at that moment, I was right back being raped and hurt."

"He hit a trigger."

"Yes. I think he did."

I stroke her arm, noting the goose bumps rising on it. *She's not at all immune to my touch.* My cock stirs beneath her, showing neither am I to hers. "I shouldn't have left you, I'm sorry."

"It's my fault; I asked you to."

And I've spent the past half-hour trying to understand why. I have to know, so ask the direct question, "Why, Mia? Why did you want me to go?"

She sighs, and takes a deep breath. For a moment I don't think she's going to answer, then, when she speaks, her voice is so quiet I can hardly hear it, and I realise she's finally admitting the truth, confirming what I'd expected, *hoped*, all along. "Because of what you make me feel."

My heart misses a beat, but I have to be sure. "And what's that?" I can't afford any more misunderstandings tonight. "Be honest with me, Mia."

This time, she draws in air so deeply I can see her ribcage rise. "You scare me. Because you make me feel alive, for the first time in seven years," she admits. She's looking down, and I suspect she's got more to say. I squeeze her to encourage her. "I feel things around you, Jon, things I write about, but have never experienced before."

Something leaps inside and my chest loosens at her disclosure. I hadn't appreciated how much it would mean to hear her admit her feelings toward me. It's time for my confession. "You make me feel too, Mia. You must know how much I'm attracted to you." The evidence is fast growing hard beneath her.

Now she looks at me, bewilderment in her eyes, "I didn't know, but I hoped. And these feelings frighten me, Jon. That's why I pushed you away. I didn't *want* to see you play with someone else, but I wouldn't be able to be what you need, to play how you would like. I'm terrified of you, of whatever this is between us. You're too much for me. You're a Dom!"

I'm still reeling from the revelation that she's as much attracted to me as I am to her, but rapidly I think through the implications. I'd told Jasim I didn't do relationships, and that's the simple truth of it. But with Mia? She clearly wouldn't be a one night stand. The thought creeps up on me that I'd already decided I wasn't looking forward to walking away at the end of the case. *Perhaps it's time I give commitment a try?* Either I end it here now before we get in any deeper, or we start something which is going to take us God knows where. I'm in unfamiliar territory here. What is plainly evident is that she's got a whole tonne of issues we will need to work through if we're going to be together. Can I commit to that? *Of course, I can!* I'm a Dom; she's someone who needs nurturing; to be cared for so she regains her emotional and sexual confidence or perhaps finds it for the first time, remembering at what young age she'd been assaulted. I'm a Dom, so how can I walk away?

I pull her up so she's straddling me. She wriggles, but can't escape the physical sign of my arousal as she's sitting right on top of it. The last time she was this close to a male was seven years ago. I hold her in place, and will myself to stay still, the only part of me moving is my cock twitching in my leathers and that I can't control. "Mia," I start gently, but firmly. "I want to be your Dom. And I want you as my sub. Exclusively."

She reaches forward, and her hand touches my bare chest under my vest, I'm not sure she realises she's doing it. "I can't be what you'd want, Jon." Her unwitting action belies the words she's repeating.

"Master." I correct her. "Here you call me Master." Her eyes widen when she realises the implications when I don't tell her to use my name. I've claimed her; I'm *her* Master. Before she can say anything else, I decide to explain how this is going to work. "You're already what I want, Mia. Make no mistake about that. As for how this is going to work, we'll go at your speed, sweetheart. As a Dom, I'll want to push your limits, but as the sub, you'll have all the control, you can stop me at any point."

She starts to protest. Placing my fingers over her mouth, I stop her and continue, "I know you think I have a lot of experience, and you're right. I won't deny I've played with a large number of women. But that just means that I've the knowledge that I'll be able to use to help you." It some ways it's refreshing and, I have to admit, exciting to have someone so new, so *innocent* to train. But I lay it on the line for her, and as the pledge leaves my mouth, I know it's the truth. "I want you, Mia, not anybody else. Whatever this attraction is between us, I'd like to explore it further."

A tentative smile appears on her face, and there's a moment's pause before she answers shyly, "Okay," Gently, her fingers trace the scars on my chest, her soft touch making me want to explode. She hasn't finished, "I want to try for you, Jon. You'll have to understand if I use my safeword if I want to slow down, or stop. I can't promise anything won't freak me out, hell; I didn't see what happened with Donavan coming. But I trust *you*." Her words impress the hell out of me.

She trusts me. Or think she does. That's something to work on, but we're certainly in a good place to start. Examining her carefully, seeing a glimpse of excitement and anticipation flare in her eyes that wasn't there before, I think she's ready.

"I'm going to take you into the dungeon in a minute, and you'll be perfectly safe. *You* will have all the power. There are dungeon monitors all around. And you're right; you have your safeword." Placing my hand under her chin, I raise it until she's looking straight at me. I wait for her nod of affirmation before continuing, "Remember, what I told you when we were driving here. Say Green if you're okay to continue, Yellow means back off, and we'll discuss it, and Red means Stop. Nothing else means Stop, little one, but if something's upsetting you, or you can't take any more, you shout out Red. I guarantee you'll have the dungeon monitors over within seconds."

"I've written about that." She seems happy enough with the arrangements that ensure everything is consensual.

"Yes, I know. And you realise if you ever call Red that I'll have failed as a Dom? I won't have read you correctly?"

She sits up on my lap, the pressure on my cock almost unbearable. But I'm happy to suffer. "Why are you going through all this? What have you got planned…" she hesitates, looks down, and then finishes her sentence, "Master?"

God, that sends a shudder right through my body triggering, even more, blood flowing to my already engorged cock. *No woman has ever affected me quite like this.* Shaking myself, I force myself to continue the conversation and answer her, but indirectly, "You can say Red at any time, and I'll take you home." And then as the next words leave my mouth I realise how true they are, I *want* Mia. Any way I can have her. "If you don't want to try, or can't continue, I won't mind, Mia. I honestly don't know if I could have a vanilla relationship with you, but I'm willing to give it a darn good try. You can say the word right now if you want and I'll take you home. But that doesn't mean I'll leave you. I mean it Mia. I'll attempt to keep it vanilla. Do you want to go home?" Fuck, I hope she doesn't, but I mean everything I'm saying. I want this woman any way I can have her, and if kink needs to take a back seat, so be it. "What's it to be, Mia?" I hold my breath.

"I don't want to go home," she whispers. Her eyes widen as if she's surprised herself.

With immense relief, I nod slowly. "Okay, this is what is going to happen. You insulted and struck a Dom, baby. I need to discipline you for that."

"How?" I feel her muscles tense.

"We're going to go into the dungeon, and I'm going to put you on a spanking bench. I won't tie you down; you won't be restrained, except by your desire to please your Dom." Now it's my turn to hold my breath. Am I pushing her too far? "Will you try that for me, sweetheart?" She's staring at me and biting her lip. I let her have the time to decide.

"Yes, I'll try." Her reply is tentative, but it's a positive response. My cock almost jumps out of my leathers and my heart leaps and swells with pride. It's an enormous step for her to take.

"Now, I'm going to kiss you." Having warned her of my intention, I put my hand behind her head and gently pull her towards me conscious that this is our first kiss, our first real intimacy, so I take it easy. How long since she's even kissed a man? Has she ever been kissed before? *Christ! This is untrodden ground for me.* Our lips meet. My tongue flicks over her mouth, willing her to give me entry. Tentatively her mouth opens, and she allows me in. I control the kiss, my tongue gently playing with hers, advancing and retreating, encouraging her to take an active part. It's as if even this is novel to her, and if possible I get even harder thinking I'll be the first to teach her. I deepen the kiss, taking hold of her hair so she can't escape. Instead of protesting, she pushes forward, taking all I have to give. As she starts to respond, matching my actions I begin to realise I could become addicted to her taste.

It's some time before I even think of pulling away. I release her hair and gently push her away. Her lips are swollen, but her eyes sparkle.

"Jon, I…"

I put my fingers to her mouth. "Shush," I tell her. And then I smirk. "And it's Master!"

"Master." She tries it out again and smiles that beautiful smile.

Picking her up, I put her on her feet. "Ready?" She hesitates and stiffens. I wait. Is she going to call a halt now? Have I already blown it? But then she puts her small hand in mine, and with that small gesture she's demonstrating how much she does trust me. I need to make sure I continue to deserve it. *Fuck, it's like walking on egg shells.* I want to make this so right for her, but I'm only too well aware how easily it could all go wrong.

I lead her out into the dungeon which is busy and buzzing now. At first, all the stage areas appear to be in use, but I'm lucky enough to spot a spanking bench which has just been vacated and cleaned. Leading her over to it, her fingers tighten around mine, and her pulse becomes rapid. She's full of nerves, but I'm still going to push her, I can't back off now, I've told her what to expect and have to follow through unless she safewords out.

I gesture towards her corset. "You'll be more comfortable if you take that off."

She shudders, and looks around at the crowd surrounding us. "Jon, don't make me. Please, I can't," she says, quietly adamant.

"No one's looking at you, Mia."

Again her glance surveys the room. She sees what I said was right; most people are too involved in what they are doing to bother about what we're doing, and many are naked, or nearly so. When she looks back at me, she asks in a shaky voice. "You really want me to?"

"Yes," I reply, firmly.

A brief pause, then bravely, she starts to undo the laces. When she's finished, she whips it off and almost jumps on the spanking bench as if hoping to hide. Her luscious breasts fall to either side; they're not hidden, but not consciously on display. It's the first time I've seen them, and I'm eager to get my mouth on them, but hold back on that impulse; now is not the time. I lay my hand on her back, and my earlier theory that my touch appears to relax her is proven as immediately some of her tension drifts away.

"I'm going to take your skirt off now," I tell her, I don't ask. My voice is low and authoritative, showing I will tolerate no argument. Again she tenses but doesn't object. In seconds, she's lying naked before me. I move her knees so they are resting on the supports, and widen them a little. She's completely exposed. I pause briefly, relishing the sight I never expected to see. Mia, naked in the dungeon. *Fuck, that's a beautiful sight. She's got even more courage than I gave her credit for.*

"Give me a colour." I move to her head and examine her. Glancing down at her face, I see her eyes tightly closed.

"Yellow," she replies hesitantly in a weak voice.

I lean down, planting a quick kiss to her head, and stroke her hair. I move around her again, but make sure I'm keeping a hand on her at all times. Noticing Donavan has come up to watch, I address Mia, but keep my eyes on him. "It's a count of twenty, Mia. If you move, I'll wait for you to get back into position before I continue."

Donavan nods his head approvingly. Then, in a gesture that surprises me, puts his hand on my arm as if to stay it. Leaning forwards so he can speak quietly in my ear, "Go easy on her; I didn't realise she was such a novice. It's my fault; I rushed in." I suspect he might have been speaking to Diamond. But however much I'd like to forgo it, she's earned a punishment. As co-owner and a Master Dom, I have to lead by example, and violence of any form is strictly against the club's rules. But at least he's making it easier for me. If only he hadn't been such a prat earlier, we wouldn't have come to this. I shake my head to remove such thoughts and calm myself, as I would never raise my hand to a sub with anything but equilibrium.

Taking a breath, I start to gently caress Mia's butt cheeks. She leans into my soothing touch. I rub a little harder to bring the blood to the surface, taking my time to make sure she's fully relaxed, and then raise my hand.

CHAPTER 16
Mia

Seven years ago

Now they've pulled me off the bed, dragged me across the room, and forced me to stand, faced against something on the wall. With a rough touch, they bound my hands up high, stretching me up straight, my legs viciously kicked apart and my ankles secured with rope. My toes barely touched the ground; most of my weight was on my arms. Already my shoulders were starting to burn.

"Hand me my whip." A barked command.

Oh God! No! A whip? No more, I won't be able to endure it!

"Which one?"

"Single Tail, the six-footer."

If it was possible to be even more terrified, then that's where I was heading at that precise moment as the crack of a whip sounded behind me. "Just getting a few practice strokes in, bitch," he said. "Don't want to ruin that pretty back now, do we?" His laugh was evil and almost manic.

At the next crack, I screamed as the whip sliced across my back, knowing it had to have cut open my skin. It fell twice more.

"Nice!" Number Two said with obvious approval in his voice, "Very nice."

But they hadn't finished. Then the lashes started falling on my buttocks and thighs. I'd never known such pain in my life.

Present day

I should be scared; I should be out of my fucking mind with fear. I've been in this position before, forced to take spankings, whippings and canings, unable to escape. So how is it I find myself voluntarily lying on a bench, completely naked and exposed in a room full of people? The touch of Jon's hand on my back is comforting, and I put all my faith in him, reminding myself that I trust him. If the memories of my past overwhelm me, and I can't continue, I have a safeword to use. There's no comparison with my past; *he's not going to torture me.*

I'm nervous because I don't know what to expect, but amazingly not scared. *Will it hurt? Well, of course, it will bloody hurt! But how much?* I'm more worried I won't be able to take it and will disappoint Jon. My Dom!

Shaking with anticipation, perhaps, but not fright, as I'm armed with the knowledge I can stop this at any time. While Jon's tactile reassurance continues, I hear someone come up and speak to Jon. In my position, it's not possible to see who, but I recognise the voice and shiver as I realise it's Donavan, he's talking quietly, but I'm just able to catch what he is saying,

He's taking some of the blame. According to Diamond, Donavan's a novice Dom. She'd suggested he might have been as nervous asking me, as I was to hear him, and that had made him over brusque in how he'd approached me. In her view, it had been mostly his fault. He'd gone about it all wrong and had been totally out of line. But she'd also confirmed what I already knew; my reaction had been over the top, and that Jon wouldn't be able to let me get away with that. I like Diamond; she's frank and honest.

Lying still and waiting, wondering when he's going to start, knowing I'm about to be spanked, all manner of thoughts going through my head. I don't want to take the easy way out, despite him offering it to me.. I'm still trying to process that he's as attracted to me as I am to him and how that makes me feel.

I never would have believed I'd be in this position. I suppress a giggle, as I realise what excellent research this is, though I never thought I'd be taking the practical! How much better I'll be able to write if I know what would be in my character's head at this precise moment. Though I'll still have to make up the pleasure side of it, I really can't see how being spanked could be enjoyable, especially if it's punishment. I'm glad Jon didn't restrain me; I think I would have flipped if he had, that definitely would be another trigger. Knowing I'm staying here of my own free will is enabling.

He's given me the time I need to settle, letting me churn things around in my head and come to terms with the situation I'm in. Not once has his hand stopped touching me, soothing me. Now, I'm anxious now for him to start. The sooner he begins, the sooner it will be over and done with.

He's rubbing me now. I've written about this and know he'll be bringing the blood to the surface of my skin of my buttock cheeks so I don't bruise. No one's ever touched me so intimately and so gently. *I like it.* Before I can process that thought, without warning, his hand lifts and comes down. Hard. *Fuck that hurt!* It was harsher than I was expecting, the whack pushing me out of position. Now I tense, waiting for the next one, not sure if I'll be able to take much more, but willing to give at least another try. When nothing happens, I remember that I have to move back into position. I shift my bum and steady myself.

His hand gently touches my back. "Relax, don't tense."

I take a breath and try to let the tension leave my body. Easier said than done.

Thwack!

I move forwards again with the blow, but get back into

position quicker this time, and relax without the prompt. The third one follows. My skin feels alive, stinging and burning, but as my body processes the pain it has an effect I didn't expect. I get a tingling feeling in between my legs and realise I'm wet with arousal and the knowledge makes me squirm in embarrassment, remembering my exposed position.

"Give me a colour." His voice breaks into my concentration.

For a moment it's I have difficulty understanding what he's asking, then it's the truth that comes out when the word leaves my mouth in a gasp, "Green."

I'm not moving so much now, almost leaning back into his hand as it contacts with my rear. He spanks me on the upper thigh, and that one hurts, and he quickly follows it up with another on the other side. Warmth floods through me as more blows come; raining down one after the other. I begin to move into them; my clit is throbbing now, my womb contracting. I don't know what I'm thinking, it's impossible to do anything other than feel. There are tears on my face, but I'm not upset. I don't know why I started to cry.

Then all of a sudden, he stops, "All done, Mia." He leans over me, massaging and caressing my sore bum cheeks, "Colour?"

I'm almost upset it's over and have no hesitation in telling him, "Green."

He whispers into my ear. "I'm going to touch you now."

I'm uncertain, not grasping what he means so nod, not quite sure if he was asking permission or warning me what he's going to do, but he seemed to be waiting for my gesture. And then I find out why he cautioned me, his hand moves slowly down my back, over my burning backside until he slides it below me, into that private place that has been untouched for seven years. I freeze, the word Red coming to my lips, but the desire to utter it retreats as he begins to stroke gently from my clit to my opening;

his fingers gliding smoothly with no resistance, and I try to hide my face as I know I'm blushing deep red.

"You're very wet, sweetheart."

I'm well aware of that and mortified he must realise how much the spanking turned me on.

"Will you stay here for me? There's something I want to try, something I think you'll like. I won't hurt you."

At the moment, I'm frightened to move, scared he might be able to read my expression and know just what he's doing to me. Then I remember he's an experienced Dom, he's probably very much aware without me voluntarily giving it away. I want to please him, more than anything. I don't feel capable of producing words, so I again, I just bob my head to indicate my compliance.

He leaves me briefly but returns before I have a chance to become worried. Again he brushes his hands over my back, and then he lifts them. The next thing is a light dusting of something, and I'm puzzled for a second before I realise he must using a flogger. But oh, so gently. The feeling is incredible, as though he's massaging my entire back, bum and thighs. I lean into the flogging; the sensation almost too good. Seeing my reaction he puts more force into the blows, but it's not causing pain, just a slight stinging that's making my back feel warm like being exposed to the sun. My womb and every internal muscle start to pulse, and quivers run up and down my spine as my arousal increases tenfold. My clit feels swollen; I'm tingling all over.

As though from a distance I hear the sound of the flogger hitting the floor as he throws down. Then his hand touches me once more. I no longer have the energy to be embarrassed, even though I know I'm so wet my moisture is starting to run down my legs. I let out a moan, unable to hold it back as his touch feels so good. He keeps stroking me, gently, circling his fingers around my clit, getting closer and closer to where I need them, but not invading me, not pushing inside. As I relax, trusting him not to go further than I'm ready for, I move instinctively, trying to get him to the right spot, but he's the one in control, putting his other hand on the middle of my back, holding me still. Expertly he circles his fingers, getting nearer, until finally reaching that bundle of nerves where I so desperately need his touch. His fingers start strumming. My tension builds again, but this time not from apprehension. I've never felt anything like this before; my womb is clenching rhythmically, and every muscle in my body goes taut. I'm completely out of control, and I don't know what to do.

"Let it happen; I've got you." His voice both commands and soothes me, "Come for me."

My lungs stop inhaling air; an intense feeling rises inside me like an explosion, and suddenly I'm falling, waves and waves of ecstasy flooding over me. Then he's stroking and soothing me, bringing me back down to earth. My tears start to fall in earnest, wracking sobs shaking my body, and my mind floats away.

I come to slowly, consciousness gradually returning to find I'm lying cuddled close on Jon's lap covered with a soft blanket. We're sitting on a couch, and he's holding my head tight to his chest, his warm, smooth skin wet with my tears. I turn even closer into his body and wrap my arms around him. Never before have I felt this emotional, nor had the desperate need to be in such intimate proximity to anyone. As soon as he realises I'm awake he kisses the top of my head. He speaks to someone, thanking them: I feel, as well as hear, his voice rumbling against my ear.

Now he returns his attention to me, lifting my chin until reluctantly I'm forced to look at him, I'm embarrassed, and fearful of what I'll see on his face. But he's smiling, he looks pleased and happy. "Alright?" he asks me, reaching around me to get a bottle of water and bringing it to my mouth. As he tells me to drink, I realise I'm parched. Taking hold of the bottle, I greedily quench my thirst.

As the cool liquid refreshes me, I realise exactly how much he's done for me; he's given me something I never thought I'd have. He's pushed me to experience things I've only ever read and written about, leaving me beyond grateful. Abruptly I realise he's awoken a craving inside. *I want more. I want it all.* Pushing the bottle of water away, I grab what little courage I have, getting out the words before I have a chance to change my mind. "Fuck me, Jon."

His face doesn't change as he shakes his head, still looking at me oh so gently, as he resolutely refuses my request, "No, Mia."

At once I'm ashamed, my feelings of euphoria vanish. Jon's rejecting me. *What's wrong with me?* My thoughts of not being enough for him were obviously right. *He doesn't want me.* "Why? Why not?" It comes out as a whisper, but I have to know, have to hear him say he doesn't want to get involved with someone as inexperienced as me. Let's face it; I didn't exactly show myself in a good light tonight.

He strokes his hand over my face, "Not here." He tells me softly.

What does he mean? Then I remember what he's said to me, no sex in the main room. "What about the private rooms?" I have one more try; it kills me that he's turning me down. *Doesn't he know how much nerve it took to ask?* I look away from him, humiliated.

He doesn't let me get away with that, turning my head so I'm forced to face him again. "For one thing, sweetheart, it's against the rules of the club because you haven't submitted your test results yet."

"But I haven't had sex…"

He lays his finger on my lips to silence me. "I know. But rules are rules. I'm a Master Dom here, Mia, and co-owner of the club. I can't be seen to disregard the safety measures we've put in place."

I start a little. He *owns* the club? My eyes narrow in confusion.

"And anyway, I'm not going to fuck you, sweetheart. When I take you to bed, we won't be fucking; we'll be making love. At least, the first time." With those words, he reaches down and touches his lips to mine. I'm so taken aback by his words, which don't appear to spell out the rejection I feared, that I allow him easy access, and his tongue sweeps into my mouth. I may be inexperienced but there's much more than just lust in his kiss, there's emotion too. Responding with everything I have, I try to let him know through the mating of our mouths that my feelings run deep for him as well.

It's some minutes before we break apart. Pulling my head into his chest he rests his chin on my hair, after staying in that position for a few seconds, he then gently pushes me away.

"Time to go," he murmurs. Stretching out his hand, he picks up the clothes that had been so thoughtlessly discarded earlier and, loosening the blanket slightly to give him access, slips my corset back on and gently starts lacing it up. "Second time tonight, Mia." He laughs. "I'll be getting a reputation for putting clothes *on!*"

I sob and laugh all at the same time. He hands me my skirt, and I wriggle into it, and then accept his help to rise to my feet. Cognisant I'm missing something, I hold out my hand. He cocks his head to one side as though he doesn't understand.

"Thong?" I prompt him.

He chuckles. "I'm hanging onto that."

CHAPTER 17

Jon

Three years ago

I was declared fit and returned to full duty some five months ago, delighted to get back to my role of providing close protection to Nijad, jet-setting all over Europe, and even a couple of flying visits to the States. My life was never dull.

Now I was returning to Paris with the sheikh, having spent the last couple of weeks making one of his obligatory family visits to Amahad. Seated in the comfort of the Kassis family jet, I was enjoying a quiet laugh to myself at Nijad's expense. The, admittedly very attractive, flight attendant was blatantly making her availability for a quickie in the bedroom at the rear of the plane quite obvious to him. I had to grin. His draw for women was legendary with his devastating good looks which even I had to admire, even if I was a fully paid-up member of the het club myself. Of course, his vast fortune didn't hurt either. But I knew he wouldn't take her up on the offer, he'd got a girlfriend in the French city at that time, and while he could be a womaniser, once Nijad was committed to someone, he practised strict fidelity while he was with them.

After I had watched him turn her down with the ease of long practice, I thought about the weeks ahead in Paris. In this European city, my workload would be light. Nijad enjoyed his independence and relative, fiercely protected anonymity there so I wouldn't need to be with him twenty-four-seven, only *accompanying him when he had an official engagement. Of course, the palace assumed I was with him full-time, but I'd long given up trying to argue with him. He was adamant he didn't need that level of protection in that city. But I was never far away, staying close by his apartment in a small but comfortable pension.*

I parted company with Nijad at the airport. He collected his beautiful Agusta motorbike which he'd left in storage, one so rare, even with my new fortune I wouldn't have been able to get my hands on the same model. So I watched, with not a little envy, as the leather-clad biker sheikh disappeared into the distance. Then I went and collected the standard Grade A owned SUV from the long term car park. It was just another return to Paris, exactly like any other.

Present day

Grinning, I see Mia wanting to protest when I refuse to part with her thong, but as she's still partly dazed from the events of the night she accepts it with just a little show of outrage, followed by a huff of a laugh. I couldn't have been more proud of this woman tonight; I've pushed her boundaries far beyond anything I'd expected to. I took a risk in touching her so intimately, all the time watching in case my touch parachuted her back into her nightmares, but her reaction was more than I could have dreamed.

I'd been monitoring her closely, more judiciously than I'd ever observed a sub before. My total concentration on every minuscule response of her body, reading her reactions second by second, ready to stop the instant I took her too far. My complete absorption in her reactions shooting me into Dom space, something I didn't expect to achieve tonight. After years of working with a vast variety of subs I've become jaded, and with anyone else getting me to that same level of satisfaction would have involved a complex and lengthy scene. But with Mia? Her reactions had been so genuine, her surprised pleasure in the response of her body affected me on a level deep down inside me, and not purely in a physical way.

Her tears seem to have been liberating. She shows no guilt or remorse after her very public display and that out of the blue offer to take things a step further blindsided me. Although I could do with the release she was offering, I can go without for now. Yes, before long I'll be fucking Mia, but it will be at the right place, at the right time, so I can make it special for her. She deserves that. But I won't be waiting long; it will happen, very soon. And tonight we'll be sleeping in the same bed. She'll have no say about that.

Diamond was, well, a real diamond tonight, reading the riot act to Donavan, taking care of Mia and even offering to clean the equipment so I could focus on my girl and make sure she came down gently from the subspace she'd so obviously achieved. As I lead Mia across the main room, I seek out Diamond again, asking one more favour of her, to go and get Mia's coat with her, staying to keep her company while I'm changing back into my street clothes. I remain anxious not to leave her alone.

When I come back out to the lobby, I grin as I see Mia's writing down Diamond's phone number. It pleases me she seems to have made a friend. Whether she'll make contact for support or knowing her, it might be for research, but either way, the girls appear to get on.

And thus Mia's first visit to Club Tiacapan, *my* club, the place I'm so proud of, is over. I hope it won't be her last.

The ride home is uneventful, hardly any traffic this time on a Saturday night, or rather early Sunday morning, so I take the route passing through the city of London, taking advantage that there's no congestion charge on a weekend. A few revellers are still out in Piccadilly Circus, but that's only to be expected. Once back at Docklands, as we take the lift to my apartment she leans on me; it's not hard to tell she's already half asleep. Inside, I take her straight through to my bedroom. She sways, as I leave her briefly to turn back the bed and I can tell she's dead on her feet. I take off her coat and start to undress her. Her eyes widen, and she puts on hands on mine. Her earlier courage has fled her, and she's now worried about how this night might end so hurriedly I reassure her.

"You're sleeping with me tonight, sweetheart. Just sleeping, lying in the same bed. Nothing else is going to happen."

She gazes at me as if determining whether I'm being honest, while at the same time, trying to stifle a huge yawn. It's noisy, and as she puts her hand over her mouth, in embarrassment, she giggles as she tries to suppress it. It breaks the tension of the moment. "I'm going to fall asleep before I get into bed." She tells me with a tentative smile.

I move my hands, and she takes hers away and lets them fall to her sides, giving me non-verbal permission to continue what I was doing. I'm honoured by her trust, as I take off her corset and skirt. Then I lift her naked body and place her on the bed. This last day has been an all too welcome interlude from the unwanted attentions of the person threatening her, but tomorrow's another day, he won't have given up. But at least, for now, those horrors seem far away. And the events of tonight have helped her forget them; she's more at ease than I've ever seen her.

Once she's settled, I remove my own clothing, just slinging them over the back of the chair rather than putting them away as I'd usually do, deciding I'll bother about it all in the morning. I'm too eager to hold the woman who's caught me unawares with her gorgeous looks, her warm character, and her bravery.

She's ensnared me. My cock's throbbing and is as hard as nails — I'm a man after all — so I keep on my boxers to ensure I don't scare her, and try to send a stern message to that errant part of my body that there'll be no playtime tonight. Climbing into bed, I pull her against me so she's spooned, her back against my front. She struggles with a slight resistance, but I'm not letting her go. It feels so right to hold her. Gently I kiss her neck, telling her softly to go to sleep.

Within moments her breathing levels out, and all the tension in her limbs disappears. She's out like the proverbial light. I'm not so lucky. I close my eyes, knowing sleep is going to evade me for some time. Lying this close to her, my dick is trying to work itself out of my underwear, berating me for not losing my control and acting on my baser instincts. Not wanting to disturb her, I don't move away, and so lie in torturous agony, wishing I could be deep inside her. It's not doing me any favours concentrating on the naked woman by my side. To distract myself, I try to force my thoughts away from the softness in my arms and onto less stimulating matters instead. Her stalker.

While she was in the beauty salon today, I'd gone back to the office but despite spending all day on the problem, we ended up only a smidgeon closer to finding out who her rapists were so many years ago. Vanessa and Nafisa have had some luck contacting the list of people that Mia and Anna supplied, and getting more names to follow up, but so far they've come up with only a few not particularly promising, leads. We know they had a van, so at least one of them must have been over seventeen, as we're working on the assumption that they were driving legally. Of course, even that assumption could be wrong. But a couple of party-goers had told us that some of the gatecrashers were older and possibly not from the same, or, indeed, any school at all. One person remembers seeing two men who seemed out of place, but so far we've got no description to go on. But we're still exploring that avenue.

And then there's the idea of the wannabe Dom. Could someone have thought she based her last book on them? I haven't had any feedback from Sean yet from his trawl round the BDSM clubs, but that could take a bit of time. And of course, it's still only conjecture that one of Mia's abusers and the wannabe Dom are one and the same. Mia thinks she protects her identity, but there are ways to find out if someone has a reason to do so. What if the wannabe Dom found out the connection between Dexie and the young girl he abused so long ago? *Or am I making too much of a leap?* Of course, it could be a wannabe who has no connection with her past at all.

Even though she's sleeping, I pull her closer to me, knowing I'll do anything to keep this woman safe. The thought of someone taking her by force, causes cramping in my guts.

Although in clubs like the one I co-own we make sure anyone joining with suspect motives is quickly weeded out – and that's if they get past our robust screening process in the first place – there are a few types who think BDSM is legalised abuse, and unfortunately, a handful of clubs have the environment that lets them get away with it. It's a dangerous world, and there's a thin line to be walked between a true D/s relationship, and an excuse for someone to mistreat the person who's giving them their trust. The thought there could be a rapist hanging around BDSM clubs and preying on innocent women is a chilling one.

And getting back to the threats themselves. What's his end game? Does he want money, recognition? Or, if it is the same man who took her before, does he want to abduct her again? Is he out to cause her physical harm or, as those fucking lilies suggest and messages suggest, is a real threat to her life?

Once again, I get angry about the gun regulations in the UK. I'd feel far happier if I knew I could put down a potential killer before they could cause harm. If I want to keep my job and my freedom, I'm bound by the laws of the country. A criminal has no cares about such restrictions, and guns, if you know where to look, are not too hard to find. Even in England. As a private CPO, I'm not allowed to carry a weapon even to protect a diplomat unless I went back to the SAS or joined the police. If a real threat against Mia's life were recognised, I wouldn't be able to be armed, despite my military service and long years of protecting high-ranking officials in other countries. Even carrying a knife could get me in trouble! If I find myself up against someone with a gun, my only legal option is to call on the armed police to help but by the time they arrived I'd probably be looking down a barrel and it would be too late. So to protect her, I'll have to make sure I keep her out of her unknown stalker's way. There's no way of telling just how capable or how prepared he is.

He's going to strike again. Deep down, I know it. Just as I'm certain, his actions are going to escalate. I run my hand down Mia's arm, silently vowing that while there's breath in my body I'll look after her. I've put my life on the line in my job before now but never have I felt the same sense of personal responsibility and commitment as this. No one is going to hurt Mia. No one.

I don't know what time I eventually fall asleep, but I wake with the sun streaming through the window having forgotten to draw the curtains the night before. Mia's beginning to stir in my arms, and I move slightly back from her, not wanting to scare her with my predictable hard-on. Let's be honest; my morning wood would have been there had there been a woman in my bed or not, but it's throbbing with greater urgency as if it can sense an available target. Pushing her gently out of my arms, I swing my legs over the side of the bed as she wakes and stretches, emitting a delightful little moan. My cock twitches, trying to tell me to get back under the covers. Discreetly I look away, as she realises her state of undress and pulls the sheet up over her breasts.

"Hi." Apparently feeling suitably covered she greets me, but there's nervousness in her voice.

Thinking it's probably safe to look, I turn back. "Hi, yourself. Sleep okay?" She looks mussed from sleep, with a bad case of bed hair and the makeup she was too tired to remove last night has smeared across her face so she resembles a panda. I've never seen such a beautiful sight in my bed in the morning.

She nods. It was a rhetorical question; I know she slept soundly. It's me who's bleary eyed from lack of rest. But I notice she's agitated, uneasy. She's like an open book, and I can tell the exact point when the memories of the night before come back to her.

"Jon, I…"

I go to her and place my finger over her lips. "You were wonderful last night, Mia."

She looks up at me, her eyes wide, moisture in the corners showing she's trying not to cry, "But I messed up," she whispers.

I shake my head firmly, compelling her to believe me. "No. No, you didn't. If anyone did, I did. I won't leave you alone again. I'm your Dom, Mia. No one else touches you."

My words seem to sink in, and a tentative smile replaces the threat of tears. She thinks about it for a moment. "Are you going to take me to the club again?"

"Do you want to go?"

She looks down, her cheeks flushing as she remembers. What happened last night must have been overwhelming for her. I hold my breath, waiting for her answer. I want her so badly, want her in my life. But my life includes the club, and it will be hard for me to stop being a Dom. *Would it be better to sell my shares in Club Tiacapan, if I can't personally play there?* When she speaks again, I give a huge sigh of relief.

"I'd like to, I think," she murmurs. "Yes, I want to. Jon, I *enjoyed* it! I'd have never have thought it, but I did!"

Unable to help myself, I reach over, putting my hand in her hair, pulling her towards me and kissing her so she's left in no doubt how much that pleases me. The touch of her lips has a predictable effect, and I shift to try to ease myself, knowing now is not the time or the place to take things further. So I draw away slowly. "I'm going to get dressed," I tell her, "Then I'll get some breakfast for us."

A shower revives me, and I go and busy myself in the kitchen while she's getting washed and ready.

I'm an old fashioned guy and still have Sunday papers delivered preferring the hard copy to reading them online. I go down to the foyer and collect them. Mia's dressed when I return, and I soon find she's so easy just to be with; no uncomfortable silences, no need for unnecessary conversation, just a relaxed atmosphere and a companion I enjoy having in my home. We spend a lazy Sunday morning reading the news, discussing our views on events and laughing over the exploits of celebrities. I find her company easy to enjoy; her sense of humour matches mine, and while not all of our opinions coincide we amicably debate those where we differ. I take her to lunch at a pub on the waterfront, and then we take a leisurely drive back to her cottage in Epping.

As we turn off the M25, she starts to fidget in her seat, and I know she's becoming anxious, worried in case her stalker has visited her home again. I'd checked the camera feed before we left the apartment and had seen nothing except for those blasted, but admittedly adorable deer once again, munching on her plants, and the security alarms have been quiet, so I'm not too concerned and tell her so.

Pulling the McClaren up behind her Fiesta, I leave her

waiting with a worried look on her face, while I check out the house, but find everything exactly how it should be. There's nothing waiting for her in her letterbox that's of any interest, just a few flyers and a couple of official looking letters. She noticeably relaxes, as I wave her inside. It's been three days now since we've had any contact from her stalker. I don't take much comfort in that, convinced that he's not just going to go away. But Mia seems reassured, and her pleasure at being home is evident.

She offers to cook for us, and I don't hesitate to agree, seeing she appears to be relishing the task and looking forward to seeing what she's going to make. I sense she enjoys being creative in the kitchen. Having a number of emails to check and work through, I stay in the lounge but can hear her pottering about, rummaging in cupboards and rattling pots and pans. After a while, she comes in, smiles at me, delves into her bag to find her iPhone and takes it with her. Shortly I hear music playing. She's got it on shuffle, and it appears she's got an eclectic taste. There's some of the heavier rock I enjoy, but also lighter stuff. She seems particularly fond of anthems. Suddenly I hear her singing along to Robert Palmer's 'Doctor, Doctor' and I can't resist going through the small hallway to the kitchen at the end. I pause in the doorway, and suck in air rapidly to steady myself; she's not only singing along, but dancing to the rhythmic beat as she peels and chops vegetables. She's shaking her bum in time to the music and twisting her hips. Her voice might not be quite in tune, but boy, can that girl move! I stand, entranced by the undulating movements of her arse, unable to keep a grin spreading over my face as my dick grows harder by the second, very much in approval of the view. Just before the song ends she turns and sees me, her cheeks reddening.

"Don't mind me," I say, chuckling.

"Huh!" She huffs, then with a grin, goes back to what she's doing, ignoring me.

I stay where I am, anticipating the next song, and hoping she'll dance for me again. In my mind, I have a vision of her dancing naked. If the throbbing in my cock can be caused by simply seeing her dancing fully clothed, one day it has to happen. But when the next track starts it's a slow song and one of my favourites, 'Waiting in the Weeds' by the Eagles. It's so appropriate I can't hold myself back, as the music plays I go over to her, carefully remove the paring knife from her hands, clasp my arms around her, and we start to sway in time to the music. I put my hand behind her head, lift her chin, and pull her lips to mine. As I hold her close, I know she has to feel my hardness against her showing how much I want her, but she doesn't try to move away. If anything she holds me tighter and rubs herself against me. She shivers, but instinctively I recognise it's not from fear. I'm lusting for her, but there's something else, something so much more. Something I never thought I'd feel, and that I didn't even know I was capable of.

I draw back. My hand is keeping her head in place, so she's looking up into my eyes. "I've been waiting in the weeds, Mia. Waiting for you." I move my hands down until I'm touching her hips and pull her tight into my body, letting her feel me so she's left in no doubt about my intentions, giving her an opportunity to stop this. My hands run up and down her body, eliciting a soft moan from her mouth as she clings to me as though she doesn't want to let me go. "It's time, Mia. I want to make love to you." I gently nuzzle the top of her head.

"I'm scared, Jon," she whispers against my chest. "I don't know what to do." She tenses, just a little.

"I do." I chuckle softly. Then reassure her, "We'll take it slow. I won't do anything you don't want me to. You've still got your safeword, remember? You'll always have your safeword."

Moving my hands up and down her back, I gently caress her until she relaxes in my arms again. Pulling back I take her hand, pause for a second, relishing the sight of this beautiful woman beside me, before leading her upstairs to her bedroom.

I'm going to take this very slow. In her room, I take her into my arms again and gently bring my lips to hers. She responds by opening her mouth, and our tongues dance together. Her taste enthrals me, and I deepen the caress, clearly showing my desire as I hold her tightly, demanding more of her as she responds. When we can't get enough of each other, can't get sufficient satisfaction from just the meeting of our lips, I step back and reach down, taking the ends of her T-shirt, and I hold it gently, my intention all too clear. She doesn't resist. There's a look of trepidation in her eyes, but definitely excitement there too. Encouraged I pull her top off over her head and throw it away, not caring where it lands. I put my lips on her neck and let my teeth gently touch her skin, nibbling and abrading, and then sucking, tempted to leave my mark there, but somehow able to resist. She trembles again, and I smile against her skin. My hands are unsteady as I reach behind her back and unclasp her bra, an action I've had much practice at now becoming awkward with my nerves. I have to make this good for her. I'm going purely on instinct, I've never taken anyone so innocent before.

She was naked before me, yesterday, but this is different, more personal and intimate. So I proceed slowly, gently drawing the straps off her shoulders, not wanting to scare her. Automatically she puts her hands on her chest to stop it falling away, embarrassed to expose herself. I kiss her again, sweeping my tongue into her mouth, gradually increasing the pressure. She tastes so sweet and, as I deepen the kiss, she presses against me. Putting my hands on hers, I move her back, and lightly pull her arms down to her sides. Her bra drops away, and her breasts are exposed. If I didn't consciously make the effort to inhale, I wouldn't be getting air into my lungs as the sight is utterly breath-taking. They're not overly large but completely perfect. Perky, with dusky pink nipples. Taking another deep breath, I lean forwards to kiss each nipple taking my time, pulling one into my mouth and sucking it, swirling my tongue around the peak until it hardens, then I change to give the other the same treatment. She gasps, and staggers as if her legs have gone weak. Her nipples are erect, slightly reddened and standing out from her breasts after my attentions. She looks absolutely stunning.

"Give me a colour." I murmur against her skin, remembering to check.

"Green," she answers without hesitation, her voice husky and low, "Very green."

I continue mouthing her breasts, using my teeth to give a gentle nip. It's hard to stop, but my dick throbs, encouraging me to hurry up and move onto the main event. Still nuzzling her I drag my hand down her stomach, taking the time to circle her navel, causing her to jump and give a little giggle. *She's ticklish!* Filing that thought away, my fingers continue their journey until I reach the button on her jeans. I pause for a moment, to give her time to object if she wants to, but she says nothing. Fumbling to complete an action I've done a hundred times before, until eventually, I undo it and then draw down the zip. Her shallow breaths show her excitement as I put my thumbs in her waistband of her jeans and slowly ease them down her legs. Folding to my knees, I lift her feet one by one, taking off her shoes and removing her trousers completely. She's standing there in plain white pants, nothing fancy. Right now they have to be the sexiest garment I've ever seen. My hands shake as I touch the last item of clothing she's wearing. She puts her hands on my shoulders and stiffens as I go to remove them, but utters no protest.

I take a second to admire the sight in front of me, shaking my head slightly at the way this woman affects me. My pre-cum dampens the denim around my crotch, and I can't remember how long it's been since I've been so turned on— if I ever have. My cock's throbbing, twitching, constricted in my jeans which feel a size too small. But I don't want to rush this. Proceeding cautiously, ultra-conscious of any stiffening of her limbs, I put my hands on her arse and gently pull her naked body into me. Her unique scent of arousal fills my nostrils as I press my mouth against her newly waxed mound. "You're so ready for me, Mia." I want to bury my head between her thighs, and not emerge for days, but she has different ideas.

"I want to see you," her breathless voice interrupts me.

At this moment, I'm not a Dom; I'm just a man. I don't want to frighten her with my control; *I want to make love to her.* So, fair's fair, if she wants, *needs* to see me, who am I to argue? I stand, and putting my arm over my head grasp the collar of my T-shirt and pull it off in one fluid moment, dropping it, letting it lie where it falls. Her hand reaches out and strokes my chest, toying for a moment with the hair I have growing there, then tracing my scars, coming to rest on the evidence of the gunshot wound. Her fingers circle it as though assessing the damage the bullet caused.

She looks up in consternation and observes softly, "It was so close."

I give a gruff laugh; I know what she's thinking. An inch over and it would have gone straight through my heart. A few broken ribs and a punctured lung seemed a small price to pay for my life. And for the life of a friend, the man who became a brother to me. I'd do it all over again for the same result. But I don't want to dwell on the past; it's the present that needs my attention. "I'm alive," I tell her quietly. Nothing else matters.

Her hand continues to explore, she toys with my nipples and

then glances up as if wanting assurance she's doing the right thing. My gut clenches as the realisation hits me again that she's a virgin. Perhaps not untouched, but I'm the first man she's fondled voluntarily, and the first who'll treat her with the love and respect she deserves. For a second, the responsibility of making this a good experience all but overwhelms me. Nonetheless, I'm determined what we do here today will erase more memories of her past. Then, when her hand moves down across my stomach following the thickening trail of hair leading down to my waistband of my jeans I forget everything but the need to be inside her. She inhales sharply and gets up the nerve to undo my belt, then quickly unfastens the button at my waistband as if she doesn't want to pause and lose her courage. Holding the zip, she moves it down gently, as if afraid she might catch me, but I've not gone commando today, so there's no need for concern. She copies my actions, sliding my jeans down my legs, falling to her knees to remove my shoes and socks, and lifting my feet until I'm free. She hesitates, throwing a glance at me as though asking for consent, then takes hold of my boxers and pulls them down.

And I'm free at last, my cock springing up ready and willing, almost reaching my navel. Distressed, she rears back, clearly startled and afraid of my size.

"Jon, I..."

Raising my hand gently to her cheek, I try to reassure her. "We'll fit, sweetheart. There's no need to be worried. We'll go at your pace, as slow as you want. And you know how to stop it if it gets too much." She locks eyes with mine for a moment and then remembers to breathe again. "Touch me," I instruct, remembering that her abductors kept her blindfolded, so she's probably never seen a cock in the flesh before, and even then it was used as an instrument of pain. Understanding why she's nervous, I decide to give her time to familiarise herself with my body, knowing I'm well endowed, larger than average in length and girth.

After casting me another nervous glance, she tentatively reaches out her hand and fondles my cock which jumps at her touch, and she backs away as if faced with an untamed animal, something not too far from the truth at the moment. I grit my teeth, forcing myself to hold back the commands which come naturally to me, allowing her to take this at her pace. Almost immediately she returns and tries to wrap her hand around me. Her fingers don't quite meet, but she grasps me and gently strokes from head to root. I stand straight, sucking in my stomach as her untutored touch isn't far off making me lose control, and triggering another few drops of pre-cum to ooze out. I clench my fists at my sides. I've had many women pet my dick, but never one who's moved me quite like this. Then, she leans forward, and her tongue comes out to lap at the salty drops glistening from the slit. My nails dig into my palms to stop myself exploding.

"You don't have to," I tell her gruffly, proud that I'm still able to speak.

"Can I?" *She's asking my fucking permission?* Taking a second to glance down to check this is something *she* wants, rather than thinking it's expected of her, but when I see her tongue come out to lick her lips in anticipation, my answer is to grasp her hair and pull her towards me. She opens her mouth and takes me in, her lips swirling around the head, tasting my next bout of uncontrollable pre-cum and licking down the seam. She can't take me in very far, but she uses her hands as well. She massages my balls, then strokes up the shaft while gently sucking me in the whole time.

"Jesus, woman! Where did you learn that?" I'm on the verge of coming, so have to push her away.

Knowing she's pleased me, she looks up with a satisfied grin on her face like the cat who's got the cream. "From my research. I've written about it, but I've not put it into practice before." Her husky voice and playful answer almost do me in, and then she has to go and add, "Am I doing it right?"

I help her to her feet. "You're definitely on the right track, honey. Your technique's pretty fucking good." Before she has time to think, I sweep her into my arms and carry her to the bed, dropping her in the middle with enough force that she bounces. It makes her laugh. Good. Sex should be fun. I come down on top off her, my mouth covering hers, letting her know the depth of my desire in my kiss. She responds eagerly; she's as aroused as I am and as I taste myself on her lips I'm seconds away from exploding.

Breaking away, I put my weight on my arms, and shuffle down the bed slowly, taking my time to enjoy all that's on offer, pausing to kiss her neck, then loitering to take another opportunity to enjoy her lovely breasts, teasing her nipples into even harder peaks with my teeth. She squirms beneath me. I trail my lips across her flat stomach, noticing how firm and fit she is. I try to touch and taste every part of her, noting for future reference where she's ticklish or sensitive, learning her body and her responses. As I move lower, I rise so I'm kneeling and place my hands behind her thighs to pull up her legs and bend them at the knees, pushing them open, exposing her completely.

Her muscles tighten, and a fearful squeak escapes her lips, so slowly I stroke her inner thighs until she releases her tension again.

"Colour, Mia?"

She takes a second to respond, and then says hesitantly, "Greeeeen."

I'll take that as a Yellow, and stay vigilant to her reactions. Fuck! She's so wet, it's soaking through the duvet cover, her juices coating her in a shiny sheen. Like petals her labia surround her gorgeous cunt, it's the prettiest I've ever seen, a slightly darker shade of dusky pink, but almost matching her nipples. Unable to resist I have to have a taste. With a quick glance to check she's still on board with this, her chest rising and sinking as she pants with desire, not fear, I lower my head and my tongue sweeps from her clit to her opening. The taste of her goes straight to my brain, making me feel like an addict with his first taste of heroin, knowing from the sweet and salty tang I'll never be able to get enough. She gives a surprised gasp as I start to lick in earnest, my tongue dipping inside her, and then swirling around her clit. She moans, and grabs at my head, but I'm relentless. She starts moving her hips, and I know she's trying to get me exactly where she needs me, but I stop and wait. I lift my mouth away and mumble. "Be still." Now I'm taking back control.

She obeys, and I start to give her what she wants again, but just as she starts to go rigid I move so my tongue sweeps into her opening knowing the longer her orgasm is held off, the better it will be. She groans incoherently pulling at my hair, and I chuckle into her sweet pussy. I'm determined to make this as amazing as I can, to make her forget her name, just who she is, and where she's come from, and all of her past. Lifting my head again I put one finger gently to her opening, moving it around to get her used to the feeling. She's still trying to push me down and seems unaware of what I'm doing. I put one finger inside her, and then a second. She stills and her body stiffens, but not with pleasure.

"Red!" she screams and struggles to get away. "RED! Get off me!"

I reel back in disgust with myself. I didn't read the signs! Knowing I have just a split second to make this up to her, I force my feelings of inadequacy into the background.

CHAPTER 18
Mia

Seven years ago

I was beyond shame. The agony unbearable; hurting all over from their vicious beatings and the perverse activities they'd submitted me to. When they started again, mercifully I passed out.

I came round, a sharp agonising pain in my chest as I gasped air into my starved lungs. I could barely move; there wasn't one part of me that didn't throb with pain.

"She's no fucking fun anymore!"

As if to prove his words, the crueller of the two didn't hesitate in giving me a sharp kick to my ribs Unable to register the new pain; I didn't react.

"What we going to do with her?"

There was a pause while the one in charge decided. "Put her back where we found her. She's no fucking use to us now." I heard footsteps, clothes rustling, and then felt breath against my ear. "Hope you enjoyed yourself, bitch! Never forget it was me who taught you everything."

Present day

Jon's making me feel so good. I try to writhe, but he won't let me and I quickly get the message. He's in charge and wants me to stay still. I'm so close to coming, so try to force myself not to move, understanding he won't continue until I obey his unspoken command. He starts pleasuring me again, and I'm almost there, reaching for that elusive high...

But then he moves his fingers *there*, inside me, touching where only my rapists had been before. Instantly I'm transported back in time, and Jon disappears, and it's one of my abusers probing my private place, and he's going to rape me!

My mouth opens, and I'm screaming and struggling to get away. "Red! RED! Get off me!"

The hand moves away immediately I speak, then strong arms enfold me, I push and shove, my legs trying to kick, wanting to escape but I'm unable to get loose.

"Shush. I've got you." The voice is soft, carrying authority, "Be still, Mia."

I'm lost in the past; I'm going to be hurt again.

"Mia, it's me. I'm not going to hurt you." As he reads my mind, homing in on my fears, his voice starts to break through the memories trapping me in the past. "Don't panic, I'm with you."

He stopped. Realising I'm not back in the dank building, grasping exactly who it is who's holding me tight, my tension begins to ease away, and I start to calm. Gently he kisses my forehead, and then my cheeks, and then my lips. His mouth takes mine, so softly at first, his touch so tender, then, as I start to respond, his lips press down more forcefully, forcing mine open, and sweeping his tongue inside. It's his taste that finally gets through to me, cutting through my fear. *I'm with Jon, not back with my abusers.*

As he continues to make love to my mouth, I return his kiss. Gradually I'm able to control and still my frantic efforts to escape, as visions of the past recede and then fade away. He relaxes his hold on me as my struggles lessen, and then lets me go completely, leaving me feeling bereft and cold. The last contact of our bodies is our lips, and then he breaks even that, pulling away from the kiss and sitting back on his haunches, watching me carefully, a look of distress on his face.

Tears start to trickle down my face, I look away unable to meet his eyes. "Oh my God, Jon, I'm so sorry."

Reaching out a slightly shaky hand, he turns my face towards him. "Nothing to be sorry for," he murmurs, "It's my fault, Mia. I pushed you too far, too soon. I should have read you better; you shouldn't have needed to use your safeword." His posture is stiff, and he seems disappointed.

I feel so awkward that I've ruined everything. What happens now? Should I get up, dress? Stay? My hand's flutter, I don't know what to do with them.

"Do you want to try this again?"

Looking up as I realise he's asked me a question, and his tone of voice, so full of regret and, for the first time from him, confusion and uncertainty. I see him watching me, and know he doubts himself, concerned he took me too far, too fast. But it was me, my stupid mind that ruined this for us. All at once I know if I end this now, my abusers have won. *Again.* It takes all my courage, but tentatively, still unsure my stupid memories won't get in the way, I nod.

After a second's more scrutiny, he seems to shake off his indecisiveness. As if he's carefully considering his every move, he touches my stomach, his hand gently trailing up and down. The sensation is soothing. He leans over and nuzzles my breasts, licking and sucking, while his fingers travel downwards. As if he's thrown a switch there's a fluttering in my womb as he arouses me all over again. He lifts his head.

"Look at me, Mia. Stay with me." His tone is commanding. "Eyes on me. Keep watching me. Don't think, feel."

He toys with my clit, his thumb circling, then, faster than I could have thought; he quickly brings me back to the point of no return. His gaze locks with mine; I can't look away, even if I had the inclination. He puts one finger inside me, and then another. All the time he's taking me higher and higher. His fingers curl round, and he reaches that special spot inside. *It's him; it's Jon. There's no one else here.* The feelings that start to overwhelm me keep me in the present, and then there's no room for thought at all as I start to come fast and hard, screaming out his name, and then screaming it out again.

"That's it, sweetheart, let it go. Come for me."

His words push me over the edge, and I give my all to him as he stays with me, continuing the intimate caress until my muscles stop pulsating.

Now he's moving over me, pushing my still quivering legs open, drawing up my knees and settling himself between them, not once taking his eyes away from mine. Keeping one hand in contact with me, he reaches the other to the bedside table and picks up a condom I hadn't noticed him place there. I hear the rustle of a packet opening, and then I see him smooth a condom down his hard and throbbing cock. A twinge from my womb as the sight of him confidently handling his large dick enthrals me. I take a deep breath, preparing myself for what's coming next. My body is still throbbing from the after effects of my tremendous orgasm; my limbs feel limp. Saying my safeword is the furthest thing from my mind.

When he starts to press into me, I have a moment of panic and close my eyes. "Eyes on me!" He's watching my every reaction.

Opening them again, I recognise the man who's vowed to protect me. The man who's done nothing to hurt me. As my tense muscles relax, he takes advantage, thrusting forwards until he is part way in. I gasp, he's so big. His width stretches me, the burn making me feel like I'm losing my virginity all over again. *And in some ways I am. This is how it was meant to be.* He stills, waiting for me to become accustomed to his size. With my eyes on his handsome face, his expression so caring, instead of wanting this to stop, *I want more*. With an unconscious movement, I squeeze my vaginal muscles.

"Fuck, Mia. That feels so good!"

His response sends a thrill through me. Experimentally I squeeze again, and it inspires him to move, slowly pulling out and back in again, all the time he's continuing to monitor my reactions. It's not enough. *I want more.* Reaching my hands behind him I grab his backside, pulling him into me. Encouraged, he thrusts, but with carefully controlled movement, moving further in with every pass until eventually he's in to the hilt and touching my cervix. Then he pauses to let me become used to the unfamiliar sensation. Slowly the pain and burn disappear, and now the feeling's so incredible I let out a loud moan.

He stays, and chuckles. "Tell me what you want."

Why isn't he moving? It takes me a few precious seconds to realise he's asked me a question. "More," I groan, greedily.

"More what?" There's mirth in his voice; he knows exactly what he's doing to me.

I take a breath; he wants me to be explicit. "I want you to fuck me," I gasp out. The desperate dirty words that I've only used on paper before, come from my mouth with no filter, catches me by surprise. The declaration he's torn from me incites him and he starts to drive into me, gently at first, then as I encourage him by my instinctive movements, speeds up until he's pumping in and out fast. Then as another orgasm is building, when he hits my g-spot but I can't quite get there, I need something more. Without me having to ask, he knows and reaches down to toy with my clit. Suddenly he pushes hard on top of it and I splinter apart, my internal muscles clutching at him. He hammers into me, once, twice more then stills, gasps and roars out his completion, his body jerking as he empties himself inside me.

"Oh, Mia, Mia." Tenderly he presses his forehead to mine, then rolls to his side, keeping his weight off me but pulling me close. We're both out of breath, our lungs heaving in time. I feel a sense of rightness, coupled with euphoria. His gentle, caring lovemaking has finally laid my ghosts to rest.

"Fuck, Mia. That was fantastic." His quietly spoken words sound genuine, making me gratified that it seems it was as good for him as it was for me. "I'm glad I was your first."

"Not technically…"

"Yes, I was. They don't count," he states firmly. "They're in the past. This is the first time you've made love. And I'm glad it was with me."

I snuggle into him, breathing in his unique manly scent, coupled with the aroma of sex. His arms tighten around me, as though recognising I never want him to let go. It's not just about sex or the amazing experience he's given me; it's the man himself. I want time with him; want to learn everything there is to know about him. So far he's shown me he's brave and caring. He's a Dom, and he certainly knows what he's doing in bed. And he cooks a mean breakfast! I want to get to know *him*, the man inside that handsome exterior; I want more from him than just his spectacular body. *But what does he want from me? Is this just a one night stand?*

Admitting my emotions are already involved, and that he already has the power to hurt me, I'm afraid to ask. But I'm also scared not to. I don't want to go on making this into something it isn't if he doesn't feel it too. He'd told me he wanted me as his sub but did he mean just in the club? What were we together out in the real world? And did he just mean until the case was over?

"I can hear your mind racing, Mia. What are you so busy thinking about?"

If this is just a one-time fling, now he's had me, and he's satisfied that itch, I need to know; I have to protect myself before I get in too deep. And I want to take that leap; already I know this isn't just about sex for me, however fantastic that was. Swallowing, I summon up the courage to ask, trying to prepare myself for rejection.

"What is this between us, Jon? I don't know how this works."

He gives a chuckle, "Neither do I."

Pulling out of his grasp, I sit up, braced on my elbows, and look at him concerned. "What do you mean?"

He sighs, laying back and putting one arm under his head. "I don't do relationships, Mia. Hey, hush!" He reaches out, his free hand holding me prisoner, "What I'm saying, is that I have no experience of committing myself to one woman. You know the lifestyle I live; my relationships with subs have all been time limited and contractual. But Mia, it isn't the going to be that way with you. I want more; I want to be your man and your man only." He sits up and hugs me to him, "I think you've bewitched me."

I hardly know what to say. This is new ground for to me, too.

"Right now, I'm not promising you a forever, Mia. We've not known each other long enough for that." He pauses, and covers his heart with my hand, "But for the first time in my life I've feelings that go deeper than what you do to my cock." A cheeky grin now spreads over his face, "Although I happen to love what you do to that particular part of me."

I snort a laugh; that's pretty obvious.

"I want to be exclusive with you, and I want it all. I won't see anyone else, and I don't want you to, either."

I immediately think of Diamond and the way she offered herself to him. "Won't you be disappointing a lot of subs?"

"Possibly." He shrugs, being honest. But he doesn't look like he's got any regrets.

I'm lost for words, a wave of intense emotion floods through me. I'm elated and on such a high that I want to make sure I haven't misunderstood him. "Are we in a relationship, Jon?" I hold my breath as I wait for his answer.

He gives me a broad smile. "Don't think I could stop now, even if I wanted to. You alright with that?"

Am I alright with that? This gorgeous man who makes me feel so good, who makes me feel so safe, so wanted. *Yeah, I think I'm just about alright with that.* My answer is to initiate a deep long kiss. When we break apart, he leaves the bed, going to the bathroom to dispose of the used condom. Returning to the bed, he manoeuvres me until I'm lying on my side, with him spooned behind me. His arms close around me. Gradually his breathing slows and I find myself mimicking him, then my eyes close, and without meaning to, I drift off to sleep.

"Hey, babe."

I don't know how long I was dozing, but now he's nudging me awake.

"Sweetheart," he tries again. When I roll over and murmur a protest, he grins at me, "I need feeding, babe. You going to cook, or shall we order in?"

"Shit!" I jump up having forgotten all about the meal I was going to make for him. I hadn't gotten very far with the prep, so I decide that another takeaway would be quicker. And besides, I don't have any energy to cook at the moment.

He's laughing at me. "Filthy mouth you've got there, sub. I should give you a swat for that, but I have a feeling I won't be getting fed anytime soon if I give you a spanking now."

My face goes red as I remember how turned on I'd been at the club when I felt his bare hand on my backside. *I never thought I could enjoy something like that.* Then I giggle, admitting that even the memory is starting to get me wet all over again. And he's probably right. If he carried out his threat that we wouldn't be leaving the bed for a while, and I'm already a little sore. So I make a rapid change of subject. "Indian, okay with you?"

He's still chuckling, as he lies there, butt naked, watching me try to scramble clumsily into my clothes; unused to having an audience. When I eventually get my T-shirt on the right way out, he deigns to start getting dressed himself.

Relaxed in each other's company, the evening passes swiftly with a tasty meal from my favourite local takeaway, followed by another memorable bout of lovemaking. All my appetites fully sated, I'm so tired that it takes no time at all after I get back to bed before I fall into a dreamless sleep.

* * * *

Monday mornings are typically dreary, but when I wake alone and hear the sounds of the shower running, a big sloppy grin comes to my face. It's not just the start of a new week; it's the beginning of a new life. *I've had a man in my bed, and I enjoyed it. And he's sticking around.* I stretch, wincing at the soreness in muscles unaccustomed from such exercise the night before. The grin's still there when he leaves the bathroom and comes into the bedroom. He's already fully clothed.

Coming across to the bed, he kisses me. "How are you feeling, sweetheart?"

"Fine," I answer him. Then expand, "Great!"

He gives me a critical look, assessing me, and then nods and smiles. "Get dressed, and then I want to talk." With that, he leaves me, and I hear him going downstairs.

Uh oh. That sounds ominous. I try to shake off a sudden burst of apprehension but shower and dress as quickly as possible. When I get down to the kitchen, he's just dishing up scrambled eggs and toast, and to top it off he's made coffee.

"Need to keep your strength up." He smirks as places a piled plate in front of me. As he leans over to steal another kiss, the gentle expression on his face reassures me.

I laugh. "I could get used to this." Then, as I take a mouthful of the perfectly cooked breakfast, I'm unable to suppress a moan. I take another and glance over to see he's still standing by the cooker. "You said you wanted to talk, you haven't had second thoughts, have you?" I put my fork down, as worry returns.

"Not about us, Mia. No." The words, accompanied by an intense look, compel me to believe him. He seats himself. "I just want to get things agreed up front. I'm a Dom, I can't help that, it's the way I'm wired. If I've spent time with someone in the past, we've usually had a contract agreed so we both know the expectations."

His words worry me; I know about contracts. And they usually have an end date. *Is he going to ask me to sign one?*

As if he knows what I'm thinking, he gives a quick shake of his head. "No, Mia. I don't want to have a contract with you. For the first time in my life, I just want to take things as they come. But I do want to get some things straight." He pauses to take a mouthful of eggs, washing it down with coffee before continuing. "I need control in the bedroom and the club, but I don't want a slave, so we'll be mostly equals outside of anything to do with sex." Another bite of his breakfast, then he carries on, "I don't want to tell you how to dress, how to act or what to do." He throws a sideways glance at me before he continues, "But I do want to take care of you, and that means I'll be looking out for your best interests. So sometimes I might break those rules, but only for your own good."

I smile, there doesn't seem to be anything wrong in what he's saying. From what I've already seen, I've no objections to him being in charge in bed. Heck, I wouldn't have a clue what to do.

We'd end up lying there like two logs if he waited for me to initiate anything. I decide to be cheeky.

"If you break the rules, Jon, do I get to punish you?"

He snorts a laugh and shakes his head, "I'm sorry, it doesn't work that way, pet." He puts more scrambled egg into his mouth, chews and then swallows, "Communication is key to our relationship, though, and you have to promise to speak to me, to tell me if I'm making you uncomfortable. I know what you need, Mia. Sometimes you might think I'm pushing you, but I'm only trying to stretch your boundaries, to explore something new. You're mine. You belong to me."

"Does that go both ways, Jon? Do you belong to me?"

He rubs a hand through his hair, and smiles ruefully, "Oh babe, if only you knew. You captivated me from the first day; I've been yours ever since I saw you." Then, his demeanour changes slightly.

Tilting my head to one side I look at him, and see he's looking a bit on edge which makes me suspicious. "What's up, Jon?"

"I'm going to push you today, Mia, and this comes under the heading of me caring for you, and doing what's best for you." His brief pause suggests it's something I'm not going to like. Inhaling deeply, he tells me, "I've made an appointment for you to see a doctor." He holds up his hand to stop me interrupting. "She's a good friend of mine and does a lot of testing for the club. She runs a private clinic. I rang earlier this morning."

All at once, my pleasure in the day disappears, and my hands start shaking. Going to a doctor is a hard limit for me. "No. I don't need to go, and I won't." I make my refusal adamantly.

"Mia, sweetheart," he comes over and kneels in front of me, brushing my hair out of my face. "You've never seen a doctor, have you? Fuck knows what those bastards did to you, but it's time you found out." His touch, the way he's rubbing his thumbs over the back of my hands is calming, and the shaking lessens. "There are other reasons too. Firstly, you need to get tested if you're going to play in the club; I stretched the rules for you last time, but I don't want to do that again. And lastly, there's a selfish reason. I've never had an exclusive relationship before; I've never taken anyone without a condom, never felt my cock inside a woman skin to skin. But I'd like that with you. I'd like that very much." Squeezing my hands he stares into my eyes, waiting for my reaction.

I put two and two together fast, "Are you asking me to go on the pill?" I break in. Goosebumps breaking out all over me as my nerves take hold, "Jon, I don't mind that, but I don't want to go to a doctor…"

Leaning forwards he presses his forehead to mine. His voice deepens, "I want my cock inside you shooting my cum up into your sweet cunt with no barriers, I want to see my spunk running out, mingling with the juices from your pussy. I want to feel you, with no barriers between us."

His dirty words are turning me on. None of his words upset me; that voice he uses makes me realise that's what I want too. To feel him, every part of him. *But to do go on the pill, I've got to consent to an internal exam.* Bastard, he's tempting me.

"So the doctor's appointment is for you?"

He looks a little sheepish and shrugs again. A smile slowly appears, "I admit I'm a bit selfish. I don't want to use condoms with you. But you need to get checked out; that's the most important thing." Leaving me, he goes back to the counter, picks up his by now cold cup of coffee, and drains it in one go. His face grows serious. "You need to have the full range of tests if you're going to come back to the club. We can't use the private rooms unless you do. I thought it would take a couple of weeks to get the appointment, but a friend of mine who's a doctor had a cancellation today, and as I called so early, I was able to take it."

Now sweat starts pouring off my brow; my hands grow clammy. The thought of a stranger examining *there* is terrifying. He's right; he's pushing me. And it's a step too far. He'll have to cancel. "Jon," I hesitate, wondering how to tell him, then just blurt it out. "I'm scared of having an examination."

I hear him let his breath out; it whistles through his teeth. He gets up, taking his empty plate and mine. "It's well past time you got checked out, sweetheart." He opens the dishwasher and begins to stack the dirty plates inside.

"But…" I begin.

He comes over to me, raising my head so I'm looking up at him. "No arguments. Mia, she's a decent woman, she'll understand and be careful with you. I'll make sure of it; I'll be with you, I promise. But this is something for your good, which you have to do. I have to push you. Do this for me, Mia." He uses that voice that makes my insides curl, the tone I have no defence for.

CHAPTER 19

Jon

Three years ago

After parking the SUV behind the pension, I grab my bags from the back seat and walk in. Registration was a brief formality thanks to the numerous times I'd stayed here. After that, I made my way to my normal room, removed my shoes, jacket and holster and settled on the bed. Nijad didn't need me today, so able to relax I close my eyes; after the early start and long journey the chance to have a nap is welcome.

I couldn't have slept long before I was woken abruptly by an alarm going off on my phone. Immediately on fully alert I jumped up, swiped the screen, putting my fingertip on the home key for identification. The security app came up—someone had set off the alarm at Nijad's apartment. FUCK IT! I should have ignored his orders and stayed close to him.

Setting a new world record I stepped back into my shoes, strapped on my holster, flung on my jacket to cover my gun and exited through the door in one seamless move. It was quicker to run the single block to Nijad's apartment than to take the car, so I was there in little more than a few minutes. I'd been trying to call him on the way, over and over, but every time it just rang through to voicemail. I was growing increasingly worried that I wasn't getting an answer, and my concern in no way lessened when I arrived at his apartment block horrified to see two ambulances and three police cars *had beaten me to it. What the fuck was going on?*

I raced inside and took the lift to the fifth floor, impatiently pushing the buttons hard as if that would make it rise faster. At the entrance to the Sheikh's home, two gendarmes stood guarding the door, one unsuccessfully trying to turn off the blaring alarm. After I had identified myself and shown my credentials, I quickly disarmed the system, and silence reigned. Finally, I was let in to find the person I was supposed to be protecting lying unconscious on the floor; one paramedic is checking his vitals, while another was preparing a stretcher to take him down to street level. Another pair of medics were treating a woman who I recognised as the Sheikh's girlfriend, Chantelle. Someone had viciously attacked her; her face was a mess, her eyes already blackening, one arm looked like it might have been broken and the other hugged across her ribs. The way she was holding herself suggested she'd taken blows to her torso as well.

As she was at least conscious, my first thought was for Nijad, anxious to know how badly injured he was. I started to go over to him but a man, who I assumed to be the detective in charge, moved in front of me to stop me.

"What happened?" I asked even though it was obvious there had been a break-in, and I was full of guilt that I hadn't been stood right outside the door on guard to prevent it.

But when the detective spoke, he stunned me as he indicated Nijad, lying unconscious behind him. "That's your employer?" I noticed the curious emphasis he put on the word employer as if he couldn't bring himself to refer to the man by name. The look on his face was one of disgust, and I got a dreadful sinking feeling in the pit of my stomach. I nodded in answer to his question and raised my eyebrows asking a silent one of my own.

"Your employer, that bastard over there," he waved his hand behind him again. "It would appear he is responsible for the woman's injuries. If she hadn't had managed to grab the lamp

and crack him over the head, we might have had a murder on our hands. It was a nasty attack."

"She said Nijad did this to her?" My mouth dropped open. "But he couldn't. He wouldn't."

The detective shook his head. "The woman is quite definite in her statement. And looking around, all the visible evidence points towards that as the most plausible explanation."

I narrowed my eyes, unable to believe it. Nijad would never do hurt a woman. "You'll be securing the flat, and examining the forensic evidence; I take it? There are security cameras…"

He stopped me there. "Let me assure you I've done this job a long time. We'll do a full investigation. But there are no security tapes. The system wasn't alarmed."

"But the alarm was sounding…"

"We set it off when we arrived. It was all quiet when we got here. We were only alerted when the woman called for help."

That would explain why the police had had time to get here before me. But why? Why was Nijad so lax as to not arm the system? A hideous thought came into my mind, but I suppressed it. No, it couldn't be true. Shaking my head, I told him again, "The woman must be lying. Nijad is not capable of something like this."

Present day

I know she's not at all keen, but it's imperative that she gets checked out as she's not been to a doctor since her attack. Who knows what damage might have been done as a result of her savage and repeated rapes? Using my most authoritative voice, I let her know there'll be no further discussion, merely that the appointment is at eleven o'clock. The pain and hurt in her eyes are clear to see as if I've betrayed her. She's gone so pale, the only thing I can do is take her in my arms and hold her close.

"You have to do this, Mia; you know that, don't you?" I try to turn her to face me, but defiantly she keeps her head turned down. "I was lucky Mary Broker had a cancellation this morning. If we don't take this appointment, you might be waiting for weeks. And the wait will only make the anticipation worse."

I feel the point when she gives in; her body relaxes with an air of defeat. She isn't enamoured by the arrangements but has to know it's a sensible step. Her voice betrays her nerves, "Will you come to the doctor's with me, Jon?"

"I'll be with you," I confirm. Mary's not only an old friend but a doctor in the lifestyle, and won't turn a hair when I wish to stay with her for the full examination.

By the time I've finished clearing up after breakfast, it's time to get moving. Mia hardly speaks in the car, and my attempts at conversation go to waste, so I make do with holding her hand and giving her squeezes of reassurance. I appreciate how difficult this is for her; being touched by any stranger is invasive, even if it is a female doctor. And in any event, I doubt I'd know anyone who would say they enjoy an intimate examination. When we arrive at the private clinic, Mia is visibly shaking as we take a seat in the waiting room, and her hand feels clammy. Luckily the timing worked out well, and we arrive so close to her appointment that she's called through almost the minute we sit down. Her palpable fear causes me pain; I hate knowing I'm upsetting her so much, but I sincerely believe it's more than time for her to be checked out. And I doubt she would ever have gone on her own.

As she goes towards the surgery door, I put my arm on the small of her back to guide her. When it becomes apparent I mean to go in with her, she looks up questioningly. "Jon? I'm perfectly capable of doing this on my own. You can wait here." She doesn't seem to have understood when I said I'd be with her all the time that I meant, *all the time*. And though she's trying to disguise her fear, she *needs* me.

She doesn't know me well at all yet. "I'm your Dom, Mia. You're mine. You're not doing this alone. Your body belongs to me."

"My body? Like heck, it does! In the bedroom, perhaps, but not here!" Her tone is almost a snarl, but quiet. It's not an argument she wants others to overhear.

I stare her down. "Certain parts belong to me at all times. I'll never have another man touch you, Mia. And if a woman does, I'll be present. You've researched the lifestyle; you must know how possessive us Doms can be." I smile to take the sting out of my words.

She tenses for a second, looking like she's going to continue to disagree but then looks down. When I take her hand, she holds onto it tight and as I lead her through the door, she makes no further protest. I hate that I might be making her more uncomfortable, but I need to be here to give her my support.

A nurse is in the room. She greets us, and without delay asks Mia to take off her top, jeans and pants, then to put on one of those ill-fitting backless gowns, lie on the table and to put the proffered blanket over her. It's a litany of instructions she's probably repeated often. Then she leaves the room without questioning my presence, she's an old hand and knows the score.

Turning away from me, Mia undresses and wraps the gown round her as if to preserve her modesty. I laugh softly and turn her to face me. "I have seen it before," I chuckle. She gives me a half-hearted smile, her mind more on the check-up ahead. I see the examination table has caught her attention, and she's fixating on the stirrups, imagining how exposed she'll be. Giving her arm a comforting squeeze, I gently guide her over. "It won't take long," I try to reassure her. She glances at the door as if calculating whether she can escape. Before she can have second thoughts, I pick her up and sit her on the table. She doesn't lie down.

"Yellow," she whispers, so quietly I have difficulty hearing her. I do the only thing I can; I pull her into my arms and hold her tight, planting a gentle kiss on the top of her head.

At that moment, Mary enters. I move a step away and nod at my old friend who greets me with a smile and comes across to take my hand. I place a chaste kiss on her cheek. Her white coat, greying hair and sensible spectacles give her an air of authority and competence, but her eyes are twinkling behind the glass. She's a Domme, and I know she'll be able to read Mia like a book, that's why I was particularly pleased to get an appointment with her. Having greeted me, she turns to her patient.

"Mia Fable?" She confirms. She's holding a clipboard and consulting it. As Mia dips her head, acknowledging her name, she continues with a glint in her eyes. "Well, I have to congratulate you. You seemed to have ensnared Master Jonathan! Never thought, I'd see the day."

Her loud laugh manages to coax a weak smile and question from Mia. "He's not brought anyone else to see you before?"

I hold my breath, waiting to see what Mary's going to say. *Shit!* I hadn't thought of this, but she remembers that I have an account with the salon. And Mary's as honest as I expected.

"Oh yes, he's brought subs here before. But never to go on the pill." She turns to me, her face full of amusement, "This one's a keeper, eh, Master Jonathan?" Then she looks stern, "Well I hope that's the situation if you intend going bareback."

Now I'm the one feeling uncomfortable, but there's no way for me to get out of it, and while Mia knows I've had other women, she probably doesn't need to have them thrown in her face. So I don't try and justify anything, but merely answer her question. "Yes, Mistress Mary. For definite." I grin down at Mia, looking up to catch Mary's smile and quick nod, almost as though she's giving me parental approval. Then she turns back to Mia, who doesn't seem to know which one of us to look at, and instead has settled for staring at her toes. My finger on her pulse, however, shows me that the informality of our banter and the certainty of my response appear to have taken some of her anxiety away.

As Mary consults her notes, I start to explain. "Mia's scared, Mary. She hasn't been to a doctor since her attack."

"Hmm. Yes, you told me about that earlier on the phone." She focuses her attention on her patient. "You were raped, repeatedly by two men over a two-day period. I understand they left you with a range of other injuries?" She's so blunt; I wince on Mia's behalf.

Surprisingly Mia, herself, seems to react well to such a no-nonsense approach. "Yes..." She swallows, rapidly a few times. Mary waits, reading the same signs as me. Mia has something else to say. "I'm worried they may have hurt me." She swallows again, "Damaged me." Her voice drops and shows the depth of her concern when her statement comes out as a question, "That I won't be able to have children?"

Fuck it! I hadn't realised she carried this particular burden, and rage rises in me all over again over what her attackers put her through, and the lasting effects of it. The thought of even committing to a relationship is new and strange enough for me by itself, and the possibility of having children in the future hasn't even crossed my mind. But the moment she mentioned the subject, I suddenly have a vision of Mia swollen with my baby, and it hits me all in a rush just how much when the time is right, I think I would want that. I clench my fists, incensed that actions of those bastards might have taken the chance away.

Mary contemplates her for a second and then says in a matter of fact manner, "Well, let's take a look, shall we? Put your feet in the stirrups, pet."

Swallowing down my rage, and forcing myself to be strong for her I step forwards and clasp Mia's hand. As she glances at me, I give her an encouraging smile, then, with obvious reluctance, she places her feet in the stirrups, her whole body trembling. As Mary snaps on her latex gloves and grabs a speculum, some lube and a light, I resist the urge to grimace at the firmness of Mia's grip.

"This will feel cold, but shouldn't be too uncomfortable," she tells her. Mia winces as the instrument is inserted and tightens her hold so my fingers start to feel numb. I make no complaint; I told her I'd be here for her. However, she needs me.

"When was your last period, pet?"

"About a fortnight ago," Mia replies.

"We can do a smear test then." Mary bends over, intent on her task, and takes some swabs. She's quick and efficient, and it's over in no time. Mia breathes out then quickly sucks in air, and I realise she'd been holding her breath.

The doctor then goes and pulls over a machine. "I'm going to use an ultrasound probe to see if everything looks normal up there," she explains as she inserts the probe and then puts her attention on the screen beside us. It's not more than a couple of minutes later, and she's telling Mia she can dispense with the stirrups now, she brings the blanket up over legs and pulls the gown up to expose her stomach. After using gel, she uses a different probe, moving it across Mia's skin, and studies the screen again.

Eventually, Mary puts the equipment away and passes Mia some paper towels to clean herself up. "Well," she pronounces, "Everything looks like it's in the right place from what I can see here. There's appears to be some evidence of scarring, which would need further investigation if you have any problems conceiving. You could possibly have a blockage in one of your fallopian tubes, but the other looks healthy enough." She then looks at us both. "Due to the purpose of your visit today, I gather getting pregnant is not a concern at the moment. But when you do want to try, give it a few months, then come back and see me if you don't have any success. But for now, don't worry about it too much. Fertility depends on so many factors, even on your partner. There, that's all for now. You can get dressed, pet." She steps away from the table; the examination completed so quickly Mia seems taken aback that it's over and takes a moment to react. As the doctor pulls a curtain around us, she turns her back on me before pulling on her utilitarian white pants and putting the rest of her clothes on. I smile at her audible sigh of relief.

"All over, sweetheart," I say, softly. "Come here." I hold out my hand, and she grabs it like a safety line. Pulling her to me, I envelop her in a hug aiming to convey how proud I am.

Emerging from behind the curtain we see Mary's washed her hands and had taken a seat at her desk. Mia and I sit in the chairs opposite and wait while she labels phials and writes up some notes. After a few minutes, she puts down her pen and turns to her.

"Right, just a blood sample now, and then you're done." Again she's quick and efficient, and while Mia averts her eyes from the needle, she makes no murmur allowing the doctor to extract the necessary amount of blood from her arm with no fuss. Mary writes another label, and then puts it with the other samples in a box waiting on the side.

"Okay, when did you last have sex?" Mary asks.

Mia glances at me, going red in the face and I grin at her. She answers, shyly, "Last night."

Mary shoots me an amused look but puts her professional hat back on quickly. "And were you been sexually active before then? Have you ever had unprotected sex?"

Mia looks down at the floor, and her reply comes out as a mumble. "Only seven years ago. To answer both your questions."

Mary directs her impassive gaze on Mia. "When you were raped? And they didn't use condoms?"

Mia nods in reply.

Mary breathes in sharply. "And you've never been to a doctor or clinic, nor have been tested for STDs?" As Mia shakes her head, the doctor narrows her eyes, as if thinking. "Hmm, most problems would have presented symptoms by now though so the likelihood is that you're clean but we need to rule out anything hanging over from your attack. Have you suffered from urinary tract infections at all?"

Mia shakes her head, and then looks at me quizzically as if she doesn't quite understand why Mary's asking that question.

The doctor continues speaking. "Most things would have shown up before now, but unfortunately, we can't rule out HIV, as you could be symptom-free for up to ten years. It's unlikely, but we need to find out."

Mia freezes, and throws me a look of concern, and I realise she's not afraid for herself, but in case she's infected me. I turn her so she has to look at me. She has tears in her eyes, her shame and worry clear. Suddenly I'm holding her hand again, and I lean over and whisper in her ear, "It will be alright. We used a condom. We'll just have to be careful until you get the results through." I glance over to the doctor, "But in all likelihood you're clean. Isn't that right, Mary?"

Mary is giving us a moment, and then she nods and gets back to business. "Yes, Jon, Mia. The chances of you having HIV are slim as you've not shown symptoms so far, but we do have to check. Belt and braces approach. Ok? And I'll contact you as soon as we have the results. Might even be today, or possibly tomorrow. Right now, onto contraception. Any ideas what you want to use?"

As her Dom, I answer. "The pill's the best option I think, as we discussed on the phone."

She looks at me, and then at Mia. "That would be fine." She looks down at her notes, "Now Mia, your last period was two weeks ago, so you'll be able to start taking it on the first day of your next. You'll be protected straight away."

Two weeks! I stop the inappropriately timed grin coming to my face. Two weeks and I'll be able to feel this woman in every way.

CHAPTER 20
Mia

Seven Years ago

I expected them to kill me, to finish it, and being in so much pain, I thought death would be welcome . Instead, they threw my clothes at me and instructed me to put them on. They forbade me to remove the blindfold so I had to get dressed slowly by touch. Every movement hurt, and by the amount of laughter they were finding my struggles amusing, although they soon got impatient that I was taking so long.

Once I was dressed, my hands and feet were rebound, and they stuffed a dirty rag into my mouth as a gag. Then one lifted me and carried me out into the fresh air. I heard the sound of a door opening, and then I was dropped on the hard metal floor of what I assumed was a van . The engine started, and the vehicle moved off, jolting down what felt like a badly rutted track. I was being thrown backwards and forwards, and couldn't do anything to stop myself rolling painfully around. At last, the ride thankfully became smoother. I had no option other than to lie in misery until we arrived wherever it was they were taking me.

At last, the journey ended, I froze as I heard one, then the other door of the van open, and felt the cold air flooding in. Dreading what they would do to me next, I cringed as they cut through my bindings, and felt the cold metal of a knife against my skin. Then, I was thrown out onto the road. I hit the tarmac hard, picking up grazes to add other hurts to my list of injuries. I heard wheels *spin, and a vehicle pulling away. Free at last to remove the blindfold, I pulled it off, blinking hard as my eyes adjusted, able to see for the first time in days. I watched as a white van disappeared into the distance.*

Present day

The doctor writes a prescription and then hands it to me. From the day of my attack, I'd worried whether I'd ever be able to get pregnant and always feared to ask. God knows where I got the strength from to do so today. I'd convinced myself that because of the intense pain my abusers caused me, they had to have caused some internal damage. The fear of finding out was one of the things stopping me visiting a doctor before.

But after the examination, I start to feel a little bit optimistic. Maybe they hadn't taken that away from me. Obviously, it's far too early to consider having a baby with Jon; for goodness sake it's hard enough to believe we're in a relationship at all. But somehow the thought of a little dark haired boy gets stuck in my mind… *Pull yourself together, Mia.*

I'm only half listening, lost in my thoughts as Jon and the doctor finish up their conversation. But I bring myself back to the here and now when Jon confirms the invoice should be sent to him. I should have realised this was a private practice and that there would be a bill, I should have gone to my own doctor on the NHS. But I'll have to dig into my pockets; Jon can't keep paying for things, so I protest. It was my appointment and therefore I should pay for it. I'm taken aback when Mary just laughs and tells me not to argue with my Dom.

We leave the surgery, again he takes my hand, I'm getting used to this; it seems he wants to stay as close to me as I do to him. But I need to get something sorted, "You didn't have to pay, Jon." I'm still put out.

Putting his finger to my lips, he stops me from speaking, and laughs, "My body, my bill."

I glare at him, but he ignores me, settling me in the car, then getting in him and starting the engine. To be quite honest, the appointment was over so quickly and had been so painless I don't know what I'd been working myself up about. *Seven years ago, why didn't I fight harder to go to a doctor then?* But there were a lot of reasons why. Perhaps I shouldn't keep looking back, thinking how I could have done things differently. *Perhaps it's time to start living in the present.*

We make the journey back to Epping in excellent time, and stop off for lunch at the Blazing Donkey, which now seems to have become our local. All the while, Jon never stops touching me. He's either holding my hand, squeezing my arm, or has his hand resting on the small of my back. When we enter the door, a man walks out; brushing past us and Jon pulls me in tight to his side. The intimacies of last night seem to have made him demonstrably possessive.

Once we find a table he sits close to me on the bench seat, his leg touching mine. Slowly he runs his hand up the side of my thigh, and I get goose bumps over my skin. *If my past brought me to Jon, could I regret it?* I shiver, realising perhaps for the first time that it's what happened to me that's brought me to where I am today.

"You cold?" he asks me, grinning.

"Actually, I'm feeling a bit hot," I answer, fluttering my eyebrows, daring to flirt with him and pretending to fan myself.

His grin widens. "I might be able to do something about that a bit later."

He brushes back his hair which has fallen over his forehead. Damn, this man only has to twitch his little finger for me to find the action sexy. My stomach clenches and I lose my nerve to continue the conversation. I know I'm blushing so turn my head away, and pretend to stare out of the window. Our food arrives, we eat, and then, neither of us wanting to delay, return to my cottage. For the first time in a week, I'm not worried about going home; I'm more concerned how long it will be before Jon gets me into bed again!

There's some mail sitting in the letterbox, so I pick it up as I walk in and throw the envelopes down in a pile on the hall table. The one on top is offering me a loan I don't want, so I doubt the others are any more exciting. Jon pulls me to him and puts his mouth over mine. The kiss starts gently, but soon he's thrusting his tongue into my mouth in the promise of what is to come. His hands move down to my waist, and then slide up underneath my T-shirt. He cups my breasts through my bra.

"I can't wait to have you." He pulls back a bit, and I see he's breathing fast and looks like he's trying to get himself under control as he draws his hands out of my top, and takes hold of my arms. "First, though, I've got to check in with the office and Detective Coulten. We're going to have to put this on hold for a moment." He's reluctant to move away, his eyes making contact with mine.

I'm wet and ready, but I know he's right. I nod as he goes into the sitting room to make his calls. I'm still carrying my handbag, so I slip the strap off my shoulder and throw it down on the hall table noticing the letters again. *Oh well, I might as well deal with these now.* I collect them and take them with me into the kitchen. My mind is more on what I'm going to cook tonight, and what might be in the fridge or freezer for the makings of dinner. I stand by the counter, quick and simple recipes going through my mind, and idly slit open the first letter. It goes straight into the bin, the second likewise. The third is from my bank explaining some changes to my account which don't seem to affect me, but being an official communication; I glance through it just in case. The fourth has a typewritten envelope, but no custom franking mark, just a stamp. I tear it open and then gasp. Oh shit! I drop the contents on the floor, and then bend to pick them up. The peace of the last few days shatters as I read the words:

GONNA SMOKE YOU OUT, BITCH! COUNT YOUR DAYS!

"Jon!" I scream out but don't wait for him to come to me. I tear into the other room and throw the typewritten page at him.

He stands up and glowers as he reads the message, his arms come around me. Tears fall from my eyes; I'm crying, but I'm not sure whether it's more from fear or frustration. I just want this over and done with. Who the hell is this bastard who's messing with my mind and my life?

As Jon jumps into action, getting back in contact with Coulten and his colleagues at Grade A, informing them about the latest missive, I sit with my head in my hands. Over the past few days, I've been lulled into a false sense of security, even beginning to wonder whether the stalker had given up. I hate the weakness that makes me give into tears, but I just haven't got it in me to be strong anymore.

Jon spends most of the afternoon on the phone. From his side of the conversations he's as pissed off as I am, but it doesn't sound like anyone's any closer to finding the identity of the man who's making my life hell for me.

My joy in the day having been blown to the four winds, we end up having yet another takeaway for dinner, Thai this time, but I'm unable to eat much. Jon's worried about me and keeps throwing me looks full of concern.

"What bugs me most is that I'm powerless to do anything!" I tell him as we sit having a drink after the dinner I could only pick at.

Putting his arm around my shoulders, he pulls me close. "I know, sweetheart. But don't be worried. I'm here with you, and this house has got the top of the range security. You're safe."

His closeness comforts me. I snuggle into him, breathing in his unique aroma. I needed this man to hold me. "I'm so glad you're with me, and I don't have to handle this alone, I don't think I could do it," I tell him then add, "I just want to get back to normal, you know? I hate how he's making me feel so helpless!"

"What normal do you want to get back to?" he asks, seeming concerned, "With, or without me?"

My head swings round. With him, of course. "I want to explore what my new normal might be. With you." I offer, tentatively, still anxious about our relationship, still a little nervous that things might be different between us when they catch my stalker.

He sits up and regards me, his eyes shining. "That sounds excellent to me, sweetheart." As if in slow motion he leans forwards and puts a gentle kiss on my lips.

Suddenly I have to know. "Have you had a relationship with anyone else like me?"

He chuckles softly. "There's no one like you, Mia."

I brush his comment off. "You know what I mean. Had a relationship with the person you're protecting?"

My comment seems to hit a chord with him. "Never." His response is adamant. "I've already told you; I've not had what you'd call anything like a relationship before at all. And if I had any sense I'd be leaving you well alone."

That stings. I make as if to move away, but he holds me down. "I'm here to provide protection for you, Mia. But you distract me." He looks away, rubs his hand across his face as if he's thinking. "I won't leave you, but I need to think how best to handle this situation. I refuse to put you in danger 'cos I'm staring at your fucking fantastic arse instead of keeping an eye out for the motherfucker threatening you."

I start to glow, and can't stop my mouth broadening, "Fucking fantastic arse?"

"Yeah." He grins back. "And then you've got these fucking fantastic knockers as well." To make his point he leans forwards and tries to suckle my nipples, but it's not too successful as I'm still wearing a T-shirt and bra. He nuzzles my neck, and speaks so quietly I hardly hear him, and it takes a second for his instruction to sink in. "Take off your clothes, Mia. I want you naked." He moves to my side and sits, waiting.

At first, I hesitate, waiting for him to take over. It's one thing for him to undress me, another for me to give him a personal striptease. Although his voice might have been soft, his tone was dominant. I glance at him, and he just raises an eyebrow. Slowly I get to my feet and draw in a deep breath for courage. Keeping my eyes on his, I cross my hands over my front and take hold of the hem of my T, and slowly pull it up over my head. My bra is plain, a simple white one from a chain store. I've never bothered with fancy underwear, and it dawns on me that that's something I'm going to need to rectify. His eyes narrow appreciatively; he's concentrating on what I'm revealing, not what I'm taking off. Inhaling another breath, I undo the button on my jeans, then the zip. In as sexy a way as possible, I shimmy them down my legs, kicking off my shoes at the same time. My knickers match my bra, plain, simple and not particularly attractive.

I falter, but he waves his hand for me to continue. So I reach behind me, undoing the clasp of my bra I let it fall free. I hear him whistle through his teeth, and his evident admiration spurs me on. Not allowing myself time to reconsider I take off my knickers, pulling them down and stepping out of them. He holds out his hand, and I give them to him, and watch, wide-eyed, as he brings them up and sniffs them.

"Hmm." He breathes in my musk. I flush; it seems an oddly intimate gesture.

I'm feeling awkward now. Do I go to him, will he come to me? But he doesn't leave me much time to worry, and I realise he is taking control. The Dom is in the room.

"Stand still." He rises. "Spread your legs, and put your hands behind your head."

He's going to do a Dom's inspection.

I'm nervous. In all the time I've been writing about such things I never expected experience this situation myself. Nevertheless, I do as he instructed, remembering as a Dom he'll want to push me out of my comfort zone, and he's certainly accomplishing that! He steps forward, softly stroking my breasts which have been pushed out by the position I'm holding. "Beautiful." He tells me.

He lets his fingers trail down my stomach. It tickles, and I flinch, but try to keep still. "Remember your safewords, Mia?" His eyes take hold of mine.

"Yes." The word comes out as a husky gasp.

He cocks his head, waiting for more.

"Red means stop, yellow means slow down, and green's good to go." I expand.

He's still gazing straight at me, trying to read my expression. "Give me a colour."

"Green." The way he regularly checks in helps to put me at my ease.

Once satisfied with my response, his hand moves further down, across my waxed mound and between my legs. His fingers probe me, and then he removes them, my arousal evident and glistening on his fingers. He puts his fingers in his mouth and sucks my wetness from them. "You taste fucking incredible." He does it again, this time holding his fingers out to me. "Taste yourself," he instructs. I open my mouth and lick. I'm not sure I like the taste as much as he does, but it pleases him that I obey, and the very thought of the dirty things he's doing causes a new rush of wetness through me.

Next, he moves around to stand behind me. "Bend over and grab your ankles." He waits for me to get into position, and then reaches forwards to put his fingers on my clit. He toys with it, and it's hard to resist the urge to stand up and reach for him. But he moves his hand again, putting a finger inside my pussy. Then he puts in another. Unlike last night, I don't freak, but he checks to make sure. "Give me a colour."

"Green." Again it comes out as a gasp.

He moves his fingers around, gathering up as much of my moisture as he can, placing one hand on my back as if to hold me in place. He's moving his finger around the rim of my arsehole. I start to tense, having to remind myself this is Jon and not one of the monsters. Gently he pushes against my hole but doesn't try to get inside.

"This will be mine, Mia, not yet, but one day." It's a statement, not a question. Then he pulls his finger away. "Kneel in front of me."

The sudden instruction takes me by surprise, and I take a minute to react. Then I'm kneeling before him, me completely naked, him fully clothed. I'm more turned on than I would have thought possible, my pussy throbbing as though it needs to be filled. He puts his hand under my chin and lifts my head. He's looking at me searchingly. "You can stop at any time, Mia. I don't want to make you feel the slightest bit uncomfortable. I'm pushing you, but you need to talk to me if I'm taking it too far or too fast for you."

I find it difficult to answer verbally, so I just nod. I suspect I know what is coming, and to my immense surprise find my mouth watering in anticipation. I want Jon. I want all of him. I want to taste him as he's tasted me.

He waits until he's certain of my mental state. "Take my cock out."

His jeans are button up, so I fumble a bit getting them undone, but at last I do. Realising he's gone commando today, I take care as I loosen the denim and put the material down just over his hips. His cock springs free. I want to examine it properly, and I feast my eyes on it greedily. It's thick and long; the head is bulbous and an angry purple-pink colour, it has a sheen, almost like satin. Thick veins run along it, and I itch to touch it and see how it feels. He reaches down and fists himself, stroking long strokes from his heavy balls to the head, making a pre-cum ooze from the slit. I lick my lips.

He chuckles. "Like what you see?"

"Can I?" I wait for him to grant permission.

For an answer, he puts his hand behind my head and gently pulls me forwards. My tongue flicks out and collects the moisture gathered at the tip. It's salty, and I press my legs together to try to get relief from the pressure building there.

"Suck me, Mia."

I open my mouth as wide as possible and still can only get the head of him inside. I run my tongue around it, then pull away, and lick the sides of his cock following the path of the veins. I cup his balls in my hands, rolling them between my palms. I'm doing something right as I hear a moan escape him. Running my fingers along his length, I discover it's as hard as marble, yet the skin feels soft like velvet.

Suddenly his fist is in my hair, and he's holding my head to him, pushing his cock against my lips. For an instant, I get a flashback, but then I smell his musk, taste his pre-cum again, and know this is Jon, that he's not going to hurt me, or force me to do anything I don't want to do.

"Relax your jaw," he instructs as he pushes into my mouth. "Breathe through your nose." Gently he pushes in and out, gradually going further and hitting the back of my throat. I instinctively swallow my throat muscles spasming against him.

"Fuck, you're killing me!" His obvious pleasure spurs me on. He picks up the pace and starts fucking my mouth. I gag; immediately he pulls out before I start panicking.

"I need you, Mia. Now!" He pulls me to my feet and then pushes me forwards, bending me over the couch. He's behind me, but his touch leaves me, and I hear a crinkling of a foil packet. He's putting on a condom. Once ready he reaches round with his hand and touches my already stimulated clit, making me gasp, my reaction showing how close I am to coming. I'm so wet and ready he thrusts inside me in one go and then stills to accustom me to his invasion. It feels so good; I'm almost ready to come. Sensing my closeness he pulls out and then starts pounding into me. This is different from last night; he's no longer holding back, and I'm elated that he's using me so hard. It feels so real. With each plunge into my depths, he stimulates that spot inside me so I'm almost going crazy in my effort to go over the top. He presses one finger against my arsehole, and pulls my hand down, so I'm playing with my clit. As he pushes his finger inside my arse, I barely notice anything except that it propels me close to climax, and I feel him expanding inside me.

"Come for me."

I explode, unable to breathe, my muscles continuing to contract in seemingly never ending waves. Everything goes black. As last, with a gasp, my starved lungs steal in much-needed oxygen.

"Fucking hell!" Jon's lying across my back as though he's collapsed there.

Carefully he pulls himself out of me and pulls me back towards him. I shake my head, trying to clear it. I think I might have blown a few brain cells that time.

"You're going to be the death of me, woman."

"Me? You?" My breathing is still fast, my heart pounding in my chest. "I think I just died."

He chuckles, hugging me close, and a huge belly laugh comes from him. "It's not called *le petit mort* for nothing. Hang on; don't go anywhere, I've just got to go and clean up." I hear him go upstairs to the bathroom to dispose of the condom. I couldn't move if I tried. He's back quickly, and puts us both onto the sofa with me lying on top of him. I let my head rest back on his shoulder.

He runs his hand up my stomach, caressing it then, whispers in my ear, "Ever since we saw Mary, I've got strange thoughts in my head. I'm wondering what it would be like to see your belly swell knowing my child is growing inside." His hand moves up to caress my breasts, "And to watch my son or daughter suckling here."

I give a short laugh. "And would you like watching me puke up morning noon and night? Shuffle around 'cos my back is killing me, wobbling on swollen ankles? Will you be there for the birth when I'm trying to push something the size of a football out of my pussy?"

"Christ! I didn't think about any of that." He's rubbing my arm as if deep in thought. "I never want to see you hurt or in pain."

"Anyway, we've only known each other a week. It's a bit too early to start thinking about a family." My words are sensible, yet inside my heart races. Is he that serious about me? Serious enough to start thinking about a family? And suddenly, I realise I could want that.

He gazes at me; his pupils still dilated from our recent pleasure. Then he says in a solemn tone. "I know it is, Mia. I don't know what's come over me. Fuck, I've never had this kind of feeling before. What the fuck are you doing to me, woman?" He doesn't bother to wait for an answer, but stands up, pulling me with him, and then lifts me in his arms. "Bed. I'm knackered, and I think you are too."

I could get used to being carried, I ponder, as he takes me upstairs. It stirs something primitive inside to be with a man who's strong enough to carry me in his arms. He only puts me down to open the shower door and holds me upright until the water runs hot enough. He notices my old fashioned shower cap hanging on the door and offers it to me, and then has a good laugh at my expense at the picture I make when I put it on. But he's right; I'm dead beat, and I don't want to bother about washing and drying my hair tonight. He steps into the shower with me, gently soaping my body. I take hold of the shower gel and return the favour. In some ways, this feels even more intimate than the sex we've just had. When he turns the water off we manage to manoeuvre ourselves out; my shower wasn't built for two. He wraps me in a large fluffy bath towel that's been hanging over the radiator and dries me, before taking the smaller towel and drying himself. He leaves me alone for a moment while I complete the rest of my pre-sleep preparations, and then uses the bathroom after me. By the time he's returned, I'm already curled up in bed. I notice he's been down and collected our clothes from the sitting room which was thoughtful. Then he gets in beside me, quickly adjusting his position until he's spooning behind me. Already I'm getting used to his warmth nestling against my back and know I would miss it if he wasn't there. It's only moments before I fall asleep.

Sometime later I'm disorientated as the sound of a crash downstairs rudely wakes me, along with the shrill sound of the alarm system. Before I have a chance to register what could have disturbed my rest, Jon's already leapt out of bed, and is getting into his jeans. With a fraught whispered instruction for me to stay put, he leaves the room.

I'm naked, so I reach for my clothes as well, wanting to be prepared if necessary. I'm only half into them when I hear his panicked shout.

CHAPTER 21

Jon

Three years ago

Nijad was unconscious for almost two days. While the police had him cuffed to the hospital bed, Jasim, his brother, had flown over from London, the family lawyer arrived, and I stood in the doorway in guard mode, my legs apart, and hands behind my back. When I forced myself to look at my former friend it was with disgust that only deepened when, with obvious reluctance, the police officer removed his restraints. It emerged that the Kassis family had bought the woman off with such a large sum that she was now saying it had been an accident that caused her injuries. No one believed her revised story, but there was nothing anyone could do unless she again changed her mind. Nijad was claiming to have convenient amnesia and said he couldn't remember a thing.

Watching from the doorway of the hospital room, I saw Nijad turn his eyes up to his brother's face. "Tell me this isn't true, Jas," he pleaded. "I couldn't have done this!"

Jasim shook his head sadly, his despair plain to see. "It would appear that you could," he told him. "And that you did."

Then Nijad's eyes landed on me. "Jon, my friend. How the fuck could you think it was me?"

I shrugged, my brow furrowed at his reference to our relationship knowing it would be impossible to continue our friendship. "There was no one else there. Chantelle had been *afraid of her life. Before she was encouraged to change her story she told me and the police that you were the one who attacked her." I shifted awkwardly and, at last, looked him in the eye. "Nijad, I've spent the last two days while you've been unconscious trying to find another explanation. I couldn't shake Chantelle; she's is adamant you attacked her, and the available evidence backs it up. Blood from your knuckles was on her face and her blood was on your clothes. There's no doubt."*

Then Jasim steps in, and summed it up. "You did this, Nijad. Just like you lost your temper with St John-Davies. You're out of control." Sadly he shook his head. "Fuck knows what's going to be done with you."

I tossed my head with repugnance, and sadness. The man I had protected for three years, the man who I took a bullet for is not the person I thought he was. I had saved the life of a man who was violent and out of control. Attacking another man under provocation would have been, perhaps, easier to accept. But harming a woman? Never.

Present day

The alarm system is belting out a shrill warning as a quick glance at my watch shows it's twelve-thirty am. I've been asleep, and I shouldn't have been. I shouldn't have relaxed my guard and given into the temptation to stay with Mia.

I'm only halfway down the stairs when the acrid smell of smoke reaches me; something is on fire—we've got to get out. Investigating what's actually burning or the cause can come later. Giving a desperate shout for Mia, I race back up to find her already getting dressed.

"There's fire. I want you out now." I bark out the order.

That's my girl. She's scared and shocked but doesn't argue. Right now, I haven't a clue as to how bad it is, but there is one heck of a fucking lot of smoke that seems to have followed me back up the stairs, so rushing to the bathroom I grab the small towel I used earlier. It's too dry, so I wet it under the tap for a second. Without wasting any more time, I return to the bedroom and take her arm. Together we go down the narrow, steep stairs, having to feel our way by touch.

The smoke's getting thicker by the second. Along the downstairs hallway, the fire is taking hold; if I was to hazard a guess someone's poured petrol through the letterbox. I pull her the other way to go into the kitchen, and here I find the cause of the crash we heard. It looks like a Molotov cocktail has been thrown through the kitchen window, and flames are already licking up around the cupboards. The house is old, and being made of a wooden frame, is like a tinderbox. We have to get out, and the only available exit is via the sitting room where the windows open wide enough to let us escape, or would do if they hadn't just had new window locks installed. Mia is keeping calm and makes me proud when she doesn't give into panic. Though she's coughing from the smoke filling the room, she has the presence of mind to grab the keys from their place on the mantelpiece. I take them from her and exchanging them for the wet towel, telling her to hold it over her mouth and nose and breathe through it.

It's hard to even find the window now. Forcing myself to take only shallow breaths, it takes a couple of attempts to fit the keys into the locks and turn them. Once the window is open, I jump up onto the window sill and outside, reaching back in to help Mia through, catching her in my arms as she comes out, noticing she's had the presence of mind to grab her handbag from the hall table as she came past and has slung the strap over her shoulder. Taking her hand, we run across the front garden to get out of the way of the heat and sparks. Even as I'm on the move, I extract my phone out of my pocket to call 999, reporting the fire, and receive the welcome news that the police are already on their way having been alerted by the alarm. Now, at my request, they'll dispatch fire engines too.

Having done everything I can, my attention turns back to the house. It's going up fast; the fire has taken hold, and already it looks like there will be little left to salvage unless the fire brigade gets here fast and can work some magic. Realising we've had a lucky escape, I'm just grateful to be alive. Having acted purely on survival instincts up to now, my brain kicks into gear. *This should never have happened!*

The gunshot ringing out across the garden shocks me out of my thoughts, whizzing past so close to my head I felt the displaced air brushing past my ear. Swinging around, I try to push Mia behind me, but she fucking steps in front of me. A second shot fires before I'm able to pull her out of the fucking way. Mia falls at my feet, and instinctively I drop, covering her with my body. Christ! She's been hit! *She got hit instead of me!* For a split second, I freeze in horror. *Can't afford that, I've got to keep my shit together.* Automatically my hand goes for my holster, but of course, it's not fucking there. I've no weapon to return fire. Touching her, with immense relief I feel her breathing and gratefully hear her moan of pain. *She's alive.* "Mia, where did he get you?" I ask urgently. Thank God for small mercies, the flickering light from the fire allows me to see her; I immediately notice blood coming from her shoulder.

"My shoulder, my arm." Her voice stutters, she's weak from shock and quite possibly loss of blood. The poor light doesn't allow me to see how bad it is.

Another shot blasts across us, again I feel the whistle of another bullet far too close. If I'm able to see Mia, so can our attacker. We have to move to a safer place. I feel sick to my stomach that she's been hurt, but force the nausea down, now's not the time for remonstrations.

"Sorry, sweetheart. We've got to move. Can you walk?"

She answers with a weak yes, so I help her to her feet. "Keep your head down." Glancing around to find a place of safety, I find the only option is to go towards the garage where we'll hopefully be out of sight. Crouching down, I take her with me, moving crablike across the garden, unable to avoid the illumination of the flames. Another shot misses us; thank Christ his got terrible aim. We get to the garage and ease behind it where the light from the fire doesn't reach, but I know he'll have seen where we're heading so we can't stop. Feeling like a bastard, knowing the pain she's in, I make her continue, doubling round to the back. There I discover the wheelie bins, so I wedge her in between them. "Stay put." She's still holding onto the damp towel, so I shove it against her wound. "Hold that there."

Without waiting for a response, I get to my feet in the shelter of the wall and cautiously peer around, greeted by another shot. I'm counting; if I can get him to waste all his ammunition I might have a chance. He won't beat me in hand to hand combat, whoever he is. Trouble is I don't know what model of gun he's got, and how many rounds it holds. But my aim is to get him to waste as many as possible. By his random firing, I doubt he's used to handling a weapon. I bend down and pick up a large stone, throwing it away from me. It's hard to see anything at all as my night vision was killed by the fire, but he'll be at the same disadvantage. The stone does the trick, and he shoots blindly in the direction of the noise. Picking up another stone I throw it again, trying anything to divert his attention away from us.

In the distance, but fast getting closer I hear sirens coming. So does he. He's got a gun; he doesn't have to be quiet, so he doesn't take any care as he turns and runs. I try to give chase, but he jumps into a car and fires up the engine, roaring off with gravel flying in his wake and I don't have a chance of catching him. I can't even see the fucking number plate in this light. The good news is that he's gone, the bad is we've still got no fucking clue to his identity. I stand for a second after the taillights fade in the distance.

Fuck, Mia! Mia, who took a fucking bullet for me. Grabbing my phone out of my pocket again, I call for an ambulance even as I race back to her. My adrenalin levels are dropping fast as I run, fear rising, hoping and praying to every god there is that her injury isn't serious. Bile churns in my stomach as I reach her to find she's still and unmoving, but when I touch her, she looks up quickly, checking it's me. Breathing a loud sigh of relief, I sink to my knees. Gently I place my hand on her uninjured shoulder to reassure her.

"He's gone. Now we've got to get you sorted out." At last, I hear the fire engines arrive, and knowing they'll have a first aider on board, I sprint over, calling out for help and return with a fireman carrying a medi-kit and a bright torch. Lifting the towel, with the aid of the bright light we can see the wound bleeding freely. I've seen injuries before, but nothing has prepared me like the sight of Mia's blood, it feels like a knife's twisting in my gut. Quickly the fireman gets out a pressure bandage and applies it. While one hand keeps the wound covered, with the other he used his radio and checks that an ambulance is close by. Then, after making sure I'm going to look after her until it gets here, leaves to assist his colleagues.

Mia tries to talk, but I shush her. She needs to conserve her energy.

It seems like hours but in reality, it's only minutes before the ambulance arrives. The paramedics assess Mia, then put on a stretcher and carry her inside. She's been so brave, my girl, but now help is here she's almost passed out with shock and blood loss. She's hanging onto consciousness by a thread, as I stand by the doors of the ambulance watching the paramedics make ready to leave, and check which hospital they're taking her to. They ask if I want to travel with her, and it's at that point it suddenly hits me.

This is all my fault and I've let her down. I let my emotions get in the way of doing my job. I was asleep when her house was set on fire, and not quick enough to move when she put herself in front of me. I'm a failure. One more time in my life, I've fucked up. Completely. And for the exact same reason.

"You coming, mate?" The paramedic is anxious to go, but he gives me one last chance.

I shake my head, staring at Mia as if I'm taking my last look at her. *It should have been me!* "I've got to wait for the police."

It breaks my heart as Mia stretches out her hand, reaching for me, but I can't bring myself step inside. As the doors slam closed, and the ambulance pulls away, I'm unable to stop watching until the flashing blue lights disappear around a bend. *Fuck, Mia, you're taking my heart with you, and I don't think you'll be giving it back.*

I'm covered in blood. Her blood. The police arrive and, in the backdrop of her dream cottage burning down to the ground, take my statement. I give the facts coldly and calmly. I'm at least professional enough for that, even though I'm crap as a CPO. I leave out the fact that her bodyguard was standing behind her when she got shot, and was fast asleep by her side when the cottage started to burn. Looking around the site is distressing; already hardly anything remains except the fire-scarred bricks of the inglenook and chimney. Mia is going to be devastated, and I'm bloody gutted on her behalf. I couldn't protect her; I couldn't protect her home. *But I should have. I made the wrong choices, just like before, let emotions get in the way and cloud my judgement.* Lost in thoughts of my guilt I relate everything I can remember to the police, which isn't much more than the basics, so it's not too long until I'm free to go.

But to go where? Luckily the wind blew the fire away from the cars, and while the Fiesta, being nearer, has some bubbling paintwork, my McClaren is relatively unscathed. It would be. Just like me. Reaching my hand into my pocket, I find my car keys. Boy, am I in luck tonight! I haven't fucking lost anything, except for my work laptop that had been in the lounge and can easily be replaced. Unlike Mia, who's fucking lost everything.

Getting into the car, I start it, then, to navigate past the fire engines which are still dealing with the glowing embers, I have to drive the sports car over the flower beds and grass. There's no house left, so cutting up the garden won't make a difference. Once I hit the tarmac of the road I put my foot down and gun it up the road, wishing I was on my bike and able to burn off more energy. But as I shift roughly through the gears, over-revving the engine, I take out my anger on the innocent machine.

Glancing at the clock, I see it's only three o'clock. Only two and a half hours since the drama started. Not giving a damn I'll be waking him up, I pull over and call Ben, unable to trust myself to use the hands-free when discussing the news I'm about to tell him. At first sleepy, Ben quickly becomes alert as I recount what's happened. When he hears my request to arrange protection for Mia, I have to brush off his questions about why it's not me that's with her. Why I'm not the one beside her hospital bed.

I know he doesn't understand, who could? I don't have a clue what I'm doing myself. If I'm going to be able to protect Mia, I've got to get these blasted emotions out of my head. *I've got to become nothing more than a robot, doing my job.*

Now I'm going to get drunk, and that's none of Ben's business. When he protests and starts to argue, I end the call, turning off my phone so he can't ring back.

Resuming my journey, turning off the A roads, I head down

south to an all-night bar, one with a dubious reputation, often frequented by bikers—the kind you don't want to meet in a dark alley on a dark night. Just right for the mood I'm in tonight. That bullet would have been a kill shot if it had been a couple of inches over. And it had my name on it. *I only wish it had been me he'd hit.*

I screwed up. And Mia could have died as a result. I fucked up, just like in Paris when betrayal cut me to the quick, and I failed to do my job. This time the emotion might have a different name—a name I'm reluctant to even voice in my head—but the effect is just the same. I failed.

Entering the bar I find, as expected, that it's still half full even considering the time of night or to be accurate, early morning. At the fringes of my mind, I'm conscious of the jukebox is playing an archetypal biker song, 'Born to be Wild,' but I'm not here to listen to music. I stand, swaying in the doorway, and notice I'm attracting even more attention than normal.

"You alright, mate?" One leather-clad biker comes up to me, concerned and wary.

Glancing down at myself, I only just remember everything I'm wearing must reek of smoke and that Mia's undried blood is still glistening on my leather jacket, and is soaking my jeans, and. I raise my hands nonchalantly and explain dismissively, "It's not mine."

He takes a step back re-joining his mates. They don't look at all amused to see me, all offer of help is gone. Ignoring them, I walk towards the bar, "Whisky. A double." I down it in one, and hold my glass out for another, unable to speak for a second as wracking coughs assail me. I breathed in too much smoke, but I don't give a damn. The second whisky doesn't even take the edge off. *I've cocked up, just like last time.*

It had all gone so fucking wrong! I knew from the first instance I saw her I should have kept well away and assigned someone else. Someone else, who'd have had her safety in mind rather than how fast they could get into her fucking bed. At the very least I should have had another team member working on the case. Unable to keep it zipped, I could have still enjoyed Mia, but with another person assigned to watch her back, she would have been safe. I should have done my job, should have been out checking the grounds, staying awake downstairs not in her fucking bed asleep. But I'd been too selfish, wanting to keep her to myself. So letting myself believe the threats were just words on paper. I saw what I wanted to see, didn't analyse it enough, just like last time. *I'm a fucking waste of space!*

I take a third whisky; I won't be driving anymore tonight but sod the expensive car I've left parked in this rough part of town. I've just left the woman I love—Jesus, did I really just admit that to myself? *Yeah, I did.* And reeling as if a bolt of lightning hits me, I realise it's true. I've just left the woman I love abandoned and hurting, because I'm unable to cope with the guilt inside me. *What if she dies?*

I freeze, realising I don't even know how badly injured she is. *What the fuck am I doing here?*

But that's all the introspection I'm allowed. I knew it would happen, was waiting for it. I'm in a bar surrounded by bikers; I'm wearing a leather jacket, but unlike them, no patches, looking surly and tense, covered with blood and clearly itching for a fight. There would be no other reason for me to come here. But they give me a chance, starting off slow. I get shoved, accidentally on purpose. An intelligent man would just move aside. But I'm not in the mood to be smart tonight. "What's your problem, motherfucker?" I growl.

"What did you call me?" A heavy-set biker, bearded and covered in tattoos looks at me incredulously.

"You heard. I asked 'What's your problem, *motherfucker?*'" I stir it up some more.

"Take it outside!" the barman shouts over. Knowing what's going to go down before it even begins.

Beardy looks at me, and I nod. I go to the door, not surprised that his two mates follow us. Three against one, that's the sort of odds I was looking for. Only a few minutes later I'm left lying on the ground having taken a good kicking. One of my eyes is swollen; my nose is bleeding, but I didn't hear the crunch that would tell me it's broken. I'm probably going to be pissing blood for a week, and any thought of sex is out of the question. And to top it all off, my lungs feel like they're burning from the smoke inhalation. But I relish the pain. I deserve it.

As I stagger to my feet, the pain helps to clear the fog in my mind and I limp back to my car. Technically I'm over the limit, but the fight has sobered me up, even if I wouldn't pass a breathalyser test. Taking out my phone, I turn it back on. There are a dozen or so messages and voicemails from Ben. I ignore them all, taking the quicker option of simply ringing him.

"Where the fuck are you?" he hisses once he realises it's me.

I tell him and hear his intake of breath.

"I'm not even going to ask why but I take it you're still alive as you're speaking to me." He pauses, "I'm at the hospital. You've got to get here. Now."

"Why? What's happened? How is she?" Concern floods through me, reminding what a bastard I am to have left.

"She's in surgery now. They waited as they had to make sure her lungs were clear enough for the anaesthetic. They're removing the bullet. She was in pieces before she went in, man. She needs you."

I shake my head, a useless gesture as he can't see me, "I fucked up, Ben. I…"

He speaks over me, not wanting to hear anything else I have to say, "Then get your arse back here and make it right!" He hangs up.

I reach the McClaren which is still where I left it. The tyres haven't been slashed and it's not been keyed, I count myself lucky. Yet again. I'd give everything I have to be able to pass that sort of luck onto Mia. Leaning my elbows on the roof and bowing my head for a moment before getting in, I remember how the car came into my possession; the grateful sheikh rewarding me for giving him back his life. Forgiving me for a mistake I shouldn't have made in the first place. *The same man I let down. Just as I let Mia down.* And then it comes to me, the fire, Mia's shooting had put it to the back of my mind but now it's at the forefront, banging on my head hurting worse than the blows to my face. Not only had I failed to protect her, the first time I took her to bed she used *her safeword.* For the first time in my fucking life, a sub safeworded out on me. Even as her Dom I botched it up, failing to recognise I was pushing her too far, too fast. Too fucking eager, to get inside her. The difference, with any other sub, is that it was always just play. Of course, I care about their needs and comfort, and there is mutual respect but nothing more than that. I made the same mistake as I made with Nijad. *I got emotionally involved. And my emotions blinded me.*

The pulsing pain all over my body gives my thoughts the clarity I didn't have before. I wasn't there for Nijad, but I've still got time to make things right for Mia.

My guilt feels a heavy burden as I drive back across London and to the hospital where the ambulance had taken her. Stopping off in a bathroom to clean the worst of the blood off my face, I examine myself in the mirror cringing at the mess I'm in. I've several cuts, and one of my eyes is swollen. My nose has stopped bleeding, but my blood, as well as her's has stained my T-shirt, though now it's dry it doesn't show too badly on the black material. Trying to ignore the pain in my back, and the throbbing in my swollen balls, I adjust my jeans in an effort to make myself more comfortable and then set off to face the music.

CHAPTER 22

Jon

Three years ago

W e didn't talk much about it, my partner Jasim and I. Never addressed the elephant in the room. It was as though Nijad was dead to both of us, our brother who'd turned out not to be the man we thought.

At first it was awkward returning to Club Tiacapan, which we owned with our third but silent partner, Jason Deville. Although anonymity is guaranteed in the club, it was impossible to hide that the Savage Sheikh, as the newspapers had named him, was in fact a well-known and previously well-liked member and more to the point my friend, and Jasim's brother. And, of course, on everyone's lips was the incident a few weeks ago when a Dom ignored a safeword and had to be pulled off his sub. Though right to stop the abuse, many could bear witness to the fact Nijad, the first to the rescue, had lost his temper and over-reacted, the level of violence used excessive, even given the provocation. The Dom, though it's doubtful he's worthy of that title, a certain Ethan St John Davies came very close to causing trouble for the club as a result. But luckily St John Davies had backed down from a court case, knowing certain facts about his lifestyle would have been disclosed in the public arena if he'd gone ahead.

We'd weathered that storm, but, of course, it fuelled speculation about whether Nijad was guilty or not, even after the papers had printed a retraction —at more not inconsiderable *expense to the Kassis family —when the woman had changed her statement.*

Jasim and I refused to comment; just gritted our teeth as we kept what we knew had to be the truth deep inside. Gradually the gossip died down, and the errant sheikh was forgotten when whatever next delicious scandal reared its head.

But I was unable to forget. Or to forgive.

Present day

Ben's made sure she's in a private room—I should have been here doing that. *Another strike against me.* He's sitting outside in the corridor and gets up when I appear. He looks me in the face, scrutinising my injuries for a moment before saying anything.

"You've looked worse." He tells me.

To say he's extremely unhappy with me is an understatement, and we'll probably be having a further discussion about my behaviour tonight at some point in the future. But right now I've got other things on my mind. "How is Mia?"

"In recovery. She should be back in her room very soon." He indicates the door behind him. "They removed the bullet without too much trouble, it didn't hit anything vital, but she lost a lot of blood."

"I let her down, Ben. Last night shouldn't have happened."

He glares, "No, it fucking shouldn't. But that maniac might have succeeded even if you'd been more on the ball."

"That bullet was meant for me."

He gives me a strange look, and I realise he knows something that I don't. "Yes, it was meant for you, but if he'd have killed you, Jon, it would have been worse for Mia."

I regard him curiously as he takes a phone out of his pocket.

"Mia's phone. She thought it was a text from you; it arrived just after she'd been admitted."

Another wave of guilt washes over me. I'd been so self-absorbed I'd left her to go through everything alone. I hold out my hand to take the phone and read the text message realising somehow the bastard has got hold of her mobile number.

YOU WON'T ESCAPE FROM ME AGAIN. NEXT TIME YOU'LL BE MINE BITCH. IT'S TIME TO PAY!

Raising my eyes to Ben, I nod, realising what he means. If he'd taken me out of action, he could have got away with Mia. The thought is chilling. "She needs more people on her. Twenty-four-hour protection. And somehow we need to flush this bastard out. The police know about this?"

He nods. "Yes, they interviewed her before she went into surgery. They've got their forensic people at the house," he pauses and grimaces, "Or what's left of it, but they're leaving protection to us. I've spoken to that detective, Coulton, and he'll be the liaison. They suggested a safe house, but I said we'd use one of ours. You'll be with her." The last was a statement rather than a question.

I shake my head. The realisation that her stalker very nearly got her due to my incompetence hits me all over again. Lowering my head into my hands, trying to think what's best for Mia, how to protect her and keep her safe. The answer hits me like a sledgehammer, and I know what I have to do. I need distance to be able to do my job, if I stayed close to her, I'd only lose myself all over again. Lifting my chin I look him straight in the eyes, and say as firmly, "Don't ask that of me. You know I'll only let her down."

His eyes flash with sudden anger. "You'll fucking stay with her, Jon. You've mucked up enough with her head. Admit you have feelings for her and accept that you're just like the rest of us. Human. We all make fucking mistakes! But most of us learn and move on." He leans forward, getting into my personal space. "Just fucking grow a pair and start behaving like a fucking adult for once!" He turns and storms off down the corridor as if wanting to be out of my presence.

It's unlike Ben to lose his temper; his words take me by surprise.

Suddenly he turns back. It seems he hasn't finished with me yet.

"And another thing. She fucking needs you, Jon. I got here as soon as I could, but it wasn't me she wants, it's you! You walk away, and you'll destroy her. I don't know what's happened between the two of you, but she depends on you. She needs her protector; she needs her Dom."

If I were a proper Dom, I'd have had her best interest a heart. If I were a proper Dom she wouldn't have had to scream Red at me. And I can't be her CPO. Because of my ineptitude, she's lost her home and almost her life. *No, I'm not good for her.* "She got hurt because of me." I'm too embarrassed to admit to him I made her say her safeword; that would remain our secret.

"She fucking chose to put herself in danger. It was her fucking choice, Jon. Just like when you took a bullet for Nijad, and before that, when you almost died for your country. *Her choice!* And why did she do that? Just stop a minute and ask yourself why? She fucking loves you, man!"

He doesn't know the half of it; I try to cover it up, "I'm just the first man…"

Again he interrupts me, getting right up into my face. "Yes, you're the first fucking man she's trusted in seven years! And why does she trust you? For your exceptional cock? She's a woman, Jon. She trusts you with her heart, and you'll rip it out if you walk away."

I realise that they must have had quite some conversation before she was taken into the operating theatre. I bow my head. "I don't need a fucking lecture, Ben."

His rage starts to cool, but somehow his quiet pronouncement is worse, "You're off the case, Jon. Take some time off."

My eyebrows raise, I'm not sure what he's getting at now.

"I'll assign a round the clock team to watch her. You'll stick with her like glue, but we won't let him creep up on her again. You can't resist dipping your wick—we'll be there to blow out the candle while you're otherwise engaged."

He's offering a chance for me to be with Mia, but taking away my responsibility for keeping her safe. But I won't take him up on it. I'm the wrong man and the wrong Dom for her. If I'd been stronger, had more control I'd have stopped Mia putting her life on the line for me. That's why she's fucking under the knife right now. Because I'm weak.

I glare at him, "I'm going to do my job, Ben. There was never anything between Mia and myself except for good healthy sex. She might think there's more to it, but as you said, I'm the first man she's had in seven years. She won't be able to trust me again. I'm a Dom, Ben. In our lifestyle, as you're well aware, trust is the key. You don't need to tell me how stupid I was to start something with her, but it was always going to end sooner rather than later. I don't *do* relationships; you know that. So it's best I hurt her now. Rip the plaster off quickly. She'll get over it. I have no more feelings for her than any sub I've played with." If I keep telling myself that maybe I'll start to believe it. "Put me back on the rota."

His eyes have been opening wider and wider as he's been listening to me, now he shakes his head in despair. "You'll back off? Really?" He's not able to believe it.

Our conversation is interrupted when a bed is wheeled down the corridor and into the room behind us. A sleepy Mia on it, her face almost as pale as the white sheet she's lying on. She's got a drip running into her arm. It breaks my heart to see her so weak and looking so forlorn and lost, but I don't let my emotions show. I nod at Ben, keeping my face impassive, trying silently to convince him I can separate the personal from professional and follow her into the room. The nurses look like they are going to shoo me out, but my glare discourages them from making the suggestion.

The constant beeping of the monitor is getting on my nerves, but I keep up my vigil sitting beside her. She's still sleeping; the anaesthetic is taking a while to wear off. As I watch her, even though I fight them, emotions flood me. Guilt and regret. She's the first and only woman I've allowed to get close to me, and how did it end up? *She could have been killed.* Looking down at her body, I remember how I'd thought about her carrying my child, seeing her belly swell with the seed I'd planted there. My gut clenches, and pain like a punch hits me harder than any the bikers threw. If I had got her pregnant, then she'd have had me tied up tighter than any form of bondage I've ever used. And I'd have had the excuse I need to stay. But we'd been careful; there's no possibility of that.

I hear her stir, and then cough to clear her throat. I get to my feet and stand over her. Her eyes widen, full of horror, and she screams. "Get away from me! Get away, get away!" She's hysterical.

The door opens behind me, and a nurse rushes in, quickly followed by Ben. The latter grabs me by the arms and pulls me away from the bed.

"What the fuck did you do?" he rasps out. He attempts to get me out of the room, but I'm not going to go, shrugging his hand off my arm and glaring at him.

"I didn't fucking do anything!" I hiss back.

The nurse throws me a disgusted look and tries to calm Mia. She's stroking her forehead, talking to her quietly and softly. Mia seems to relax and turns her head to look at me; she's shaking and panicked. *This is the reaction I sought, I needed her to see me as the fallible man who let her down, wanted her to blame me.* But now it's obvious she knows how much I failed her, I crave her forgiveness.

I try to go to her, but Ben holds me back, not releasing me until Mia puts out her hand reaching for me, her eyes full of tears.

"Jon…. I'm sorry. I was dreaming."

It's impossible not to offer her comfort; I go to her.

"Oh, Jon," she raises her good arm and pulls me to her, looking aghast at my face. "What's happened to you?" She gently brushes her hand across my cheek.

Fuck! She's still thinking about me, rather than herself. I shrug off her concern. "I got into a fight."

"What does the other guy look like?" She doesn't ask me why. *Does she know me that well?*

"The *three* of them," I emphasise, "Look worse."

She tries to laugh, but it starts her coughing. The nurse comes across; she's been observing us carefully. After giving me a sharp look, she turns to Mia, explaining to her how she can use the pump to give her more painkillers if necessary, and, passing her the call button, how she can summon help if she needs it. After one last look of disgust directed at me, she leaves us alone. I figure she doesn't approve of fighting.

Mia pulls back from me and looks across at Ben, who seems reluctant to leave us alone. Her gaze turns back to me, "My throat. It's sore."

"It's the tube they use when you're under, Mia. It will get easier soon." Ben's comforting her; I should be doing that. *No, I've got to distance myself.*

She nods. "It triggered a memory."

Ben moves closer to the bed. "What did you remember?"

I turn and glare at him. "Not now, Ben. She doesn't need it to go through it right now."

She swallows, talking is obviously painful for her. I can't help taking her hand and squeezing it as she looks between Ben and me. "Yes, now. While it's fresh, in my mind."

I don't think she needs to be put through anything else tonight, she's suffered enough. But as she continues to stare at me intently, I give her a reluctant nod to proceed.

"I remember a lot of what happened to me, but it's usually in flashes, those bastards using me."

She's brave, starting to talk about things that she's kept hidden. I already know most of it, but I'm impressed she's opening up in front of Ben.

"One of them was the worst, the most violent. I don't think he cared what happened to me. Like I was some sort of toy?" She glances up, making sure we understand. "When he was…" she licks her lips.

"Do you want some water?" I hand her the glass by the bed and place the straw to her mouth. She takes a few sips, and then coughs.

"When he was *raping* me he'd put his hand around my throat, cutting off my air. He didn't care if he killed me."

"It's alright Mia; you don't have to say anymore." My suggestion is as much for me as for her; having to listen to what she went through is killing me.

"But I want to. If it's one of my abusers is the stalker, surely anything I remember might help?"

She's right. I glance at Ben. He makes a gesture as if to ask me whether he should leave, but I shake my head. If Mia doesn't mind, then I think he should stay. I'm not even sure I want to hear anymore.

"They had these gadgets. One was a dental gag." She looks up at us both, "I looked into BDSM toys for my books, but I never wrote toys being used to hurt people. Not until the last book." She shrugs self-depreciatingly, "I thought it meant I was stronger and getting over it. Anyway, he used the dental gag and said he was going to fuck my mouth and choke me until I was dead. He said, 'You're going to die, bitch, then I'll bring you back and do it all over again.' My throat is sore, and my chest hurts. It just brought it all back."

"Your throat hurts from the tube, Mia, and you breathed in a lot of smoke," I explain how her memory could have been triggered even as Ben and I are exchanging glances. We never allow breath play at the Tiacapan—it's too dangerous. And I've seen dental gags used as a punishment, but frown on them as they seem too much like abuse. In a seedy club abroad, I've also seen a woman accidentally suffocated until her heart stopped, needing CPR to bring her back—she ended up with a couple of broken ribs. I recalled Mia's recollection of her injuries when she was freed, and with disgust, wonder if that's what happened to her.

Ben steps forwards. "In your last book, you wrote about a wannabe Dom?"

"Can I have some more water?" She takes a longer drink this time before waving it away. "Yes. Before my books have focused on pleasure, but this time, I was exploring what could go wrong if the Dom didn't know what he was doing."

"The way you wrote, were you describing your experiences?"

She looks away as if she doesn't want to answer, swallows, and then answers quietly, "I didn't think so when I was writing it. But I think I'd probably blocked out some of the worse details. The dental gag and breath play. Yes." she admits, her croaky voice even softer and hard to hear. "I didn't consciously remember it as something that actually happened to me. It's only just come back."

Ben and I exchange glances. "Did you include anything else in your book?"

Mia thinks before replying, "The whipping scene?"

I flinch, remembering the silver white scars I saw on her back.

"The character I wrote about, he's a sadist, Jon, with no respect for any real power exchange."

I nod. I've read the book—the story's good, but I hadn't realised the significance at the time. There was no way I could have known she'd been retelling actual incidents, especially as she hadn't even realised herself.

"I'll tell Sean what to watch out for," Ben suggests. I agree with him; it sounds like we're on the right track sending him out round the clubs.

I put my head on one side, trying to remember the plot. "He has male subs."

Her head shoots round. She grimaces with pain at the sudden movement. I'm by her side in seconds, handing her the gadget to give her another dose of painkiller. She pushes my hand away, "No more morphine, Jon. I don't want to go back there."

I nod, the narcotic can cause hallucinations, and I understand why she'd rather suffer. Even so, it kills me to see her in pain; she closes her eyes for a moment. She opens them again and looks straight at me. Something's triggered another memory.

"The other man was his sub. He had anal sex with him, whilst..." Her manner is matter of fact, but I know it costs her.

While the other man was raping her. I complete the sentence in my head. I can see Ben doing the same when he turns and takes his leave.

"I'm out of here, mate. I'll get this followed up." Ben can hardly speak through his disgust.

Left alone with Mia all I want to say is how sorry I am, but I don't know where to start. It's my fucking fault that she's lying there, pale, wan, and in pain. If I hadn't been so fucking possessive of her, I'd have had another man in the house looking out for her, but no, I wanted her all to myself. Fucking excellent close protection I provided, sleeping a satiated sleep while her bastard stalker escalated the action and burnt her house to the ground. She's lost everything, and all because of me. I put my head in my hands and harden my heart, and my resolve. She's better off without me.

"You look done in," she says, sympathy clear in her voice. "I want you to hold me, Jon. Can you get on the bed?"

"I don't want to hurt you." My response is stiff.

"You won't." She shifts over so she makes room on the side of her good arm.

"I'm okay here, Mia."

"Make me feel safe, Jon."

She's asking the impossible. How could she ever feel safe with me again? Not unless I played the role I should have been fucking playing all along.

"I'm here to protect you." I kept my voice cold. "You've been hurt because I took my eye off the ball. It won't happen again

"Shush." She reaches for my hand and brushes her fingers gently across it.

"Why did you, Mia? Why did you move in front of me?" I have to ask.

"Why did you do it for Nijad?"

"It was my fucking job. It wasn't the same."

Her head shakes. "He was your friend, Jon. More than a friend, just like you are to me. It was impulsive, instinctive. I didn't want you hurt."

Her hand's on mine, but I don't respond in any way. I have to stop this now. "I'm sorry Mia; things should never have gone as far as they did. I was supposed to be doing my job, and I failed. Unless you want me completely off the case, I'll stay on to provide protection, but our relationship will be purely professional from here on in.

I hear her gasp and feel her distress. I know that I'm a bastard, but also that I have to let her go.

"What about when the stalker's caught, Jon?"

I decide to play dumb. "I'll have done my job."

"And you'll move on? Just like that? Couldn't you give us a chance?"

No. I can't allow someone to have that much power over me. I *care* god-damn-it. For the first time in my life, I care about a woman, and it hurts so fucking much. Forcing my features to stay neutral, I say the bitter words she has to hear. "I think it's best we make a clean break. This isn't going anywhere, Mia. I'm not the kind of guy you need. You care for me, and I'm sorry, I can't reciprocate in the way you'd like me to. I don't do relationships. It's best to put a stop to it now."

"But you said…"

"I said a lot of things. I got carried away, Mia. I'm sorry. But this is me; it would never work between us. I'm not the right man for you."

She turns her head away from me and so misses the look of desolation on my face. It's going to be the hardest thing I've ever done to walk out of here. But I won't have her putting herself at risk again. Better she hates me.

"What about the club?"

I'm not expecting that question. "What do you mean?"

"I'd still like access to it." Her voice that started soft gets a bit stronger. "For my research."

"Are you suggesting I play with you there?" I still don't grasp what she's getting at. "I'm not sure that would be a good idea. I can't be your Dom, Mia. You had to use your safeword, remember?"

"Jon, that wasn't your fault!" She looks surprised I'd brought that up. "It was another trigger, but you got me through it." A tear runs from her eye, "It was wonderful."

I shrug, "I should have stopped before it got that far. But yes, the sex was good, very enjoyable. But sex is sex. You haven't got any experiences to compare it to."

She's staring at me; her mouth falls open as I shock her with my cold statement. Her eyes turn steely. When she starts speaking, I'm not expecting the words. "No, I'm not suggesting I play with you," she sounds adamant as she adds, "But there are other Doms at the club. And as you say, I could do with the sampling a variety until I find what I like."

I'm caught. I see red and want to fucking hit something. The thought of anyone touching her causes me such rage I clench my fists trying to control myself. The one good thing is that she's not looking at me so doesn't see my reaction. So I come up with the first answer that comes into my head. A cruel response, showing what a motherfucking sonofabitch I am. "You can't afford the fees, Mia."

She turns back and looks me straight in the eye. "Then I'll find another club. One that's within my price range." Her eyes narrow, she's furious, and I don't blame her. "I took a bullet for you Jon, but all you can fucking think about is yourself. Would you rather he'd killed you and then kidnapped me again? I don't think he'd have made it quick and clean.

"But oh, no. This has to be about fucking Jon Tharpe. Well, get the fuck out of here you moron! And get someone else to protect me. Or I'll go to another company. I never want to see your fucking face again!"

I was going to say something, but her eyes narrow, and it's clear she's not finished yet. "You're great in the sack, Jon, but that's not surprising considering all the women you've had. I'm not stupid; I know I'm just another in a long line. I'm grateful for your attentions, but don't confuse lust with emotions. You were convenient and an easy lay!"

Jesus! She's got claws. The look on her face sears me. An easy lay? Did she actually just say that to me? Does she fucking mean it? I swallow down the words that would refute her declaration before they can escape my mouth. Isn't this exactly what I want? To be free of her? She's just given me an out, enabling me to walk away free of any guilt. *And I fucking hate it!*

Pulling myself from the chair, I hide my wince at the pain in my back and the throbbing in my balls. My head's aching like a bitch, but I'm careful not to let her see the agony I'm in, especially the mental hurt that hits me like a twenty-ton lorry. "I'll be outside. Until someone relieves me." I want to reassure her I'll do my job to keep her safe.

She hides her face from me and doesn't even watch me go.

I walk to the door, open it, and make a point of closing it noisily, so she knows I'm gone. I take out my phone and text Ben, advising him he needs to get someone else here as soon as possible. Then I stand outside, military style, my legs apart, my hands behind my back, reverting to my early days in the army when I'd stand for hours on guard, my mind, of necessity blank, focusing only on my surroundings and ignoring any discomfort. I'll guard her with my body. But I don't know how to guard my heart.

CHAPTER 23

Mia

Seven years ago

The sun just beginning to rise over the horizon told me it must be early morning; my thoughts confirmed when I heard the electric whirr of a milkman's van in the distance. Looking around, I recognised the triangle of green grass at the end of the road where that fateful party had been held. Once I had my bearings, I very carefully pulled myself to my feet and started the thankfully short, but painful trek home.

I'd lost my bag; I had no keys, so had to knock on the door of my house, clinging on to the frame so I didn't fall over. After what seemed like forever the door opened.

"Mum." I burst into tears; it was hard to stand unaided, but I reached out for her. I needed comfort and kindness and believed she must have been so worried when I hadn't come home.

But she didn't move, didn't pull me to her. Showing no particular relief after I'd been missing for two days, she, just stood there, staring at me, taking in my appearance. Then she hissed, "Get inside, now!" and pulled me roughly into the house uncaring of my injuries. "You don't want the neighbours to see." Once through the door she stepped back and took a proper look at me. As she did so, her eyes narrowed in disgust.

"I think I need a doctor," I told her, my voice breaking as I sobbed. "And the police."

She drew herself up to her full height. "You're seeing no one *and going nowhere, Mia Fable! Do you want to bring shame down on this house? Do you think I want everyone gossiping about the slut I have for a daughter?"* There was no sympathy in her voice at all.

"But I've been raped, Mum." I decided to spell it out for her. *"The police need to find the men who did it. And I'm hurt, hurt badly."*

She shook her head, as angry as I'd ever seen her. But all her rage was directed at me, as was all the blame. *"You went out looking like a whore, no wonder someone took advantage of you. You're a dirty girl, a slut; you got everything you deserved. Now get up to your bedroom. And stay there!"*

My mouth fell open in horror and dismay, unable to believe she hadn't the slightest drop of compassion for my plight.

Present day

Jon's gone. For good. Any chance of a relationship developing between us had been killed stone dead by the words we'd hurled around, verbal arrows designed to hurt their target. With a sob, I wonder how much of what he said was true; not much of what came out of my mouth was. *Oh, my God, what have I done?* When he said those hurtful things to me, I had to retaliate, couldn't just lie there and take it. And then it escalated so fast! There can no way to get back from this; there's no point in trying. Not now, too much has been said. Had he riled me on purpose? Or had he meant what he those words? However much truth those spiteful comments held, they've caused irrevocable damage. As they were meant to do.

The pain throbbing through my arm is a distraction, vying with the emotional hurt to take first place. Briefly, I look longingly at the morphine pump beside me but refrain from pressing the button. Although relief from the pain and a drug-induced sleep would be welcome, I want no more hallucinations or dreams.

The clock on the wall lets me know it's midday, and as I didn't get much sleep last night, I'm tired as well as woozy from the effects of the anaesthetic and loss of blood, and, I suppose, I'm in shock. You don't expect to lose your house, and stop a bullet all in one night. And on top of that, I've now lost Jon.

I've lost everything I own. My house, my lovely little cottage. Ben had told me it's completely gone, utterly destroyed with only the chimney left standing, but I don't give a damn about bricks and mortar. Although it's the house I proudly purchased with the earnings from my writing and was comfortable and cosy, I could never feel secure there again. And the only memories I'd want to keep had been made there had been with Jon, and now I'll have to try to put those behind me too.

Possessions can be replaced, a new house bought with the insurance money, and the future can take care of itself. I don't need my cottage, but I need Jon. *Oh God, why can't I get him out of my mind?* How can he end it like this? He's done so much for me, helping me to escape from the self-imposed prison cell I'd locked myself in for so long, showing me how to be a woman, how to enjoy my body without the pain or shame. How can I conceive of moving on?

I won't cry. I won't. With great difficulty, I fight to hold back the tears, forcing myself to concentrate on other matters, the practical things I have to do. As well as sorting out the insurance, I have to do something about my work. I'll need to ring Val and get an extension from the publishers; I won't be able to use a keyboard with both hands for a few weeks. The bullet didn't damage anything vital, but my muscles are torn and need to heal. All my work's backed in the cloud, so once my laptop's replaced I'll be up and running again. But what frightens me is that the voices that usually reside in my head are silent; my characters have abandoned me. Will I ever be able to write again? And if I do, would I ever be able to write about relationships and intimacy without thinking of Jon?

Oh, for heaven's sake! He won't get out of my head! Perhaps I'll risk some morphine; it might quieten my thoughts.

There's a quiet knock on the door, and then it opens, and Ben enters the room. His look of sympathy is unwelcome, so I nod a greeting, struggling to keep myself composed, and carefully school my features; glad I'd been strong enough to hold back my tears.

He gives me an intense stare which I return, showing I'm strong enough to take anything he wants to tell me. With a quick shake of his head, he imparts what he's come to say. "Jon's off the case."

"Good," I reply, sharply, incline my head then lift my chin, hoping I'm conveying satisfaction.

"That's what you want?" He waits for my confirmation. The doubting look on his face suggests I haven't fooled him.

"Yes." I'm proud my voice portrays more strength than I feel.

He continues to study me intently. "He cocked up."

I'm not sure what to say. Yes, he did, but we could have moved past that if Jon's guilt hadn't made him turn tail and run. "I don't blame him. No one could have predicted the stalker was going to get up close and personal."

"We should've been prepared, though. That's what we're paid for." As Ben looks down at the floor, he seems embarrassed on behalf of Grade A.

There's no answer to that.

"I've assigned Ryan and Sean as your protection. They'll stick with you like glue. When you're out of here, we'll see if we need others. We're going to keep you safe." His unspoken words came across. Clearly, he's determined they won't cock up again.

Opening the door, he waves in the two men in question and makes the introductions. As he does so, I recall I've met them before, at the Grade A security offices. It seems a lifetime ago now, was it only last Saturday? Without much interest I examine my new bodyguards, seeing they both look competent. Each must be well over six foot and gifted with more than average good looks which makes me idly wonder whether that's a requirement to work for Grade A. Ryan's broad, but with muscle not fat, and has his hair trimmed short in a military cut. He nods at me then takes on a vigilant stance. Sean is slim but appears lithe, strong, and fast. His blond hair is longer, just touching his shoulders, but perfectly styled. I'm a sucker for long hair, and when he turns his megawatt smile on me it should have produced a spark inside me but I have no reaction at all. I manage to say a simple 'hi' to verify we've been introduced, then Ben opens the door and ushers them back out.

"You'll be going to a safe house when the hospital discharges you." Ben resumes speaking almost before his employees leave the room.

I'd been so torn up about Jon, surprisingly I hadn't given much thought to the fact I'm now homeless. "I could go and stay with Val," I frown, even as I suggest it. I count her as a friend, but not one I'd feel comfortable imposing on in that way.

Dismissing my suggestion with a wave, he explains, "The safe house is easier to guard. It's secure and alarmed."

I huff, unable to stop my sarcastic comment, "So was my house."

He shrugs, conceding my point, but continues to explain his preferred option. "The safe house has better security; steel shutters can be lowered over the windows, and there's no access from the garden. Lots of features all designed to keep the bad guys out."

Moving closer, he takes the chair Jon so recently vacated. "I'll send Vanessa out to get some clothes for you. She'll just get you some basics to get you started." He takes a box out of his pocket and waves it at me. "This is a new phone for you. I've put Vanessa's number in and she's expecting your call so you can discuss what you want her to get for you." A grin transforms his face, "I know you ladies are particular when it comes to make-up and such like," he smirks, "And she'll want to know whether you want thongs or bikinis, high legs or whatever."

Though I hadn't expected it his wry comment forces a laugh to burst from me. Something I didn't think the misery of the day would allow. "You know a lot about lady's underwear, Ben!" I'm impressed with the way he's covering all the basics. It shows how confused my head is. I hadn't even thought about the fact I only have the smoky, bloody clothes I was brought in with. They'll never be able to be worn again. I thank him.

As he tosses a box on the bed and I see it's a brand new iPhone, I can't think why he's giving it to me. "I've got a phone, Ben," I tell him, curious. I don't know how, but I'd had the presence of mind to grab my handbag before leaving the burning house.

"Somehow he's got your number, Mia. I'd like to keep hold of your phone. If he tries to contact you again, we can try and track him. You can wipe anything you need to do, first, if you like. Oh, and give me the code to get into it."

I shudder, receiving a text was bad enough, I wouldn't want to receive an actual call. So I've no problem with Ben taking custody of my phone, and there's nothing on it that I wouldn't want him to see. I've no issue giving him the pin number he needs. I don't want to be kept out of the loop, though. "You'll tell me if he makes contact? I need to know what's going on. Please don't leave me out of it, Ben; I'd go mad if you kept me in the dark."

"Don't worry; I'll personally make sure you're kept fully briefed." His face grows serious, "I've been speaking with Detective Coulter. We both believe the fire wasn't meant to kill you, just get you out of the house. By attacking both front and rear, your only exit was via the lounge windows; he must have been keeping watch for you to come out. And that the bullet was meant to kill your bodyguard." He rubs his hand over his face, pausing with his fingers resting under his chin. Idly I notice he needs a shave. "He wanted you, Mia. Neither Coulter nor I think this is about money."

"He was going to take me." A simple enough statement, but one that fills me with horror.

He moves his hand from his face, and it comes to rest on mine, it doesn't soothe me like Jon's touch would have done. "It seems a fair assumption that he wants some up close and personal time with you. But don't worry, my team will do everything possible to prevent that happening, so that means keeping you out of his way until we've caught him."

I shiver. Deep down I think I've always known the stalker wanted me; it wasn't hard to interpret the notes that way. But if the stalker was one and the same with one of my rapists from seven years ago… *Shit!* I wouldn't be able to go through that again. And this time, if he gets me, from the wording of the notes I'm sure he won't be letting me go.

Ben notices my consternation. "We *are* going to keep you safe."

"But how long will it take to find him? It might be weeks, months? I can't hide forever!" Ten days ago I was living my nice quiet life, no threats, no one after me. Now I'm being forced into hiding.

"We're working on it, and so are the police. But just as a precaution…." He reaches into his other pocket and brings out a small packet. As he opens it, I see some small buttons. Confused, I try and sit up for a closer look and grimace as the action pulls on my wound. Ben notices, "Don't move; I'll bring them over."

He sits on the bed, careful not to jolt me. "These are GPS devices. I've got three here that you can keep with you, in your bag, a pocket, a shoe. In the unlikely event he manages to get through all the security and takes you, we'll be able to track you. We're trying to cover all bases."

Though hopefully, it's doubtful he'd get through both of my newly assigned protectors, the thought they'd be able to find me fast if he did is a comforting one. "Thank you, Ben. That makes me feel a lot better."

Just the action of trying to sit up has made me dizzy and ill. All at once everything seems to catch up with me, and a myriad of emotions hit me. Despair, confusion, fear and anger; the mental and physical pain combined with exhaustion hits me. I don't want to talk anymore. Leaning back on the pillows, I shut my eyes, hoping he'll get the message. It's not long before the sound of the door softly closing reaches me.

I sleep for a while and wake to feel a little stronger. I deter Val from coming to visit. I don't want her or anyone to see me in this state. As I am, I'm struggling to keep it together, with Jon's desertion going round and round my head. A friendly face offering sympathy would probably make me lose it.

The doctors decided to keep me in the hospital overnight but assess me as fit enough to be discharged the next day. I leave, kitted out with a sling. When I open the bag Sean had given me, I find Vanessa's bought me a button up sleeveless top that is loose enough to fit over my bandage, and a pair of sweatpants. I'm glad she didn't go for jeans; I always have to try on a few pairs to get ones that fit properly, tending to hover between a size six and eight, and different shops seem to cater for different builds. The underwear I've asked for is there. I went for bikinis; there's no point suffering an uncomfortable thong if no one's going to see it. Likewise, the bra is plain and functional. Everything's brand new, complete with tags.

She's also bought me a leather jacket, similar to my old favourite which is now probably cinders in the remains of my home. Choking back a sob as I realise how much I've lost, I wonder how she knew which one I wore. The suspicion that Jon might have had a hand in choosing it goes through my head. But I dismiss quickly it as wishful thinking. He'd made it plain he wanted nothing more to do with me, however much my heart would like to think he's there in the background, still watching out for me.

Sighing, I remind myself I've pulled myself back from worse things, so when Sean and Ryan open my door to check I'm ready for the off, I even manage a smile as I take my leave of the nurse who's just been helping me dress.

"Morning, boys." I succeed in sounding at least part way cheerful.

Sean makes a mock bow, "Your chariot awaits, ma'am." He grins, while Ryan, the more serious of the two, just acknowledges me with a lift of his chin before stepping forwards to take charge of my meagre collection of belongings. Sean takes my arm, and I exit, with great pleasure, the sterile hospital room. It crosses my mind that I've an incredibly handsome man touching me, his hand cupping my elbow. And I don't feel a bloody thing.

It's not a long journey to the safe house. It's small and in the middle of a terrace, with a back and front door, the houses on either side preventing more entry routes. The back garden is plain grass fenced in with six-foot panels—all alarmed they assure me—with no hedges or shrubs to hide behind. Likewise, the front is paved and open. I'm shown so many security gadgets inside I start to suspect Fort Knox could learn a few lessons from this place. The tour helps me feel safe, and the bedroom I'm assigned is comfortable, clean, and fresh albeit stark and utilitarian. I realise I haven't any personal possessions to made it feel like my own.

After a quick look round and having put away the one other set of clothing Vanessa had bought me, I go back down to the lounge, disoriented and unsure what I'm going to do. There's a TV, but that doesn't excite me; having lost everything I suppose I'm relegated to reading books on my phone. So I'm surprised, and pleased to find, sitting on a coffee table, a new laptop still boxed up with a note on it addressed to me. And it's the same model I lost in the fire. Picking up the paper on top, I read the few words written there: *To get you started and help you get back on your feet.* I wonder. *Did Jon have a hand in this?* But whether he did or not, I'm not going to look a gift horse in the mouth. The ability to work is a normality I need, even if I'm limited as to how much I'll be able to do at this stage.

My arm's aching like a bitch, but having internet access will keep me occupied. Impatient to get it up and running, I have to ask Sean to help me get it out of the box, resentful at being so weak and helpless. A feeling I haven't felt for seven years.

No, I'm not going to think that way again. I'm not the person I was then. Pulling myself together, I plug in the charger and sit with the laptop resting on my knees. Painstakingly I go through the registration process, entering all my details from scratch feeling like I'm beginning my life all over again. I've still got all the important stuff held in the Cloud; all my books, completed or in progress stored there along with notes and vital documents. But everything I'd saved locally is lost forever; photos, music, emails going back years. Suddenly I'm overwhelmed by what's happened. I have the clothes I stand up in and a change for tomorrow, but that's all. A sob rises in my throat and the tears well in my eyes and fall down my face. In just a few seconds I'm crying hysterically, and I don't know how to stop.

I'm not sure quite how long my crying jag lasts, but after a while, a box of tissues magically appears by my side and, wiping my eyes, I see Ryan hunkering down in front of me. He reaches out his enormous hand taking my much smaller one in his; his pained expression, the slight shake of his head conveying sympathy. As he crouches in front of me, staying silent, the fact I've got an audience is embarrassing and gives me the encouragement I need to try and stop the flood of tears. As my sobs gradually fade, I start to apologise.

Ryan takes the laptop, which was still on my knees and puts it to one side. "You've been shot, Mia. You're in shock and need to rest." He looks at me with his serious gaze. "You've held it together amazingly up to now. I'm not sure many people would have been as strong as you."

The gentle words from such a burly, taciturn man help me suppress the last few involuntary sobs from my bout of tears.

CHAPTER 24

Jon

Six months ago

To get a phone call from Jasim out of the blue, when his greeting was simply his disowned brother's name, was fucking unreal. And it got worse as I listened to what he had to say. By the time he'd finished, I was hardly capable of forming any words at all, his news hitting me so hard I could barely keep hold of the phone. I managed to stammer out my agreement when infected by his sense of urgency; I agreed to drop everything and leave on the first available flight to Paris.

I met him at Charles de Gaulle airport. Although Jasim had been attending a meeting in Germany, our planes landed only an hour apart. While I'd been waiting I hadn't stopped pacing; the implications of the little he'd told me so far completely screwing up my head. When I heard the details he'd waited to divulge in person; I was shocked to the very core; the news hit me as hard as a punch to the gut.

As I easily read the guilt written all over his face, I knew his expression only matched mine. If what he told me was the truth, we'd facilitated a grievous wrong. A wrong for which penance was still being paid, three years later. Had we misjudged the situation? Misjudged our brother? His true brother in blood, mine by friendship.

In the middle of the busy airport, we grasped each other's hands, and I'd felt the slight tremble in his. "Cara may be wrong," I told him.

He shook his head, "That fucking hole in the wall, Jon. We all missed that. His bruised and grazed hand, his blood on his knuckles, his blood on her."

"If she was lying…" I start, unable to believe I could have missed the signs. Chantelle, Nijad's girlfriend, had been so credible.

"She's lucky she's a woman," he growled in response.

Together we trawled the backstreets of the French capital. It took surprisingly little time to track down Chantelle, who we found whoring herself out to survive. And that's when we discovered everything had been a lie; the scene set up to incriminate Nijad. Orchestrated by her boyfriend who'd appropriated the six-figure payoff she'd received from the Kassis family for himself. A set up that was so cleverly enacted that even Nijad had believed the evidence against him and had spent the last three years in physical exile and mental anguish over a crime he'd never committed.

I should have known my friend wasn't capable of such an attack, despite the forensic evidence and the unshakeable story the woman had given, I should have realised my blood brother could never have committed such a crime. I should have trusted in him, instead of letting his supposed betrayal get to me. Should have calmly balanced what I knew of the man against what I saw in front of my eyes. But I hadn't.

It kept me awake at night, the guilt I held inside. My sixth sense had kept my men and me out of danger so many times, my premonitions had warned me of the attack in Paris in time to save many lives, so how could I have judged Nijad so wrongly? His presumed actions had offended me on a deeply personal level; having felt betrayed that I'd given my friendship and love to such a man. If I'd just been his CPO, I might have been able to see through the emotional fog that had clouded my mind, but I'd become more than that.

I'd become his blood brother, and that had made me blind.

Present day

Putting my hand over my mouth, unsuccessfully trying to stifle a yawn, I realise just how long it's been since I last had more than a couple of hours of sleep. As soon as I close my eyes everything swirls around my head, leaving me feeling like I'm on a never-slowing merry-go-round, missing Mia like I'd miss a part of my body. The errors I'd made were Paris all over again, but this time the my emotions caused the error of judgement that almost got a woman killed. I should have known not to get involved. When I do, I only end up making one mistake after another. I'd underestimated my opponent, and Mia got hurt. On my fucking watch! I've no option but to stay away from her; I failed to keep her safe.

Ben's furious with me, he doesn't understand; it caused our first ever stand up row. When he demanded I get right off the case and go to the States to oversee a new contract, he was incensed at my refusal. But even now I can't distance myself completely. I have to know what is going on with Mia, overseeing her safety if only from a distance. After a heated argument, he reluctantly agreed; the threat of having to find a new partner being the final and dirtiest card I played. So that's why I'm sitting here today, taking the lead in Mia's case, but remaining firmly in the background.

I yawn again and rub my tired eyes, forcing myself focus back to the meeting going on.

"That's three clubs now, and I've not come up with anything." Sean finishes up his report, glancing across at me. He's spending his days at the safe house guarding Mia; nights he's trawling round kink clubs looking for something that doesn't look right. So far he's come up with zilch. Sean's a great choice to investigate the clubs, not only is he a switch and happy to either top or bottom, but he's also bi-sexual. His pretty boy looks have broad appeal.

"Enjoying your work, Sean?" Vanessa grins.

Sean smirks. "It's dirty work, but someone's got to do it."

His response gets a laugh from them all. Going to a club and not playing is like going to a bar and refusing to drink; it would raise suspicions, so I've no doubt he's mixing business with pleasure.

"I've made a bit of progress," Vanessa starts, and my attention swiftly shifts to her. "We've got a name from a couple of the partygoers. It seems there was a guy called Miller there, and he was seen leaving with a girl who one person remembered looked pretty drunk. No one knows much about him, though. He sounds like the proverbial gate crasher."

"Miller the surname?"

Vanessa shrugs. "Could be a first name I suppose, but it would be an unusual one." She glances down at her papers. "We're assuming it's the surname, so we're going back to the electoral registers for the surrounding areas. A couple of families in a twenty-mile radius were called Miller, but none with a young person of the right age at the time. We know he drove so he'd be seventeen at least, and from what we've been told he didn't stand out from the crowd so was probably not much older. So we're assuming he had to be late teens or early twenties. Therefore we're looking for someone in that age group."

"Keep searching," I tell her, then, turning to Sean again; I ask a question, not sure I want to hear his answer, "How's Mia coping?"

After giving me a sharp look, he takes a deep breath in and lets it out before he speaks, as though trying to gather his thoughts. Is he going to censor what he tells me?

"Outwardly, man? She seems to be okay; she's started working again. Val, her agent, came to visit her yesterday, and she seems happy enough with her new deadlines. But I think she's struggling. She wants to get on with her life, but can't until we sort this bastard out." As he finishes speaking, the look he throws me suggests he wants to add something more but refrains when he catches my glare.

"I asked Nafisa to help her sort out her insurance etc.," Vanessa breaks in, "It's one hell of a thing to deal with when everything's literally gone up in smoke. Just sorting out the utility bills is a pain. Nafisa spent an hour on the phone yesterday. They were insistent they couldn't do anything without an account number, and all her paperwork was destroyed! Nafisa's hopefully taking the pressure of the drudgery off her a bit at least."

"Thanks for doing that, Vanessa. And thank Nafisa for me." I'm pleased they're helping Mia out and guilty that I'm not doing anything tangible myself. I couldn't even go to the clubs with Sean as Mia's stalker would recognise me. The only thing I'd been able to do was to replace her bloody laptop.

"We'll continuing trawling the clubs," Ben broke in, informing us. "Sean's going to Satan's Kinks tonight."

I know of it. It's a popular club in Soho and would attract a large crowd on a Saturday night.

After throwing a few more ideas around, I close up the meeting, but remain in the room on my own, ostensibly to finish my cup of cold coffee, but in reality using the time to think. We're making some progress, but it's all too slow. Too fucking slow! There's been nothing from the stalker all week—no phone messages or any contact made through her agent or publisher, the only other two ways he could try to get in touch. But as long as Mia's in the safe house I know she's out of danger. But she can't stay there forever. Sean's right, Mia needs to be able to move on with her life. *And then perhaps I'll be able to move on too.*

"Time to call it a day, Jon."

I start and look over my shoulder to see Ben's returned. "I'm just going." I frown, wanting to be alone with my thoughts.

Looking at me carefully, he takes the chair opposite. For the past few days, he's barely spoken to me, except when he has to. I know I shouldn't have pulled that stunt about selling up partnership in Grade A. It wasn't fair to him. I watch as he runs his hand across his face. His eyes look at me, searchingly.

"It's called survivors' guilt, Jon." Ben's words jolt me.

I stare at him, my eyes narrowing. I want to tell him just to go, but something in what he says touches a chord.

"Jon, you're starting to worry me. You're a prat, but why? Think about it! What did Nijad do, Jon?" He prompts me. "You took a bullet for him."

I shake my head. "Totally different. It was my job."

"But you're his friend. He felt guilty." Ben continues to push, "What did he do, Jon?"

My hands rub my chin; the stubble is coming through and it's rough to the touch. It's easier to concentrate on the fact I need a shave than to consider Ben's question; he's well aware of the answer, he's just forcing me to acknowledge it. Nijad had wanted to give me something for surviving unscathed when I took a bullet for him, so he'd given me my fortune. Not directly, of course, but in such a round-a-bout way I'd had to accept it. It was a way to assuage his guilt, not that he had anything to feel any blame for, and I was receiving a salary precisely for that reason, to protect him. And then that fucking judgement call that went so wrong, my acceptance of the evidence banishing him to purgatory for three years. And what did Nijad fucking do then? For my small part in proving his innocence, despite my protests Nijad had given me his treasured bike and car; shipping them over from Amahad with the excuse that as he rarely came to the Europe anymore, he didn't need them.

I'd spent the last three years building my life; Nijad had spent the last three years in hell.

But the situation with Mia was entirely different, wasn't it? It was totally my fault that Mia had even been put in the line of fire. I should have been on my guard. I should have protected her, should have never let her get in front of me to take that bullet. I'd fucked up. Again. If I hadn't been asleep, if I'd been watching out for her…

"She should never have been put in danger, Ben. That was all down to me."

"Perhaps. Possibly. Who knows what could have changed the outcome? But she's alive, Jon." Another searching look comes my way. "But I'm not so sure about you. She doesn't blame you. So why do you keep blaming yourself? She needs you."

"She needs someone who can protect her. She doesn't need me because I always make the mistakes! Fuck it, Ben, you warned me yourself. I should never have got involved with her. It fucked up my mind. Is that what you want me to say, Ben? That you were right? Well, I'll say it. You were right, and now I'm doing what you wanted. I'm steering clear." As I spit out the words they seem to hang in the air. Not wanting to continue this conversation, I stand up and make a move to gather my paperwork and laptop. Glancing at the clock I see it's already seven-thirty in the evening. We've all been putting in the hours trying to identify Mia's stalker and to keep her safe. "I'm going home, Ben."

He nods, slowly. "I may have been right at the time but things changed. You *did* get involved. Think about what I've said, Jon. Don't make hasty decisions now. They might be the wrong ones."

Shaking my head, I go to leave the room, but he stills me with his hand on my arm. He's not finished, yet. "If you'd been cleared as medically fit, would you have gone back to active duty with the SAS, Jon?

Narrowing my eyes, unsure what he's asking, my depressive mood lets the answer slip out that, on another day, I might have kept to myself. It's a simple, "No."

He nods, as though he's onto something. "You thought you missed something, didn't you?"

I don't answer; he's hit the nail on the head.

"You blame yourself for missing the vital evidence that would have cleared Nijad, and now you're castigating yourself for underestimating Mia's stalker! It's not all on you, Jon. We all make mistakes, but only realise them in retrospect. You did the best you could at the time."

"I was Mia's Dom."

He snorts, "You weren't her Dom, Jon. To use a juvenile term for it, you were her boyfriend. You got too deeply involved."

"I was her Dom!" I protest, "I scened with her in the dungeon."

"I heard about that, but it wouldn't have happened if you hadn't been pushed to do it by her behaviour. You wanted her as your woman, not just your sub."

Running my hand through my hair, I blurt out, "Jasim's worse than an old woman for gossip!"

Ben smiles, and then grows serious again, "If you pull your head out of your arse long enough you'll see you can have Mia again. She doesn't bear any grudges. And she *needs* you."

Shrugging his hand off my arm, I continue towards the door without saying another word. I've done the right thing, the *only* thing I could have done. I have to stay away from Mia. Whatever anyone thinks, I failed her, both as a man and a Dom. Two strikes against me; her injury, and that she had to use her safeword. I'm not going to let there be a third.

I go home, change, and then start some further analysis of the messages sent, the phone call, the fire investigator's report, just trying to find a thread, a pattern, something that will lead us closer to the stalker. A few hours later, my eyes are burning from squinting at the computer as I endlessly look stuff up online, and my head's pounding. I shower and throw off my clothes, ready to go to bed. But I'm still lying wide awake when the phone rings at three am. When I hear what the voice on the other end of the line has to say, all residual tiredness slips away and I'm out of bed, dressed, and ready to go within minutes. *Finally, we might have a fucking lead!*

Driving through empty streets to Ben's place, I know I'll be lucky to avoid a speeding ticket tonight. At least one camera flashes me, but I don't care about picking up any fines, too anxious to get to my destination. Ben answers his door at first knock and ushers me quickly inside. Sean's sitting awkwardly on the couch, and the drink in his hand appears to be whisky. He looks done in, suffering from physical discomfort. I'm impatient to find out what's going on, but manage to throw him a glance of sympathy.

I don't bother with any greetings. "What happened?" Flicking my eyes between Ben and Sean, I move into the room.

Ben nods at Sean and then looks at me. "I wanted to wait until you got here. Sean won't want to go through the details twice. He's had a hard night."

The man in question is watching us, and dipping his head in agreement. I know he can sense my agitation as he takes a deep swallow of his drink to prepare himself, and starts to speak. "I think I found him."

Those five words are enough to excite me. Ben motions me to a chair, but before seating himself pours us both a drink. I take the glass automatically, my focus on Sean.

"You sure?"

"Well, I can't be certain," Sean shakes his head, "But if it's not there's some other sick bugger hanging around the clubs who needs to be dealt with."

I wave my hand in a come hither gesture to encourage him to continue.

He sighs. "I went into the club as normal and parked myself down with the unattached subs. I got my first drink of the night."

So far it all sounds fairly typical; I fold my arms, hardly able to contain my impatience for him to get a move on with his story. But he's holding himself as though he's in pain, so curbing my curiosity and impatience; I let him proceed at his own pace.

"After a while, a chap comes up to me. He was mid to late-twenties I'd say, his hair already thinning on top. Carrying a bit too much weight but his face is surprisingly lean and sharp. Obviously full of himself." He pauses as he remembers. "One of the other subs seemed to back away; she turned to avoid his eyes. It was plain she didn't want him to approach her, so I gave him a bit of a come on look."

Ben gets up to refresh Sean's drink. After thanking him, and taking a gulp from the new glass, Sean resumes his story, "He was abrupt and rude, but it could have been his way of taking control, so I went along with it, you know how some Doms can be. He asked me if I was looking for a Dom or Domme, and I just shrugged and said I wasn't bothered either way. He pulled himself up at that, and seemed interested, asking me if I wanted to play. When I agreed, he got hold of my hair and pulled me to my feet." Unconsciously Sean strokes his hand down the length of his dirty blonde hair which just touches his shoulders. Then he gives an abrupt laugh, "He was a bit shorter than I am, so it wasn't quite the grand gesture he planned, having to let go when I stood to my full height, but fuck did he pull it. I think he was left with a handful. Anyway, by his expression it was clear I'd offended him, simply by being taller than he thought I'd be. Taller than him." He pauses, and frowns at the memory. "The game was obviously still on, though, as he led me across the main area. Once we got to the other side he quite properly asked me my hard limits—which you know with me, aren't a lot. Then without further ado, he instructs me to kneel at his feet. Without any procrastination, he pulls out his cock and tells me to suck it. No introduction or fanfare, and it certainly wasn't a polite request." Sean's face twists with disgust at the memory, "I told him I wouldn't unless he put on a condom. He complained saying he was clean, and that he knew I had to be too, othcrwisc I wouldn't have been given admission to the club. I told him, no go without covering up, and he called me a pussy."

"Wanker," Ben spits out.

Sean shoots him a nod of agreement. "He huffed and puffed, but eventually he gloved up. I let him face fuck me, can't say it was the greatest experience I've ever had, but I was taking one for the team…"

"You've got our thanks." I butt in, dryly.

"Cheers mate." He winks at me. "Anyway, he was rough, didn't care about his sub as long as he got his rocks off. He was choking me and tried to put his hands round my neck, but I wasn't having any of that. But a person with less strength than me…?"

As his unfinished question hangs in the air, Ben and I exchange looks. Sean is built like a beanpole, and but is stronger than he looks.

"I told him breath play was a hard limit. He called me a fucking pansy again and then said if he'd wanted a whinging cunt tonight he'd have chosen one of the bitches. Then he finished off."

"Nice guy," Ben comments drily. "You get his name?"

"Master Hatcher."

It didn't ring any bells with me. But he could have been

using a club name for anonymity.

"So," Sean resumes, "He looks at me and confirms that flogging and light whipping are on my agenda. I wasn't keen, I didn't trust him, but I agreed. Something seemed very off about the man, so I wanted to hang around to see where he was going to take it. And I didn't want him to impose himself on anyone else." He pauses to take more of the whisky. It looks like he needs it. "He told me to take off my shirt and then fastened me to a St Andrews Cross. The bindings were pretty tight, too tight. But when I remarked on it, he told me to stop complaining, saying he'd never come across such a wimp." He holds out his wrists allowing us to see the angry red marks. Sean looks down at the drink in his hand and then shivers. I realise what's coming next won't be pleasant.

"He picks up a single tail and does a couple of practice swings. Then, without any warm up, he lashes me. Hard. I tell him, 'What the fuck, man? Take it easy!' He just laughed. A horrible fucking laugh. And then the bastard does it again, and again!" Sean is getting riled at the memory. He lifts his eyes first to Ben, then to me, "I did something I've never had to do before —I safeworded out. But he ignored me."

I look quickly at Ben. That's unthinkable. "Sean..."

He shakes his head to stop me, so I stay quiet, allowing him to complete the story in his way. "Luckily the place had dungeon monitors, and one heard me. He came over and stopped it." Sean shifts uncomfortably, and then looks over at me, guiltily, "While the DM was getting me down, Hatcher slipped away. I couldn't follow him, Jon. He'd disappeared by the time I was free. The club wanted to get me medical attention, but I wanted to try to find where he'd gone. But I lost him, I'm sorry."

"Jasim's on his way over," Ben informs me, Sean apparently already knew. As if on cue the doorbell rings, and Sheikh Jasim al Kassis enters looking tousled suggesting he'd come straight from his bed. He's carrying a black briefcase. Luckily for us, he had been a paramedic in the military back in his homeland, and we weren't above using our friend's skills when we didn't want, or feel the need, to involve the authorities.

Sean shrugs out of his jacket, but has difficulty with his T-shirt as it's stuck to his back, so Jasim takes him off into Ben's bathroom to try to help him out of it. As I hear water running, I turn to Ben. "Sounds like our man?"

Ben's eyes open wide, "A definite wannabe Dom with a sadistic streak a mile wide? Could very well be."

I think for a second. "Could Hatcher be a surname, and Miller the first name? Does the club keep records?"

"Sean had to sign up as a member, so this Hatcher chap should have done too. I'll get Vanessa to do some research. Hopefully, we haven't lucked out with a fake name."

"We'll find him, Ben. We'll follow the paper trails, and we should be able to pick him up again soon. People would surely remember someone that sadistic. He might have been kicked out of other clubs. Somewhere there'll be a clue as to whom and where he is."

We drop the conversation as Sean; now minus shirt comes back into the room. He is naked from the waist up.

"I thought you'd want to see this," Jasim says, heatedly. He's furious. As Sean turns around showing his back to us, I jump to my feet. Before the DM had managed to stop Hatcher, he'd got half a dozen hard licks in. Sean's back is criss-crossed with angry welts, several oozing blood. He'll have scars from tonight. But something catches my attention, and I lean forwards to have a closer look, gently turning Sean, so the light falls on his wounds.

"It's him." My voice is grim. "See the pattern here?" Ben and Jasim move closer and look where I'm pointing. "He's got vertical strokes and then has crossed them. And then gone over the top to define them. See what's been carved out?"

Ben examines the marred skin. "An 'H'?"

I nod, my hands tensing at my side as I explain, "Mia's got the same scars on her back. It hadn't clicked the lines formed a pattern before, but seeing this, it's clear. It has to be his trademark."

Jasim fiddles in his bag and brings out a couple of tubes. He flashes them at Sean, telling him one is an antibiotic, and the other a local anaesthetic. Then he applies the salves and bandages him up. By this time Sean looks done in, the expression in his eyes bleak. Ben tells him he'll be staying in his spare room tonight, and the fact Sean agrees without argument says a lot. Sean is an active, robust man, no stranger to fighting and violence. Like the rest of us, he'd done his time in one branch or other of the armed forces. But tonight would have been shocking, even for a man like him. In a D/s situation, the sub gives his trust over to a Dom, but retains overall control of the situation by being able to use his safeword. Sean had been robbed of that control tonight, had been put in a position where he was completely powerless. If it had been somewhere without vigilant DMs, who knows how far that bastard would have gone? Something like that is harrowing for anybody. But knowing the man as well as I do he'll regroup and bounce back in the morning. But to start his recovery he needs a good night's rest.

I turned to see Jasim looking at me with narrowed eyes, and I lift my eyebrow in question.

"This is the bastard after your girl?"

"She's not my girl." Emphatically, I deny any relationship. "But it looks like he's the one after Mia Fable. Yes."

He nods, slowly, as if considering. Then he scowls. "Kill him slowly, Jon." Picking up his bag and waves away Ben's thanks as he returns to the lounge, Jasim heads out of the door. I get up to refill my glass, put my arms on the top of the sideboard and lean forwards, my eyes closed, totally exhausted. *What a fucking nightmare.*

CHAPTER 25
Mia

Seven years ago

Mum locked me in. She actually locked the door. Which gave me no option, other than to stay hidden away in my room. I had no phone, and she'd taken my laptop, removed any chance of communication with the outside world. I couldn't even escape out of the window; my room wasn't on the ground floor, and in any event, I was too sore to attempt to shimmy down a drain pipe, even if there happened to be one handy. She didn't actually neglect me; bringing me sufficient food and drink along with painkillers, and later, that first day, a tablet which she told me was the morning after pill. I took it without argument, wanting no permanent reminder of my ordeal.

In shock and pain, I listened when she told me she'd contacted my school, informing the headteacher I'd been in an accident and needed time off to recover. It was an excuse she thought would hold until the bruises faded and I was fit to be seen in public again. Appearance was everything.

Refusing to call a doctor, she saw to my injuries as best she could cleaning, applying salve and bandages, but there was no tenderness in her administrations. As she dressed each wound, she reiterated that I'd deserved everything I'd got, that it was my fault and mine alone. She was ashamed of me and stressed over and over again how I must never speak of what I let happen. To anyone. I'd brought it all on myself.

For over a fortnight I was confined to my room, subjected to her daily mantra. I was only seventeen. I came to believe her.

Present day

Fed up and bored, I pace around the small living room, not sure what to do with myself. It's now been a week that I've been held a voluntary captive in the safe house and during those seven long days, I've not taken one step outdoors, except to go into the securely fenced back garden just to satisfy my desire to breathe in fresh air. Even then I had to have the company of one of my burly guards. I'm desperate to escape from these four walls.

And I'm dying to get some new clothes. Vanessa had bought me two sets of clothing, so one I wear and one I put in the wash, rotating daily. Wash, rinse, repeat. Literally! I'm sick to death of the nondescript T-shirts and sweatpants and want to feel something different against my skin other than leisurewear. I'm fast going stir crazy.

To try and help pass the time, I've completed the setup of the new laptop, enabling my attempts to get some work done, but I'm only managing a pitiful one thousand odd words a day—far below my usual word count—and even those are forced out. It's a struggle to get anything on the page; nothing seems to flow.

I've neither seen nor heard from Jon, but not having sight of the man doesn't mean thoughts of him haven't taken up residence in my brain, and memories of the little time we had together keep going round and round my mind. I miss the intimacy, both the emotional connection with another person, as well as the physical. He'd helped me explore my sexuality, and having had one taste I want more. And he'd been such good company to have around; I miss the easy way we seemed to fit together. Everything had seemed so right with him. I loved his wry sense of humour, his thoughtfulness. Shit, here I am thinking about that man again. I'm making no headway in my attempts to forget him. God, I miss him. *Stop thinking about him!*

Ceasing my pacing, I go to the back window and look out over the sparse garden; just an overgrown lawn surrounded by bare, high wooden fences. My CPOs take their work very seriously, preventing the slightest of risks. Yes, I've got to get out of here. If not, I'll go stark raving bonkers in the very near future. But first I need to convince my gaolers to allow me out on parole. Surely I deserve time off for good behaviour?

But there might be a chance. Yesterday I received a call from the insurance people—Nafisa has been brilliant sorting out as much as possible— but now they need me to go to the property in person to meet with the assessor. Apparently, I have to walk him through exactly what's been lost, giving me a bona fide excuse to get out of this house. No one can argue I shouldn't get on with getting the claim sorted, and then perhaps I'll be able to start moving forward with my life. At the moment I've nothing to my name, and the thought I'm going to have to start over almost from scratch is scary.

Very few things had proved salvageable from the fire, but here Grade A came up trumps, arranging to have anything worth keeping moved into storage for me. The inventory of what they were able to rescue is sparse, though; a few books that randomly escaped both fire and water damage, some kitchen utensils, the odd ornament, some jewellery and a couple of bits of furniture. The only thing of any real significance was a hard drive that seemed in fairly good nick. They've put one of their computer experts on it for me to try and recover what's on the disc, and I'm keeping my fingers crossed the expert can work his or her magic. It will be an older backup from a few months ago, but miles better than nothing.

Getting back to planning my great escape, I make a mental list of what I want to do. I'll need to go to the cottage and then can hopefully persuade my protectors to take me to a clothes shop. It wouldn't be a long detour; my favourite shop has a branch in a small out of town shopping centre just on the outskirts of Epping. That surely would be safe enough; nobody would know I was there. In my head, I run through just what I need to buy. Jeans, leggings, skirts, tops, a jacket, socks, tights, shoes, perhaps a dress and of course, at least a week's worth of underwear! The ones I've got will soon be little better than washed out rags. And I'll need make-up and toiletries. I start to feel excited. What girl doesn't like spending money on a shopping spree, especially when she can justify the need for everything she buys?

Determined they'll have to let me out of my prison, I walk into the kitchen where Sean is helping himself to a bowl of cereal and, without apology for interrupting his breakfast, tell him what I want to do. At first there's the predictable protest as he recounts his instructions to keep me here. But I keep my cool, impressing on him the importance of meeting with the assessor, even Sean can't argue with that. And he doesn't, after giving me a sharp look and throwing his hands up in defeat, he reluctantly agrees to approach Ben for permission.

Thrilled at the thought of some freedom, if only for a few hours, I find it hard to sit still while waiting for his boss' response. Hovering in the kitchen, my fingers tap aimlessly on the worktop. *Shows how tedious my life has become if the promise of a shopping trip gets my blood flowing.* When he returns to tell me Ben's agreed, I leap up and give him a hug as though he's given me the go-ahead himself.

"Whoa, there, baby." He hisses breath in through his teeth and pulls my arms from their position around him placing me at arm's length.

I cock my head on one side and frown. "What's the matter, Sean?"

When he denies anything is wrong and shrugs it off, I don't push it, even though he seems to be in pain. Selfishly, I'd been too excited about my impending great escape, and hadn't noticed how stiffly he's moving, but now I do as he leaves to do whatever bodyguards do when they're out of sight. Briefly, I wonder how he got injured, but let it go, deciding it's probably none of my business. Leaving the room, I collect my phone. Putting in a call to the loss adjustor, I arrange to meet him later this morning at noon.

I'm ready and chomping at the bit when Ryan, at last, appears and gives me warning we're leaving in five minutes. In that time he tells me Sean will be checking the car, and then they'll both reconnoitre and ensure it's safe for me to leave the house. He throws me a sweatshirt to wear which is too large and looks ridiculous on me, but at least with the hood up it helps to hide my face. I'm happy to agree with any of their instructions for the opportunity to breathe some fresh air. When Sean eventually opens the front door and tells me it's time to go, I step outside to see Ryan scanning the road while his partner hurries me out of the house and into the back seat of a non-descript, dark grey SUV with blackened rear windows. Sean then gets in beside me. Once we're in and belted up, Ryan quickly slides into the driver's seat, and without further delay we move off.

"The M25 is going slow to stop, so I'm taking the back roads," Ryan speaks over his shoulder to Sean. I let their route planning discussion wash over me, and turn my head to look out of the window, enjoying freedom for the first time in days. The journey first takes us through the suburbs, but soon we're driving across a bridge over the M25, looking down at the bumper to bumper traffic snarled up in both directions. Soon we head out through country lanes into the southwestern parts of Essex, and into the commuter belt where the property costs are sky high. The rolling hills give the impression of vast open countryside, yet it's only just beyond the motorway and close to the stations providing easy access into central London explaining why this part of the commuter belt is so expensive. It's a pretty area, and I'd bought a house I could afford as close to it as I could.

As we get nearer to Epping, I grow tense. The last time I was here it was dark and flames were shooting from my home. My almost healed shoulder throbs, serving as a reminder of everything that happened that night. I'm still unable to believe my house is gone; it doesn't seem real, and half of me is expecting to pull up outside, walk across the garden and enter the front door as if nothing has happened, as if it was all a terrible dream. Tears prick at the back of my eyes as it hits me again how much I've lost. Putting my hands to my cheeks I feel them escaping and impatiently wipe them away. It seems I do nothing but cry these days.

"You okay?" Sean's picked up on my tension, and I turn to meet his wary gaze.

"I don't know," I answer honestly.

He reaches over and takes my hand, understanding I need some physical support. His touch gives comfort, but nothing more, and my traitorous mind tells me I'd feel better if Jon was here. I swallow down the sob that threatens to overwhelm me. I hadn't realised going back would be so hard. The house might be gone, my memories of the man certainly aren't.

We turn into my driveway. My car's gone; another courtesy of Grade A as they've had it towed to get it fixed. It was just the paintwork that had bubbled and burned, but because of that it needs a new door that's still on order, and a window and the windscreen, cracked from the heat, also need replacing. As we stop, my perfidious mind shows me a vision of the McClaren sitting out in front with Jon just stepping out, and determinedly

I thrust it away. *I don't want to remember the car or the man who drove it!* Instead, I focus on the roofless garage, noting there's more of that left standing than the house itself.

Finally, I let my eyes settle on the ruin that had been my home. The lone brick inglenook fireplace and chimney stand high and proud, blackened with smoke residue making it a macabre sight. Shuddering, I thought I'd been sufficiently prepared to visit the scene, but I wasn't anything like. The garden I'd so carefully tendered is trampled and ruined. The whole plot an indescribable mess.

Ryan gets out of the SUV, carefully scanning the perimeter. Sean waits with me in the backseat until the loss adjuster arrives. It's not long before a car pulls up behind us and Sean's muscles tense as he gets prepared in case he needs to protect me while Ryan goes and checks the man's credentials. When Ryan throws a nod to us over his shoulder, it seems he's satisfied the man's who he says he is, the fact confirmed when he waves at us to get out and come over. Sean stays very close to my side as we walk up to the house, Ryan waits outside.

"Morning." The newcomer holds out his hand. "Jenkins." He informs me succinctly.

"Mia Fable," I verify my identity equally briefly. I don't see the necessity in introducing my companions; it would take too long to explain.

Jenkins regards me sympathetically. "Police confirm arson."

I gather he's a man of few words, so I don't waste any of mine and nod in agreement. Not news to me.

"Have you got any quotes for rebuilding yet?"

I shake my head. "I'm waiting for the go ahead from you." Not him personally, but his company, but he'll know what I mean.

"Walk me through."

We start picking our way where we can, and I point out the

different rooms to him and run through what the fire had consumed. He accepts I might be missing some of the minor items, but for now just wants the gist of it.

When we finish, he looks at me sympathetically. "You've got a good policy, Miss Fable. Rebuilding won't be a problem, and your contents cover should be more than adequate. Hopefully, the next step will be the go-ahead from head office to start clearing the site. Then you can get on with your life again."

I'll be able to get on with my life once the stalker has been caught, I think to myself, while out loud I just thank him. He's only doing his job. Jenkins nods a farewell at me, looks curiously at Ryan and Sean, who've stayed silent throughout the encounter, and takes his leave of us.

After he's driven off, I raise my eyes, blinking furiously to hold back the tears. "Just get me away from here, will you?"

Without delaying, Sean leads me to the SUV, and once more Ryan has a good look around before again taking the driver's seat. As we at last get underway, I breathe out a long sigh of relief that I'm leaving the ruins of my cottage behind and gradually start to regain some enthusiasm for my shopping expedition ahead. Replacing clothes seem to be my only step forwards while everything else is in a state of stagnation.

Ryan regularly checks the rearview mirror as he drives, and I hear him confirm to Sean that we're not being followed, finding comfort in knowing they are taking my safety so seriously. And it's not all that long before we arrive at the shopping centre I wanted to go to. It's one I often visit so I know it well. It has about a dozen of the usual outlets, a couple of furniture stores, a computer shop, a chemist, an electrical store, and a hobby shop. And there, in the centre, a branch of Next whose brand of clothing matches my style and, for me, generally a good fit. We park as close as we can to the clothing store, with Ryan giving verbal complaint about the curious one-way system that makes the car park almost impossible to negotiate around. I grimace in sympathy knowing well what he means. Getting out is relatively straightforward, getting in to find a parking place needs a degree in navigation!

Eventually, we get parked. Sean stays me with a touch on my arm, and now there's another short wait as Ryan gets out of the car and evaluates every conceivable potential threat he can see or even imagine. Once he's happy the car park holds no menace, he takes station by the vehicle and Sean moves to vacate his seat. "I'll check inside," is Sean's parting shot as he leaves the car and makes his way over to Next which I've told him is the one I want to go into first. Of course, after clothes I'll need to stock up on toiletries at the chemist.

Due to my impatience, it feels like an age before he's back, but in reality probably no more than a couple of minutes. He opens the car door and leans in, "We're lucky it's a weekday so the store's relatively empty, nothing suspicious in there. I've checked the changing rooms. There's a fire exit out the back, but the assistant told me it's locked and alarmed. I've had a look at it, and it's all in working order. If the fire alarm does go off, wait for me in the changing rooms and I'll come in and get you."

I nod, though I'm not taking it in, at the moment being infinitely more interested in the display in the store window. *That top would suit me.*

I think he knows he's lost me, as he chuckles and gives me his hand to help me out of the car. "Women and shopping! I'll be inside with you; Ryan will stay here."

"Thanks." I have to acknowledge him somehow, but my feet are already moving forwards to take a closer look at that top.

Replacing a whole wardrobe is turning out to be fun, I muse, as I walk around the shop picking up this and that, jeans, trousers, tops, dresses and skirts. I don't hurry; after my week's imprisonment I'm just enjoying being out of the safe house. After checking how many items can be taken into the changing room at once, I decide Sean can earn his keep and stand outside with the remainder of the armful I've collected but am not allowed to take in. Explaining to the assistant who is standing guard, she agrees to help by swapping out clothes that I've tried on with the ones Sean's holding. That will save me time getting dressed between changes. Sean does make a very kind offer to come into the changing rooms to help me with things like zips, a wide smirk on his face, but I turn him down with a laugh. *Men!* But before he lets me enter he holds me back, and questions the assistant about who's in the changing rooms right now. Only when he's satisfied I'll be the only one in there, and has another quick look himself, does he allow me to go in. Feeling completely safe and reassured, and, for once, relaxed, I enter the cubicle and start to undress while thinking how conscientious and competent Sean and Ryan are at their jobs.

Right, where to start with the business of trying on clothes? I look up at the pile I've collected, hanging from hangers on the peg. Jeans first, I decide, I'm a jeans sort of girl. Anything to dispense with these baggy sweats! The first pair I try on are no good, but the second feel like they were made for me. I check the price tag, yup, just as I thought, twice as much as the first pair. But hell, I need to have something to wear. So I take them off, and they go into my yes pile. I need more than one pair, so I try the black ones next, deciding they'll do as well. They're a bit tight and skinny and I have trouble getting them on and off, but looking in the mirrors to the front, side and rear of me, boy do they make my bum look good—I'm having those! Having difficulty getting them off, I sit on the bench and do a shimmy; that works. As I complete my struggles and put them on the pile to buy, I hear a faint scratching sound from outside the cubicle, and then a soft snick but I ignore it, figuring the assistant must be tidying up or something. Sean's waiting outside, all's good.

Dressed only in bra, knickers and shoes that I've put back on so I can get the proper effect, I reach my arm out to take one of the dresses I'd selected off the hanger. Suddenly the curtain is whipped back, and I'm grabbed and pulled, so my back is tight up against a very hard masculine chest. I smell a strong and unpleasant odour of stale male sweat. But before I'm able to let out a scream, a hand is put over my mouth. I kick and struggle, but he's too big and strong. He's got something in his other hand, and now it's covering my mouth and nose, forcing me to breathe in the fumes.

Within seconds, I know nothing at all.

CHAPTER 26
Jon

Six months ago

Three long years had taken their toll on Nijad. His physical discomfort—spending thirty-six months fighting in the desert—nothing compared to his mental anguish as he believed himself capable of a hideous act, without understanding how it was possible. Careless of his life, he had been leading the combat in border skirmishes, with no regard for his safety, ending up crashing his helicopter and almost dying. He was lucky his only reminder was a permanent limp. That's what I did to him.

Against all odds, it was his new wife who believed in him, believed in the man inside, not what everyone else could see. Unlike me, who didn't look beneath the surface. He couldn't have done it, she said, raising doubts, putting forward an alternative version and forcing us to re-examine the evidence. The woman, who had come to love him despite the inauspicious beginnings to their relationship, saw the man he really was.

And what did Nijad do? He reaffirmed I was his brother; had thanked me profusely for my part in clearing his name. Yeah, I was his brother even though I made the wrong decision, interpreted everything the wrong way and almost got him killed. I had been instrumental in changing his life.

He needed me, and I wasn't there. What I'd seen as betrayal had made me hate him. Now I just hated myself.

Present day

My phone buzzes. I'm right in the middle of answering an email, so I curse the interruption, tempted to ignore it and continue what I was doing before I lose my train of thought. But a glance at the screen shows it's Sean. Without delay, and with a sense of foreboding, I accept the call. "Hi, Sean, what's up?"

I've barely got the words out before he's interrupted me. "She's gone!"

"What?" I don't remember getting to my feet, but I'm standing up, all other work is forgotten. Unnoticed, papers fly out of the file I'd been referring to, as it gets knocked off the desk and drops on the floor, landing in a mess. "What the fuck you talking about?" I've gone cold. He can't mean Mia's missing. *Anything but that!*

"She went into the changing room, Jon, but she didn't fucking come out." Sean's voice is full of panic. "She'd taken armfuls of clothes in so I didn't worry for a while, but after a bit, I went back into check. The clothes she was wearing are all there, Jon. The fire escape door was open, the alarm disabled."

My hand runs through my hair, and I realise I'm shaking. "Didn't you check the fucking alarm?" It doesn't seem credible he'd make such an elementary mistake.

"Of course, I did! Someone must have disabled it after." Sean's indignation comes clearly down the line. "But how the fuck could he have known where she'd be, Jon? No one knew where we were going, and up to this morning, even *we* didn't have a clue where we'd end up today."

That was a question that would need to be answered, but right now there was a more important one. Where the fuck was Mia now? "Vanessa!" I turn away from the phone and yell. "Can you activate Mia's tracking device?"

"On it!" Her reply shows she's getting right down to it and not stopping to ask questions.

"Most of the tracking devices are here – her bag, her clothes."

"She's got one in her shoes. Were her shoes there?"

"I've got a trace now. She's about five miles away and moving fast." Sean doesn't have to answer; the fact Vanessa can track her means she's still wearing them. I send up a quick prayer of thanks.

Turning back to the phone, I'm having difficulty keeping my voice calm as I tell Sean, "I'm out of here. I'll bring Ben. Vanessa will conference call us all in and give us directions."

Disconnecting the call, I grab my keys and rush out into the corridor, skidding to a halt in front of, and then opening the main conference room door. I don't need to say anything, just gesture I need him. Now. One look at my face and Ben stands, excusing himself with a quickly mumbled apology and joins me, racing towards the lift without asking questions until we're on the way down. He holds back any comment when I explain the situation; his look of horror confirms he knows this is the time for action, not discussion. We take the McClaren; it's faster than his car. Once out of the garage Ben answers the incoming call, and we're all in contact. Vanessa's giving us directions.

I hear Ryan's voice. "There was a fucking tracker on the SUV, Jon."

"What?" I'm incredulous. "Why the fuck didn't you check it?"

"I did," he replied, "When we left the house." He pauses before he admits, "But not before we left her cottage."

"How the fuck did someone get a fucking tracker on the car there without you seeing them?" Jeez, am I surrounded by idiots? I thump the steering wheel in my disgust. *And I've let Mia down again!*

Sheepishly, he replies. "While Mia and Sean were in the

house; a girl came past walking a dog. She bent down by the car. Naturally, I checked what she was doing; she was picking up dog shit in one of those little black baggie things. I thought nothing of it. I'm so fucking sorry, Jon. She must have been working with him. Only way I think it could have been put there. It had to have been her."

No time now to berate him for his carelessness. "Description!" I snap.

"Petite, not much over five foot, light frame. Pretty oval face, brown eyes and brown hair in a bob. Wearing jeans, and a pink sweatshirt. She barely looked out of her teens."

"Shit!" Sean breaks in. "I saw her come into the shop. She was browsing while Mia was looking round. Then she made a quick phone call and left when Mia went into the changing room."

It's evident she was an accomplice. I wonder how someone as evil as Hatcher had got her onside, but people do strange things. That isn't the issue right now. Now we have to find Mia.

"Tracker's stopped," Vanessa informs us. I appreciate her ability to keep calm in a crisis as she gives us directions in an unemotional voice, telling us our destination is an abandoned warehouse.

CHAPTER 27
Mia

Six years ago

*L*ife changed for me after the attack. At first, I withdrew completely into my shell, nervous of any interaction with strangers, particularly males. The daily rantings and lectures from my mum ground me down even further until I started to wonder why I bothered to stay alive. I knew I had to escape, one way or another.

To escape from the thoughts in my head and the ravings of my mother, I buried myself in my school work resulting in excellent A level grades, easily sufficient to get into the Uni of my choice. Shortly after my eighteenth birthday I accepted a place in Halls on campus and moved out of my mother's house and out of her sphere of influence. I didn't know it at the time, but I was never to go back. It was either get out and live, or give up and die. More than once I contemplated suicide.

Moving away was the best thing I'd ever done. Nervous at first, I soon settled in, making friends with several girls, but continuing to avoid the opposite sex like the plague. If there were rumours that I was a lesbian I didn't mind at all. I spent a lot of time by myself, reading both books for my course work and novels for my entertainment. Many, many novels. Mainly romance.

I saw life, I read about fantasy, I began to heal, and reached the point where I started to think about things in a different way, at last becoming able to counteract my mother's brainwashing.

Finally, I saw the truth. I was not to blame for my attack. I had been the victim of a vicious, abusive crime.

Present day

When I come to, I don't know where I am but feel groggy and ill. With frightening déjà vu, as my senses return I quickly realise I'm in a moving van, my hands are handcuffed to something on the side, and there are more cuffs around my ankles preventing me from moving. I struggle to come to full consciousness and twist my head to try and see the man driving. I don't recognise him, but I know exactly who he is, his body odour triggering memories I'd rather not remember. Closing my eyes, I try and buy more time before he knows I'm awake. Panic starts to rise, but I try to force my terror back down. I'm not a seventeen-year-old girl anymore, but a twenty-four-year-old woman and this time I'm going to fight. *I will not let this happen again!* This time, I suspect he won't leave me alive. *But Jon will be coming for me. I know he'll come for me, he won't desert me now.* That thought is all I've got to hang onto.

Summoning up a mental image of the man, who these desperate circumstances now allow me to admit that I love, I try to let it comfort me. For days my efforts have been to keep him out of my head, but now I'm trying to remember all I can about him, his unique scent, his touch. Anything to drown out what's currently happening. *He'll try and find me, won't he? He vowed to protect me; he'll come.* He has to.

Having stripped off in the dressing room, I'm next to naked wearing only bra and pants making me feel even more vulnerable. Then I look down and see I've still got on my shoes. *And there's a tracker in them!* They're tracing me and will be on their way now. Sean won't have wasted time sounding the alarm. *All I have to do is to hang on until they find me.*

The lurching of the van and whatever he used to knock me out is making me feel very queasy, and the violent motion throwing me side to side is not helping, escalating my nausea as well as pulling on my arms and making my muscles scream. I can't hold back, and I retch noisily, vomit spewing from my mouth.

"Fucking dirty cunt!" He looks back over his shoulder and sees me, his face creasing with disgust. "Fucking filthy bitch pig. I'm going to punish you for that!" He curses at me loudly.

Suddenly we take a turn off the main road, and after a couple of moments of bumping over rough ground, the van comes to a jolting halt. He jumps out, next I hear him around the back, and see the rear doors wrenched open. I shrink away, automatically trying to make myself as small as possible, and am alarmed when he pulls out an evil looking knife. It's the first time I've been face to face with my abuser, but for now, I'm focusing on the weapon he's brandishing, rather than familiarising myself with his appearance. But I can see the intense lecherous expression on his face, and I become very afraid.

"I'm not stupid, bitch. You've probably got a tracker on you." He reaches over and slices through my bra straps, and then the front so he can quickly pull it away. He does the same to my knickers and then sits back a moment as if appreciating the view. I shudder, partly in humiliation at my nakedness, and in anticipation of the pain to come. "Not bad, bitch. Seven extra years look good on you." He chuckles, a sound which sends shivers down my spine and not in any pleasant way. "Be better if you weren't covered in puke, though."

He hasn't touched my shoes. *Don't touch my shoes.* If he takes them off, no one will know have any ideas where I am. Making sure I keep my eyes averted from them; I look anywhere but at my feet. He's standing, considering me, and then he's there beside me, pulling at my hair and ripping off the velvet band that I used to secure my ponytail, taking a clump of my hair with it. My hair falls around my shoulders, and he reaches out to stroke it. There's madness in his eyes. Suddenly he gives a wicked laugh and reaches for my shoes. Now a sob escapes, as I know my last chance of rescue is quickly fading.

He throws the scraps of material, all that's left of my clothing out of the van, along with my footwear. I realise he's left them here for a false trail and presume we'll be moving on. I stare at him, fearing the predatory expression coming over his face as he grabs hold of me, forcing my legs apart as far as the cuffs will allow and without any preparation shoves his fingers inside me. I'm dry and it hurts and is degrading.

"Got a tracker up there, bitch? Got to find out, you know." Next, he rolls me over, and his fingers are probing at my rear entrance. "Still as tight as fuck," he groans in annoyance. "But this time, I'll just work harder on that." Then, thank God, his fingers are gone, but as I turn the sight of him pulling them into his mouth and licking them looking like he's relishing the taste. "Hmm, nice. Got to get moving now, bitch, but don't you worry your pretty little head. I'll be able to take my time with you later."

Instead of returning to the driver's side, he climbs in beside me and un-cuffs me from the side of the van, refastens my hands, now together behind my back and picks me up. "Fuck, why did you have to puke?" I take some perverse comfort that he can't avoid getting my vomit on his shirt. Roughly, he pulls me round and forces a ball gag into my mouth. "Just don't fucking puke again with that in. I don't want you stealing my fun by fucking choking and dying. Well," he smirks, "Not until my cock's inside you, anyway." He lifts me out of the van and dumps me in the boot of a car. When he closes it claustrophobia hits, and I try to scream, but the gag stops the sound. He's right; I could choke if I'm sick again, and that thought terrifies me too.

There's no room to kick, and with my hands and feet cuffed I'm completely helpless. I try to control my rising terror knowing no one can track where he's taking me. But I've got to keep hoping. Somehow force myself to remain positive. Jon's got to find me, somehow. Grade A won't give up; *I know they won't give up!* I keep repeating it to myself, trying to believe it, clinging to that fast disappearing bit of hope!

I try to brace myself as the motion of the car flings me from side to side, but something keeps bruising my back. My vagina is burning and stinging from his rude intrusion earlier, and then to add to my misery, my hair catches on a sharp piece of metal. When I try to get free, I feel my scalp tear as another handful is pulled out. Already I'm hurting all over, but unable to kid myself there's not worse to come. Trying to control my breathing, to stay calm and strong, I keep telling myself that I'm not the weak girl I was, and renew my resolve to fight. And if the worst comes to the worst, I survived last time, and I can get through this again and come out the other side. I've done it before. *As long as he doesn't kill me.* Shit, I can't give up. Anger rises in me; I've wasted so much time over the last seven years letting what this bastard did to me ruin my life. If I get out of this, I won't live a half-life anymore. I'm going to live life to the fucking full!

The journey seems to go on forever. It's hard to breathe as the boot seems small and airless, but I haven't suffocated by the time we start bouncing up a bumpy track, the lurching throwing me this way and that, making me bang into the sides as if I needed any more bumps and bruises. Then the car suddenly stops. For a second, all goes quiet, and I hear birdsong outside. Then the boot is opened. He's brutal and uncaring as he lifts me out.

"Stinking bitch! Christ, I don't even want to touch you like that."

He catches my bruised back as he lifts me and I wince, but he takes no notice of my discomfort. Quickly, I look around me to see if I know where we are, but I don't recognise this place at all. We're outside a decaying wooden shack, a barn perhaps, with old rusty machinery around it. There's a rotting pile of logs, but nothing else of note. We seem to be in the middle of nowhere, trees all around, sunlight only just dappling through.

He half carries, half drags me to the side of the building and then throws me down. I'm still bound, so can do nothing but watch as he goes to a tap on the wall with a hose attached. He turns it on, full force, and a blast of icy cold water hits me. He hoses me down, thoroughly. I try to struggle to my feet, but he kicks me over and blasts me the other side. The hose is so powerful it's impossible to get away from it.

Eventually, he seems happy he's removed all evidence of vomit, and he turns it off. With a vicious tug, he pulls me to my feet. I'm drenched and shivering, cold water drips off me, my wet hair hanging long and heavy on my back.

As he hauls me inside the building my feet trail across the rough ground, but he's uncaring of the skin being scrapped off my toes. Pausing for a second, he extracts a key from his pocket, then opens a padlock, undoes it and pushes the door open. It's in that moment I know where I am. I've never seen the place before; I was always kept blindfolded. But I remember the smell. God, do I remember that smell; mould, decay, sweat and blood. I stiffen as blind terror sweeps through me. I've been thrown back in time to seven years ago, and I'm about to lose my virginity in the worst possible way.

As if he senses I know where I am, he pulls me to the middle of the room and forces me to look around, holding my head and twisting it this way and that. Swallowing hard, I try to stave off a panic attack.

"Good to be back?" he asks me, confirming what I already

know. He laughs loudly, the evil sound and triggering shivers down my back. "I've remodelled a bit; I don't have to improvise now." As he talks, he removes his dirty shirt but thankfully leaves on the rest of his clothes. His chest is covered with dark, wiry hair, and he's out of condition, rolls of fat quiver over the top of his belt.

I look away and take in my surroundings as it's a slightly better option than looking at my abductor. Shuddering, I realise what he means about the renovations. *Fuck, he's created a dungeon.* My gaze travels around all the equipment; the spanking bench, St Andrew's Cross, some things I don't recognise as well as old rusting machinery which was obviously part of the original building, but now adding to the gruesome atmosphere. Whips, canes, and floggers cover the walls. It's dark and cold and looks like a torture chamber. *My* torture chamber. For a few seconds, I forget to breathe.

He lets out a sigh, "You have no idea how much I've wanted to get you back here, to continue what we started." His words come out almost wistfully.

I realise that if I keep him talking it might delay the inevitable and buy me some time, time for any rescuers to discover my whereabouts. "Why? Why me?"

"Why you, bitch?" He walks around in front of me, still holding me up. Just in case I get out alive, I start to memorise his features, but as he hasn't blindfolded me, this time, I doubt he'll be letting me go. His eyes are a dull blue; his pupils dilated as though he's on something. He's almost bald and in need of a shave. His nose is crooked as though it's been broken at some point. *I hope it hurt.* I can't move away from him as he hasn't untied my legs; I'd fall if he let me go. So I'm forced to breathe in his foul breath and stale sweat, recognising personal hygiene is way down on his list of priorities. He watches me looking at him with a sneer and finally, answers my question. "Why you?

Huh!" He shakes his head in disbelief. "I gave you everything!"

What? "You gave me nothing. You took everything from me. You raped me, abused me." I spit out.

Another harsh laugh. "You must have loved it! The way you write about the things I did to you. Everything that happened here, you've written about, and your characters all love it. Being tied up, spanked. You've made money out of the experiences I gave you. I know you enjoyed yourself last time, bitch. Now we get to do it all over again."

He's mad. He must be!

He pulls me brutally again, this time towards a bed-like contraption in the middle of the room and forcibly pushes me down until I'm sitting on it. Then he takes a step back and stares at me. "And at first I didn't mind, it even amused me. I bought all your books, became your greatest fan! Every word you wrote I imagined doing that to you, every man you described was me, wasn't it? The man wielding the whip, the crop, was always me."

My mouth drops open, *how can he think that?* My characters, my Doms always took care of their subs, never pushed them beyond anything they enjoyed. I have no idea how he could be so deluded to believe for a moment that I was writing about him.

Ignoring my reaction, he continues, "But then you started describing me as a wannabe. I'm a Dom, bitch; I always have been. I was born that way. And for you to suggest I don't know what I'm doing…!" His hand whips out and slashes me across the face, and blood trickles from my nose.

"But I wasn't writing about you!" I protest. If there's a chance to somehow get through to him, I have to take it.

"Who else were you describing them?" His voice is scornful. "I taught you everything you know. Every whip stroke, everywhere you had a cock inside you. There was only ever me. There was never anyone else after me, was there? I've been keeping an eye on you, so don't tell me I'm wrong. I gave it to you so good, you never wanted another prick anywhere near your cunt."

"And your cohort. You weren't alone."

"Pah!" He slashes his hand through the air. "That motherfucker doesn't count. It was me you gave your virginity to bitch."

"I didn't give it to you; you took it. You stole it from me!" I shout out in utter disgust.

He throws me an incredulous look. "You were gagging for it! Waving your untried cunt in my face with your tight leggings, your sexy top."

I look away; I am not going to accept any responsibility. I'd moved past that years ago. The only person to blame is him. I didn't think it was possible to hate a person as much as I do this man who abducted me. I'd kill him with my bare hands if I got the opportunity, without a moment's regret.

"Enough talking. Now it's time we get reacquainted, bitch. But first, I want to see my pretty marks on you."

I want to fight; I'm determined to fight, but bound as I am, he's left me few options. He moves in front of me again, and I take my chance, throwing back my head and bringing it down on his, smashing my forehead into his nose. It works on films, but it seems to hurt me a lot more than it does him as he just jumps back, clutching his hand to his face and rubbing it vigorously, then, he grins.

"You've got more spirit now, bitch. I'm going to enjoy breaking that. You're going to do exactly what I say, when I say it. You're going to give me everything I fucking ask for."

Dragging me off the bed, he draws me to the spanking bench and pushes me over it, his weight coming down on my back, his fat shifting as he pushes against me, his flabby skin making me shudder with revulsion. As he undoes the handcuffs,

I try to buck him off, but he's so much heavier than me. I have no chance to evade him as he forces my hands into new cuffs either side of the bench. I prepare to kick out as he goes to undo the cuffs holding my legs together, and try to get one strike in, but he's ready for it and jumps back quickly. My leg only hits air and then is encircled by his sweaty palm. Prising me into the position he wants, he puts the new cuff round one ankle before undoing the original, then holds tight to my other leg as he fastens it the other side. He seems to have a method for restraining me. *Has he done this before?* I decide he has. He's set up a dungeon, and I doubt anyone would come here willingly. The thought is chilling. As he starts to turn a handle, all my thoughts return to my current predicament as the bottom cuffs separate, pulling my legs wide apart, far more than is comfortable.

Then he stands still, for a while nothing happens. Twisting my head to one side, I try to see what his doing. He's standing, just staring at my exposed parts, his zip part undone and one hand stroking himself through his jeans. I shudder, feeling sick that he's going to rape me now. *Please, no, not again.* As I watch, he seems to come to a decision and steps away from the bench, walking across to the walls covered in the hideous, cruel implements I'd noticed earlier, and I turn, closing my eyes, unwilling to see what he is about to inflict on me. *I survived once; I will survive again.* That mantra is going around my head I let my mind drift back to Club Tiacapan, and try to imagine myself back there, with Jon wielding the flogger above me. *I'm not here, I'm there, I'm scared, but Jon's in control and has my trust. I know Jon wouldn't hurt me, I know it's going to be alright...*

I scream. Loudly. What the fuck is he using? When the second slash sends fire across my thighs, I realise he's got a cane, and he's not holding back. He lifts it again and again. I scream and shriek, my voice grows hoarse with shouting. I'm begging him to stop; the pain is excruciating. I'm sobbing and crying, I can't even yell out anymore, I've stopped flinching, even ceased trying to move away as agony radiates through my body.

Then, at last, he ceases, his calloused hands moving roughly over my skin, abrading the welts which I know will be raised and probably bleeding. My thighs, arse and back throb with pain. He squeezes my butt cheeks; I try to rise to get away as pain floods through me. He laughs loudly; it's a gruesome sound.

"Fuck, bitch, but you turn me on like that. You mark so well. I wish you could see yourself." He slaps my bum with his hand again, making me jump and squeal. "The noises you make, fuck they go straight to my fucking dick."

He moves to my head and frees my hands. My body might feel like it's on fire, but I'm not giving in. Fisting my hand I thrust it into his face.

"Bitch!" he roars, his hand covering his eye. The back of his hand hits me across my face so hard I see stars. My small rebellion doesn't get me very far. Taking advantage of my temporary dizziness he undoes the cuffs around my feet. He looks at me, cane in hand, assessing. As if deciding he isn't bothered about further resistance; he barks out a command.

"Get over to the bed, bitch. Crawl."

I slowly get to my feet, my eyes flicking everywhere seeking something I could use as a weapon. The rack of torture instruments are too far away. Trying to ignore my discomfort and refusing ever to get on my hands and knees for him, I pull myself to my full height and make my stand. "No."

Before I register what he's about to do or take any evasive action the cane's pulled back and viciously lands over my breasts. "Want more of that, cunt?"

Gasping and wrapping my arms around me in a protective

gesture I realise he's taken hold of me again. Too impatient to wait for me to follow his instructions he's hauling me over to the bed like contraption. Frantically struggling I attempt to break loose, but he overpowers me, his hands holding my arms so tightly he'll leave bruises. When we get to the bed, he halts and tilts his head to one side. "Now," he starts, his voice slow and considering. "Arse or cunt? Where to start. What a decision." I turn a pleading look to him, but his face shows no mercy. His eyes seem to be glazing over in anticipation, and I realise he's asked the question of himself, rather than me. The waiting fucks with my mind, and I have to bite my lips to prevent myself screaming out for him to just get on with it.

"Hmm. On your back, bitch. I want you to feel those stripes."

He pushes me down firmly, so I lie awkwardly on the table. One kick, I'm thinking, one kick where it would really hurt him might render him incapable, at least of *that*. I try to pull back my leg but he's ahead of me and in one swift movement tips me back, and has one of my feet strapped into one of the stirrups. The bruising on my back blasts me with new pain when I land on it, but I put it out of my mind, knowing if he gets the other foot in I'll be helpless. I struggle, kicking out, moving my leg so it's hard for him to catch hold but my puny attempts are futile, he catches my leg, easily takes hold of my flailing foot and straps it into the second stirrup. Then his weight, his flab is on me again, pressing me down as he tightens another strap around my torso. All fight leaves me as I realise he's too heavy to push off. I'm completely powerless and have no way of resisting him as he binds my hands tight on either side.

He's standing between my legs, looking at the view. There's drool on his mouth, and he wipes his hand over his face to remove it while giving me a predatory grin. He looks feral and totally insane. He chuckles, the ghoulish sound echoing around the room. He steps away moving towards a chest I hadn't noticed before. When he comes back, he somehow lowers the top end of the bed, and my head hangs down over the back. He's got something in his hands, and he raises it to make sure I have a good view of it. I gasp and shake my head violently from side to side as the diabolical dental gag comes into view.

"Remember this, bitch?" Spit flies from his lips and lands on my face. "Oh we had some fun with this, didn't we?" His strong hand grasps my chin, holding me firm. I watch the gag descending. He forces my mouth open, inserts the implement then tightens the screws, so I'm open and ready for him. I hear him fully unzipping his jeans and pulling them down, freeing himself from his pants. I keep my eyes open, morbidly transfixed by the sight of his ugly penis, already engorged and dripping with pre-cum like oozing pus. With dread and trepidation rising fast I know he's going to choke and suffocate me, and I can't even plead or beg.

CHAPTER 28

Jon

Six weeks ago

The email was open before me, and it took all my willpower not to close it without reading and move onto the next. But I couldn't leave it any longer; I had to respond. Just like I had to answer his call last week, and the one the week before, I'd run out of excuses to avoid talking to him. I knew what the contents of this new communication were, just by the heading. It was an invitation to Sheikh Nijad's wedding; well, his official state wedding that was.

Why didn't he blame me? Why didn't accept it was my fault that he'd spent the last three years in exile? I was supposed to protect him, but instead, I'd let him down, he should never have been able to forgive me.

Unable to avoid it any longer, I opened the attachment, it was a standard one, personalised but no different to those sent to any other guest. The invitation was just as I expected, I closed it, and at last focused on the email content itself, the personal message I'd wanted to avoid. I read through the typical salutations and then got to the words that fucked with my head.

The last three years have brought me here, to this moment. We can't rewrite our past or change fate, and where I am now is exactly where I am meant to be. I'll forever thank you for the part you played in my destiny, my friend, my blood brother.

With sincere wishes from us both that you'll be able to attend our wedding.

Yours,

Nijad

Finally, knowing he's the bigger man, that he was able to forgive me while I was unable to find absolution for myself; I decided to reply. And accept.

Present day

Even though we're approaching from different directions, I drive the McClaren through the open gates to the abandoned warehouse only seconds behind the SUV Sean and Ryan are driving. Ben's throwing himself out of the sports car almost before I've come to a screeching halt, and running over to our colleagues. Yanking up the handbrake, but not bothering to shut the door, I sprint across to join them. They're pulled up beside a white van.

My phone buzzes. It's Vanessa. "We've pulled the CCTV from the shopping centre. He's driving…"

"… a white van." I interrupt her. "We've found it."

"Mia?"

I hear her inhale as she awaits my response, but I've no good news for her, the back doors are wide open, and the interior is empty.

"No. Pull up what everything you can about this name Hatcher." Anything's worth investigating at this stage. Though we'd luck out if it's a fake name, I have to think we might just get a break and be lucky.

"Already on it. We hacked into the club records this morning and found where he lives. Harry's on his way now to the address we've got."

Ending the call, satisfied that back at the office they're doing everything they can, I turn to see Ben picking up torn underwear, and, of course, the shoes that had concealed the tracker. He's shaking his head and looking livid. Ryan waves me closer to the van, and looking inside; I see vomit smeared into the floor. *Oh, God, Mia, what are you going through?* My gut clenches in fear.

Ryan's watching me carefully. "No blood, Jon."

"She was drugged." Sean comes up to us, his phone to his ear. "Nat's at the shopping centre and found a cloth which smells of chloroform."

"Fingerprints?"

"We're on it," he assures me. "The police are on their way and are fully briefed."

Ben's been looking at the warehouse. "No sign he's been there, it's all locked up, no evidence of forced entry, Jon. Reckon he just stashed a spare car here, and it was his plan to swap vehicles all along."

I call Vanessa again. "We're pretty certain he's changed vehicles. Any CCTV we can get into?"

"Nafisa's already looking, none in the immediate area. Oh, Jon, I'm so sorry." She sounds gutted, more emotional than on a standard case.

Why's she sorry for me? Mia's a client, just like any other. All of us will want to rescue her. It's just my job to find her, and I've only the same level of concern as Ben and the others, exactly the same as we'd have for any other person we were supposed to guard. If I keep telling myself that I might fucking come to believe it, knowing I wouldn't feel this wretched for anyone else.

Ending the call without commenting further, I glance at my companions. We've nothing to do but mill around, unable to do fuck all. And somewhere Mia is going through hell. If we're not going to be able to find the bastard quickly, there's a small part of me that hopes she's already dead. He's ultimately going to kill her in any event, I'm certain of that, and I can't handle the thought of her suffering any more than she has to. *Mia, oh fuck, Mia! Where are you? What's he doing to you?* It takes all my effort to stay on my feet and not to sink to my knees in despair.

I force myself to think professionally. I'm no use to anyone if I'm unable to focus. I'm confounded. This case has been a comedy of errors from start to finish, with me playing a significant role in our failure to protect one woman from her stalker. The blame doesn't sit solely with Ryan or Sean; we've all made mistakes. Mine being the worst of all. I fucked her instead of keeping my eye on the ball. *Shit, fuck, damn and bugger it!*

"What the fuck do we do now, Ben?" He looks as shocked as me. We've lost her. Fucking good advert for Grade A.

My phone vibrates in my hand. It's Vanessa again.

"I've got info, Jon." Immediately I put her on loud speaker and gather the guys around me. "Right," she continues. "His name *is* Miller Hatcher. He's twenty-seven years old and owns a small security company. He majored in electronics at Uni." We all exchange knowing looks. Disabling alarms would be simple with that background. "He lives in Kent now, but formerly lived about two miles from Mia's old home.

"This is the interesting bit. Hatcher's father died about ten years ago, but before that he had a small sawmill in the woods near to where Mia was originally abducted. No one has worked it as a business since; Google shows it looking run down and the surroundings are overgrown, but Hatcher's still paying the water rates and electricity for it."

Now we're getting somewhere, why pay the bills on a place that isn't used? "Where is it?" I snap out.

She gives me the coordinates, and immediately I start programming the car's sat-nav.

Ben leans forward, so the mic catches his voice. "Keep digging, Van. I don't want us putting all our eggs in one basket.

This could be a wild goose chase." He's right, but my gut is telling me we're onto something.

"On it! I'll give the info we've got to the police so they'll be on their way."

I don't delay and wait for them, knowing they'll be some time behind as the debacle at Mia's cottage showed he's in possession of a weapon and would wait to mobilise an armed response team. But it's good to know back-up is on its way. The sat-nav tells me it's going to take forty minutes to get to the sawmill without traffic delays. Forty minutes too long in my opinion so I stomp on the accelerator and do a handbrake turn to get us on our way. A look into my rear-view mirror shows the boys are right behind me.

"We'll get to her, Jon." Ben tries to reassure me.

"In time?"

He can't answer that.

"You okay?" He asks me.

I'm concentrating on driving, and take a minute to formulate my answer. "Ben, she's a client. Same as any other."

I hear him tsk. Well, fucking sod him if he doesn't believe me.

We catch traffic—of course, we do. I watch the time slip by and want to hit the bloody sat-nav as it cheerfully tells me there's a five-minute delay, but I'm still on the fastest route. Despite my protestations to Ben, my heart's pounding at the thought of what could be happening to Mia. When we come to a complete standstill, I thump my hand on the steering wheel in frustration. Shit, we've got to get there and save her!

After what seems like hours, but I know in reality is only just a little more than the predicted forty minutes, we arrive at the start of a track. Vanessa's helpfully been checking Google maps again so, following her suggestion, pull up the McClaren in a layby conveniently situated just up the road; Sean and Ryan stop behind us. My three colleagues gather around me.

"There's little doubt he plans to kill Mia," I explain my thoughts, numbly; "If we rush in he could get spooked and just do it. We've got to proceed quietly and carefully. On foot from here."

They nod in agreement. Ben's happy for me to direct the operation due to my experience in this type of situation.

"We can assume he's armed." I continue, and point out needlessly, "We're not." To maintain Grade A's impeccable reputation we strictly abide by the laws of the land. No handguns, knives, or even pepper spray. We're all experts at hand to hand combat, though. The boys are already moving towards the boots of the cars where we carry body armour as standard practice. We take the time to prepare; only fools rush in as the saying goes. Even though my stomach churning at the thought of what Mia might be going through I have to do this right. A wrong move could see her dead. As we suit up, I calm; my heart and breathing steadying as my brain shifts into professional soldiering mode. My focus is on a successful extraction, a process I've performed many times and often in environments significantly more hostile than in the UK.

We start up the track at a good pace, keeping to the edges taking advantage of the shadows offered by the trees, moving silently like ghosts. A few hundred metres up, the track bends to the right, and we approach the turn cautiously. As we pause for a better view of the wooden building that's come into view, a gut wrenching scream rips through the air. Feeling like I've taken a punch to the gut, I force myself to resist the urge just to run hell-for-leather to the rescue; the discipline of my training holding me still. At least we know we're at the right spot, and that Mia is, at this moment, alive. Moving quietly and without saying anything, Ben comes alongside me. Using hand signals, I wave Ryan and Sean round to the back of the building and indicate to

Ben he's staying with me. There's a door facing us. We wait in place. After only a couple of minutes, Ryan appears from the rear of the property gesticulating to let me know there's a window in the back, and also another entrance. I signal back 'one minute', and he knows we'll make a joint entry.

Ben and I inch forwards, keeping low and out of sight. The building isn't sited as a defensible position, so it's relatively easy to sneak up unobserved. I hear Hatcher's voice and, hoping we're going to be taking him completely unawares, try the door handle. It's been left unlocked. I push it open as silently as possible, and creep inside, Ben following me. We're in a disused office area, and the heartbreaking sounds of muffled cries and struggling are coming from the room behind a rough wooden divider.

I hear a crash from the back; the others have had to break in, taking away our element of surprise. Ben and I rush the door in front of us hoping that our joint assault will catch Hatcher out.

A split second is all I need to take in our surroundings. We're in a mock-up of a dungeon stocked with every piece of equipment a Dom could ever want, and then some. But what immediately strikes me is that the layout of the room is not in our favour. Mia's strapped down on a bed on the opposite side of the area, and Hatcher's standing over her, facing the four of us and holding a gun, his jeans loose and unfastened. It wasn't possible for any of us to get behind him.

For a moment, there's complete silence, as we analyse the stand-off. Then I take a step forward, ignoring the fact he's waving me back with his weapon. "Give it up and let her go, Hatcher," I tell him, my voice calm and controlled, "The police will be here soon." I keep my eyes on him and resist the urge to do more than shoot a quick glance at Mia. She naked, stretched out and open to our view, she's wearing a dental gag which will be terrifying and uncomfortable for her, but force myself to ignore the woman and her suffering to focus all my attention on disarming her captor.

"Let them come," he says indifferently as if it doesn't matter. "It's my dungeon, and I'm playing with my sub. My sexual preferences aren't against the law."

I'm incredulous; it's as if he believes he's acting normally. His fixation on Mia had suggested he wasn't quite right in the head, but I'm now starting to believe he's utterly insane. *We're dealing with a fucking madman holding a gun.*

Sean steps forwards beside me, his lean form coiled like a spring. His action draws attention immediately as Hatcher's eyes widen in recognition. "Huh! If it's not the chicken-bitch sub, who safeworded on me. Step back." He pronounces the last two words in a deep, commanding voice.

At this precise moment, Sean's stance doesn't show an ounce of submission. His concentration is all on Hatcher; his eyes narrowed and steady. He gives an incredulous laugh. "You trying to go Dom on me now?" He scoffs "You're not a Dom; you're merely a sadistic bastard."

Hatcher's taut, and slightly disbelieving expression shows he doesn't like anyone challenging him, and particularly not someone he's dismissing as a defiant sub. He's also stupid, underestimating Sean like so many others before him. He moves a step towards Sean, confident that he has the upper hand.

"I'll save you to last," Hatcher warns. "This time, there'll be no one to hear you bail out with a fucking safeword." I see he's incensed, and my muscles tense, ready to jump him while his attention is diverted. The almost imperceptible motion of Sean's hand stops me. The gap has narrowed between the two men. Sean has enticed him forwards so Hatcher's within reach of his lethal long legs. In a blur of movement almost too fast to see, Sean changes his pose and his right leg shoots up and out and accurately hits Hatcher's wrist hard enough it wouldn't surprise me if he's broken it. The gun flies out of his hand. Ignoring his gasp of pain, Sean and Ben rush forward to restrain him.

Instantly, I signal Ryan to go and release Mia. He throws me a sceptical glance; expecting me to rush to her myself. But I deliberately turn my attention to Hatcher, who's making a poor job of resisting the men taking him down. But out of the corner of my eye, I watch Ryan removing the gag and freeing Mia from the handcuffs and straps which hold her. She needs his help to sit up. Fucking hell, I've failed her again. Hatcher should never have been able to get hold of her. I want to be the one holding her, comforting her, but I force myself to stay put. Fuck knows she deserves someone better than me.

Using Ryan for support, she manages to pull herself up and swing her legs off that awful bed-like contraption. It's Ryan who strips off his shirt and wraps it around her. With eyes full of panic, rapidly scanning the room to ensure her captor has been secured, she pulls it on, putting her arms through the sleeves. Ryan helps her button it up. It's long on her, reaching to her mid-thighs. Suddenly her gaze becomes more purposeful, and she moves painfully and awkwardly across the room. At first, I think I'm her target and go still, not certain that my body wouldn't betray me, hoping she's not coming to hug me. I don't think I'd be able to resist embracing her in return. But she slips past me, falling to her knees on the floor. When she stands, she has Hatcher's gun in her hand. Before we can stop her, she's in front of Hatcher, who's now handcuffed and held between Ben and Sean. She puts the gun to his forehead.

Now it's Hatcher who has panic in his eyes. "Put the gun down, sub." He tries to use a Dom's voice, but it's not so effective with a quaver in it. Instead, Mia brings up her other hand to steady herself and, probably unknowingly, takes a shooting stance. Hatcher's residual confidence drifts away; now he looks apprehensive. "You won't do it," he tells her. I think he's optimistic. She looks very serious to me.

"Give me a reason why not," Mia demands. Her voice rasps, overused from screaming.

"You owe me," Hatcher spits the words. "I made you."

"You destroyed me. You stole my life so now I'll take yours." She sounds cold and very, very dangerous. I've never seen this side of her before, but then I've never previously seen her hurt, humiliated, and bleeding. Ben shoots me a look, which I interpret as him silently questioning whether we should disarm her, or let her just go ahead and do it. But she's so close, I can see the safety's off, and with her finger on the trigger, any movement could cause her to pull it.

I need to step in; I mustn't fail her now, "Don't do it, Mia." My voice is calm, deep and authoritative. I have to find a way of stopping her.

Her body is shaking, but her hand is steady, her finger curled round the trigger. "I have to." Her voice is chillingly calm.

Moving closer, I put my hand on her shoulder. She starts, and I see her trigger finger fractionally tighten. Lifting my arm, I stop touching her. "You'll have to live with it, Mia. You won't be able to do that."

"I won't be able to live knowing he's out there somewhere, that he could come after me again."

"He's going to prison for a very long time," Ben adds his contribution.

"It will never be long enough," she replies.

Assessing her carefully, I see for all her bravado she's reluctant to pull her finger back that final couple of millimetres. *There's still a chance I can get through to her.* Leaning forwards so that I can speak into her ear, I make my request, "Give the gun to me, Mia. You don't want his blood on your hands. You'll have to live with that every day of your life, seeing the bullet hitting him over and over again, having nightmares about it. Taking a man's life isn't for you. It's really not. Let us deal with him." I choose my words, carefully, "You're strong now; you'll get over this. But if you kill him you'll never recover. Believe me, I know." I don't threaten her with the police or tell her she'll go to prison. If she shoots him, I'll make sure it's only my fingerprints the police will find on the Glock.

Her arms are shaking from holding the gun steady. Slowly, very slowly, and without taking her eyes of Hatcher, she lowers the weapon. I reach around her and take from her, quickly putting on the safety.

Hatcher gives a nasty smile. "That's a good sub," he sneers.

I grab Mia and pull her back as an incensed Sean leaps for Hatcher, pulling back his arm and swinging for his jaw. His solid right hook catches Hatcher hard on the chin, causing him to fly backwards emitting a loud animalistic scream. He's fallen on the old circular saw used for cutting wood, his body, which had twisted with the force of Sean's blow, landing neck first onto the rusty metal; the saw still sharp enough to have cut through his jugular. It's a nasty wound and, from the amount of blood flowing freely, he is going to bleed out in front of us. There would be nothing we could do, even if any of us had any inclination to help.

I hold Mia tight, turning her head into my body, keeping her away from the sight of Hatcher's body flailing and twitching like an automaton. My eyes stay on him as his life blood flows away, satisfied he knows he's dying. This man who had tortured God knows how many here, in this dungeon and elsewhere, in the name of BDSM. This man, who robbed Mia of so much in her life, is now losing his. None of us make any effort to try to save him. It is only a short while before his body is still.

"Sean, go get the car." He nods, and makes a good catch as I throw him my keys. As he leaves the building, I bend my head down, "It's over," I murmur to Mia. She gives a loud sob and buries her head in my shirt. I look around at the others. "The police will be here soon. Ben, can you get Mia out of here before they arrive? She's in no state for them to question her now."

"You're not going with her?" Ben raises his eyebrows, his tone bewildered.

I try to come up with a plausible excuse. "My fingerprints are on the gun, Ben, as well as Mia's. They'll soon find that out, so best they know the truth of what happened sooner rather than later." It sounds flimsy even to me.

Ryan throws me a strange look, and Ben just stares at me. After a moment's hesitation, he steps forward and puts his hand on Mia's arm. I have to physically prise open her fingers before she lets go of me. She looks up, hurt so plain to see in her eyes, but I remain resolute. My mind's made up. I force myself to stay cold as I return her gaze. I'm no good for her.

It's only a moment, but it feels like a lifetime before, with a little disbelieving shake of her head, she steps back and allows Ben to lead her out. I hear Sean arrive with the car, hear the doors open and slam shut, and then hear the wheels spinning as they get a grip on the unmade track and hear them taking my brave girl away. I close my eyes briefly. *I'm no good for her*, I repeat in my head, desperately trying to believe it.

CHAPTER 29
Mia

Five years ago

For the third time, that morning my fingers landed on the home keys of my laptop, and I started to type. A few letters in I faltered, and pressed the delete key. Again. No, this was wrong! Standing up, I paced around the room, not that there was much distance to travel in the tiny student bedroom; just three steps forward, turn, then three back. But it was enough to feed my determination. With a resolute huff, I returned to my desk and took my seat again. This time, I ignored the angry voice in my head that had the same, rather annoying, pitch my mother would have used. Instead, I listened to the other softer, but more insistent tones, those of my characters, who were demanding I told their stories. Placing my hands back on the keyboard I took a deep breath and started to type.

The words tumbled out of my head, my emotions, long held at bay, spewed out onto the pages. Each sentence I wrote, each paragraph, cathartic and cleansing until at last I reached the culmination of the story where my characters found their HEAs and put down my metaphorical pen. As I re-read the final page tears fell, blurring my vision and my head slumped down on my arms as I sobbed the grief of the last three years out of my system.

Extract from the first novel by Mia Fable aka Dexie Sanders

Sandwiched between the two men, Della felt safer and more loved than she ever had before. It felt so right to have Damian caressing her bare breasts, sucking on her nipples while Riley, her soldier boy, rubbed his cock against her arse, promising all types of wicked rewards if she submitted to them. Society might condemn their relationship, but here, right now, in the BDSM club her men had brought her to; their actions were condoned and even celebrated. Wriggling, she tried to encourage her Doms, which only earned her a sharp spank showing they, not she, were in charge, and she would receive their cocks only when they were ready. As the warmth spread through her, her cunt oozing her arousal, she smiled a contented smile. This is where she belonged. This was home.

Present day

"More tea?" I pick up my empty mug and wave it at Ben.

He shakes his head and gestures no with his hands, "I'm okay, thanks."

I don't particularly want another drink myself, but need to take a break to try to assimilate everything he's told me. It's been a long, long week since Hatcher died, and my emotions have been shot to hell. Sky high one day, rock bottom the next. There have been hours of talking to the police, hours of talking to the therapist Ben insisted I see and hours of missing Jon. I thought he'd come back to me; I thought he'd have been the one to hold me, to comfort me, to support me through the aftermath of my ordeal. I never thought my last view of him would be him standing over a dead bloody body.

Waiting for the kettle to boil I roll my head back, then straighten and stretch my back. Physically, I'm practically healed now except for a few residual aches and pains, and there'll be no lasting damage. But my heart? Jon stole that from me, and that hurts worse than anything Hatcher ever did. Taking in a deep breath, I let it out on as a long sigh. I've got my life back now, no more looking over my shoulder. I just need to move on and live it. Without Jon. If only I didn't think that would be so difficult.

I fish the tea bag out of my cup, add some milk, and take the mug back into the sitting room of the safe house that Grade A is kindly letting to me rent free until I decide what I want to do. It's nice to have the breathing space to consider whether I want to rebuild the cottage, or sell the plot and move somewhere else. I think Ben and his partners feel guilty for the way they handled the case, but I don't attach any blame to them at all. The fact I'm safe and alive, and that the nightmare is over is all that matters. Everybody makes mistakes, but in the end, they came through for me.

Taking the seat opposite Ben again, my action a little awkward, betraying there's still a lingering stiffness in my back. A week on, and most of the bruises are fading, but one or two of the worst welts still give me a bit of pain, particularly when sitting. Ben watches and grimaces, but doesn't comment, for which I'm grateful. I've had it up to the back teeth with sympathy.

I pick up the conversation where we'd left it, the point where it was getting hard to take. "Two graves?"

He nods. "That's what they've discovered so far, just outside the old sawmill. They've called in the cadaver dogs to see if there are any more." The police have kept Grade A informed; the officials have only provided me with the briefest details as if it wasn't my business to know them. Ben reaches over and takes my hand, running his fingers gently across the back of it. "The first one was very recent and easy to find, and we had no problems with the identification. It's a man called Kevin Grower, and he used to run about with Hatcher a lot. Apparently, they were inseparable in their teens. We've traced Hatcher's parents, and they said there was always something about their friendship that they found concerning. It makes sense to think h was probably the sub Hatcher had around when they first took you."

"But why would Hatcher kill him? Do they know the cause of death?" I try to keep my voice level, shocked at what he's telling me.

Again he nods in confirmation and grasps my hand tighter. "Strangulation. His hands were still bound. It's not clear whether it was deliberate or accidental."

I shudder, and shake my head, remembering what Hatcher had put me through. *That could have been me.* I pull myself together. *It wasn't, and I'm here, alive.*

Ben gives me time to compose myself, before continuing, "Kevin Grower's little finger was missing on his left hand.."

Throwing him a quick glance, I let out a long breath, "Blue hoodie." It was a statement, not a question, but Ben nods his answer.

"Has to be," he confirms.

I think what that means. I'm not sure what I feel about his murder; it's a loose end that I no longer have to worry about, but should I be pleased that someone else is dead? I no longer have to worry that the person Hatcher employed/forced to deliver that first message was going to come after me now his Dom is gone. But part of me is sad; I don't wish any more people dead. Jon had been so right to stop me pulling that trigger; a week on and I realise that I couldn't have lived with taking a life, however much it was deserved. Witnessing his accidental death was bad enough. I look back up at Ben again and continue our discussion. "And the other body?" I have to know.

"A young girl, forensic evidence suggests she was in her late teens at most. Also bound. No identification as yet and the body's in more of an advanced stage of decomposition, so the job's going to be harder." His hands squeeze mine, "They're still searching; the cadaver dogs are behaving as though there might be more to find."

Feeling sorry for the cadaver dogs—they can't have a happy life, no one wants to praise them when they're successful in their search—I put my cup of tea back down on the table. I don't know why I was holding it; it's too hot to drink, it's just a prop, a familiar action to ground me. Standing, I walk across to the window, hugging my arms around me, trying to ward off the cold that sweeps through my body at the realisation that it's all my fault. Two people were dead—possibly more—who could have been alive had I reported my rape seven years ago. "I could have stopped him, Ben. I should have reported the kidnap and abuse… If only I hadn't been so weak."

"Now stop that!" In a second he's standing by my side, and taking hold of my arm as he gives me a gentle shake. "You can't take any blame. Yes, it should have been reported, but like so many rapes it wasn't, and for the wrong reasons. The one authority figure in your life at the time misguided you. You were seventeen, Mia; you can't blame your adult self for mistakes a teenager made. Of course, you'd report it now, but then? Apart from the fact your mother prevented you from speaking to anyone; she was constantly telling you you brought it on yourself. And not just once, but over and over again, brainwashing you until you fucking believed it!"

He looks straight into my eyes, "Mia, you're not weak, you're a strong person. *You* picked yourself up. *You* saw through the lies fed to you by your mother, the very individual who was supposed to protect and nurture you." He pauses as he summons up the right words. "You survived, honey. You didn't let him destroy you, then. Don't let him do that now."

I turn my head to face him. "Even if I could accept that, Ben, it doesn't help. Others died."

"Just concentrate on the fact that Hatcher's gone now. It's

over. He won't have any more victims." He tilts his head to one side to look at me carefully, and then grins, "Your tea's getting cold."

I have to smile back. The English cure all for all situations, tea. I go back and drink my cup, putting its curative properties to the test.

He returns to his seat. Ben's been my rock this last week, coming round almost every day to keep me updated, and we've settled into a comfortable friendship. I enjoy his visits. He's a handsome man, a little older, and different to Jon, tall with blond hair curling down around his collar, blue eyes that twinkle, and a devastatingly sexy smile which should make my toes curl when he turns it on me. Everything about him screams Dom. But there's nothing there, not even the whisper of anything between us. He's not *Jon*.

He's smiling now. "Don't dwell on what-might-have-beens. Everyone makes mistakes. We're only human."

I can't smile back, and with the man never far from my mind, I say, "I don't blame Jon." Then quickly add to hide my slip, "Or anyone else at Grade A."

The smile disappears, he can see straight through me. "Jon knows that. But he blames himself." He inhales sharply, "I've never known Jon to feel so deeply about someone as he feels about you, Mia."

"Felt. Past tense," I correct him.

"No." He contradicts me, "You mean so much to him, yet he thinks he failed to keep you safe." He's quiet for a moment as if deciding whether to continue. "Mia, I shouldn't be telling you this, but Jon's not coping well. I've never seen him like this before. He's missing you."

"I'm here!" I stand up, frustrated. *He's* missing me? *I* fucking miss *him* like hell; I want him here with me. I don't want Ben to tell me how Jon's feeling, just as I've started convincing myself

I'll be okay, able to move forwards on my own. *Have I? Have I really?*

He comes over to me and gently turns me to face him, his eyes searching deep inside me. It seems he can see into my soul. "Do you want him back?"

Inside I'm screaming *YES*, but I'm trying hard to keep control so don't let the word escape. I stay silent.

He stares at me in that Dom way, and then dips his head up and down, the corners of his mouth turn up as a knowing grin crosses his face. It seems he doesn't need a verbal answer. "Will you trust me?"

There are not many people I put my faith in, but Ben has become one of them. I'm curious what he's got in mind. If there's a chance to have Jon back in my life, should I take it? *If I didn't, wouldn't I always regret it? It wouldn't hurt to see what he's cooking up.* "What are you thinking, Ben?" I narrow my eyes, trying to read him, but he's a closed book to me.

His face lights up with a smirk as he answers, and what he says isn't an explanation but an instruction. "It's Friday tomorrow. Be ready in the evening. I'll pick you up about nine-thirtyish. Fetwear."

I take another deep breath and hesitate before replying. The inference in his few words very clear, "Club Tiapacan?" My voice shakes. I don't need the confirmation. It's written on his face. Could I bear to go back there again?

He gives me a moment to absorb the implications but doesn't give me an opportunity to turn him down. "Trust me." Leaning over, he brushes a quick kiss on my cheek, and then steps away. He picks up his coat to leave, but pauses and turns back as he gets to the door. "Nine-thirty, remember?"

∗ ∗ ∗ ∗

Should I? Shouldn't I? Was I actually planning on going to go to the club with Ben? *What if Jon isn't there? What if he is there? What if he's there with someone else?* How would I cope with any of those prospects?

I've showered, dried and styled my hair, and have carefully applied my makeup, so it enhances my eyes but isn't too obvious. I haven't yet dressed in anything other than the towel I have wrapped around me. I keep changing my mind, picking up my phone to ring Ben, and then putting it down again. *Do I want to go?* What if there is a chance to get Jon back? What if this is my only chance and I miss it? Or what if I go and he ignores me? Could I stand it if he turns his back on me? What if he makes it plain he doesn't want me? Am I brave enough for yet another rejection? I know how much that would set me back, could I bear that hurt? Picking up the phone again, I text Ben.

Mia: I'm not sure this is a good idea.

Ben: The club?

Mia: Yes.

Ben: Trust me.

I wish it were that easy!

Earlier I'd been out shopping. Buying something appropriate to wear wasn't committing me to anything, was it? I could change my mind at any time. And did; at least twenty times or more. But I'd spent time choosing a bright red satin corset, covered in black lace with suspenders attached. I purchased a red thong to go with it, and black fishnet stockings. On impulse I'd bought a pair of scarlet stilettos, heels so high I had difficulty walking in them, but I knew they made my legs look like they went on for miles. Jon would love what I'm wearing! *Fuck it; he won't have a chance to see me as I'm not going.*

At nine o'clock I make a decision and, changing my mind yet again, put on my new fetwear. Looking at myself in the bedroom's full-length mirror I know I look good. Actually, I know I'm looking fucking fantastic. I pick up my phone:

Mia: I can't do this. Sorry.

Ben: I'll be there in 30.

Mia: I'm not going.

Ben: See you soon.

Damn the man!

＊＊＊＊

It's déjà vu when I walk into the club; the only difference is that this time I'm on Ben's arm. Now I know the procedure, so leaving him I go straight to the locker room to put my coat and bag—as I'm wearing the high heels this time, I'm permitted to keep my shoes—in a vacant locker. I go back and hand my key over to Ben for safe keeping. While I was getting ready, Ben's lost the shirt and now wears only tight denim jeans that sit low on his hips and a leather vest which hangs open, showing off his muscular abs, almost, but not quite as good as Jon's. Ben hugs me in an entirely platonic way, offering me his support, and I respond in the same manner. My feelings for the man who's brought me here as his guest are completely asexual, but I wouldn't be human if I didn't take a moment to admire the view, even if it doesn't work for me. Some girl's going to be lucky tonight, but I've no inclination for it to be me. Which begs the question, why am I so fixated on the man who doesn't want me? Why do I feel that there's only ever going to be one man I'm going to want in my life? *Why can't I move on?* There's none of the excitement that filled me the first time I was here; the overwhelming emotion I'm feeling is sadness. I don't know how I'll cope if I see Jon with someone else. *Please don't let me see him playing with another woman. I'd die a little inside.*

Straightening my back, I pull away from Ben, and I give

myself a silent lecture. I had survived before I met Jon Tharpe, and I'll bloody well survive after him too. Just goes to show I was right to keep men very much at arm's length for the last seven years. Letting them close only opens the door for pain.

I try to summon up Dexie, but like a bolt of lightning it hits me, *she's already here.* Somewhere along the way my two personalities have merged, and I no longer need to play a role. Looking across at myself reflected in the glass doors I realise for the first time I have the confidence to carry this off, whatever tonight holds. *Fuck Jon Tharpe! I'll enter the club with my head held high.*

"Ready?" Ben's steely all-seeing eyes are watching me closely.

Despite my new found self-assurance I need a backup plan if this all goes pear-shaped, so I touch his arm. "Will you take me home if…?"

"I'll take you home whenever you want, Mia." His confirmation encourages me. Touching his hand to my chin, he raises my face so I'm looking at him. "I'm Sir or Master Ben when we step inside. Remember your protocols. And if you want to negotiate a scene make sure you find me."

I show my agreement and chuckle, "And no hitting Doms?"

He laughs out loud and shakes his head, "Abso-fucking-lutely not!"

He pushes the doors open, holding them to let me pass through into the main room. It feels like only yesterday that I was here but in the same instant it seems like a lifetime ago. It's taking those first footsteps into this elitist club that confirms how much I've changed. I feel sure of myself with the conviction I'm looking good. I may not yet be ready for any man except Jon to touch me intimately, but at least I look the part and if—when— I get over him, maybe I could go there. What I'm not doing is shrinking with fear at the thought.

Ben doesn't hurry me, just waits patiently beside me, letting me soak up the atmosphere of the room. Like the last time I was here, we've arrived early, so the action hasn't yet got going, and there are not too many people around. But my first test is walking towards me.

"Hello, pet." It's Donavan.

I surprise myself, feeling no hesitation as I reply respectfully, "Good evening, Sir." I even summon up a weak smile. I can't be sure whether he's forgiven me.

But he returns my tentative response with a friendly grin which transforms his face; he no longer looks stern or scary. Then, as fast as it came, the smile fades. "I read about what happened to that author, Dexie Sanders," he says pointedly, "I'm so very sorry, pet."

I start a little, but I should have realised that people would have made the connection. The death of Hatcher and my kidnap had been all over the news, and unfortunately, the newshounds had found my true identity. Lifting my head up, I look him in the eye. "I survived," I say, simply. Luckily the newspaper reports hadn't gone into the full details of my experience, only my kidnap, and kidnapper's demise. Grade A made sure of that.

He looks at me searchingly for a moment, then nods and walks away. I let out a breath I didn't know I'd been holding and am glad that I've got the hurdle of meeting Donavan over and done with early in the night.

Squeezing my arm Ben gives me a look clearly showing his approval. "Drink?" He doesn't wait for me to answer but starts to lead me to the bar. Approaching, I notice there are some familiar faces waiting there.

"Vodka tonic?" Master Ralph grins as my eyebrows go up in surprise that he's remembered my drink, and answers my unspoken question. "Photographic memory. Great bartending skill. Good to see you back again, pet."

I laugh at his explanation and thank him for his welcome. Then I turn to the two women already seated on bar stools, Gorgeous, and Diamond. Gorgeous is looking out of this world fabulous, dressed only in corset and thong. Diamond is wearing another see through diaphanous dress which clearly shows she's wearing nothing underneath. I'm overdressed beside them.

Both of them are looking at me sympathetically. I should have expected that, but the last thing in the world I need is for people to treat me differently because of *him*. I want to put Hatcher in my rear view mirror, not constantly be reminded of my ordeal.

I see Ben's frown directed towards them, and his unspoken message must have been clear as Diamond leans forward and hugs me, then, rather than rehashing what happened to me, just says how great it is to see me here again, and compliments me on my get up. I let out a silent sigh of relief knowing they're not going to be asking difficult questions I've no wish to answer. I'm all talked out on the subject of my abduction. Thanking Master Ralph when my drink arrives on the bar, I take a long sip before I remember the two drink limit and that I have to go slow. I rest my glass back on the counter and hop up on a stool Diamond has just vacated to move along to the next one so I can sit between her and Gorgeous. Ben excuses himself, and I'm left alone with the girls.

"Are you going to play tonight?" Gorgeous leans forwards and shouts in my ear. The thumping music has just been turned up in volume.

I tap my foot to the steady beat while thinking how to answer her. There's only one man I want to play with, and if that doesn't work out, I'm out of here. "Maybe," I answer evasively.

She gives me a knowing look, "Making him jealous might work."

"Fuck!" I spit out my drink. "Does everyone know?" Okay, the kidnap was common knowledge, but what happened between Jon and I was personal, and I hadn't thought it would have got around.

She shakes her head and hastily reassures me, "Only Diamond and I. Ben thought we might be able to help move things along."

They've apparently been plotting. I look at Gorgeous questioningly, "How?"

She pats my hand. "Let's wait and see how things pan out. Diamond and I are good at thinking on the fly. While these Doms believe they are in control, they forget how manipulative us subs can be."

Her undeniable optimism, coupled with the way Diamond's eyes are sparkling as she nods in agreement with her older woman, makes me feel lighter. I realise these two women could well become good friends.

We sip our drinks in comfortable companionship, and I listen to them discussing girly matters until Diamond leans forward and whispers in my ear, "Eh up! Don't look now, but Master Jon's arrived. Ignore him, Mia. Show him you're here for *you*, and not sitting waiting for *him*."

I haven't seen him since the day of my rescue from the barn when he abandoned me to Ben's care, so keeping my eyes turned away is one of the hardest things I've ever done. *I don't need him; I don't need him.* I try to keep the words repeating in my head, but as I sense him move across the room towards me, I realise I'm still tuned in to this man, and how I'm only fooling myself if I think my heart can survive him keeping away.

His scent wafts over, the intimate mixture of man and the aftershave he uses and I know he's standing very close to me. I stay turned towards Diamond as if intent on our conversation. Master Ralph appears as if by magic with a shot of whisky in his hand. I see a familiar arm snake out over my shoulder and take it from the bar.

"Thanks, Master Ralph." I hear him speak, but it's not to me. His voice sends shivers down my spine, and I hate myself for the unwanted reaction.

"Master Jonathan." The barman nods at the man standing behind me.

Jon takes his drink, and I feel him walking away. He hasn't spoken or acknowledged me in any way. My head bows, a wave of desolation floods over me. An arm goes round my shoulders; a hand touches my arm. Leaning in, one on each side, Diamond and Gorgeous pull me close to comfort me.

"He's hurting too," Diamond murmurs.

"Then why doesn't he show it?" I shake my head in despair, unable to understand him.

"We'll make him." The tone of Gorgeous' voice suggests she's got a plan. I sit up straighter, prepared to listen. "That's my girl," she laughs approvingly, "We just need to elicit a little help." She looks around, points to someone and raises her eyebrows. I turn round along with Diamond, but don't know what's caught her eye.

Diamond understands, however, as she chuckles, and waves, beckoning the unknown person over. "I think we'll need Master Ben," she suggests to Gorgeous.

"I'll go get him." Gorgeous seems to know what she's talking about even if I don't, and slides off the stool and disappears.

"Why do we need Ben?" I ask, perplexed, not understanding anything at all.

"For your negotiation," Diamond says sneakily, as she glances up to smile at the man who's approached us. With trepidation wondering who she's thinking of setting me up with I follow the direction of her eyes and am pleasantly surprised to see Ryan. I haven't seen him since I left him at the sawmill.

He moves until he's standing in front of me, a cautious look on his face. He reaches out his hand to shake mine. I'm struck again by the men I've met from Grade A, and have to admire their selection criteria as they all seem to be tall and stunning. Alpha males, of that there can be no doubt. Like most of the others, I know Ryan's background is military, but unlike some of his colleagues, he's kept the army's short back and side's haircut. I don't normally like the almost shaven look, but on Ryan, it suits him and frames his sharp features. Like so many others he's wearing the Dom's uniform of figure hugging dark jeans, and a tight black T-shirt which does nothing to disguise his muscular frame. He's got tattoos down one arm which I'd like to examine closer. He towers over me, even as he props his backside against the high stool recently vacated by Gorgeous.

When he takes my hand in his, I feel the warmth emanating from him. He holds onto it, looking at me searchingly as he asks, "Am I forgiven, Mia?"

I put my head to one side, honestly having trouble remembering what I need to forgive him for, then I realise he's referring to the bug that was put on the SUV, under his watch, enabling Hatcher to find me. "Ryan, it was a simple mistake. No worries. Have you found anything about the girl?"

His face relaxes, and he looks relieved. After gesturing to Master Ralph, indicating he'll have a drink, he turns his attention back to me. "No. We've got a good image of her from the CCTV in the shop but haven't yet been able to make any identification. She could have been his sub or someone he offered some cash just to plant the bug and then follow you into the store. If she's in the lifestyle, she'll probably turn up in a club somewhere. We'll keep looking."

It's a loose end, but I'm not going to let it unravel me. As Ryan finishes talking, Ben appears an amused grin on his face as though he's enjoying himself. He greets Ryan with a one armed manly hug, and they slap each other's backs, then he turns to me and winks.

"Ok, little subbie," Ben addresses me, "We going to do some negotiating then?"

I realise this has been a setup. I didn't come here to play, but out of anyone they could have come up with, Ryan is someone I've grown to like and respect. And he's certainly got sufficient potential to make Jon jealous. That doesn't stop a wave of apprehension running through me though.

And my concern only deepens when it becomes clear Ben is taking his role as the Dom responsible for me very seriously, as he starts running through safewords and limits, and my stomach starts to churn with nerves. *Will I have to go through with this? How far will I have to go with Ryan?* I suspect and hope they think Jon will step in and put a stop to me playing with him. But what if he doesn't? Will Ryan understand if I tell him I can't continue?

My eyes flick backwards and forwards between the two men. Ben puts his head on one side considering my reaction and glances at Ryan. As if he senses my nervousness, Ryan puts his hand on my shoulder and gives it a squeeze. He waits until I look up into his gentle brown eyes. "Red stops everything, Mia. At any time."

CHAPTER 30

Jon

Earlier today

Again I went back to the message that Nijad had written to me, and that I'd saved all those weeks ago in my special documents folder. He might have been writing about himself, but his words also applied to me. I re-read them again, "The last three years have brought me here, to this moment. We can't rewrite our past or change fate, and where I am now is exactly where I'm meant to be."

I'd been to the wedding and met Nijad's wife, Cara. It was our second meeting, but she seemed to bear me no ill-will for having been the pilot who'd taken her out to the desert to meet the stranger she'd been forced to marry. And seeing her glowing with happiness there could be no doubt that Nijad and Cara's marriage was an unlikely, but complete success, both obviously very much in love.

I recalled the conversation when Nijad had taken me aside.

"You're blaming yourself, and you shouldn't, Jon. You didn't have the time to investigate properly before Chantelle changed her story, and then I was quickly whisked away from Paris."

I shook my head, "I should have gone back to the apartment. Perhaps with a second look, I'd have seen things not obvious at first, like that bloody hole in the wall!"

Nijad laughed, "I never thought putting my fist through the plasterboard would eventually clear my name. It's ironic, isn't it?

But Jon, Jasim had closed the apartment up as soon as I left. No one thought there was any reason to return. The forensic evidence seemed unquestionable, and if I thought I was responsible for hurting her, who were you to think otherwise?" He paused and cast a pointed look across the room to where his wife stood talking to his father, Emir Rushdi. *"If it weren't for the events in Paris, I'd have never met Cara. I'd have continued my playboy ways, never regained my love for my country, let alone settled back home in Amahad."* He turned back, and I felt the force of his stare as his dark eyes narrowed and focused on me. *"I don't regret a thing, Jon. I'm exactly where I want to be."*

When I returned from the wedding, I found the Agusta and McClaren waiting for me. I didn't feel I'd deserved them but knew better than to argue with the sheikh. It was a sign that Nijad meant what he'd said. His old life was over, but he'd ended up in a better place.

The last three years have shaped me, too. Have shown I'm fallible, as any man. My experience with failure has brought me here, today. When I let people get close to me, I only let them down. And that predominantly includes Mia; she deserves someone she can rely on. Someone who won't get her shot or kidnapped.

I know she's missing me, Ben's kept me updated. But she's grown and changed; she'll find someone new, and then we'll both be able to move on. And I'll continue to have short term contract based arrangements where both parties know what to expect from the start, and where no one can get hurt.

But fuck, I miss her.

Present day

What the fuck is she doing here? Gratefully, I take the whisky from Ralph and, needing to get away from the woman who's got me twisted up in knots as quickly as possible, make my way to the VIP area, knowing full well it has to be Ben who's behind this fuck up of a situation. I know he's been seeing her almost daily for the past week, checking up on her, making sure she's healing both mentally and physically. Reporting and reassuring me she's doing fine, though why the fuck he thinks he needs to keep me updated on the client of a closed case I don't know.

I came to the club tonight hoping to get Mia out of my head. Thinking to find someone to play with who wouldn't remind me of the woman I let go. I never expected to see *her* sitting at the bar, dressed to kill and looking so desirable. Fuck, my cock stood at attention as soon as I caught sight of her! It only took that short minute standing at the bar for her to get under my skin again. Her smell, the sight of her in that corset and short skirt that immediately made my cock wake up; black and red, my favourite colour combination. And those heels! I don't even have to see her standing to know that they'll accentuate her lovely calves, her long legs leading up to a slice of heaven.

I had to get away, had to run off like a coward. I couldn't bring myself even speak to her, didn't trust myself to hear her voice. She's so much better off without me; I'm not, and will never be, the man she needs. I've shattered into pieces any trust she could have for me when I failed to keep her safe. Christ, even as her Dom I let her down when I failed to read the signs and made her safeword out...

Knocking back half of my drink in one go, I realise I might have put physical distance between us by retreating to the VIP area, but that doesn't mean her effect on me doesn't linger. I'm uncomfortable in my leathers, my cock straining telling me I need to find someone to play with, someone to take the edge off. And I need it fast. Before I do something stupid like go to *her*.

The seat I've chosen gives me a good view of the main room, and I know I'm lying to myself that I've not selected it just so I'm able to keep an eye on what Mia's doing. No, of course not, I've just placed myself in the best position to search for a suitable playmate; someone with no expectation, other than to have a bit of fun tonight. But as I look around at the available subs, my cock deflates like a pricked balloon. Shit, it seems to be programmed only to respond to Mia. *What the fuck is she doing here?* Inwardly I ask the question again while unbidden my eyes flick back to watch what she's doing. She's engrossed in conversation with Diamond and Gorgeous, and I don't trust those two as far as I could throw them. If they've taken her under their wing, they'll set something, or rather someone, up for her. Which would be excellent; she'll be demonstrating she can move on, and I should be proud of her. But something twists inside of me, as I wonder how the fuck I could survive seeing her in a scene with someone else. I have to pull myself together. She deserves better than me.

Fuck! I don't know if I can do this. I toy with the idea of going straight home, but my empty apartment holds no allure for me. Her ghost still walks there and sleeps in my bed. I drop my head into my hands. I'm so fucked up. Feet appear in front of me, I look up, and scowl, "Why the fuck did you bring her here, Ben? It was you, wasn't it?"

He shrugs and doesn't bother denying it. "It will do her good, Jon. She needs to feel like a woman again, not a victim."

"There are other ways of doing that. If you wanted to take Mia out, why not take her to a night club?" I try to dismiss the immediate vision of Ben holding Mia close on a dance floor.

"She's submissive," he starts explaining. "She needs to accept that submission doesn't lead to abuse, to understand the power exchange and exercise her power. To comprehend on the deepest level, Hatcher wasn't a Dom."

"Well, you're certainly throwing her straight into the deep end by bringing her here." Although what he says makes sense, I don't agree with what he's doing but only for purely selfish reasons.

Ben sits back and sips his drink. Then he sighs. "Jon, I'm going to be frank with you. You say you're a Dom, but are you?" He pauses to shake his head as I sit back with my mouth open, wondering just where he's going with this. "We've discussed this before; you weren't a Dom to Mia."

"You don't know that!" As I snarl, I think about what he's saying. Is he right?

Ben ignores my comment, "You've been doing things by rote for a long time now. Playing with experienced subs, repeating the same routines. You've become a Dom by habit. Your self-doubt limits you from trying anything new."

"Now wait just a fucking minute!"

He holds up his hand to stop me; there's obviously more he wants to say, "Perhaps training a new sub is beyond you. And if that's the case, maybe you should sell your shares in the club and get out of the lifestyle."

"For fuck's sake, Ben, I was born a Dom, I can't change that." *Is he really telling me to leave Tiacapan?*

He shakes his head sadly, "You've lost confidence in yourself. Why should anyone give control to someone who's so full of self-loathing? To someone who expects to make a mistake. You've lost your way, man." Again he gestures to let him finish. "I'm sorry Jon, I thought Mia was the right person for you, but now I think I was wrong. She is submissive; she needs a Dom. But first and foremost she needs a Dom who's in control of himself. And who keeps things in perspective. Sure, shit happens. But that's life."

And we're back to the subject we started with. Growing angry I spit at him, "So you brought her here to find a proper Dom? Because I'm not one?"

"Not unless you step up and prove it."

"So you don't think I'm right for her, but you've left her alone with Gorgeous and Diamond? Don't you think that's asking for trouble? She's just been through a horrendous ordeal for fuck's sake! What the hell are you thinking? What if someone like Donovan approaches her again? Who's looking out for her in case she has flashbacks?"

"I've got it covered, don't worry."

Narrowing my eyes in suspicion, I wonder what exactly has been going on during his daily visits with Mia. "You're going to play with her?" I'm surprised the words don't stick in my throat. I clench my fists and hold them tight at my sides, hoping for the strength to restrain myself from punching him if his answer is in the affirmative. Expectantly I wait, dreading the response. It's not the done thing to get into a throw down with your boss, especially in a club which I part-own and where violence isn't tolerated.

But he surprises me as he shakes his head. "I think she ought to choose someone for herself," he tells me. "I've told her I'd help her negotiate a scene so it's right for her."

He's going to negotiate for her? I don't know what would have been worse, Mia with Ben, who at least I knew I could trust, or with someone else who might not understand her. I try to make him see sense. "Even if you're right, she can't have completely healed yet. It's too early to bring her."

Again a shrug. "Most of her bruises are gone; some are still a bit yellow looking, but she assures me they're not hurting anymore. A couple of the welts are still a little painful, but it would be easy to avoid them. That info will be part of the negotiations." Having divulged that snippet of unwelcome information, he turns and leaves to go back into the club proper.

I'm stuck in the hole I've dug for myself. If I try to dissuade him, I'd only be admitting I have feelings for her. Feelings I'm trying desperately hard to keep hidden. Only I know how deep they go. I look down into my empty glass, wondering where the drink went, and consider leaving and going to get drunk. Very drunk; seeking oblivion so I'm not capable of fucking thinking at all.

The thought of watching Mia play with someone else is enough by itself to drive me crazy with jealousy and grief. Grief that I had to let her go. *And I had to, didn't I?* I couldn't trust myself to do right by her... Hang on a darn minute. Suddenly the words that Ben had spoken start to get through to me. If a Dom has no confidence in himself, how can he take responsibility for a sub? And even the best Dom in the world can't control everything. As he so eloquently put it, *shit happens.*

As I stare into space, the mental slap around the head that Ben's just given me helps me put things into perspective, perhaps, for the first time in my life. There might have been nothing I could have done to save my men, nothing further *at the time* I could have done to clear Nijad's name. I *might* have been able to protect Mia better, but who's to say the fire wouldn't have taken hold in any event? And it was Mia's love for me that ended up with her taking a bullet. And how did I reward her? I walked away. As the man, and her Dom, I walked away.

It's a couple of minutes later when I look back up into the vast play area that is Club Tiacapan, *my club,* and my eyes go immediately to the woman in the black and red corset sitting by the bar.

And then I'm consumed by rage, red fury overwhelming me, making me want to smash something. It's fucking Ryan! Ben's standing between Ryan and Mia, deep in discussion and there's only one fucking thing they could be talking about. I'm frozen on the spot; transfixed, unable to look away or even move. I see them nodding, smiling. Laughing. But as Mia slips down from the stool, I'm able to read her body language from here. She's stiff, nervous. And then I have to watch as Ryan, an experienced Dom, reads her just like I would, and draws her to him, giving her a moment to settle herself, before taking her hand and leading her away. Suddenly the invisible restraints holding me motionless drop away, and without conscious thought I'm standing, moving, *running* out of the VIP area and then I'm in front of the pair I've been watching. My hands draw up, clenched again in fists, my stance threatening.

"Take your fucking hands off her," I growl menacingly. "Or I'm going to drop you here."

To his credit, Ryan keeps Mia held tight at his side. "I think that's her choice," he says, calmly.

I'm incensed. Ryan let her down too. "You fucking bastard. If you kept your eyes on the fucking job Hatcher wouldn't have got her." Immediately I want to take back the words. It had been an easy enough mistake to make, one that I might have made myself.

Mia looks up at Ryan, and I go cold as she calmly asks him for permission to speak. *He's not her Dom. I am!*

At his nod, she addresses me, "He'd have got me at some point, Jon. And now he's dead. It's over. And I'm fine." Her face turns up, her expression pleading. "I'm *fine*," she repeats with emphasis.

I first look at the angry red scar from the gunshot on her upper arm then I look into her eyes, one still showing a fading bruise, and read the message hidden in the depths there. She's not fine, but like the wounds that are visible, she's repairing herself, rebuilding herself. The fact she's here, brave and courageous, standing upright, facing her fears tells me that. She's not fine, but she will be. And it's at that moment I know I have to prove myself to her, prove I can be the Dom, as well as the man she needs. And as her Dom it's my responsibility to help heal her. I know exactly what I have to do.

Ryan's arm drops from her shoulders. As my temper begins to cool he steps aside and stands with arms folded, legs apart, waiting for me to make the next move. I close my eyes briefly and appreciate what he's doing. Without words he's offering her to me, giving me a chance to make this right. Inhaling sharply, knowing deep in my soul this is the right thing to do; I nod my thanks to him. Quickly, thoughts run one after the other in my mind, and then I get the clarity I need and come up with a plan.

I take a deep breath. "Do you want to play with Ryan?" I give her the choice, dreading the answer. If there's a chance we can move on from here, she has to make that decision.

My heart leaps as without missing a beat, she replies. "No. I want to play with you."

I glance at Ryan, the fucking bastard's smiling. It's then I realise how well and truly I've been set up. I shake my head, slowly, and take a moment looking around the room, considering very carefully how I should proceed. She's so brave to have come here tonight, to this dungeon with all the equipment and implements that were used to hurt her. I need to change that for her, reward her bravery. I take a deep breath in and hold it, only letting it out when I know I'm in control of myself as well as her, with no doubts or second thoughts in my head.

"Mia," I begin, waiting to sure her attention is focused on me. "I want to do a scene involving sensation play. Do you understand what I'm talking about?"

It's impossible to miss the way her eyes widen and her pupils dilate. Another man might be fooled it's just with excitement and anticipation, but I can see the nervousness there, too. It's confirmed when she asks, "Are you going to blindfold me? Restrain me?"

Remembering the way she completed her limit list, I

confirm, "They were soft limits for you, Mia, I understand that. And I know why you're not sure about them." I reach forwards and take her hand in mine, squeezing it gently. At my touch, I feel her relax, "But I can help take those bad memories away? Can you trust me? Will you try for me?"

"What if I safeword out again?"

"Then I stop." That answer's simple. "But I hope I'd never go that far." Not again.

Ryan cocks an inquisitive eyebrow. "You want me to come along?"

The old me would have scoffed and dismissed the thought of another Dom helping me monitor my sub's reactions; I've been a Master for years. The new me realises that while I've tried to sort out my head, I'm still nervous about doing this wrong and that I'd appreciate someone else watching out for her, should I, heaven help me, not be reading the situation properly. I accept his support, "Thanks, mate. But *hands off!*"

Ryan grins widely, "I suspected that would be the case."

Mia's looking from one to the other of us. There's a terrified expression in her eyes, her lips are pressed together tightly, and her skin has gone white. She's experiencing a flashback and what's coming back to her isn't good. *Because it's two men.* She reverses a step, having second thoughts. "Jon, I'm…"

Ryan knows her story, and is quick to reassure her. He turns to Mia, "Pet, I'll just be acting as a dungeon monitor, I won't be touching you."

She glances at him, and then, after a moment, again finds that strength inside her and nods. It's the signal I need to start the scene.

I school my features carefully, fully in Dom mode now. I'm not going to give an inch. "It's Master Jonathan or Sir." I remind her sternly as I make it clear I'm in charge. Then I walk the few steps over to the bar and indicate to Ralph that I need him.

When he comes over, I point behind him. "Pass me my toy bag, please?"

Bag in hand I return to Ryan and Mia. I keep my voice serious, taking control. Inside I'm grinning. She's going to enjoy this.

I want to be her man, but I *need* to be her Dom. I can't deny that part of me. If she lets me, I can use what I am to replace her terrifying memories of Hatcher; can substitute them for good ones. She might have come to Tiacapan; she might have a good knowledge of what goes on here, but she's still nervous about playing herself. But after tonight she'll never fear it again. It's my duty to make this a positive and enjoyable experience if I'm going to be her Dom.

And that's exactly what I'm going to be.

CHAPTER 31
Mia

Four years ago

To my great surprise, my first attempt at a novel was quickly snapped up by an agent, and within a year I was holding a paperback copy in my hand, and the e-book was flying off the, er, virtual shelves. So proud of myself, but well aware it was probably not a particularly good idea, I sent my mother an advance copy of my book, only to receive it back with a message full of her loathing and disgust and expressing her wish that I never darken her doorstep again. It neither surprised nor upset me.

Time moved on, more books followed, and I became blessed with a modicum of success. But I couldn't bring myself to trust a man, never went on dates. I watched my friends pairing up with soul mates, and was happy for them, but knew that could never be for me.

I had a comfortable life, moderate success, and I enjoyed what I did. But something was missing. Deep down I knew I was letting the past rule my future, but I was too afraid to move on. I wanted what everyone else seemed to have, my own HEA. But until I was brave enough to face up to my fears, that was something that would remain forever beyond my reach.

Present day

As I walk across the dungeon, sandwiched between the two men, my palms are sweaty. I'm nervous, but also elated. Is this my second chance with Jon? Or does he just want to play with me? I gathered he was as upset with the thought of seeing me scene with someone else, exactly as I felt about having to watch him with another woman. Does this mean he still wants me?

As well as my hopes, I'm also more than a little scared. When I was completing that darn limit list I never expected to need to use it; I never expected to play myself. And now Jon wants to restrain and blindfold me? I might freak out like I did with Donovan, the past might overwhelm me again and the last thing I want to do is disappoint Jon.

Turning, I look at him; while his expression is full of encouragement, there's no doubt that the Dom has entered the room. His head is cocked to the side, waiting for something. My brow furrows as I realise he's leaving the decision to me. That was the negotiation. He's told me what he plans to do and is giving me the chance to walk away. I can use my safeword and never have to see him again. *But I safeworded out before.* And that had upset him. But the important thing *he'd* missed was the impact it had on me when he'd stopped. Immediately, and without question. He hadn't pushed me too far—my past had come back and ruined it for me. And then I realise. He might be my Dom, but as his sub I've as much a commitment to him, as he to me. *He needs me to submit to him, to give my power to him. To give him control. He needs this.* My trust is the gift that I, a sub, can give to my Dom.

Looking away from him, I glance over at the stage area he's led me to and can't suppress a shudder. There's a flat table, the table to which he's going to tie me in some way. This particular piece of equipment is all too similar to the contraption Hatcher had me bound to, and I flinch in memory of the things he did while he had me restrained. I shake my head. If I don't do this, my abuser is still winning; even dead I'm still giving him control over my life. So I pull myself up tall, take a step forwards, and then another. And then, more confidently, as I hear only sounds of pleasure echoing around the room and realising I have nothing to fear, one more.

"Strip. But leave the shoes."

I start, and pause as the low steady voice comes from behind me, and realise this is part of the scene. I hesitate, but not long enough for him to have to repeat himself. The command in his deep, velvety voice banishes thoughts of Hatcher, and instead sends tingles of anticipation down my spine. *I can do this.* Knowing Jon's right there helps me to remember where we are and concentrate solely on him. Slowly I untie the laces holding my corset together and let it drop to the ground. With shaking hands I unzip my skirt, letting it fall and stepping out of it. Not allowing myself second thoughts I put my thumbs into my thong, and I pull it down, carefully lifting one foot and then the other. He's behind me; I know because his hand reaches out to take the thong from my hand, I don't know how he moved close so silently.

"No underwear in the club, Mia."

Hearing the amusement in his voice, I give a tentative smile; he sounds more like the Jon I know, and that simple thing helps to settle me further. With one more deep breath to fortify myself, I take the final step towards the equipment.

"Lie on your back, Mia, and put your hands at your sides."

I do as instructed, and he puts my hands in cuffs, then I'm enveloped by warmth as he leans over me as he secures my wrists to the edges of the table, running his fingers between the fleecy lining and my skin, making sure they're not too tight. I test my restraints, and immediately try to pull back. I've little movement, and I begin to panic, I can't get loose, I can't escape. It's too much; I'm going to have to say my safeword.

A hand immediately comes out and rests on my shoulder, and a rumbling, authoritative voice directs me, "Breathe, Mia. Deep breaths. Relax."

I try to concentrate on the feeling of his fingers smoothing up and down my arm. It's not Hatcher. It's Jon.

"Eyes on me."

I hear Ryan's voice and snap my eyes open, turning my head to the side to see him. He has moved with us and is now standing close to me, not touching. Standing, with his arms folded, he's regarding me carefully. The fact there's someone else watching out for me calms me, and my panic begins to recede. Jon must feel my muscles relax as he takes his hand away. As Ryan nods at me, I hear a voice in my ear saying approvingly, "Good girl."

Hands then take my legs and pull them apart, but not so far as to be uncomfortable. As two more cuffs are fastened around my ankles, they don't cause the same anxiety as the first restraints. I keep my eyes on Ryan. He's still watching my every reaction. After a minute, he nods to Jon over my shoulder.

As instructed, I try to control my breathing, taking in a long breath, and then exhaling, and repeating the process until I become less tense. I'm tied, unable to move, and at the mercy of a man. *Can Jon really take such a dreadful experience and make it pleasurable for me instead?* I'm not sure how. Again I glance at Ryan; he gives me an encouraging smile and lifts his chin reassuringly. I can't go so far as to summon a smile back, but can feel my features relaxing from their original grimace.

Hearing noises behind me, I lift my head to see. I can't twist quite far enough, but I can just make out Jon's rummaging in the big black bag he carried in with him. *Oh my God! What implements of torture has he got in there?* Then Jon walks into sight. He's holding a blindfold in his hand.

"You're safe, Mia. Remember your safewords. No one's going to mind if you have to say them, and immediately you do, the restraints come off, and all play stops. There'll be two of us to get you out as quickly as possible." Ryan's calm, steady voice reassures me again.

I look at Jon and, as he shows me what he's holding, give a hesitant nod.

"I'm going to put this over your eyes now, Mia. By blocking out one of your senses, you'll be able to concentrate on the others. I want you to *feel* tonight. If you give me your permission, it will enhance all your experiences. But I need to hear you agree to it. Will you let me blindfold you, Mia?"

I'd been kept blindfolded for two days, and horrific things happened to me then. It's not an easy decision to make. After swallowing a couple of times, I manage to whisper out, "Yes."

He quickly fastens the blindfold over my eyes and my sight is taken away. As I begin to tense I feel a hand on my shoulder, "Stay with me, Mia. You're at Tiacapan. Remember that. You're safe."

There's another hand on my head, "I'm still here, I'm not going anywhere." Ryan's voice comforts me.

Then, before I have a chance to process anything else, I feel something soft running from my chest to my groin. It lifts from my body, and then I feel it on the underside of my feet. Just when I start to squirm from the tickling it lifts and gently brushes over my breasts. I feel my nipples peak immediately at the sensation. *It's a feather or something like that.* As Jon lifts and sweeps it down my body, so I never know where it's going to land, my fears start to disappear, and I even begin to push myself into the touch.

As the feather tantalisingly touches my clit, I almost arch off the bed. And then the gentle contact disappears, to be replaced with something harsher, something with spikes that begins to run down my torso. *It has to be a Wartenberg wheel.* My skin, which has already become sensitised by the pleasant soft touch of the feather, now starts to prickle as the wheel runs across my stomach, down my legs, thighs, and calves until it reaches my feet, with only a slight swipe across the soles. It starts the return journey will a little more pressure and I feel my whole body tingle in expectation. My nipples, already erect, harden even more as he runs it across them, one way, and then the other in a criss- cross pattern. Then, slowly, very slowly, the pricking sensation runs down my body, pauses for a second over my mound and I tense. *He's not going to use it there, is he?*

But he does, he runs the wheel across my clit but lightly. The scratchiness of the toy causes me to clench my legs as arousal sweeps through me, and I feel myself getting wet. I move my head from side to side and give a small moan, as I become desperate for release.

He tortures me with the wheel some more, and then starts alternating it with the feather. Rationally I know it's the endorphins released from my brain, but I start to feel I'm on an ever increasingly high. Now it's something different. Lips reach down and take mine in the gentlest of kisses, and then he starts licking me, a stroke here, and a suck there. Then he's over my already stimulated nipples, laving them, gently using his teeth.

"Give me a colour, Mia," he rumbles against my skin.

I can barely understand the question, but then I realise he's checking in. "Grrreen." I manage to stutter out, overwhelmed by the feelings his evoking.

Chuckling softly, causing vibrations over my skin, he moves his mouth downwards. *Yes, yes! That's where I need him!* And he's there, with the faintest of touches around my clit, escalating my level of arousal to an all-time high. And then he pulls away. *Noooo!*

My whole body is at fever pitch. But no one's touching me, and I'm blind. *He's leaving me like this?* "Jon?" I ask, hesitantly, as reality threatens to intrude on my sense of tremendous well-being.

"Hush, Mia," A hand, Ryan's hand, touches my head. "He's just getting ready."

Ready for what?

Knowing there's still someone here has immediately calmed me. I start to burn with anticipation, and all the while my clit is throbbing and my womb is clenching, but however I move I can't get enough friction to get relief.

"Be still, Mia," Jon's stern voice remonstrates.

As I obey, he reaches up and takes off my blindfold. The sudden light makes my eyes water for a second.

"I want you to see this; I think you'll enjoy it."

Narrowing my eyes I watch him tuck something into his clothing, and then, with an evil glint in his eyes, he reaches down to take my nipple once more into his mouth. As he gets closer, sparks fly from his mouth! *What the fuck?* My nipple sends a sharp tickling, stinging feeling straight down to that area between my legs. As he applies the same sensation to the other, more sparks fly. His hands reach out and hover over my breasts, and a tingle of electricity runs over my flesh. *His whole body has been electrified.*

As Jon makes me endure his sensual torture sensations are bombarding me, sending me higher and higher. He continues alternating between my breasts, then goes to my feet and starts making his way up my body. Every touch emits sparks and the whole of my skin becomes sensitised. Up my legs, over my stomach, across my nipples, then a kiss which sends tingles down my spine. And then he's working his way back down, across my stomach, over my mound and when he puts his mouth, *there*, I explode, combusting with an intensity washing over me wave after wave and that quite literally sends me out of my mind.

I hear mumbling voices around me, and I seem to be floating as I barely notice as the ankle and wrist cuffs being removed and now my hands and arms are free. Then I'm helped into a standing position, which I'd doubt I'd have been able to achieve without assistance. A blanket is wrapped around me then Jon's strong arms lift and carry me. I'm vaguely conscious of being taken through the main room and into the corridor where the private rooms are. The door is conveniently open as we enter and he kicks it closed behind us, and then I'm lying in the middle of a large double bed.

I have no idea how long I've been stretched out beside him, but when I eventually open my eyes, Jon leans over me, and his mouth takes mine. It's not a gentle kiss, but I match him, my tongue aggressively toying with his. All the missed passion of the last couple of weeks is pouring out from both of us, he bites my bottom lip, I retaliate, and my teeth touch his. He fucks my mouth with his tongue, imitating the action we both need and want. When he breaks away, we're both breathless.

Inhaling deeply he rears up. "I have to taste you," he tells me, huskily.

"Taste me then." I rasp out my permission, desperate for him. Our kiss has reawakened a throbbing arousal despite having come so hard just a short while before. I'm behaving like an animal, desperate in my search for release.

He slides down my body, roughly pulling my legs apart as if he's as frantic as me. Raising my head I see him staring at my wetness in appreciation, and then his mouth is there, just where I want it. He licks around my clit, tormenting me. I twist and thrust upwards, trying to get him to focus where I need it. He puts one hand on my stomach to still me, and then his other hand circles me, and he gently pushes one finger inside, and then it's joined with a second. I look down to see him watching me carefully as he finger fucks me while licking and sucking, raising my excitement to such a peak I don't think I'll be able to take any more.

"Jon…" I mouth, pleadingly.

"What do you want, Mia?" I hear the smile in his voice and feel the rumble as he speaks having barely lifted his mouth from my engorged bud. "Tell me, sweetheart."

I thrash wildly, I'm so close.

"Tell me what you want."

"I want to come!" Now, I'm almost screaming with frustration.

As a reward he curls his fingers inside me, hitting the exact right spot while biting down gently on my clit. I come apart, the intensity of my orgasm causing my whole body to go into spasm. He licks and sucks, absorbing wave after wave of my muscles contracting. I think I've finished, but his clever manipulations bring me to the peak again. I scream, unable to keep the sound in, and tears come to my eyes as he gently brings me back down to earth. My muscles go weak, and I don't feel capable of moving as he clambers back up the bed and lies down beside me, pulling me into his arms.

He kisses me again, a gentle kiss full of emotion and I taste myself on him. "Mine," he stakes his claim in his Dom's voice. My heart leaps. When he adds, "I think you liked the violet wand, Mia," there's laughter in his voice.

"Mmm," I reply, sleepily. Then, as my body starts to become reinvigorated, I lift my head. "I was scared Jon; I didn't know what to expect.."

He gives me an intense look. "I'm so proud of you, Mia. I wanted to take away your fear, to show you how strong you are. And how I'll never abuse the control you give over to me."

"I never stopped trusting you," I tell him, surprised he would doubt it.

Rolling over onto his back, he puts his arm across his face. "I thought I'd let you down so much; I didn't think I deserved you. That you'd never be able to put your faith in me again."

Sitting up, I move his arm away, so I gaze straight into his troubled eyes. "How the hell did you let me down?

"You got hurt on my watch; you got kidnapped when we should have been taking better care of you."

"He was waiting for his chance. Jon, you're a man, not a machine. I've nothing to forgive you for."

Reaching up his hand, he strokes my cheek, "I see that now. I wasn't thinking clearly before. I'd convinced myself I couldn't be who you needed.

"What changed your mind, Jon? Was it seeing me preparing to play with another man?"

"Would you have gone through with it?" he asks sharply.

"No," I say quickly, wanting to put his mind at rest. "And Ryan was well aware of that."

He's quiet for a moment, as though thinking what to tell me. "Ben talked to me and made me realise I can only be in control of me, not everything around me. And he told me you need me, as I need you." His hand comes up and holds my chin then he draws down my head, our lips meeting for a kiss full of domination.

When at last, he lets me go, I say emphatically, "You've made mistakes; I made mistakes. We're human." I take a deep breath and leap. "I love you, Jon. I always will. Whether things go right, or things go wrong, I'll always love you. And I'll always trust you. Even when you're wielding a violet wand." I smile at my last comment.

His eyes capture mine. "I love you too, Mia. I've never felt this way before, ever. And I'll always try to keep you safe. I hate that Hatcher was able to take you again…"

"Shush!" I instruct, putting my fingers to his lips. "I'm here, Jon. You saved me. And Hatcher's gone. For good."

He seems to consider that for a moment.

"I didn't realise how incredible sensation play could be; you were so gentle." I change the subject. "Will you show me the toys you used…?"

He puts his hand over my mouth, "You can research for your next book another day."

I giggle; he's sussed me out quickly.

Sitting up, propped on one elbow, he places his lips over one of my nipples, gently biting and sucking, and his fingers twist and pull the other one. It's as if there's a string of nerves connecting my breasts with my clit as, unbelievably, my arousal grows all over again.

"I want to clamp these; it's a shame I haven't got any with me right now." He pinches each peak, and at the small burst of pain, I feel another rush of wetness. Leaving my breasts with a final caress, he moves his hand down, slowly across my stomach, until he reaches my clit and his talented fingers start winding me up again. It's only moments before I'm taut as a bow and ready to come all over again.

"I need you inside me," I tell him, hoarsely.

As though he was waiting for the words, he leaves me bereft as he stands up. My body suddenly goes cold, but the sight of him throwing off his vest exposing his chest, his abs, his pecs and that delightful V leading down to the waistband of his leathers makes me glow inside. He notices my attention, and oh, oh so slowly, undoes the button on the waistband, and, as if he is in no hurry at all, unzips. He's gone commando, and his throbbing cock springs free, the head angry and red, pre-cum already glistening as it leaks from the slit.

I lick my lips, and he grins. Then, with more urgency he

pushes the trousers down and he's naked before me. Just the sight of him stimulates me even further. I watch as he reaches across to a bedside table and opens a drawer. He pulls out a condom.

Reaching out my hand, I place it on his arm. When he looks at me questioningly, I enlighten him, "No need for that, Jon. The pill should be working by now. And I got my test results – I'm clean."

His loud intake of breath, the jubilant expression on his face shows just how much that means to him, "Fuck, Mia. And I thought this night couldn't get any better." Brushing his hand over my cheek and leaning in for a brief kiss, he double-checks, "You'll take me bare?"

When I nod, he pauses, just for a moment as though soaking in the sight of me. "Mia, you're the most beautiful woman I've ever seen."

I very much doubt that, but don't bother to contradict him as in one quick move he comes over me, pushes my legs apart and drawing me towards him. He's on his knees, and he raises my hips, pulling me against him. He swirls his hand around my entrance and then wipes his now well-lubricated hand up and down his unsheathed cock. Watching his slow masturbation turns me on even more. His eyes meet mine, and I know I'm unable to hide anything from him as he smirks, and, in a single motion, positions himself and slides deep inside.

At first, his movements are slow; tantalising enough to keep my arousal high, but not enough to send me over the top. I moan, no longer able to form coherent words. Then, just as I think I'm reaching the end of my endurance, he starts thrusting hard, his strong hips pumping aggressively. He's hitting my cervix, and with every stroke he takes me higher and higher. His hands are holding my hips so hard, I expect to have bruises, but this animalistic coupling is so right for us; he's fucking all my bad memories away. It's a new beginning us both, he's staking his claim. Quickly the stimulation on my G-spot takes me to the edge, and intuitively he knows it, stopping, almost pulling out.

"Fuck!" I yell in frustration.

He just laughs, and then pushes back in, resuming his pace, hammering into me. He doesn't stop as he takes me to the peak and pushes me over the top. A loud, almost tortured scream escapes from my mouth, and he joins me with a triumphant roar as he empties himself deep inside, his cum pushing up right into my cervix, his pumping extending my orgasm until he collapses on top of me, his arms keeping his weight from my body. He stays still as his cock softens, extending our moment of intimacy.

We stay like that, joined for some time, until eventually he pulls out, and sits back, staring for a moment at our combined juices leaking out of me. Then he stands up, and goes quickly into the small en-suite, and returns with a cloth. Completely at ease with him now, I feel no embarrassment as he cleans me up and then discards the flannel. Coming back to me he lies on his side, pulling me into his body. For a few minutes, we lay still, both satiated, relaxed and recovering.

After our breathing slows and our heartbeats return to something like normal, he puts his weight on one arm, his head resting on his palm, giving me a serious look, staring at me as if deep in thought. He seems to come to a decision as he nods and asks me, "Why did you pull that stunt tonight, Mia?"

I turn my head away, biting my lip. I don't want to have this conversation now, preferring to start afresh from this moment.

When I stay silent too long, he prompts me, "Hmm?"

I reach for his flaccid cock and stroke it; it comes back to life in my hands, and I smile.

He knows what I'm doing, and stills my actions by putting his hand on mine. "Answer me, sweetheart."

I haven't got a choice; he won't be leaving this alone. So I admit to him in a mumble. "I missed you, Jon. More than I thought I would." I missed him like a fish would pine for water. "Ben convinced me you were missing me too. I was so miserable without you, and if there was a chance to be with you, I had to try."

I steal a quick glance at him, but am unable to decipher what he's thinking, then feel my heart beat faster as he responds, "Fuck, Mia, I missed you too. So badly. More than I imagined I'd miss anyone. I've never hurt that badly before. Christ, I wanted you every fucking minute of every fucking day. I never want to feel like that again."

I shrug, leaning forwards and burying my head in his chest, "So what happens, now?" He's told me he loves me, but he's left me before. As insecure as I am, I want a clear answer.

"Look at me." He puts his hand under his chin and turns my face towards him. "Eyes on me!" I've no option but to obey his commanding voice. He waits for my compliance before continuing. "Mia, you hit me like a freight train—from the first glance I had of you I knew you were something unique. So special, that when I let you down, I didn't think I was worthy of you."

I go to speak, but he puts his finger to my lips to shush me.

"You know I'm a Dom, Mia, and trust is at the very heart of a D/s relationship. Out of the bedroom, I'll always be there for you, your protector. In the bedroom, I'll need control. But tonight proved how that could work between us." He brushes his lips over mine. "I assure you, I love you more than I thought it would ever be possible to love anyone."

My eyes mist over at the depth of the emotion pouring from him. It's not just the words; I feel it in his touch, in his caress.

Moving me with him he pulls us both up until we're sitting, then he swings my legs off of the bed and gets to his feet. To my astonishment, next he drops to one knee on the floor and takes both my hands in his. "I know this has happened fast, but it feels so right. In my thirty-five years, I've known a lot of women, sweetheart; I'm not going to hide that from you. But I've never had this connection with another person; never felt that I'd only be living a half-life if I didn't have you by my side." He pauses and places a gentle kiss on the palms of each of my hands. "Maybe it's too soon; I don't know. I'm way out of my depth here." He grins, "But I know I don't want to lose you, I can't let you go again. If you hadn't come here tonight, I'm certain I'd have come to find you, once, as Ben so articulately put it, I'd pulled my head out of my arse. I'm not interested in anyone else, and now the caveman in me wants to tie you to me in any way possible."

Again a pause while he draws in a deep breath. The hands that hold mine are shaking, and I realise this big strong man at my feet is nervous. I let him take his time, knowing better than to interrupt.

Now he lifts his head and looks straight into my eyes. "You're going to be my permanent sub, Mia. And you're going to marry me. Mia, you're going to be my wife."

I stare, unbelieving. I have no words; I don't know what to say. A rush of emotion makes my eyes blur with happy tears. He's surprised me; it's the last thing I expected him to say. His sub, perhaps. His wife, not in a million years did I expect that. But all of a sudden I know how right that feels.

He looks concerned when I don't immediately respond, and his fingers rub across my palms. Any touch of his makes me tremble, and especially now that my heart feels like bursting with happiness. "Well?" he prompts softly. "Aren't you going to answer?"

A slow smile comes to my face as I decide to toy with him. "I wasn't aware you'd asked a question," I start to grin as his proposal sinks in. "I thought it was a Dom's command."

Barking out a laugh, I'm pulled in close to his body and hugged tightly. "You know, you can be a brat at times."

"Your brat," I tell him, shyly, while thinking about what he's asked me. "It's so soon, Jon. And," I pause to get the strength to say, "I might never be able to have children."

Taking my face between his hands, he looks at me intently, and then reassures me, "Do you think that fucking matters to me? I want you, Mia. You. Only you. There's never been anyone else that's made me feel anything even half deep as what I feel for you. I don't want to lose you, lose the chance to make a life with you. We've lived through so much in these last few weeks." His hands stroke my face, "If we have kids, great. The thought of your belly swelling with my child, well, I can't fucking find the words to describe how that would make me feel. But if you can't—or even if I can't. Well, what the fuck would that matter when we have each other? It doesn't matter. I just want you."

No reply comes to me; I'm having difficulty processing how so much love and happiness is mine to take if I want it.

"Mia, I know it seems too fast, but I've never been so sure about anything in the whole of my life, these last couple of weeks without you have seen me in a hell I never want to revisit. Mia, sweetheart. Marry me." His eyes crinkle, a smile stretches across his face as he changes his demand, "Give me a colour."

"Oh, Jon!" I hug him; hug him as hard as I possibly can. This man, this wonderful man is offering me a life with him. A lifetime of waking up beside him, of sharing everything with him. He's taking me with all my flaws, as I'll be taking him with his. This amazing, wonderful man. "Ah, yell…" As I start to speak his smile starts to fade, and I realise it's cruel to tease him.

"Green." I change my answer quickly. Then I repeat, my voice ending on a shout, "Green! Green! GREEN!!!"

Fuck! *I'll suffocate if he keeps holding me this tight!* With a laugh he releases me and takes my lips in a ravishing kiss. Then he pulls back just far enough to whisper into my ear. "You really are a brat, aren't you?"

SECOND CHANCES

Zoe

I've become <u>that</u> woman, the woman who lets herself fall under the influence of a man who only gradually reveals the monster that lies beneath his civilised veneer. By the time I know I have to get away it is already too late. Ethan St John-Davies is one of the richest and most powerful men in the UK, virtually impossible to escape. I have to use all my wits when I leave him, my only chance at freedom to take a job far away in the Arabic state of Amahad.

Promising myself I'd never fall under the influence of a dominant man again, I meet Kadar and find it hard to fight my attraction to him. But whatever my feelings, he is already married – to his country, and soon to be wed to a political bride.

Kadar

I'm not ready to be the emir and admit some sympathy with the tribespeople who question my readiness to take on the role. Needing to appease them I agree to a marriage to a woman of their choice. But then I meet Zoe and take her under my protection. Little do I know as I teach her the difference between Dominance and abuse, she will find a place in my heart.

As Amahad plunges into a civil war, I soon find myself fighting not only my own tribespeople but the man who would do harm to the woman under my protection. Can I win all my battles? Can I keep my country united, the woman of my choice alive and have the relationship I desire?

Blood Brothers #3: Second Chances

ACKNOWLEDGEMENTS

Thanks must go to my beta readers, Beverly Holland, Alex Clark, Kirsten, and <u>Christy</u> who helped me get the plot in shape and gave me the encouragement to continue, and of course to Kate from The Ribbon Marker Services for another in-depth beta-read report.

Cover design and formatting by Freeyourwords. Lia, it was great working with you as always!

Editing by The Ribbon Marker Editorial Services – thanks Kate!

Finally thanks to my husband for letting me have the freedom to write and so much encouragement, and to my wonderful son who didn't seem to get bored when he listened to my ideas.

And of course, I'm grateful to everyone who's taken the time to read *Close Protection*. If you enjoyed it, please leave a review.

ABOUT THE AUTHOR

After commuting for too many years to London working in various senior management roles, Manda Mellett left the rat race and now fulfils her dream and writes full time. She draws on her background in psychology, the experience of working in different disciplines and personal life experiences in her books.

Manda lives in the beautiful countryside of North Essex with her husband and two slightly nutty Irish Setters. Walking her dogs gives her the thinking time to come up with plots for her novels, and she often dictates ideas onto her phone on the move, while looking over her shoulder hoping no one is around to listen to her. Manda's other main hobby is reading, and she devours as many books as she can.

Her biggest fan is her gay son (every mother should have one!). Her favourite pastime when he is home is the late night chatting sessions they enjoy, where no topic is taboo, and usually accompanied by a bottle of wine or two.

Email: manda@mandamellett.com

Website: www.mandamellett.com

Connect with me on Facebook:

https://www.facebook.com/mandamellett

Sign up for my newsletter to hear about new releases in the series:
http://eepurl.com/b1PXO5

Photo by Carmel Jane Photography

www.ingramcontent.com/pod-product-compliance
Lightning Source LLC
Chambersburg PA
CBHW070742120726
47910CB00001B/147